BIRTHRIGHT

VOLUME FIVE
BELLY OF THE BEAST

IMAGE COMICS, INC.
Robert Kirkman *Chief Operating Officer*
Erik Larsen *Chief Financial Officer*
Todd McFarlane *President*
Marc Silvestri *Chief Executive Officer*
Jim Valentino *Vice-President*

Eric Stephenson *Publisher*
Corey Murphy *Director of Sales*
Jeff Boison *Director of Publishing Planning & Book Trade Sales*
Chris Ross *Director of Digital Sales*
Jeff Stang *Director of Specialty Sales*
Kat Salazar *Director of PR & Marketing*
Branwyn Bigglestone *Controller*
Sue Korpela *Accounts Manager*
Drew Gill *Art Director*
Brett Warnock *Production Manager*
Leigh Thomas *Print Manager*

Tricia Ramos *Traffic Manager*
Briah Skelly *Publicist*
Aly Hoffman *Events & Conventions Coordinator*
Sasha Head *Sales & Marketing Production Designer*
David Brothers *Branding Manager*
Melissa Gifford *Content Manager*
Drew Fitzgerald *Publicity Assistant*
Vincent Kukua *Production Artist*
Erika Schnatz *Production Artist*
Ryan Brewer *Production Artist*
Shanna Matuszak *Production Artist*
Carey Hall *Production Artist*
Esther Kim *Direct Market Sales Representative*
Emilio Bautista *Digital Sales Representative*
Leanna Caunter *Accounting Assistant*
Chloe Ramos-Peterson *Library Market Sales Representative*
Marla Eizik *Administrative Assistant*

www.imagecomics.com

SKYBOUND

Robert Kirkman *Chairman*
David Alpert *CEO*
Sean Mackiewicz *SVP, Editor-in-Chief*
Shawn Kirkham *SVP, Business Development*
Brian Huntington *Online Editorial Director*
June Alian *Publicity Director*
Andres Juarez *Art Director*
Jon Moisan *Editor*
Arielle Basich *Assistant Editor*
Paul Shin *Business Development Assistant*
Johnny O'Dell *Online Editorial Assistant*
Sally Jacka *Online Editorial Assistant*
Dan Petersen *Director of Operations & Events*
Nick Palmer *Operations Coordinator*

International inquiries: ag@sequentialrights.com
Licensing inquiries: contact@skybound.com

BIRTHRIGHT VOLUME 5: BELLY OF THE BEAST. ISBN: 978-1-5343-0218-1. First Printing. Published by Image Comics, Inc. Office of publication: 2701 NW Vaughn St., Ste. 780, Portland, OR 97210. Copyright © 2017 Skybound, LLC. All rights reserved. Originally published in single magazine format as BIRTHRIGHT #21-25. BIRTHRIGHT™ (including all prominent characters featured herein), its logo and all character likenesses are trademarks of Skybound, LLC, unless otherwise noted. Image Comics® and its logos are registered trademarks and copyrights of Image Comics, Inc. All rights reserved. No part of this publication may be reproduced or transmitted in any form or by any means (except for short excerpts for review purposes) without the express written permission of Image Comics, Inc. All names, characters, events and locales in this publication are entirely fictional. Any resemblance to actual persons (living or dead), events or places, without satiric intent, is coincidental. Printed in the U.S.A. For information regarding the CPSIA on this printed material call: 203-595-3636 and provide reference # RICH – 740023.

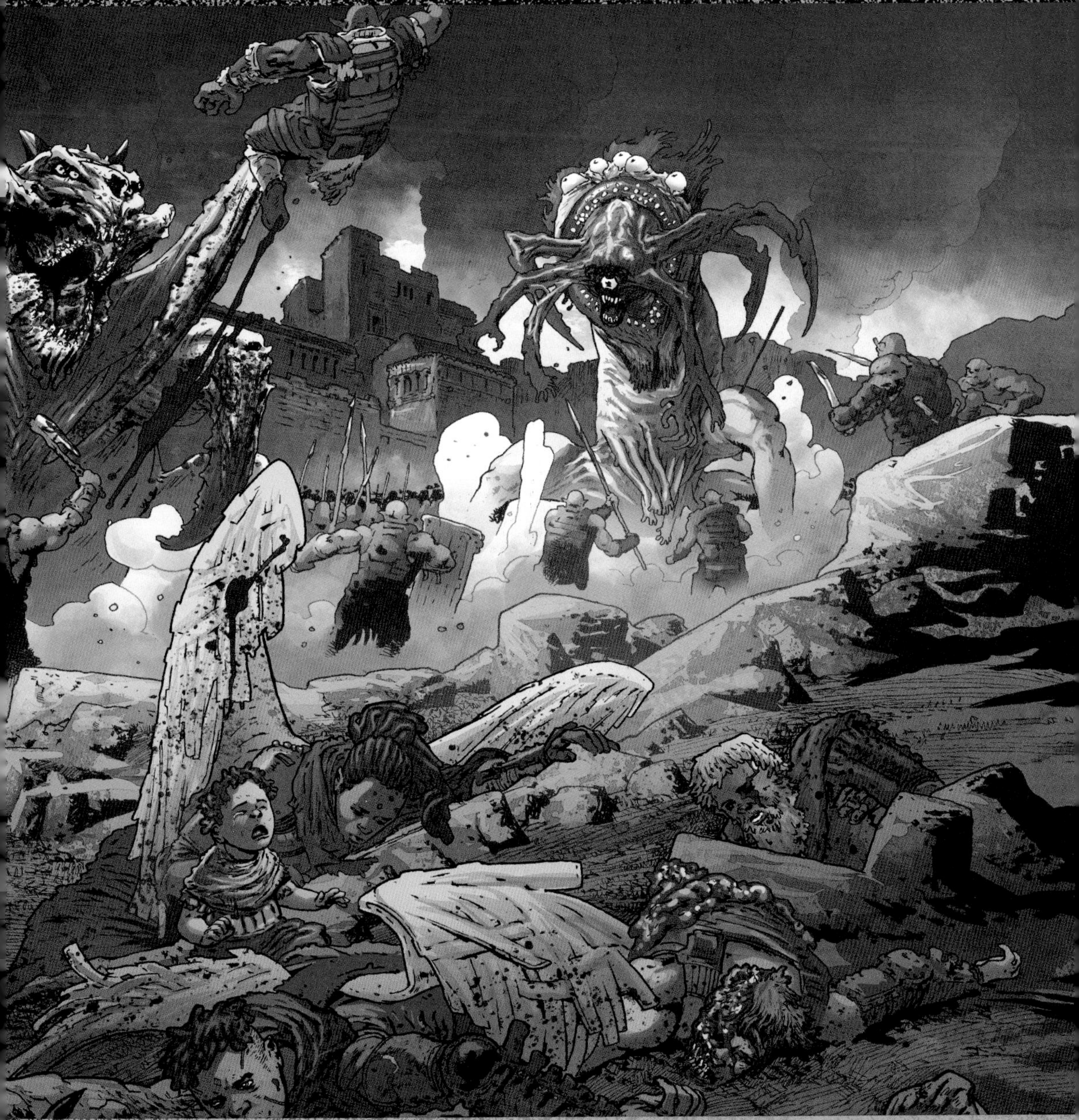

Joshua Williamson
creator, writer

Andrei Bressan
creator, artist

Adriano Lucas
colorist

Pat Brosseau
letterer

Arielle Basich
assistant editor

Sean Mackiewicz
editor

logo design by Rian Hughes

cover by Andrei Bressan *and* Adriano Lucas

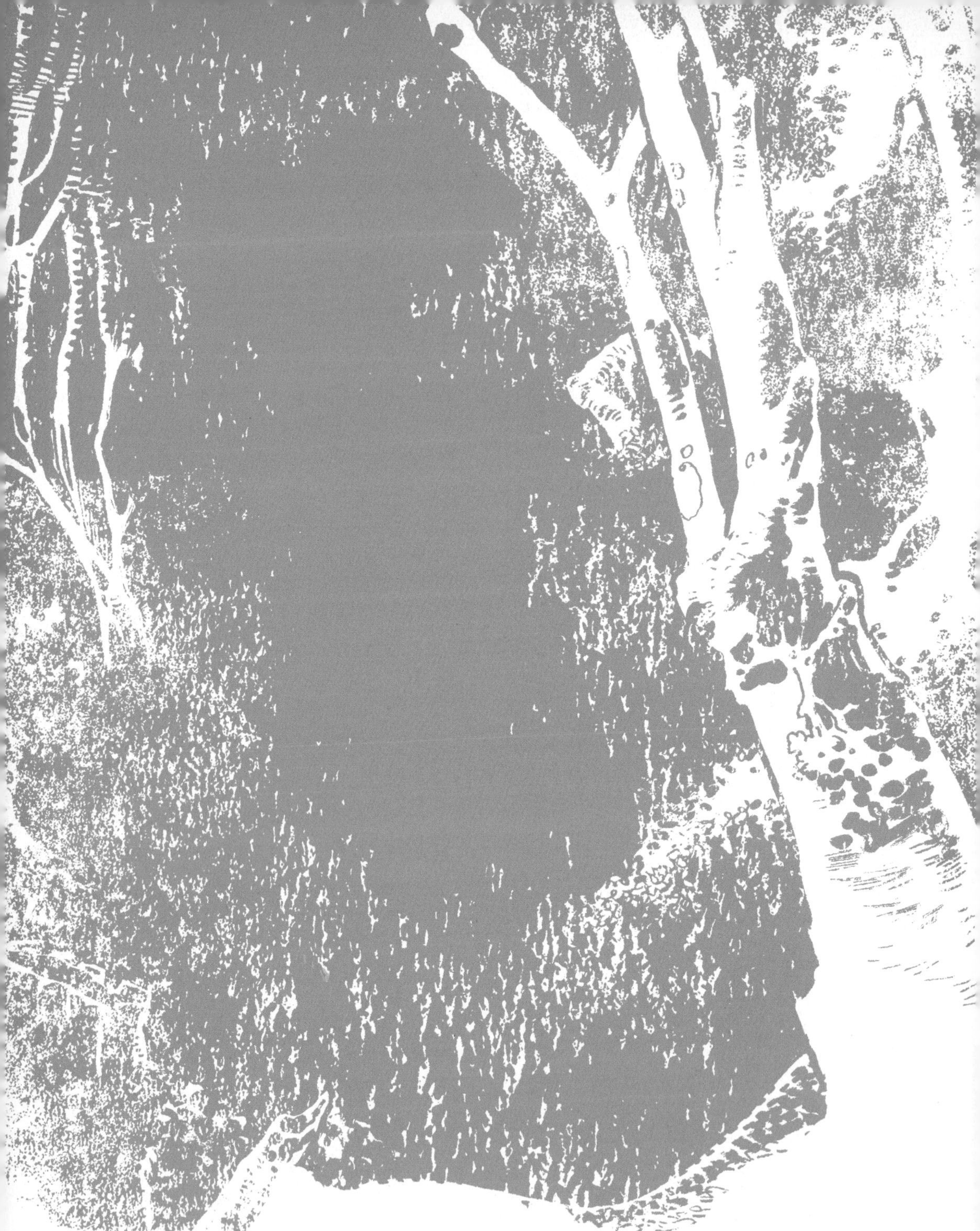

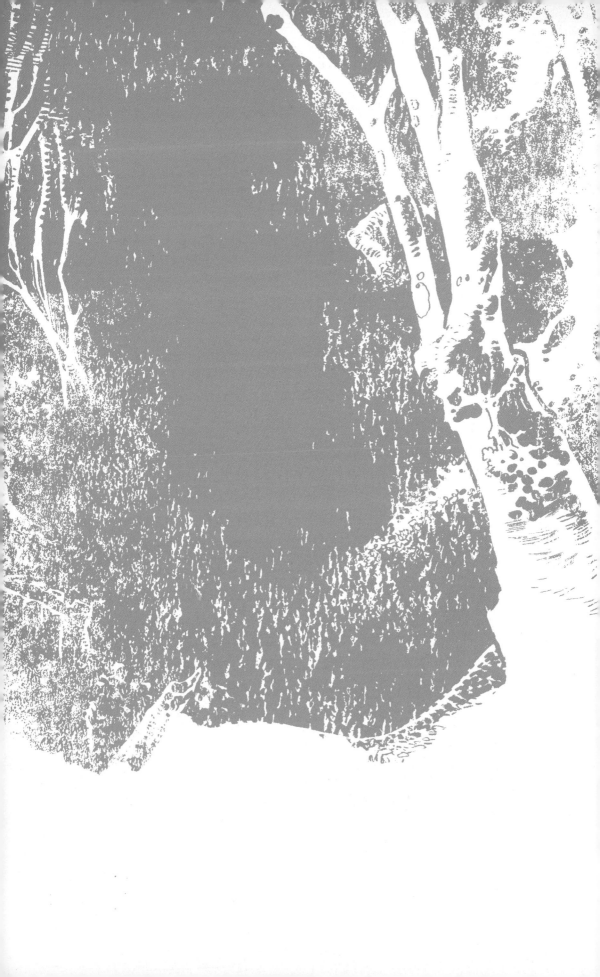

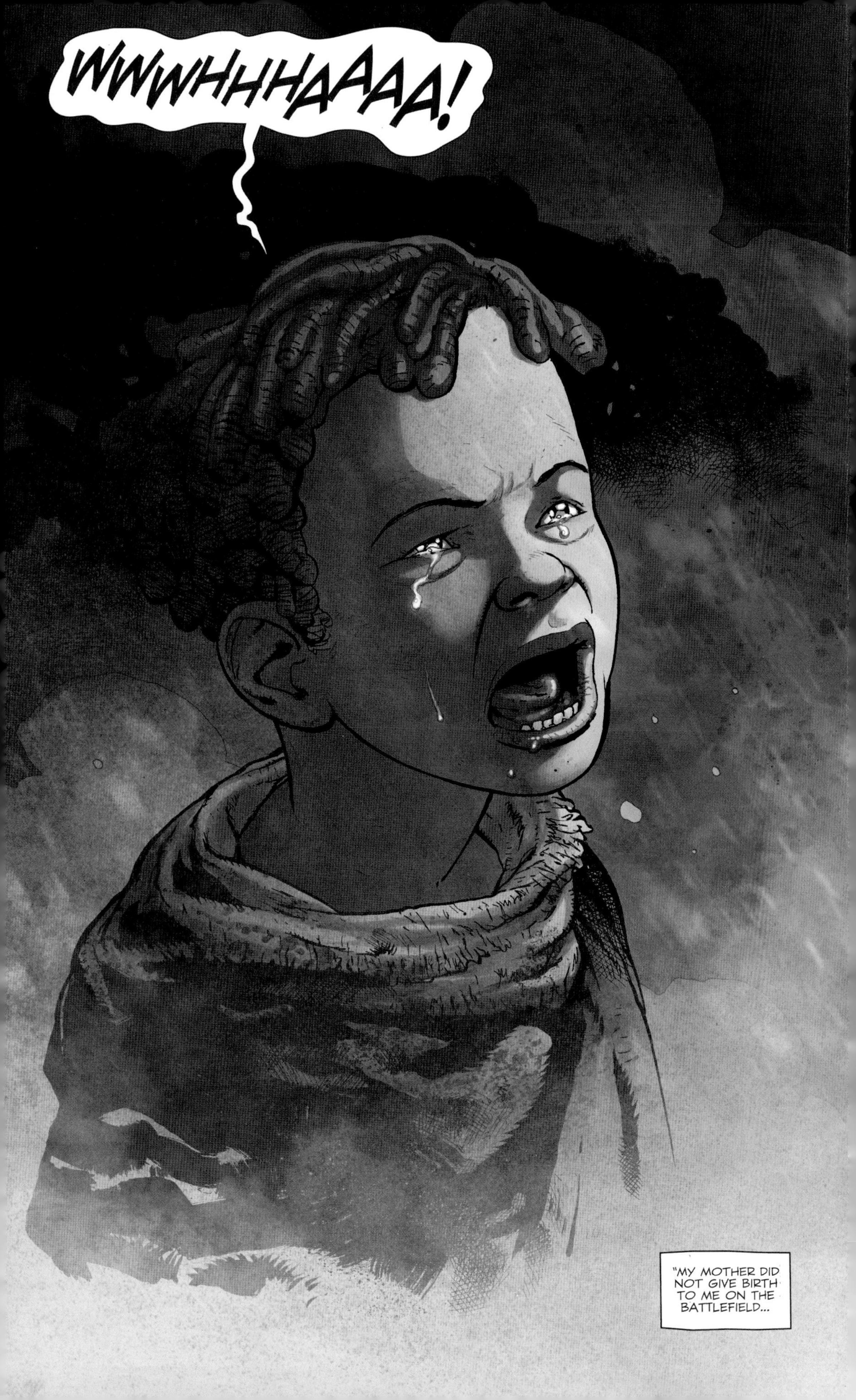
WWWHHHAAAA!
"MY MOTHER DID NOT GIVE BIRTH TO ME ON THE BATTLEFIELD...

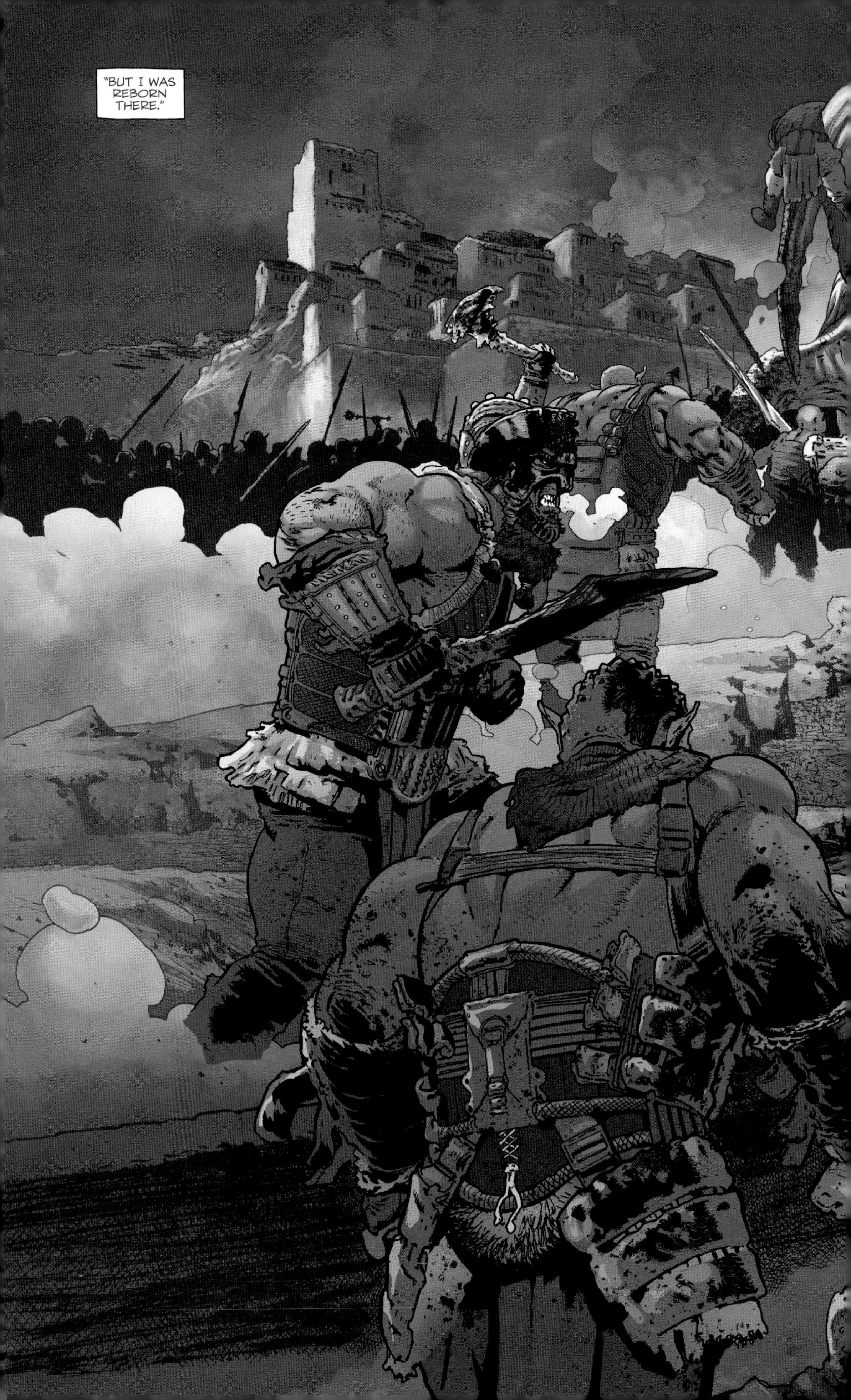
"BUT I WAS REBORN THERE."

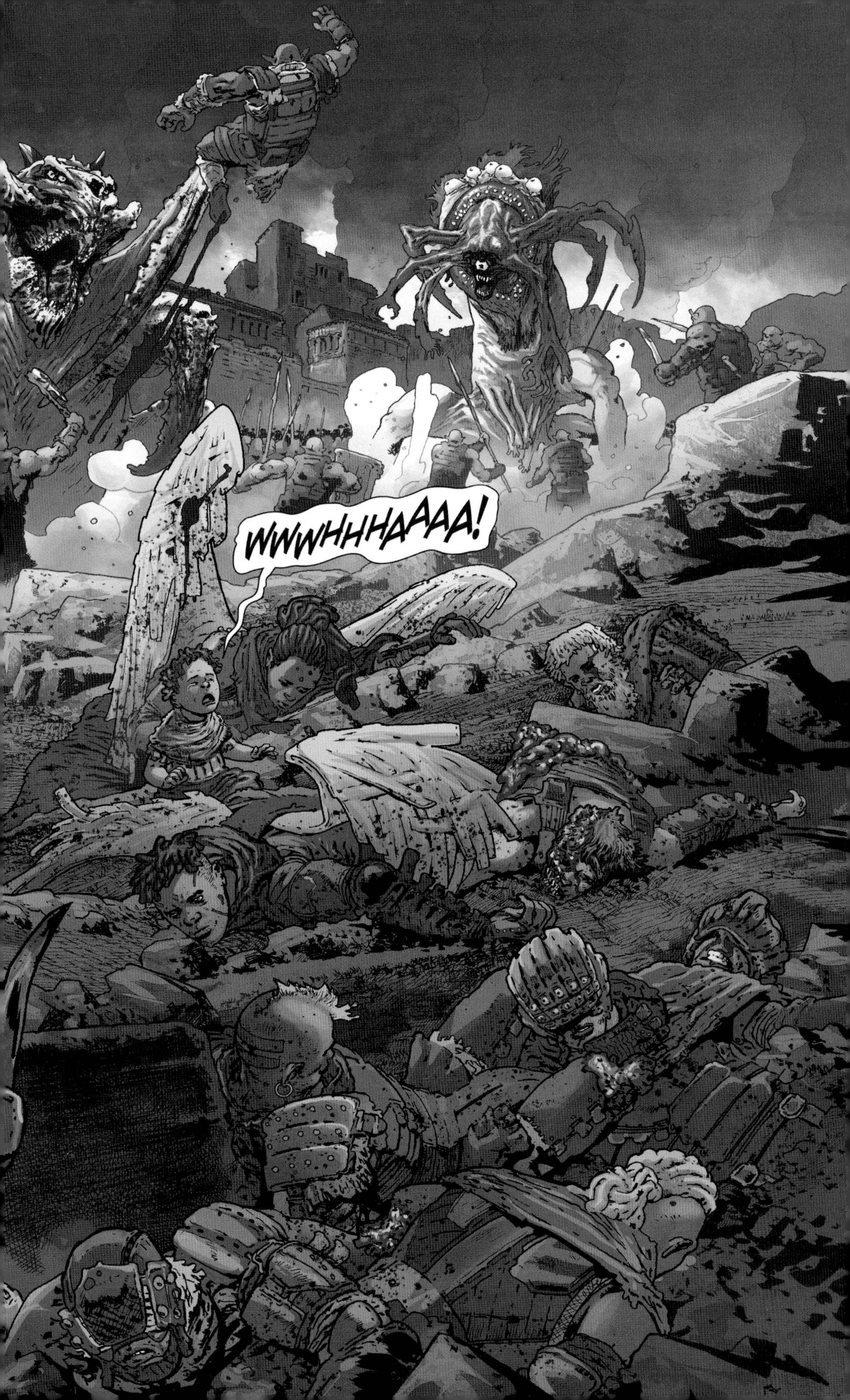
WWWHHHAAAA!

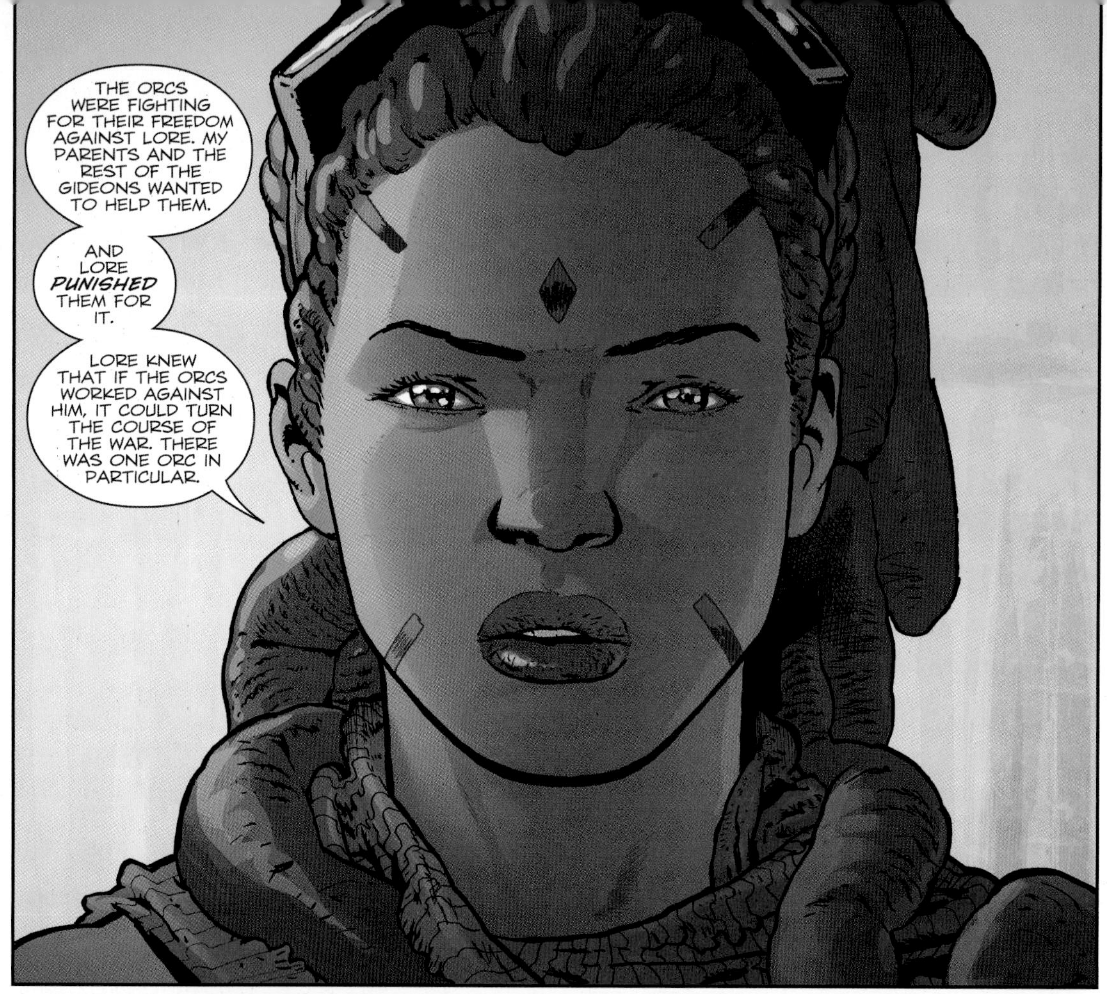
THE ORCS WERE FIGHTING FOR THEIR FREEDOM AGAINST LORE. MY PARENTS AND THE REST OF THE GIDEONS WANTED TO HELP THEM.
AND LORE *PUNISHED* THEM FOR IT.
LORE KNEW THAT IF THE ORCS WORKED AGAINST HIM, IT COULD TURN THE COURSE OF THE WAR. THERE WAS ONE ORC IN PARTICULAR.

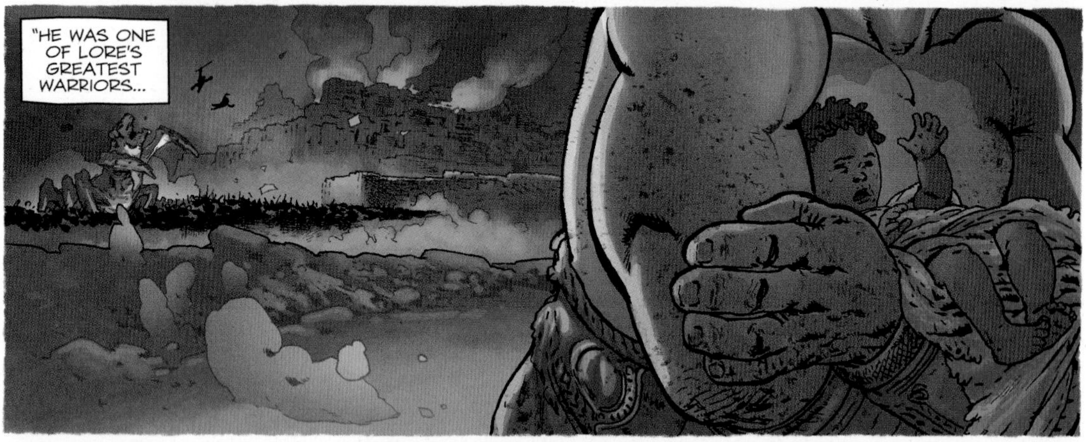
"HE WAS ONE OF LORE'S GREATEST WARRIORS...

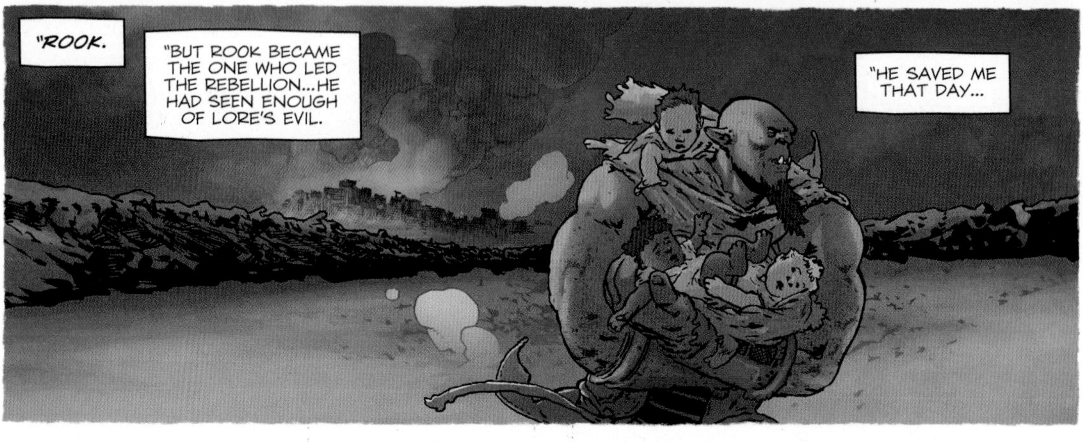
"*ROOK.*
"BUT ROOK BECAME THE ONE WHO LED THE REBELLION...HE HAD SEEN ENOUGH OF LORE'S EVIL.
"HE SAVED ME THAT DAY...

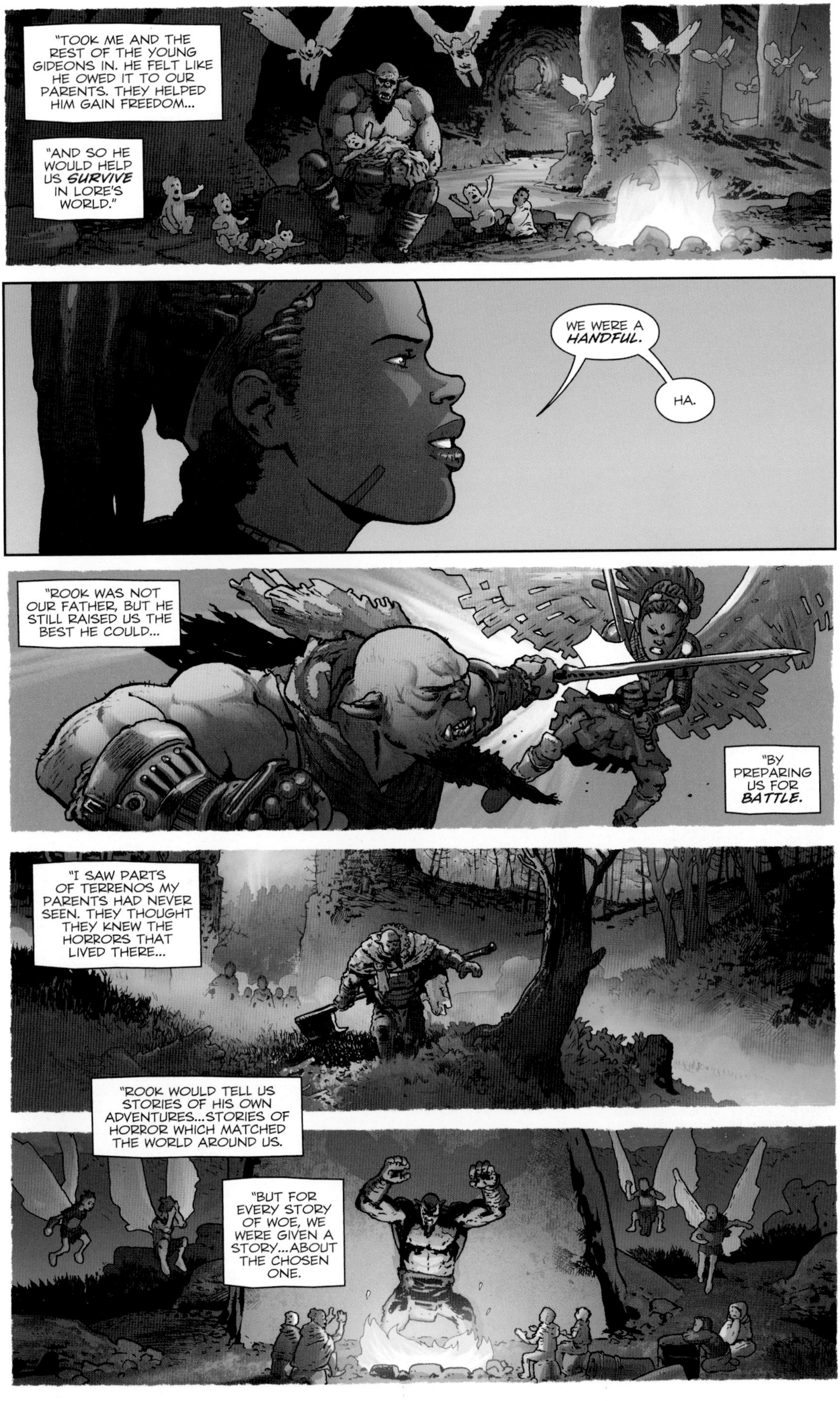

"TOOK ME AND THE REST OF THE YOUNG GIDEONS IN. HE FELT LIKE HE OWED IT TO OUR PARENTS. THEY HELPED HIM GAIN FREEDOM...
"AND SO HE WOULD HELP US SURVIVE IN LORE'S WORLD."
WE WERE A HANDFUL.
HA.
"ROOK WAS NOT OUR FATHER, BUT HE STILL RAISED US THE BEST HE COULD...
"BY PREPARING US FOR BATTLE.
"I SAW PARTS OF TERRENOS MY PARENTS HAD NEVER SEEN. THEY THOUGHT THEY KNEW THE HORRORS THAT LIVED THERE...
"ROOK WOULD TELL US STORIES OF HIS OWN ADVENTURES...STORIES OF HORROR WHICH MATCHED THE WORLD AROUND US.
"BUT FOR EVERY STORY OF WOE, WE WERE GIVEN A STORY...ABOUT THE CHOSEN ONE.

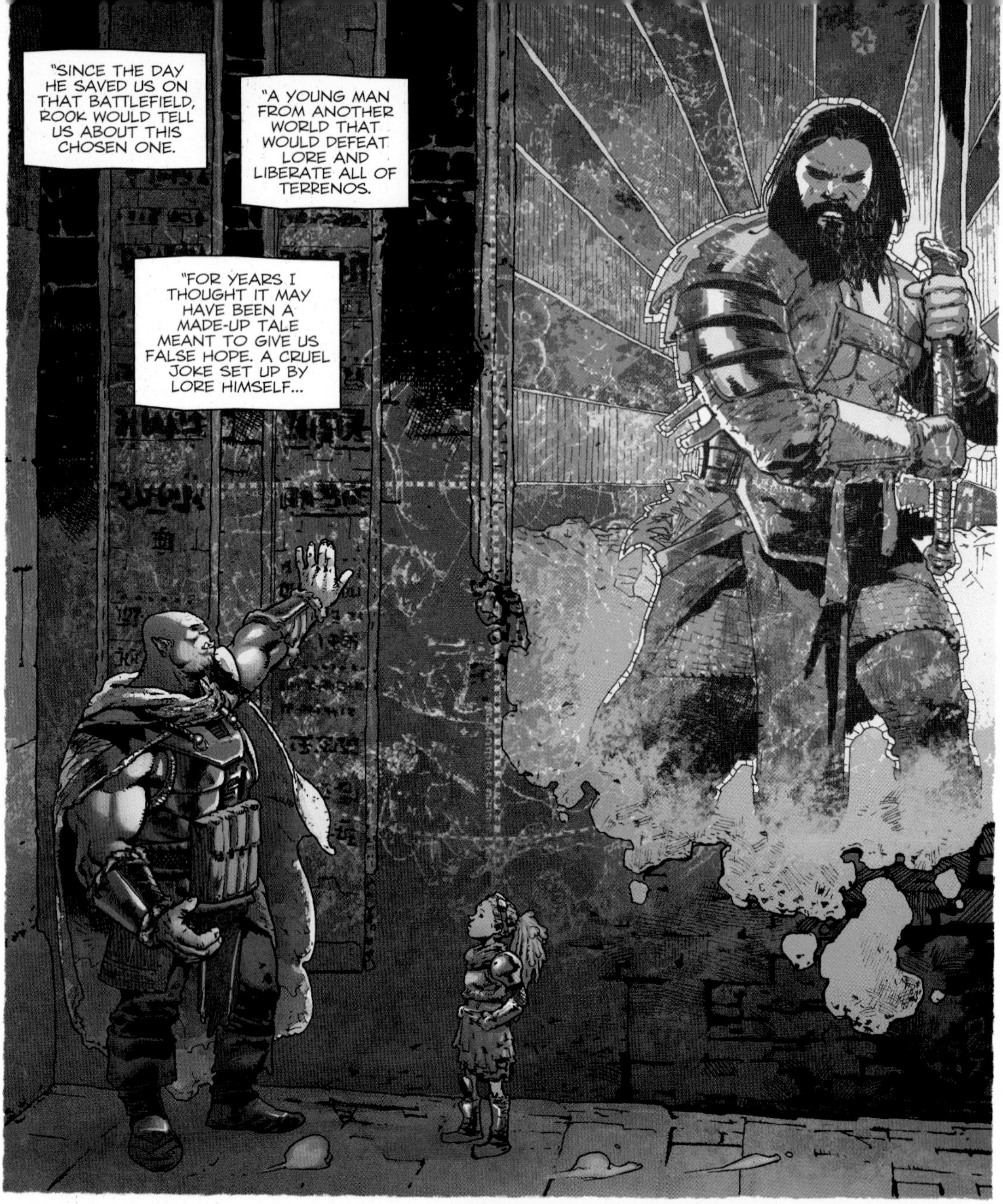
"SINCE THE DAY HE SAVED US ON THAT BATTLEFIELD, ROOK WOULD TELL US ABOUT THIS CHOSEN ONE.
"A YOUNG MAN FROM ANOTHER WORLD THAT WOULD DEFEAT LORE AND LIBERATE ALL OF TERRENOS.
"FOR YEARS I THOUGHT IT MAY HAVE BEEN A MADE-UP TALE MEANT TO GIVE US FALSE HOPE. A CRUEL JOKE SET UP BY LORE HIMSELF...

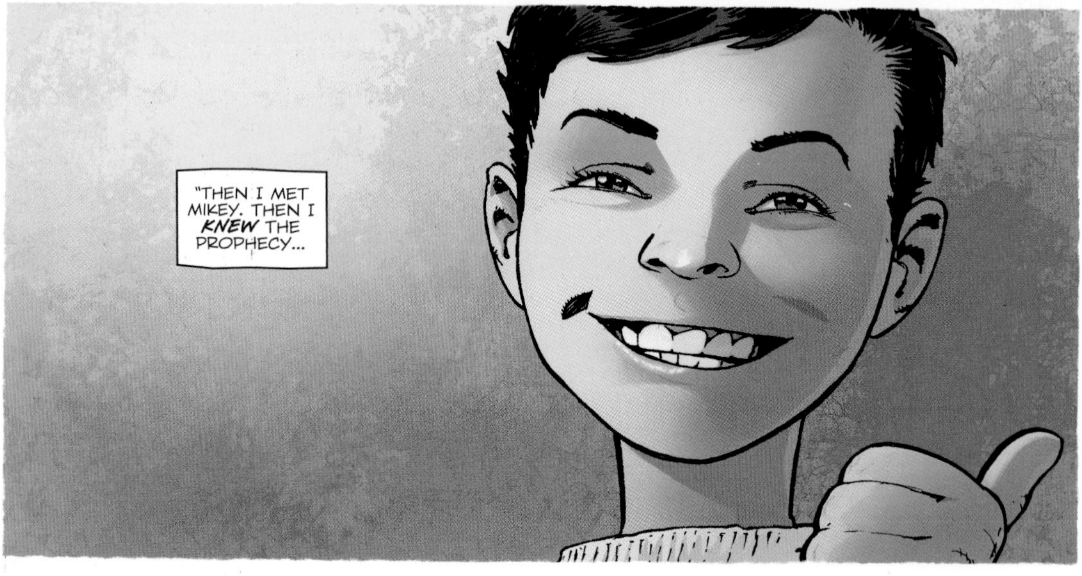
"THEN I MET MIKEY. THEN I *KNEW* THE PROPHECY...

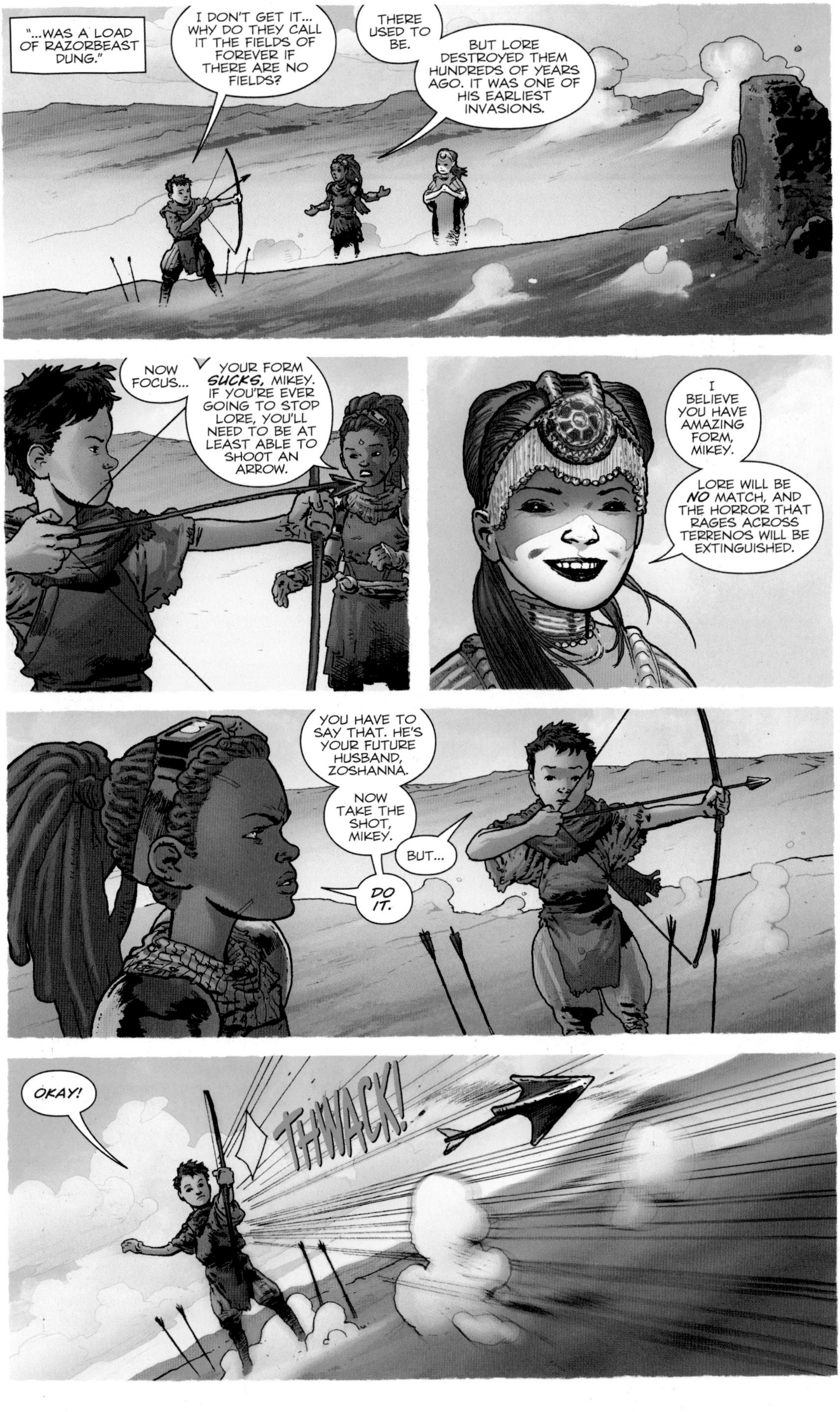
"...WAS A LOAD OF RAZORBEAST DUNG."
I DON'T GET IT... WHY DO THEY CALL IT THE FIELDS OF FOREVER IF THERE ARE NO FIELDS?
THERE USED TO BE.
BUT LORE DESTROYED THEM HUNDREDS OF YEARS AGO. IT WAS ONE OF HIS EARLIEST INVASIONS.
NOW FOCUS...
YOUR FORM SUCKS, MIKEY. IF YOU'RE EVER GOING TO STOP LORE, YOU'LL NEED TO BE AT LEAST ABLE TO SHOOT AN ARROW.
I BELIEVE YOU HAVE AMAZING FORM, MIKEY.
LORE WILL BE NO MATCH, AND THE HORROR THAT RAGES ACROSS TERRENOS WILL BE EXTINGUISHED.
YOU HAVE TO SAY THAT. HE'S YOUR FUTURE HUSBAND, ZOSHANNA.
NOW TAKE THE SHOT, MIKEY.
BUT...
DO IT.
OKAY!
THWACK!

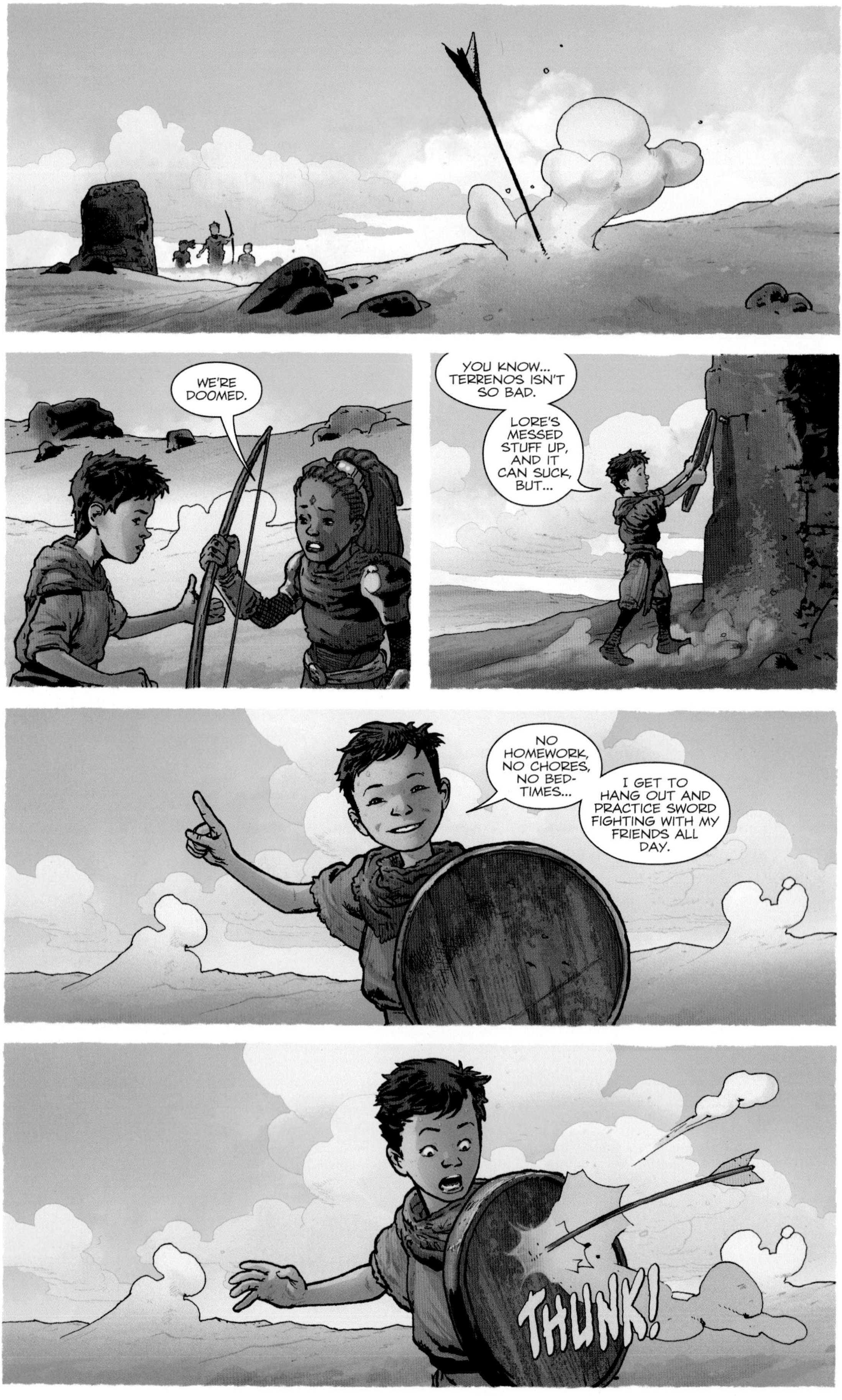
WE'RE DOOMED.
YOU KNOW... TERRENOS ISN'T SO BAD.
LORE'S MESSED STUFF UP, AND IT CAN SUCK, BUT...
NO HOMEWORK, NO CHORES, NO BED-TIMES...
I GET TO HANG OUT AND PRACTICE SWORD FIGHTING WITH MY FRIENDS ALL DAY.
THUNK!

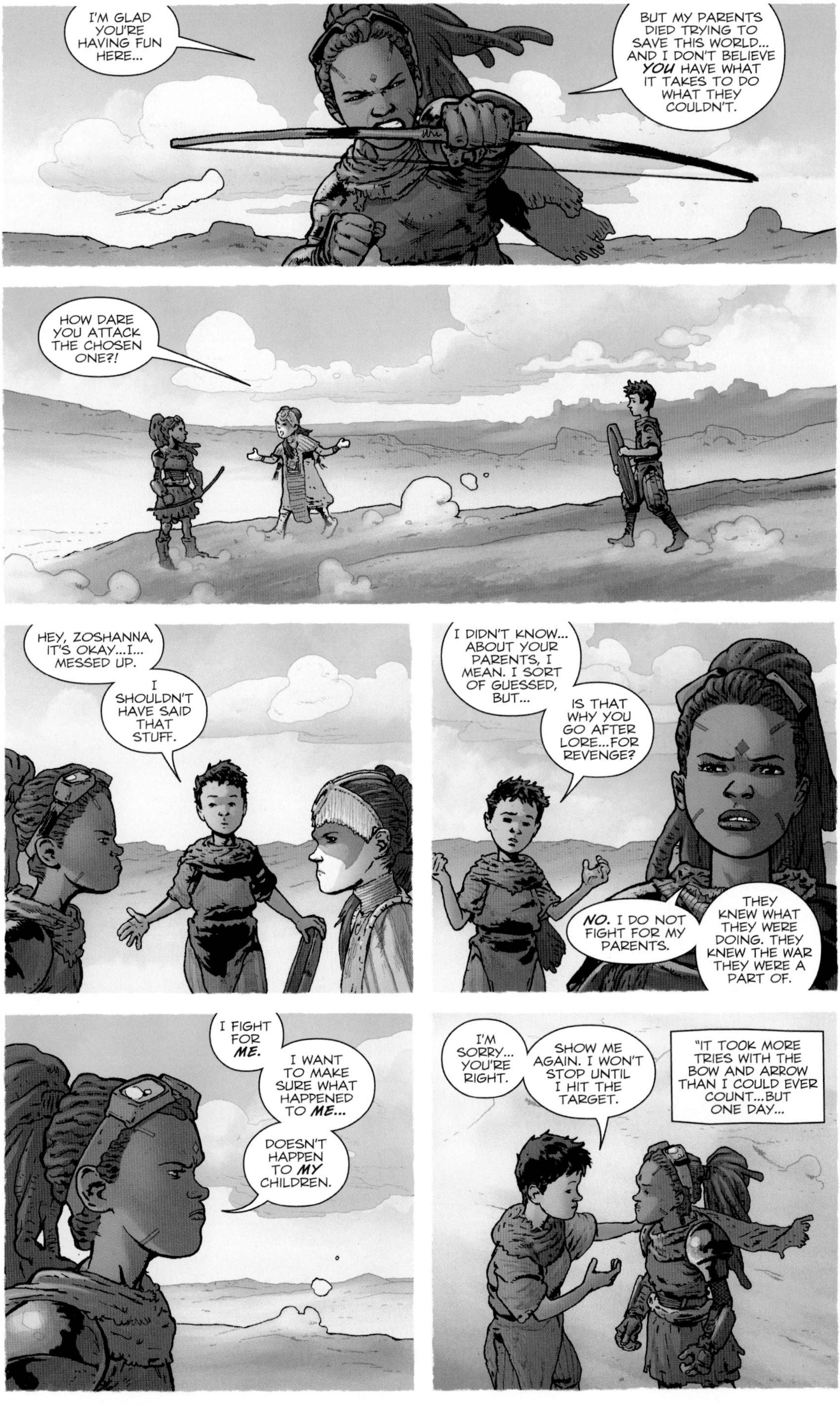
I'M GLAD YOU'RE HAVING FUN HERE...
BUT MY PARENTS DIED TRYING TO SAVE THIS WORLD... AND I DON'T BELIEVE *YOU* HAVE WHAT IT TAKES TO DO WHAT THEY COULDN'T.
HOW DARE YOU ATTACK THE CHOSEN ONE?!
HEY, ZOSHANNA, IT'S OKAY...I... MESSED UP.
I SHOULDN'T HAVE SAID THAT STUFF.
I DIDN'T KNOW... ABOUT YOUR PARENTS, I MEAN. I SORT OF GUESSED, BUT...
IS THAT WHY YOU GO AFTER LORE...FOR REVENGE?
NO. I DO NOT FIGHT FOR MY PARENTS.
THEY KNEW WHAT THEY WERE DOING. THEY KNEW THE WAR THEY WERE A PART OF.
I FIGHT FOR *ME.*
I WANT TO MAKE SURE WHAT HAPPENED TO *ME...*
DOESN'T HAPPEN TO *MY* CHILDREN.
I'M SORRY... YOU'RE RIGHT.
SHOW ME AGAIN. I WON'T STOP UNTIL I HIT THE TARGET.
"IT TOOK MORE TRIES WITH THE BOW AND ARROW THAN I COULD EVER COUNT...BUT ONE DAY...

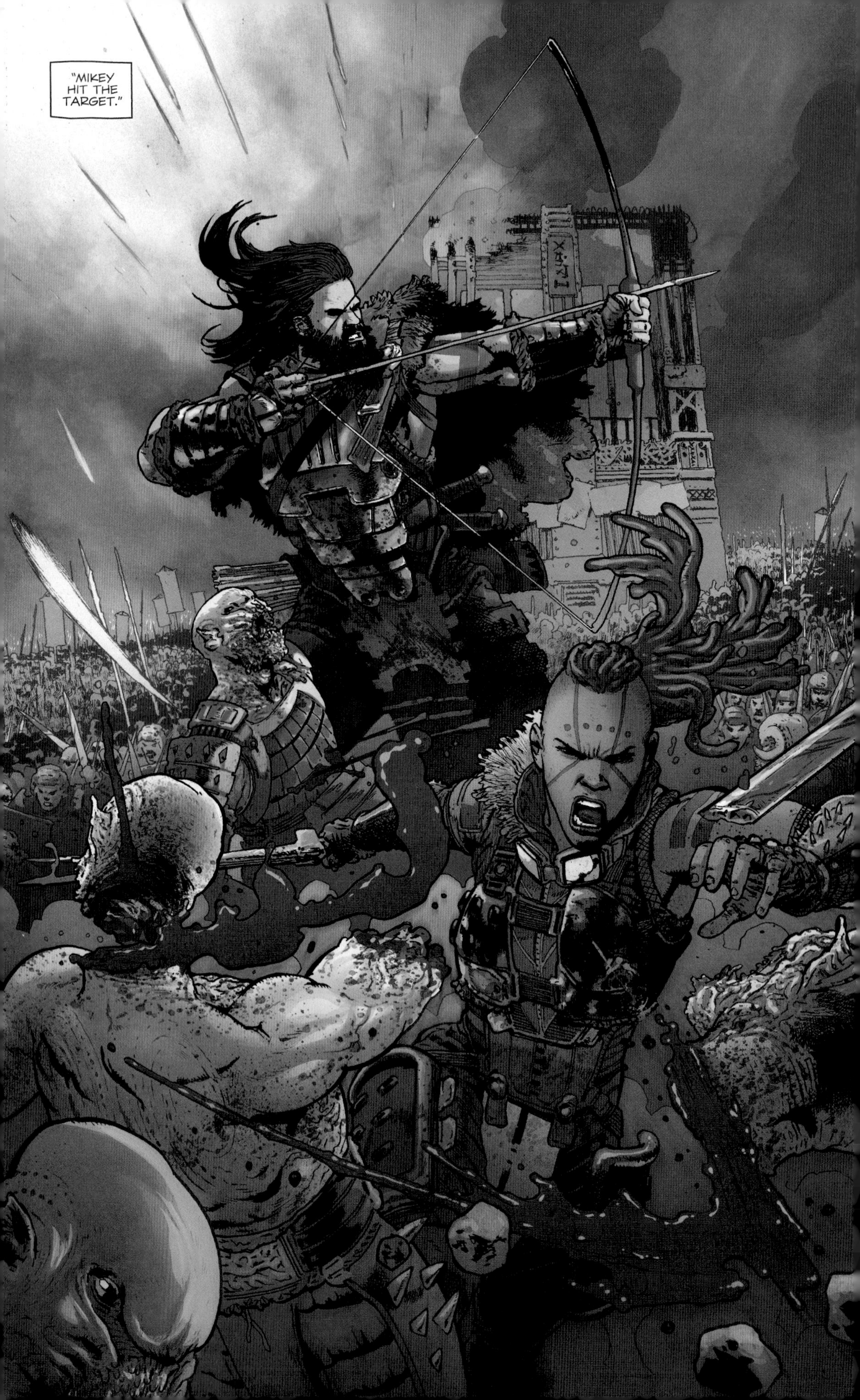
"MIKEY HIT THE TARGET."

BUT THEN MIKEY DISAPPEARED... ON THE DAY HE WAS SUPPOSED TO GO UP AGAINST THE GOD KING LORE.

THE RUMOR WAS THAT LORE HAD KILLED HIM.

BUT I KNEW...I COULD FEEL IT IN MY *HEART*...

"THE FIGHT WAS FAR FROM OVER."

WHAT ARE WE DOING HERE, RYA?

WE NEED TO FIND THE ORC YOUNGLINGS AND MOVE THEM BEFORE LORE'S FORCES OVERTAKE THESE PARTS.

WHY ARE WE TRYING TO SAVE ORC BABIES?!

HOW COULD YOU ASK THAT, SHAVO? ROOK RAISED YOU AS WELL...

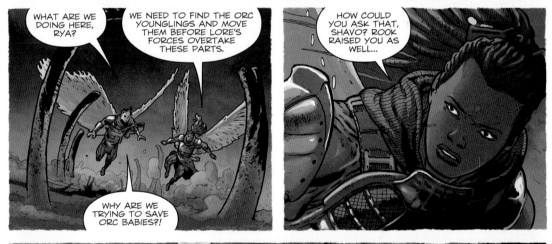

C'MON... WE DON'T HAVE MUCH TIME!

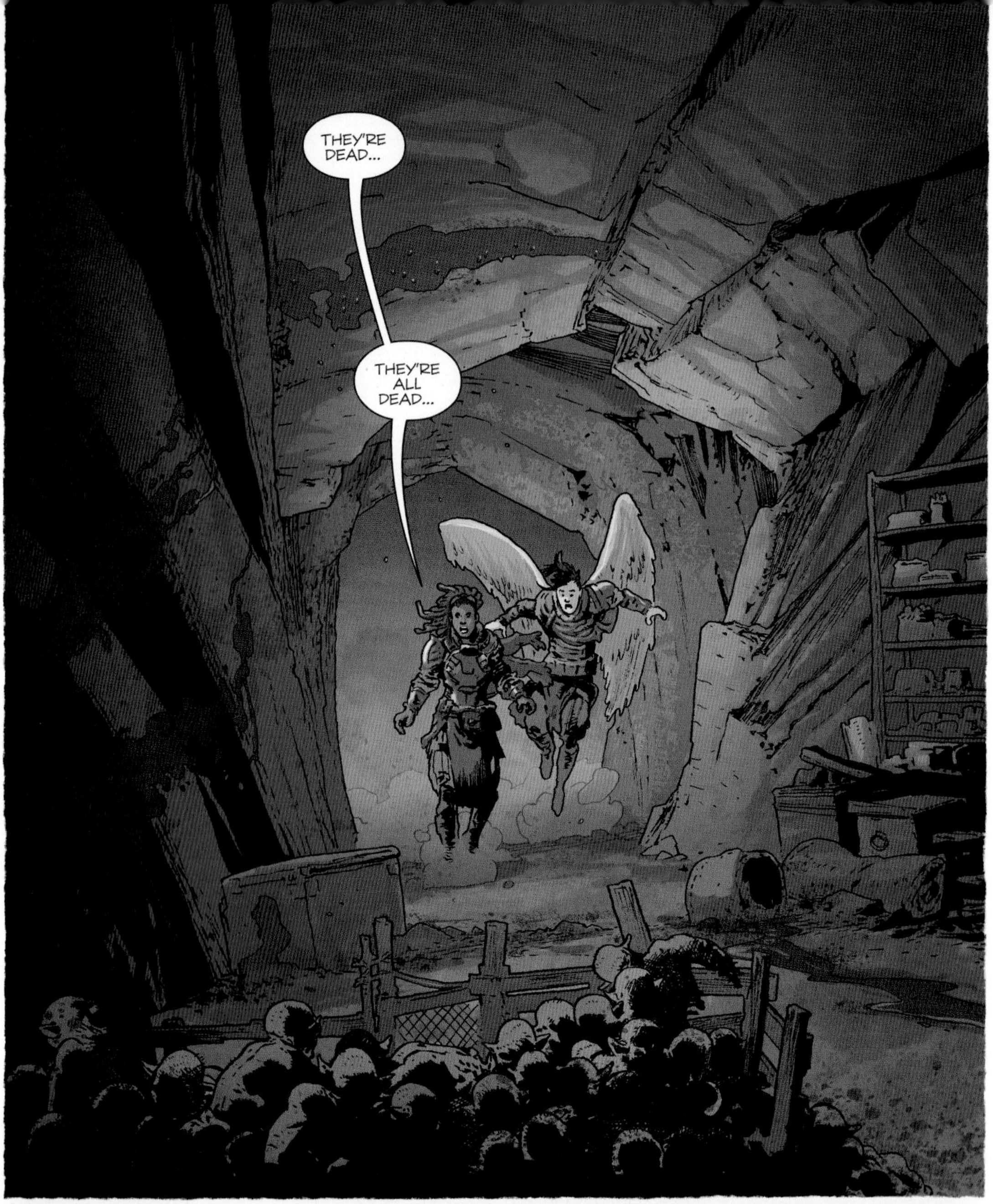
THEY'RE DEAD...
THEY'RE ALL DEAD...

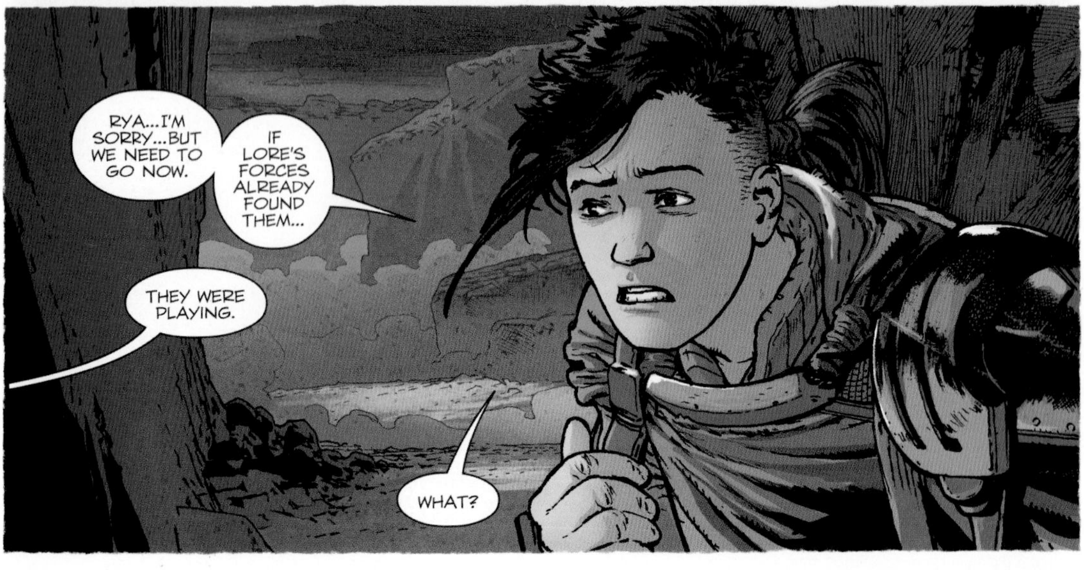
RYA...I'M SORRY...BUT WE NEED TO GO NOW.
IF LORE'S FORCES ALREADY FOUND THEM...
THEY WERE PLAYING.
WHAT?

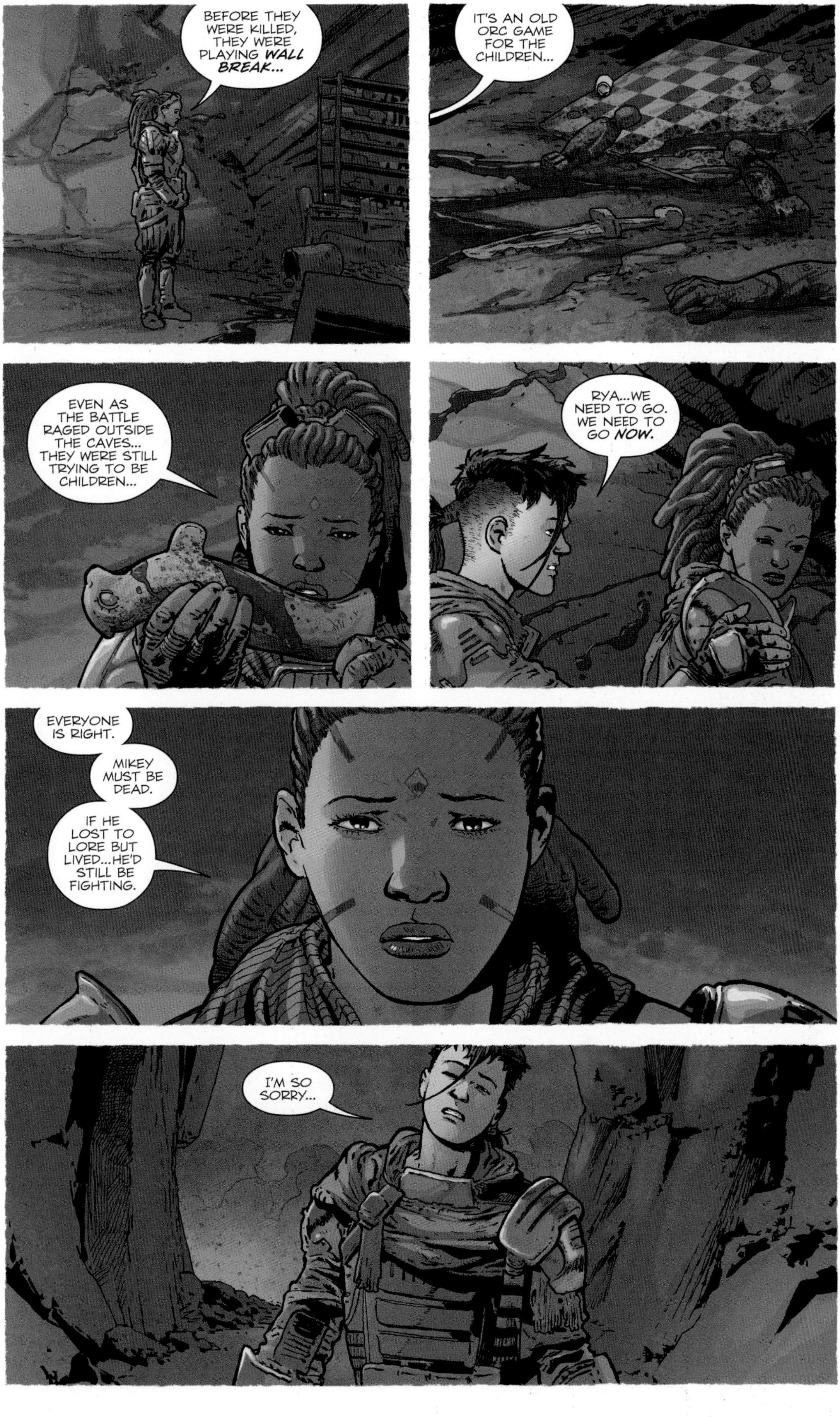
BEFORE THEY WERE KILLED, THEY WERE PLAYING WALL BREAK...
IT'S AN OLD ORC GAME FOR THE CHILDREN...
EVEN AS THE BATTLE RAGED OUTSIDE THE CAVES... THEY WERE STILL TRYING TO BE CHILDREN...
RYA...WE NEED TO GO. WE NEED TO GO NOW.
EVERYONE IS RIGHT.
MIKEY MUST BE DEAD.
IF HE LOST TO LORE BUT LIVED...HE'D STILL BE FIGHTING.
I'M SO SORRY...

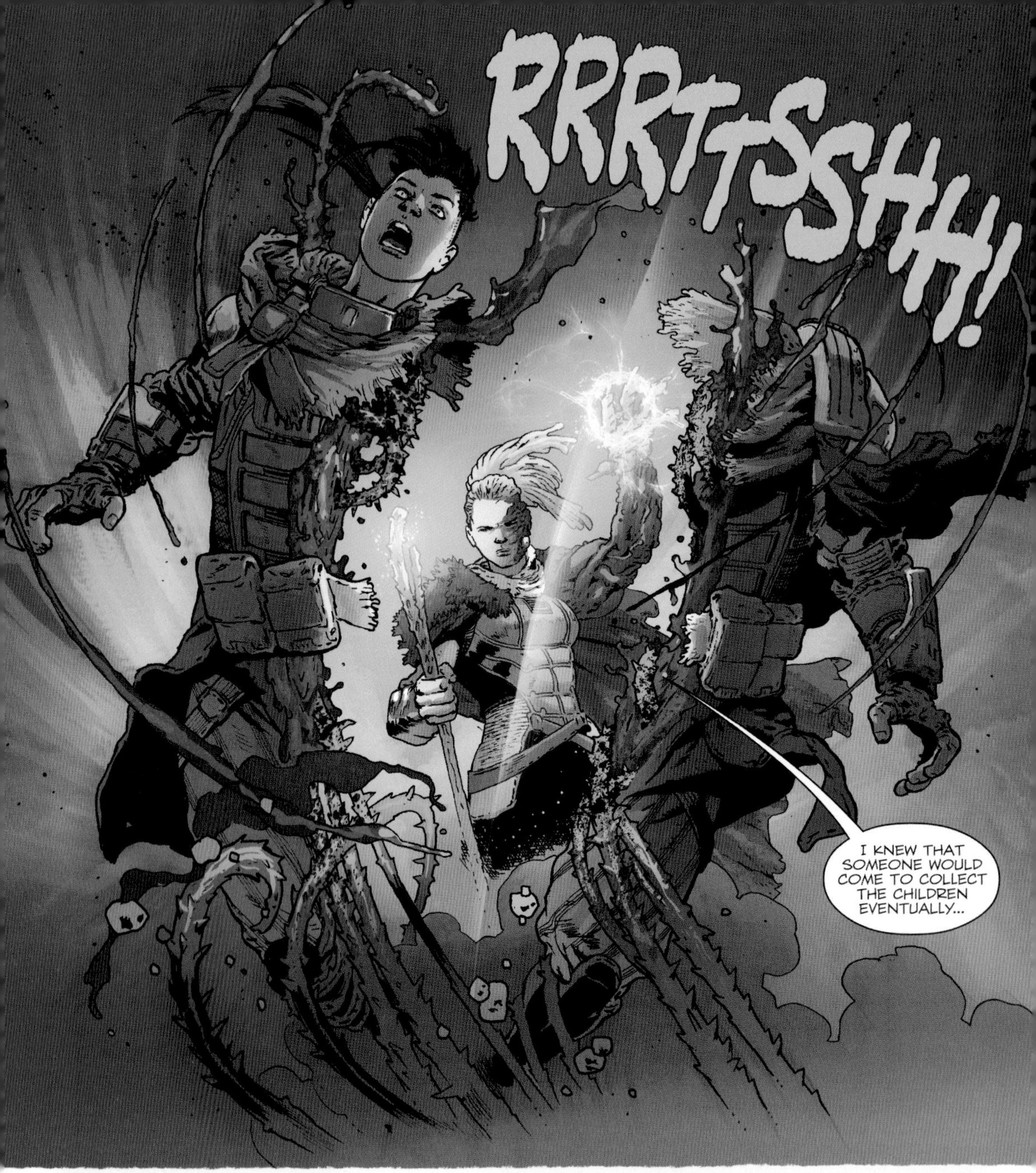
RRRTTSSHH!
I KNEW THAT SOMEONE WOULD COME TO COLLECT THE CHILDREN EVENTUALLY...

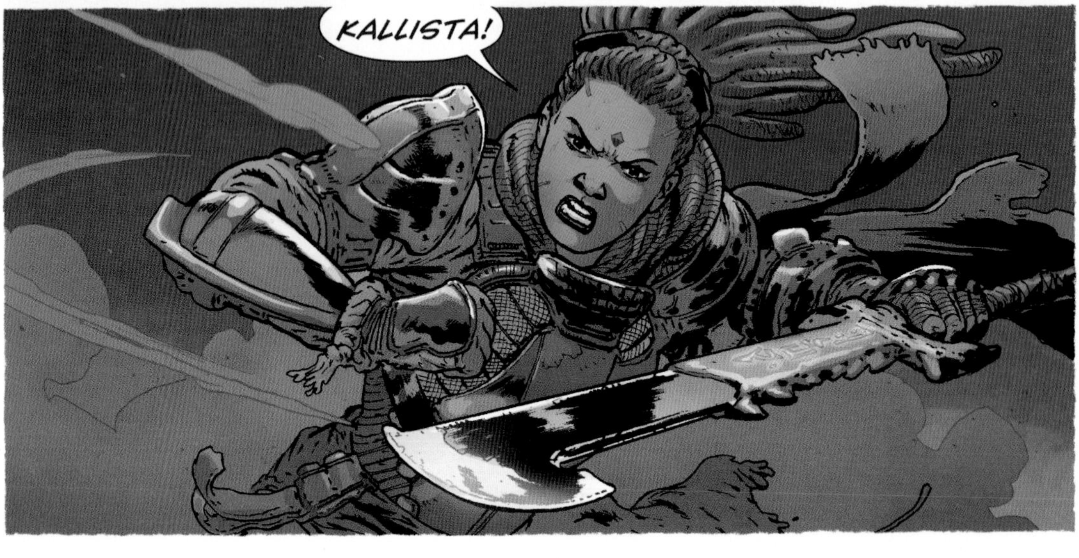
KALLISTA!

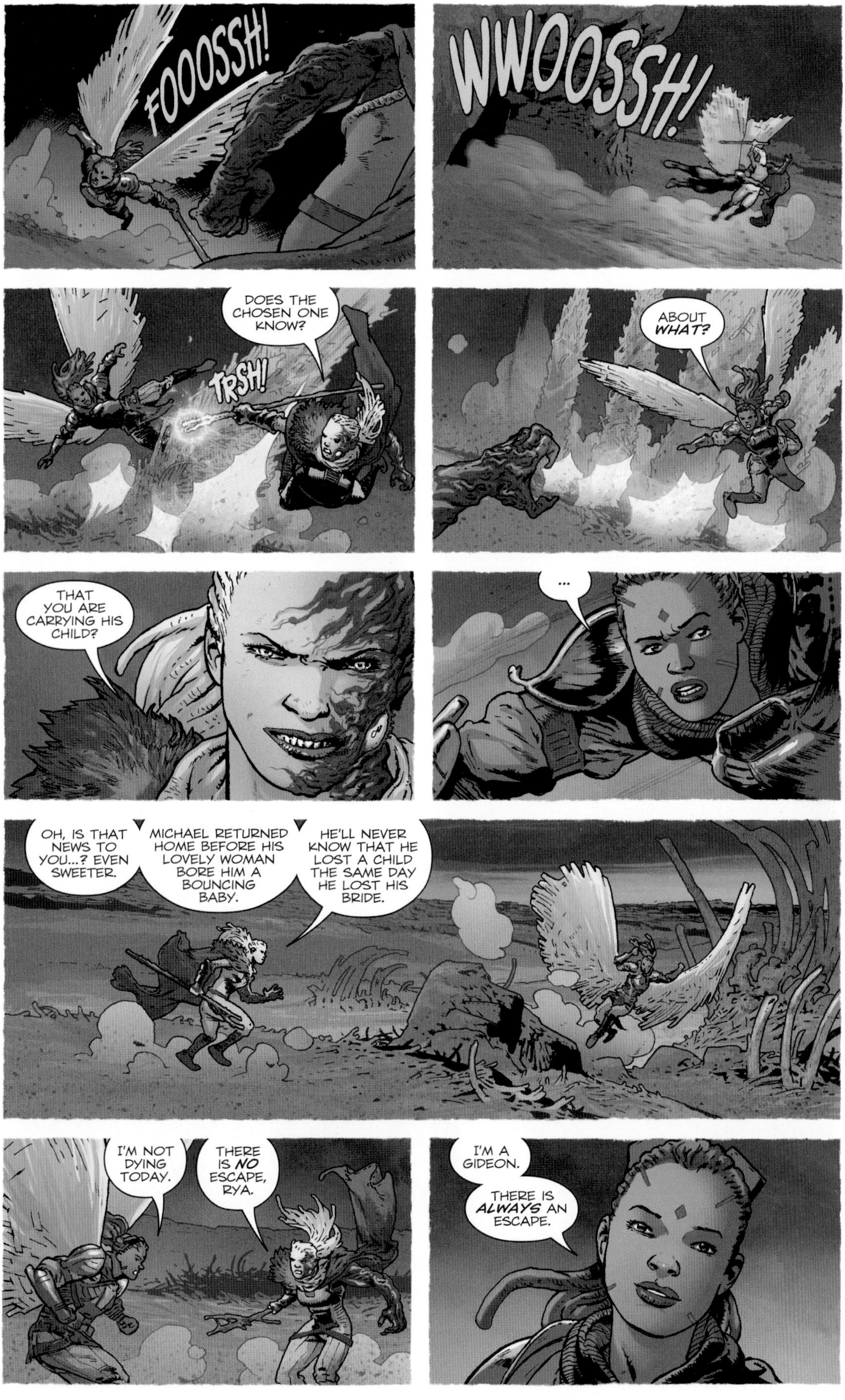
FOOOSSH!
WWOOSSH!
DOES THE CHOSEN ONE KNOW?
TRSH!
ABOUT *WHAT?*
THAT YOU ARE CARRYING HIS CHILD?
...
OH, IS THAT NEWS TO YOU...? EVEN SWEETER.
MICHAEL RETURNED HOME BEFORE HIS LOVELY WOMAN BORE HIM A BOUNCING BABY.
HE'LL NEVER KNOW THAT HE LOST A CHILD THE SAME DAY HE LOST HIS BRIDE.
I'M NOT DYING TODAY.
THERE IS *NO* ESCAPE, RYA.
I'M A GIDEON.
THERE IS *ALWAYS* AN ESCAPE.

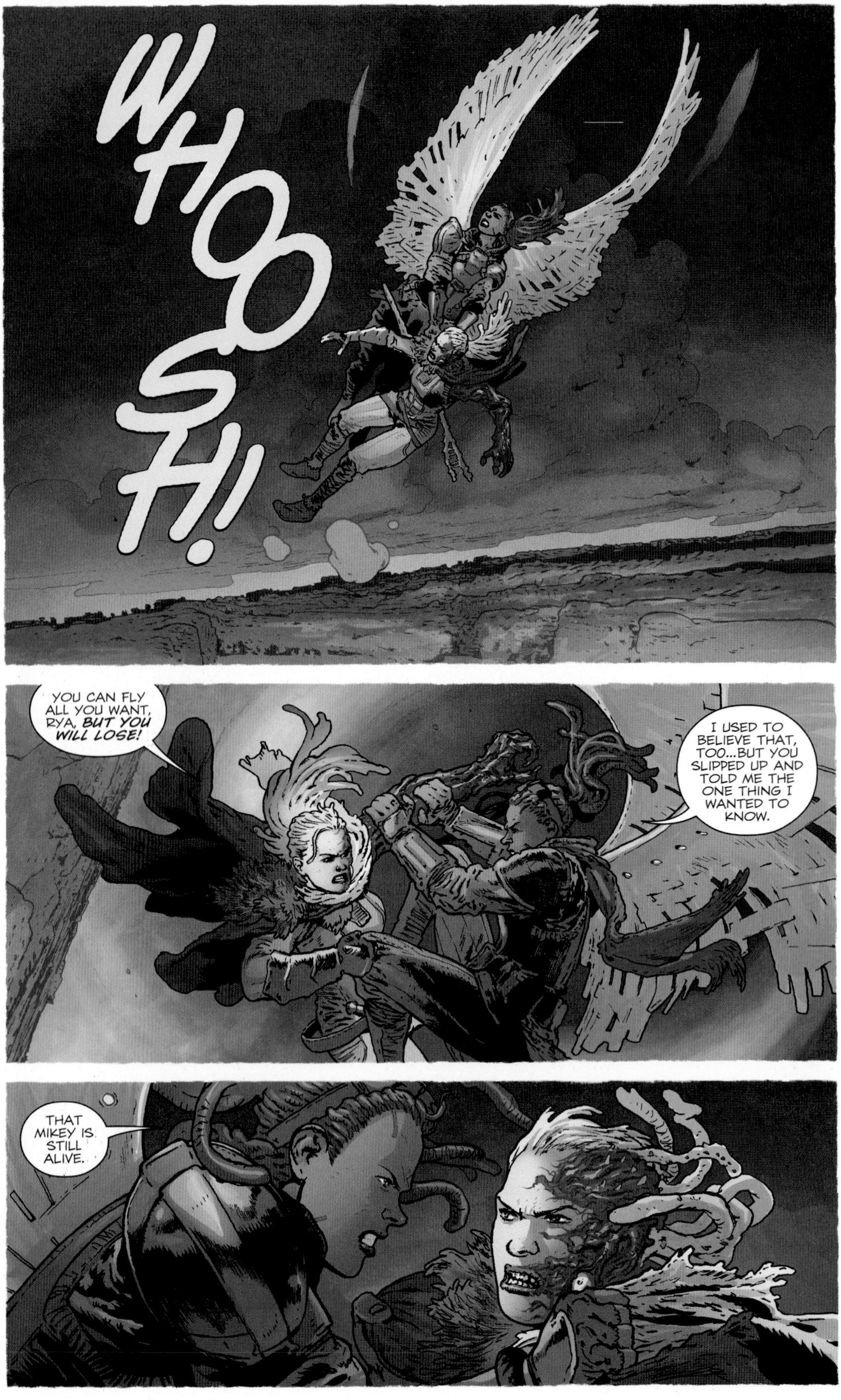
WHOOOSH!!
YOU CAN FLY ALL YOU WANT, RYA, **BUT YOU WILL LOSE!**
I USED TO BELIEVE THAT, TOO...BUT YOU SLIPPED UP AND TOLD ME THE ONE THING I WANTED TO KNOW.
THAT MIKEY IS STILL ALIVE.

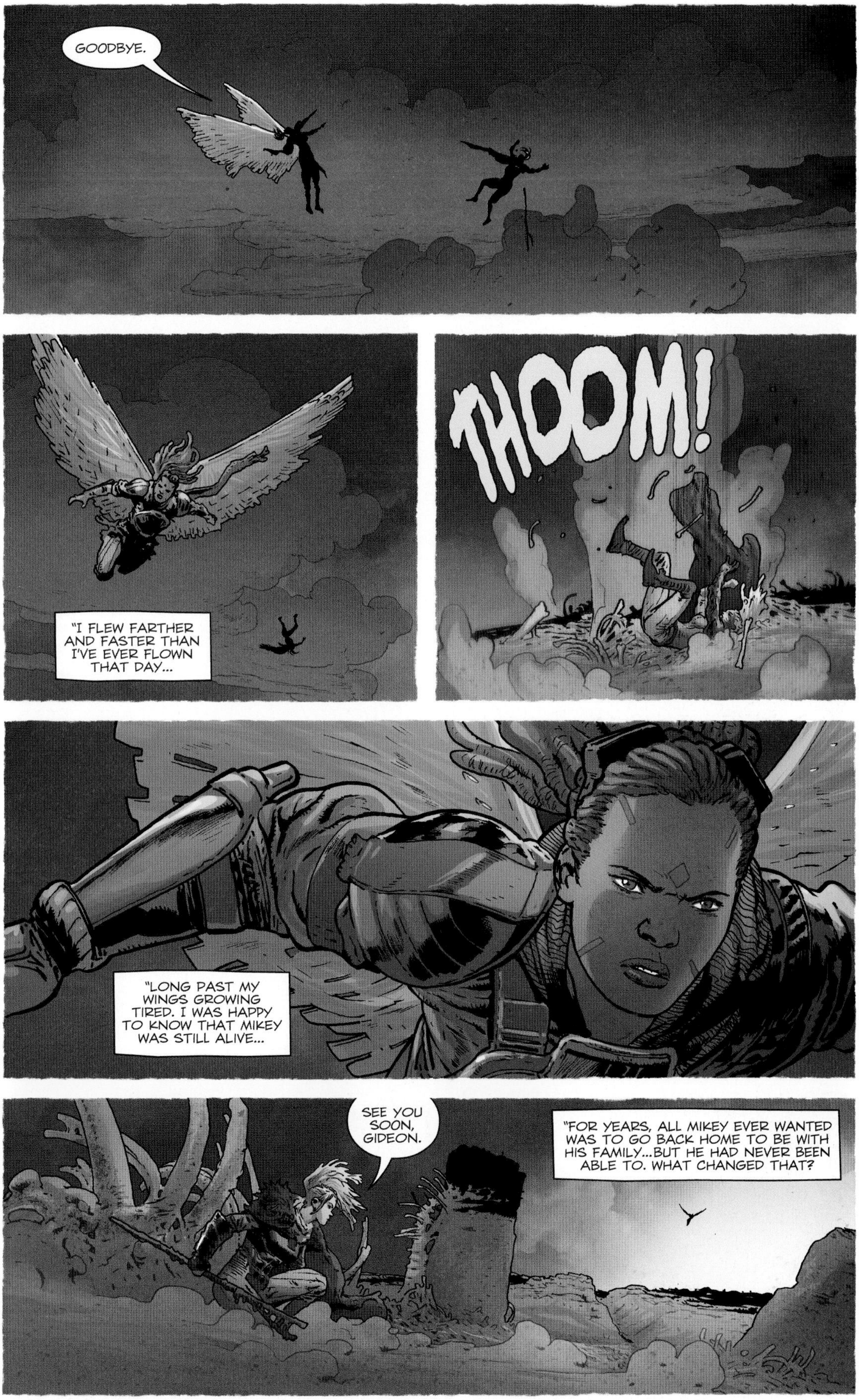
GOODBYE.
"I FLEW FARTHER AND FASTER THAN I'VE EVER FLOWN THAT DAY...
THOOM!
"LONG PAST MY WINGS GROWING TIRED. I WAS HAPPY TO KNOW THAT MIKEY WAS STILL ALIVE...
SEE YOU SOON, GIDEON.
"FOR YEARS, ALL MIKEY EVER WANTED WAS TO GO BACK HOME TO BE WITH HIS FAMILY...BUT HE HAD NEVER BEEN ABLE TO. WHAT CHANGED THAT?

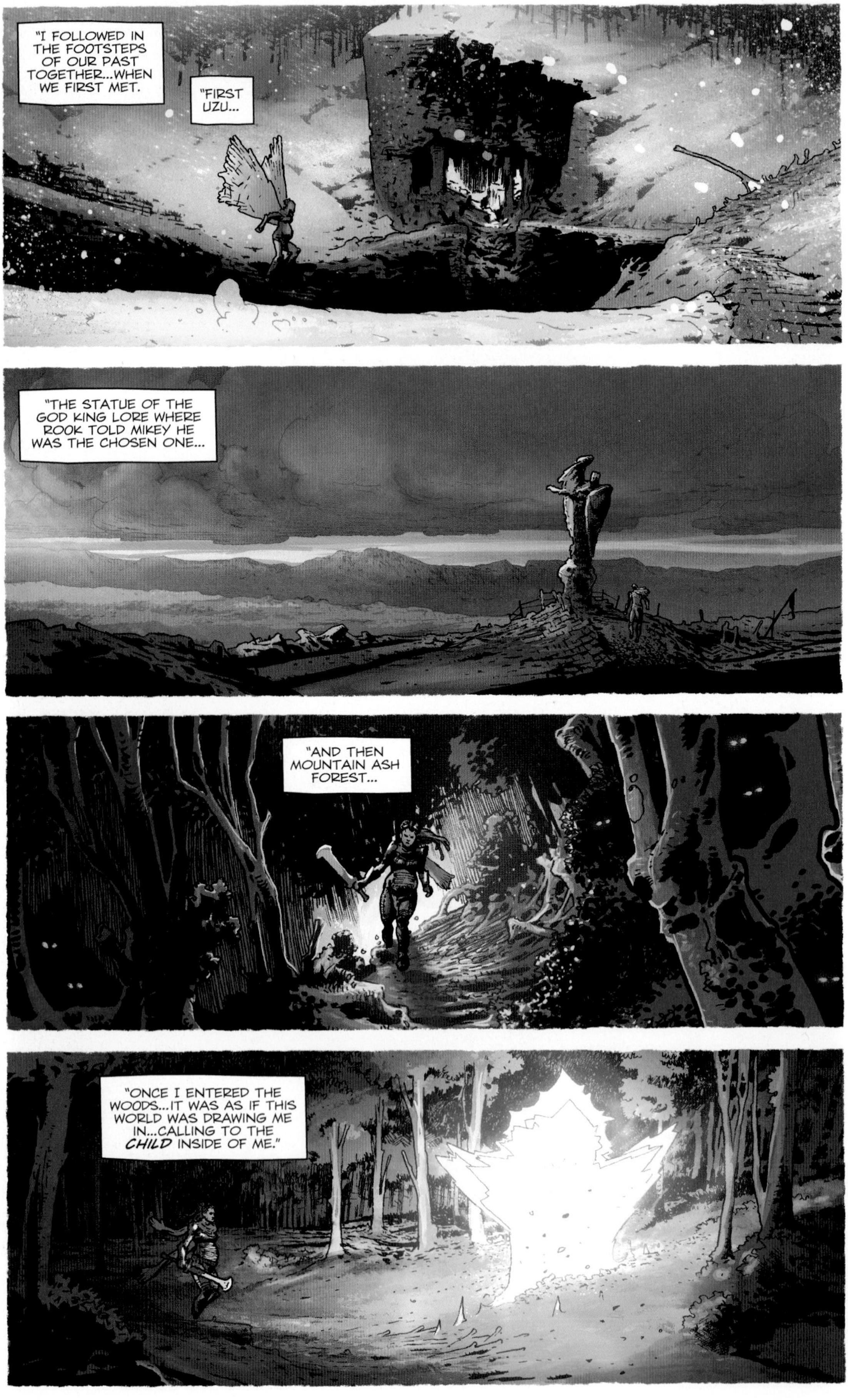
"I FOLLOWED IN THE FOOTSTEPS OF OUR PAST TOGETHER...WHEN WE FIRST MET.
"FIRST UZU...
"THE STATUE OF THE GOD KING LORE WHERE ROOK TOLD MIKEY HE WAS THE CHOSEN ONE...
"AND THEN MOUNTAIN ASH FOREST...
"ONCE I ENTERED THE WOODS...IT WAS AS IF THIS WORLD WAS DRAWING ME IN...CALLING TO THE *CHILD* INSIDE OF ME."

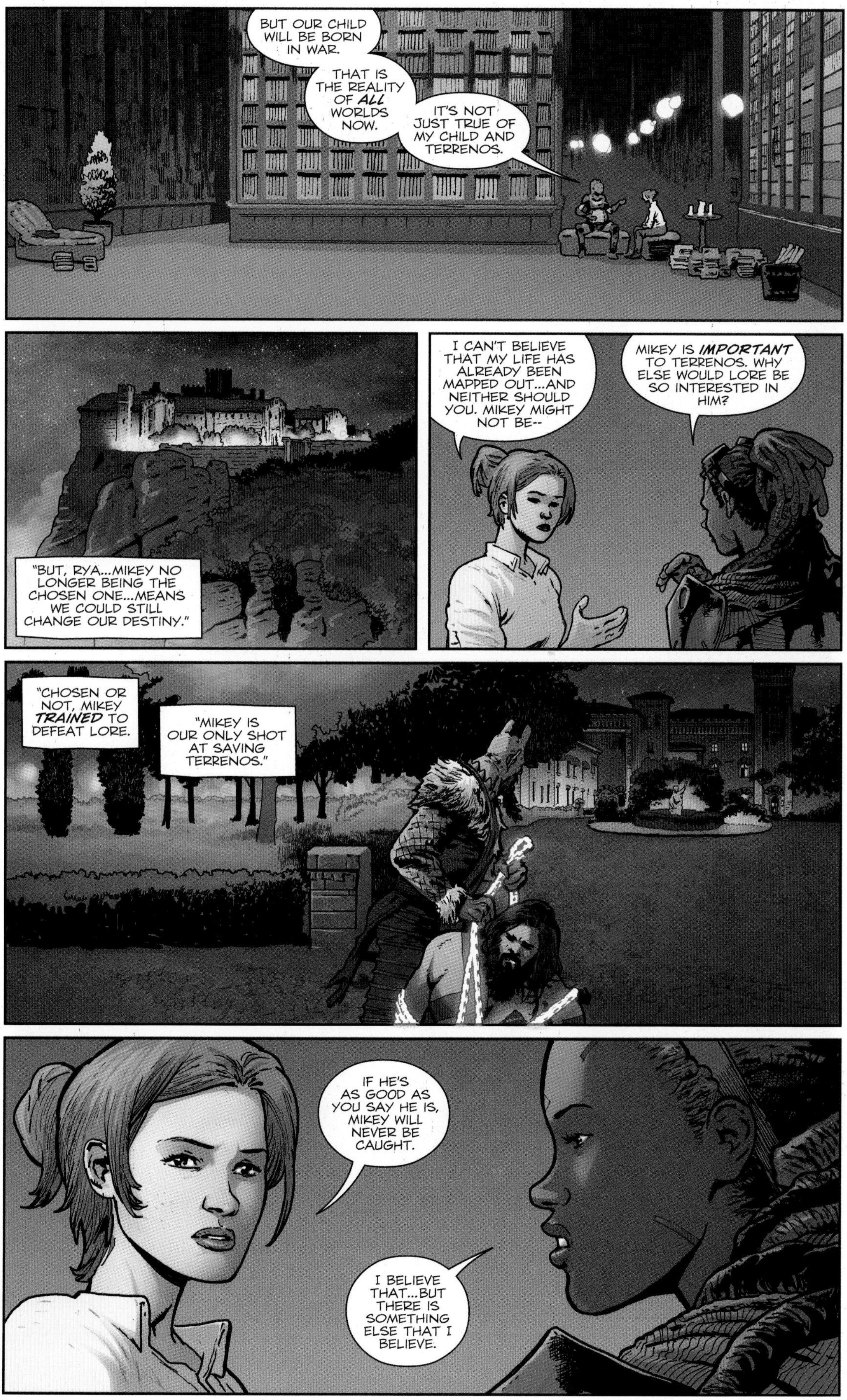
BUT OUR CHILD WILL BE BORN IN WAR.
THAT IS THE REALITY OF *ALL* WORLDS NOW.
IT'S NOT JUST TRUE OF MY CHILD AND TERRENOS.
"BUT, RYA...MIKEY NO LONGER BEING THE CHOSEN ONE...MEANS WE COULD STILL CHANGE OUR DESTINY."
I CAN'T BELIEVE THAT MY LIFE HAS ALREADY BEEN MAPPED OUT...AND NEITHER SHOULD YOU. MIKEY MIGHT NOT BE--
MIKEY IS *IMPORTANT* TO TERRENOS. WHY ELSE WOULD LORE BE SO INTERESTED IN HIM?
"CHOSEN OR NOT, MIKEY *TRAINED* TO DEFEAT LORE.
"MIKEY IS OUR ONLY SHOT AT SAVING TERRENOS."
IF HE'S AS GOOD AS YOU SAY HE IS, MIKEY WILL NEVER BE CAUGHT.
I BELIEVE THAT...BUT THERE IS SOMETHING ELSE THAT I BELIEVE.

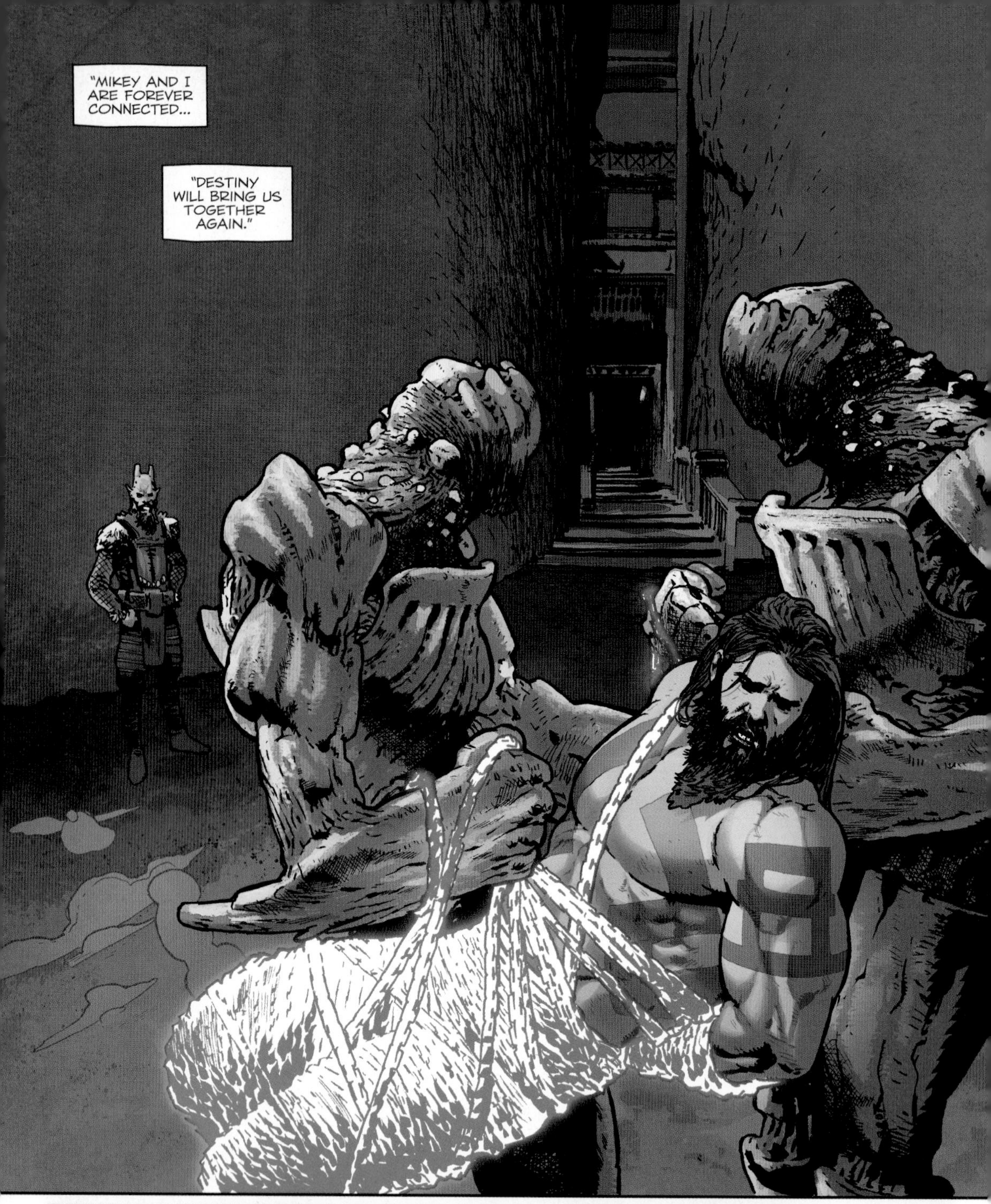
"MIKEY AND I ARE FOREVER CONNECTED...
"DESTINY WILL BRING US TOGETHER AGAIN."

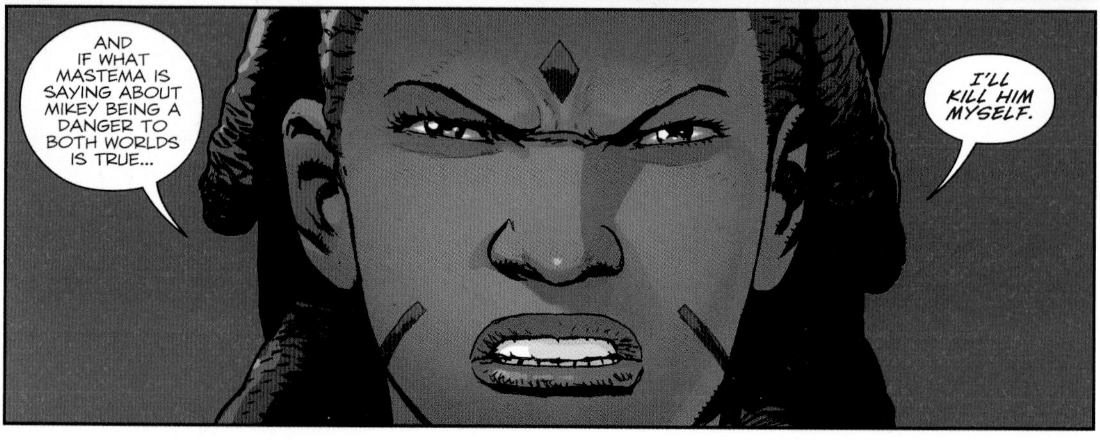
AND IF WHAT MASTEMA IS SAYING ABOUT MIKEY BEING A DANGER TO BOTH WORLDS IS TRUE...
I'LL KILL HIM MYSELF.

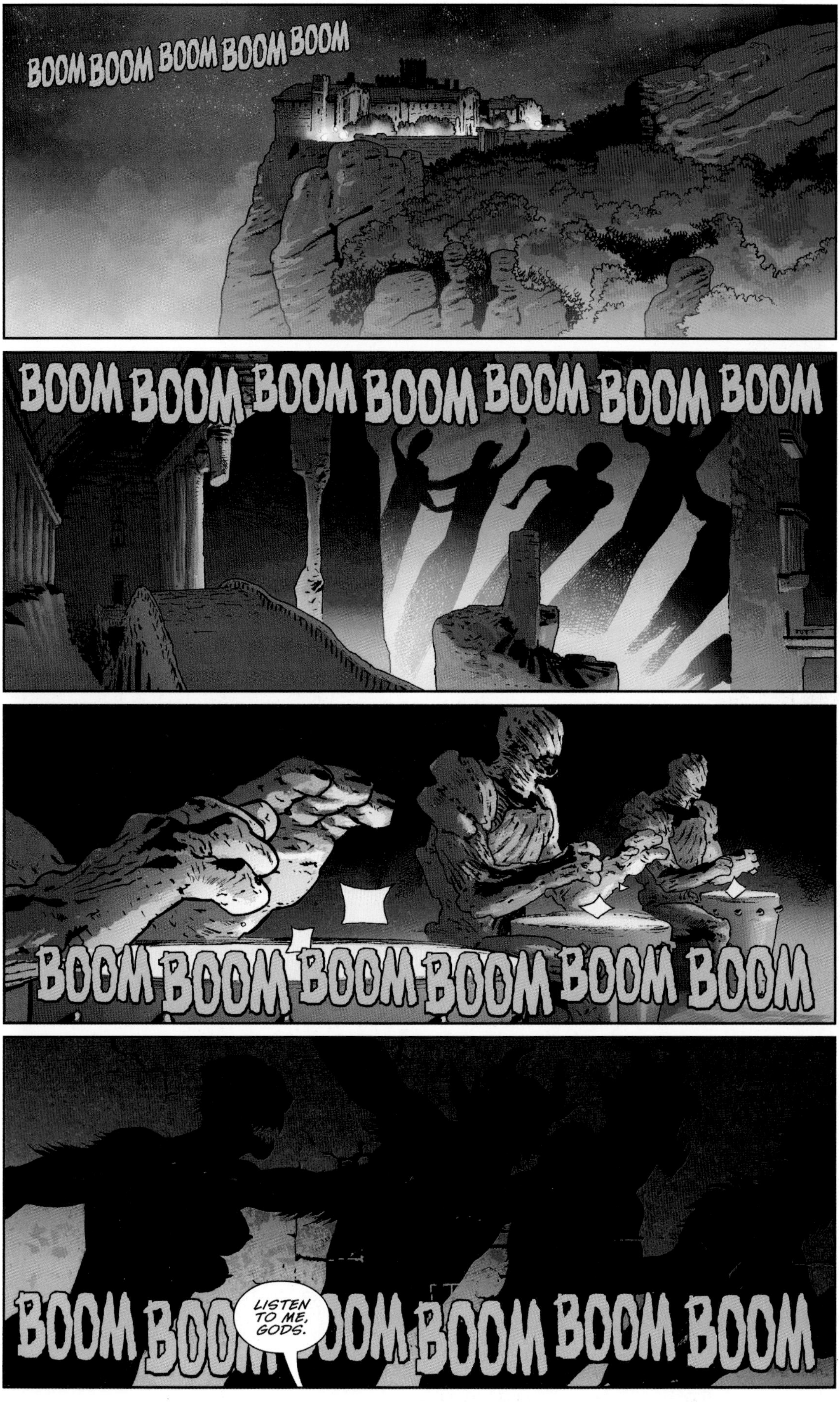
BOOM BOOM BOOM BOOM BOOM
BOOM BOOM BOOM BOOM BOOM BOOM BOOM
BOOM BOOM BOOM BOOM BOOM BOOM
BOOM BOOM BOOM BOOM BOOM BOOM
LISTEN TO ME, GODS.

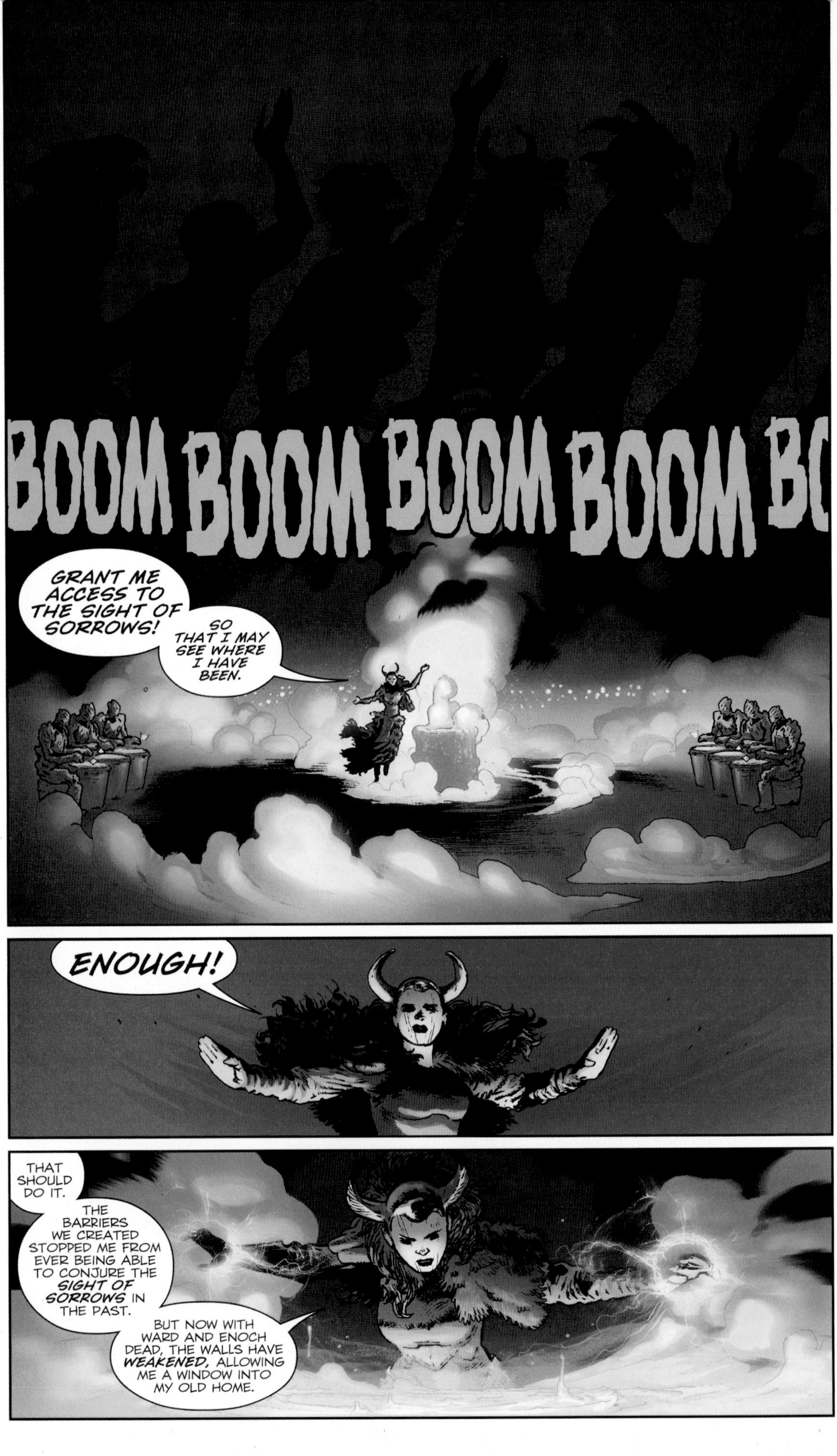
BOOM BOOM BOOM BOOM BO
GRANT ME ACCESS TO THE SIGHT OF SORROWS!
SO THAT I MAY SEE WHERE I HAVE BEEN.
ENOUGH!
THAT SHOULD DO IT.
THE BARRIERS WE CREATED STOPPED ME FROM EVER BEING ABLE TO CONJURE THE SIGHT OF SORROWS IN THE PAST.
BUT NOW WITH WARD AND ENOCH DEAD, THE WALLS HAVE WEAKENED, ALLOWING ME A WINDOW INTO MY OLD HOME.

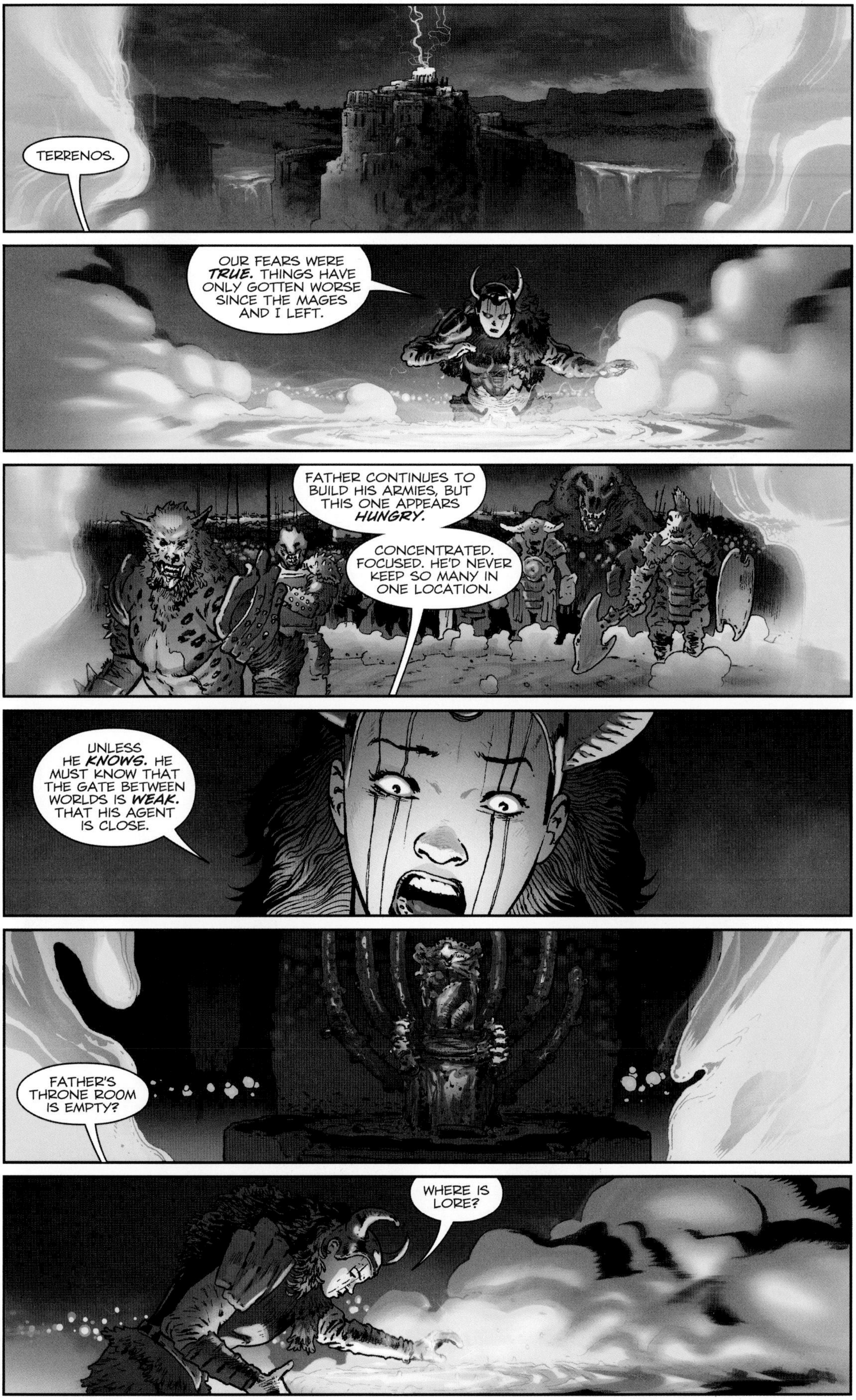
TERRENOS.
OUR FEARS WERE TRUE. THINGS HAVE ONLY GOTTEN WORSE SINCE THE MAGES AND I LEFT.
FATHER CONTINUES TO BUILD HIS ARMIES, BUT THIS ONE APPEARS HUNGRY.
CONCENTRATED. FOCUSED. HE'D NEVER KEEP SO MANY IN ONE LOCATION.
UNLESS HE KNOWS. HE MUST KNOW THAT THE GATE BETWEEN WORLDS IS WEAK. THAT HIS AGENT IS CLOSE.
FATHER'S THRONE ROOM IS EMPTY?
WHERE IS LORE?

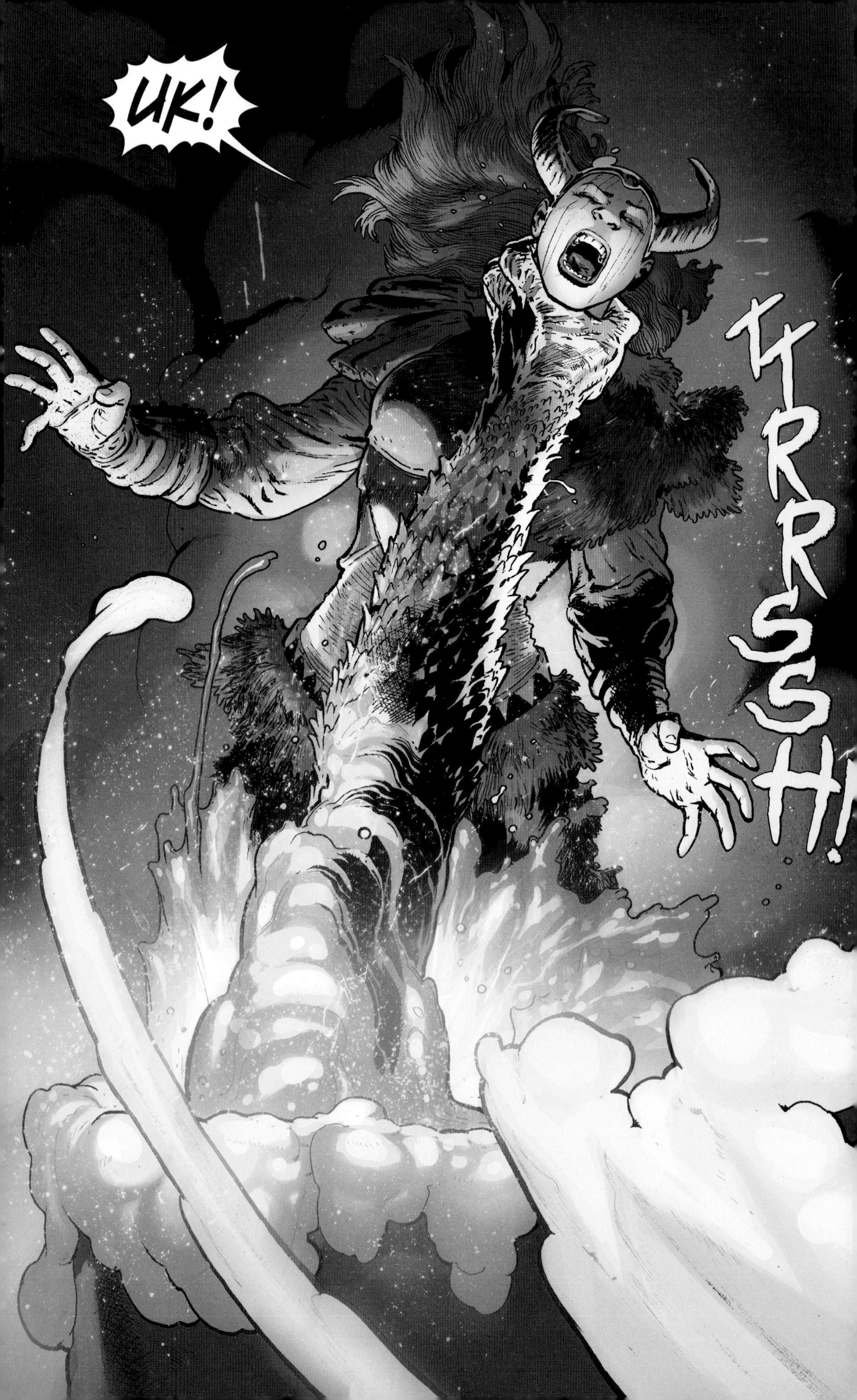
UK!
TTRRSSH!

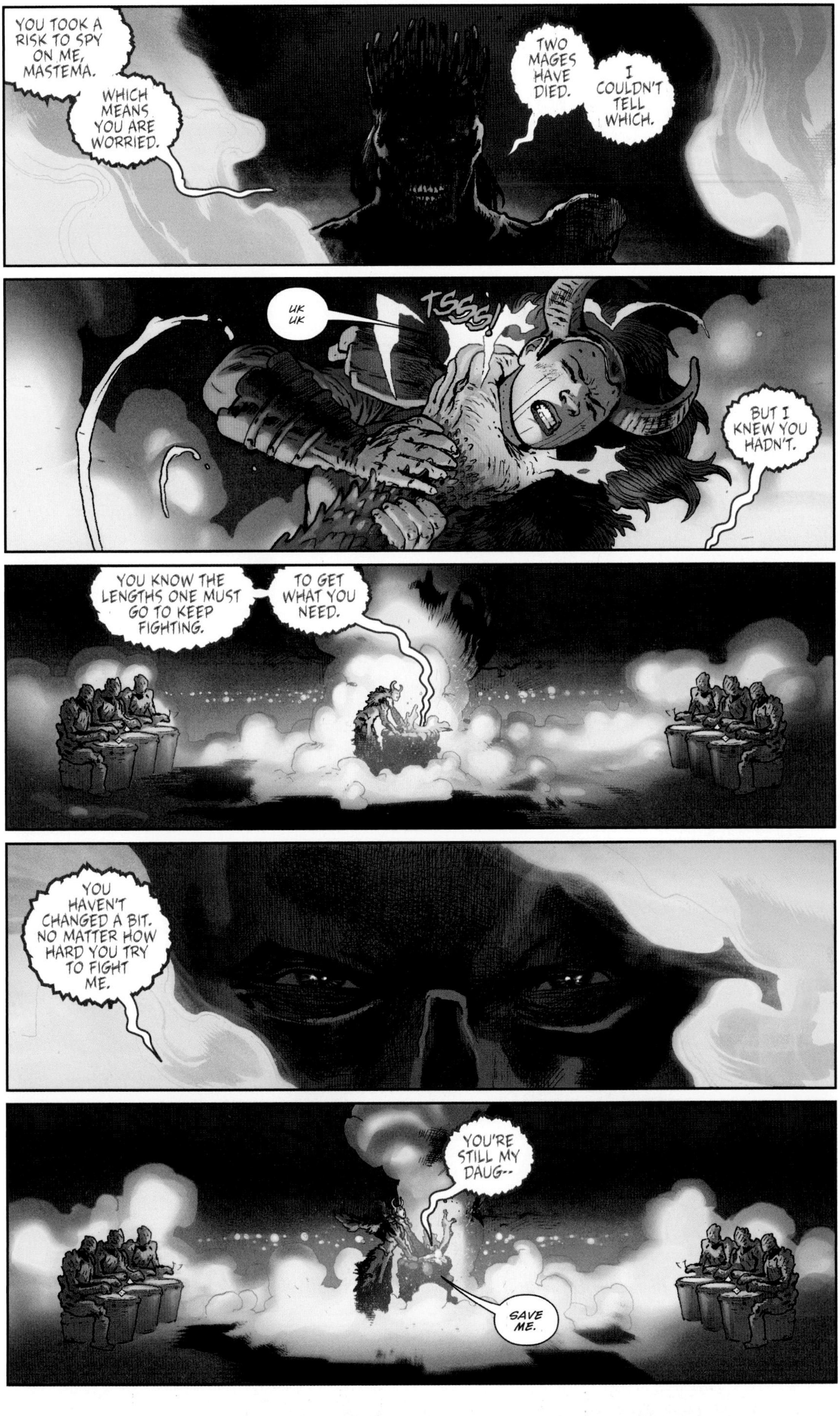
YOU TOOK A RISK TO SPY ON ME, MASTEMA.
WHICH MEANS YOU ARE WORRIED.
TWO MAGES HAVE DIED.
I COULDN'T TELL WHICH.
UK UK
TSSS!
BUT I KNEW YOU HADN'T.
YOU KNOW THE LENGTHS ONE MUST GO TO KEEP FIGHTING.
TO GET WHAT YOU NEED.
YOU HAVEN'T CHANGED A BIT. NO MATTER HOW HARD YOU TRY TO FIGHT ME.
YOU'RE STILL MY DAUG--
SAVE ME.

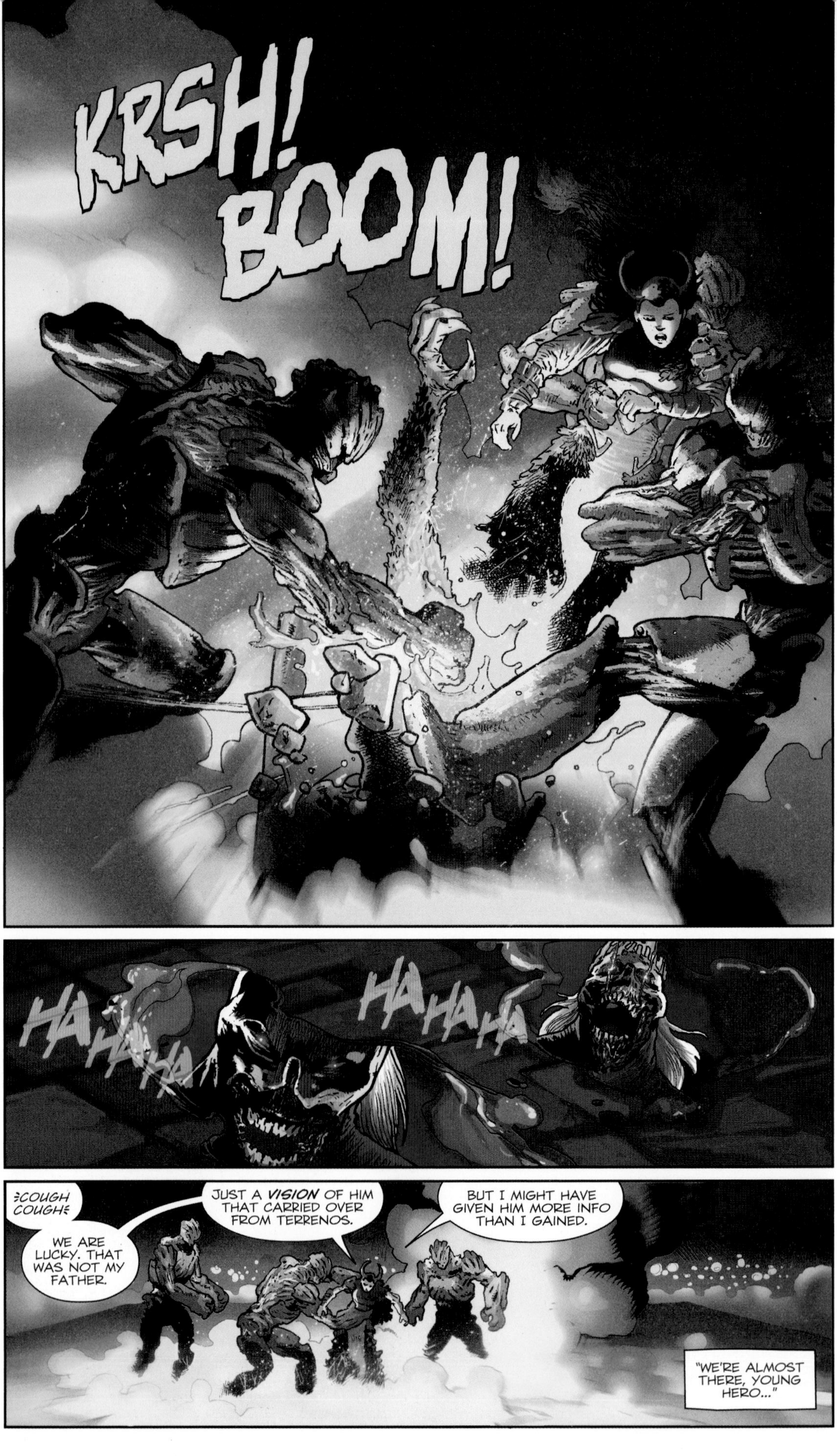
KRSH! BOOM!
HA HA HA HA
HA HA HA HA
COUGH COUGH
WE ARE LUCKY. THAT WAS NOT MY FATHER.
JUST A *VISION* OF HIM THAT CARRIED OVER FROM TERRENOS.
BUT I MIGHT HAVE GIVEN HIM MORE INFO THAN I GAINED.
"WE'RE ALMOST THERE, YOUNG HERO..."

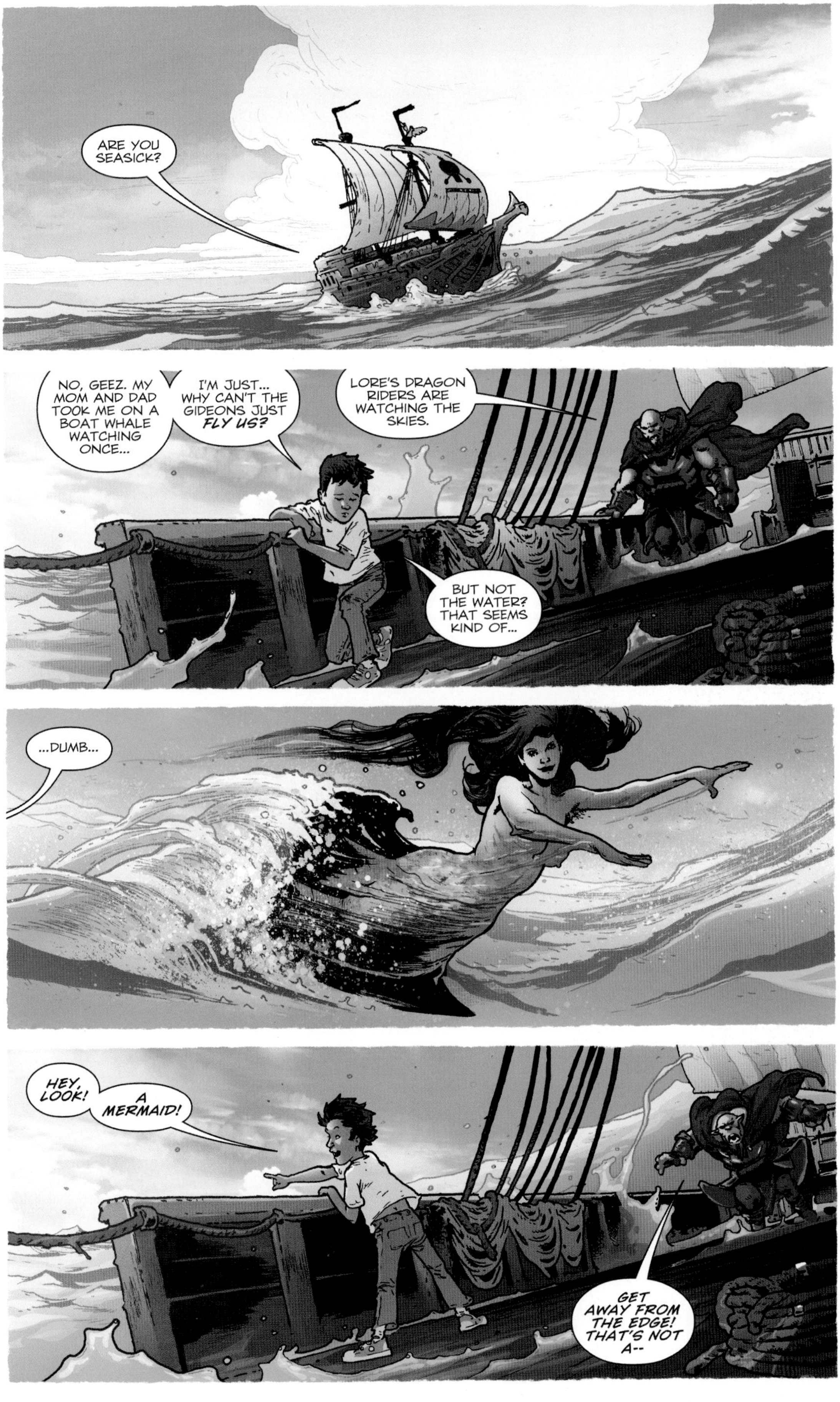
ARE YOU SEASICK?
NO, GEEZ. MY MOM AND DAD TOOK ME ON A BOAT WHALE WATCHING ONCE...
I'M JUST... WHY CAN'T THE GIDEONS JUST *FLY US?*
LORE'S DRAGON RIDERS ARE WATCHING THE SKIES.
BUT NOT THE WATER? THAT SEEMS KIND OF...
...DUMB...
HEY, LOOK!
A MERMAID!
GET AWAY FROM THE EDGE! THAT'S NOT A--

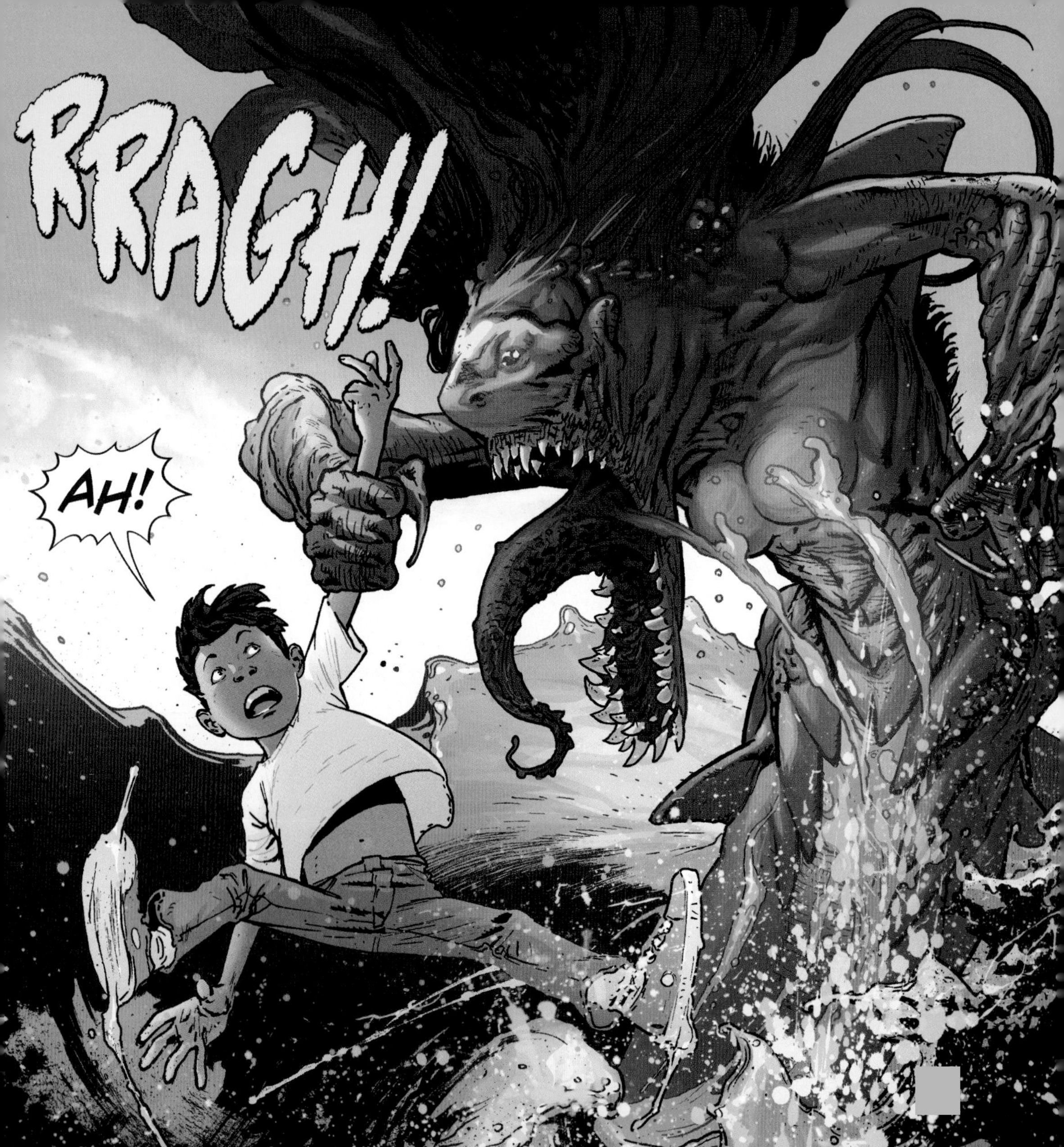
RRAGH!
AH!

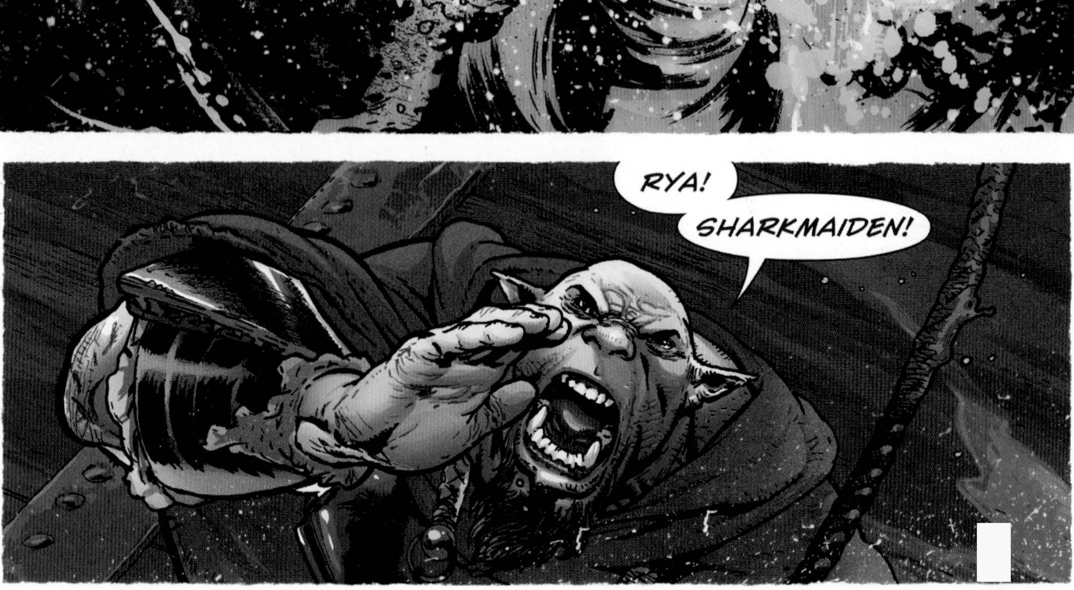
RYA!
SHARKMAIDEN!

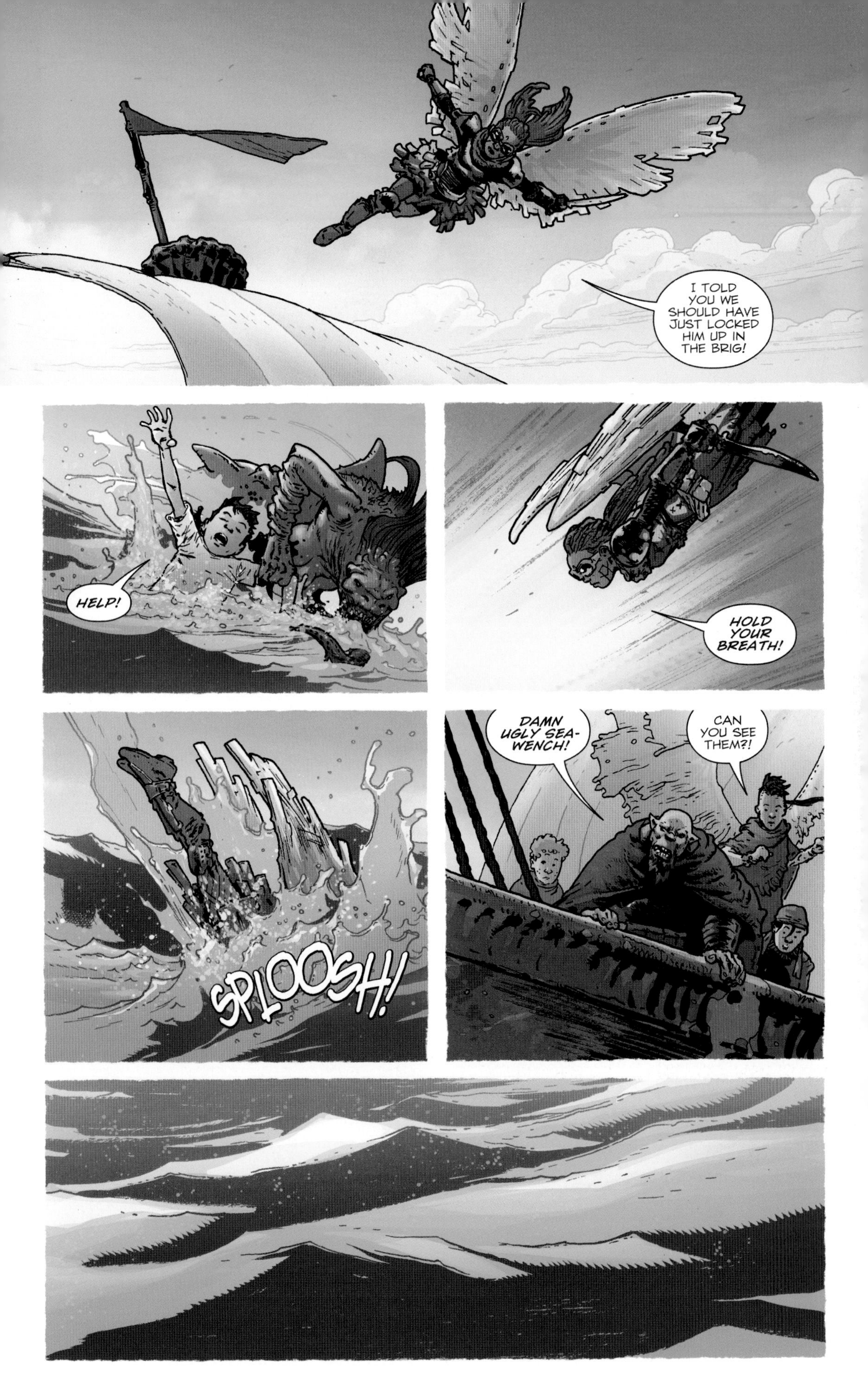
I TOLD YOU WE SHOULD HAVE JUST LOCKED HIM UP IN THE BRIG!
HELP!
HOLD YOUR BREATH!
SPLOOSH!
DAMN UGLY SEA-WENCH!
CAN YOU SEE THEM?!

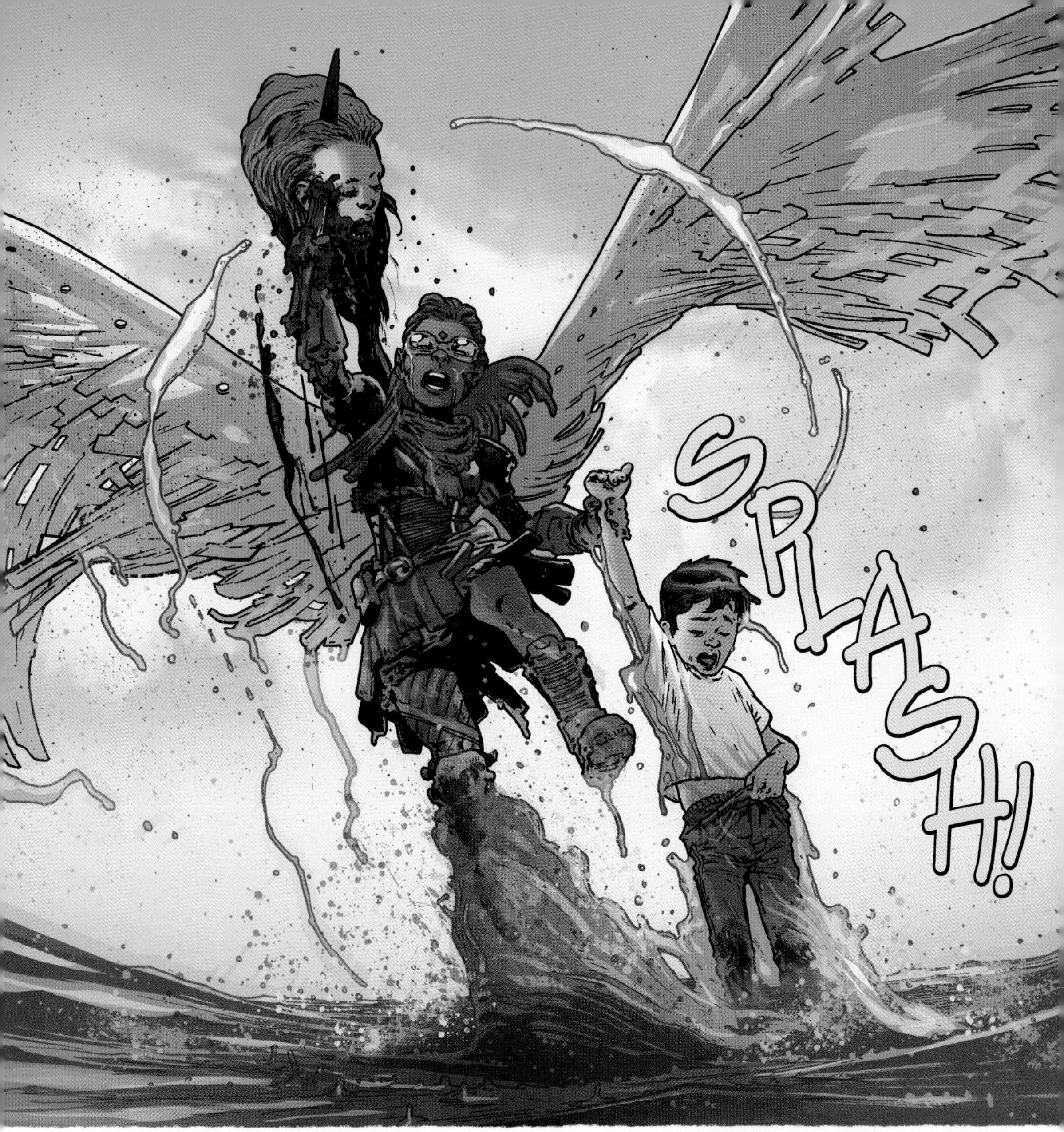
SPLASH!

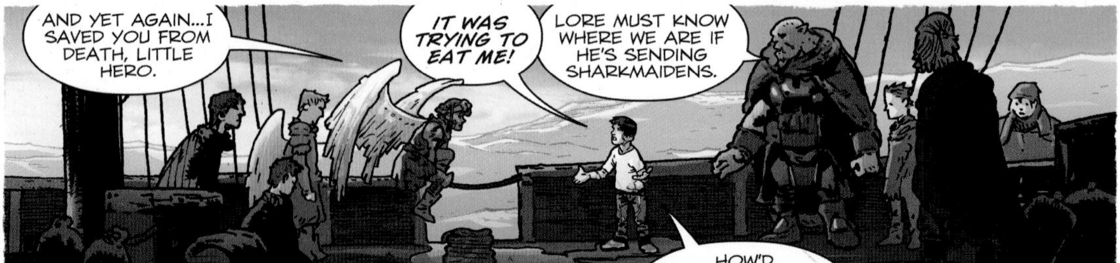
AND YET AGAIN...I SAVED YOU FROM DEATH, LITTLE HERO.
IT WAS TRYING TO EAT ME!
LORE MUST KNOW WHERE WE ARE IF HE'S SENDING SHARKMAIDENS.
HOW'D YOU FIND ME UNDERWATER, RYA?

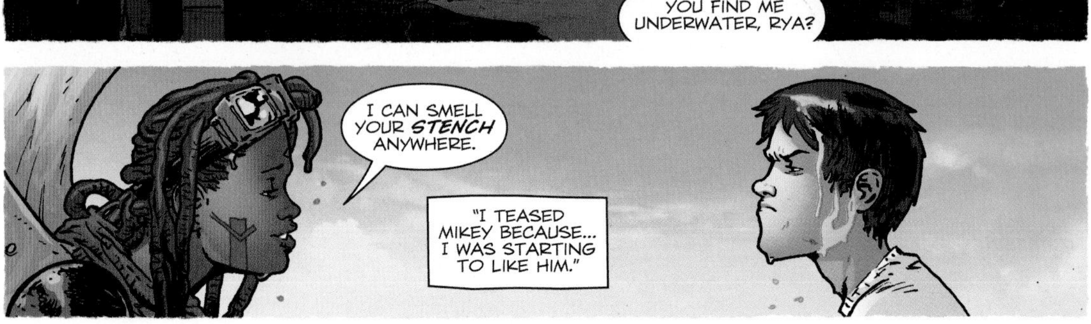
I CAN SMELL YOUR STENCH ANYWHERE.
"I TEASED MIKEY BECAUSE... I WAS STARTING TO LIKE HIM."

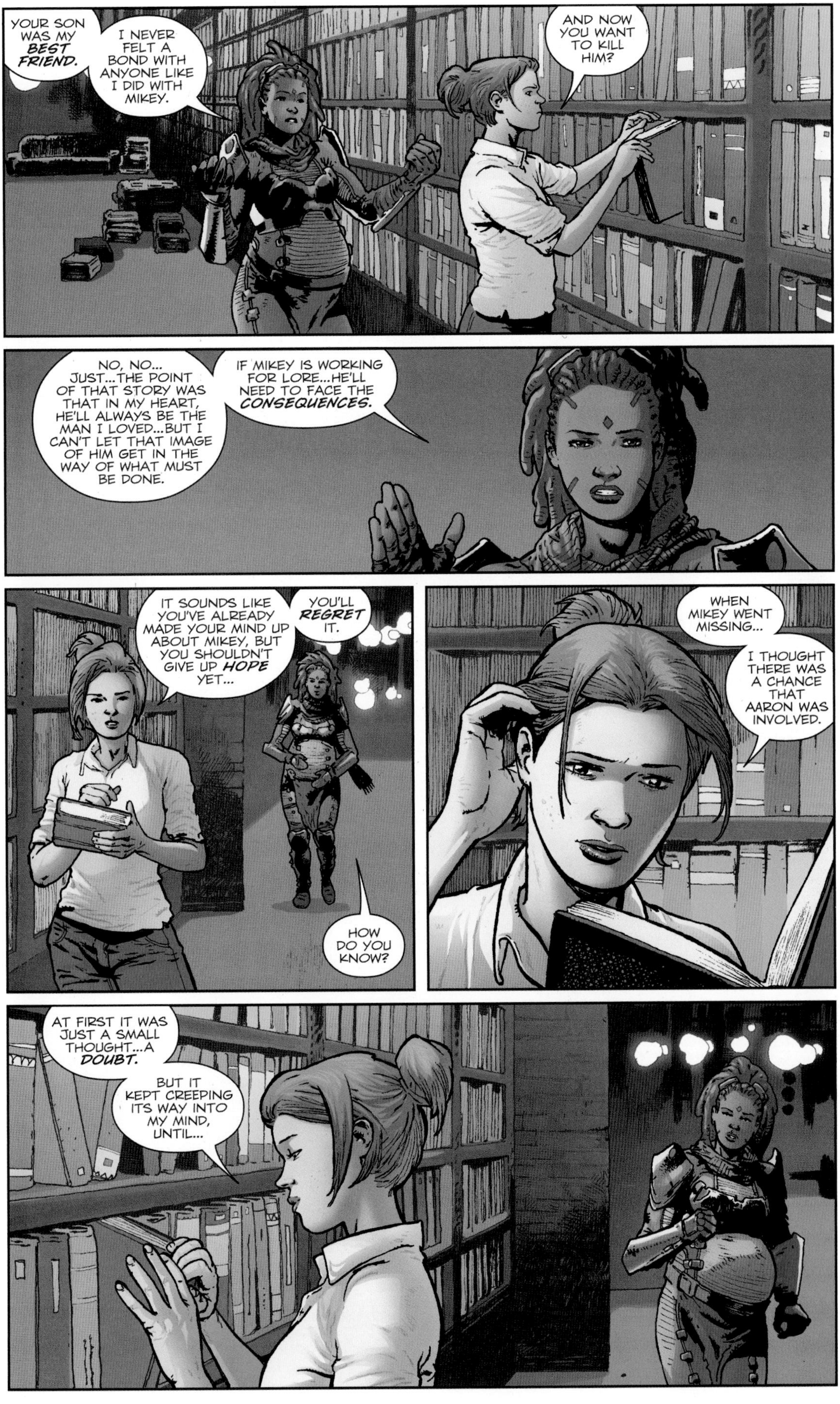
YOUR SON WAS MY BEST FRIEND.
I NEVER FELT A BOND WITH ANYONE LIKE I DID WITH MIKEY.
AND NOW YOU WANT TO KILL HIM?
NO, NO... JUST...THE POINT OF THAT STORY WAS THAT IN MY HEART, HE'LL ALWAYS BE THE MAN I LOVED...BUT I CAN'T LET THAT IMAGE OF HIM GET IN THE WAY OF WHAT MUST BE DONE.
IF MIKEY IS WORKING FOR LORE...HE'LL NEED TO FACE THE CONSEQUENCES.
IT SOUNDS LIKE YOU'VE ALREADY MADE YOUR MIND UP ABOUT MIKEY, BUT YOU SHOULDN'T GIVE UP HOPE YET...
YOU'LL REGRET IT.
HOW DO YOU KNOW?
WHEN MIKEY WENT MISSING...
I THOUGHT THERE WAS A CHANCE THAT AARON WAS INVOLVED.
AT FIRST IT WAS JUST A SMALL THOUGHT...A DOUBT.
BUT IT KEPT CREEPING ITS WAY INTO MY MIND, UNTIL...

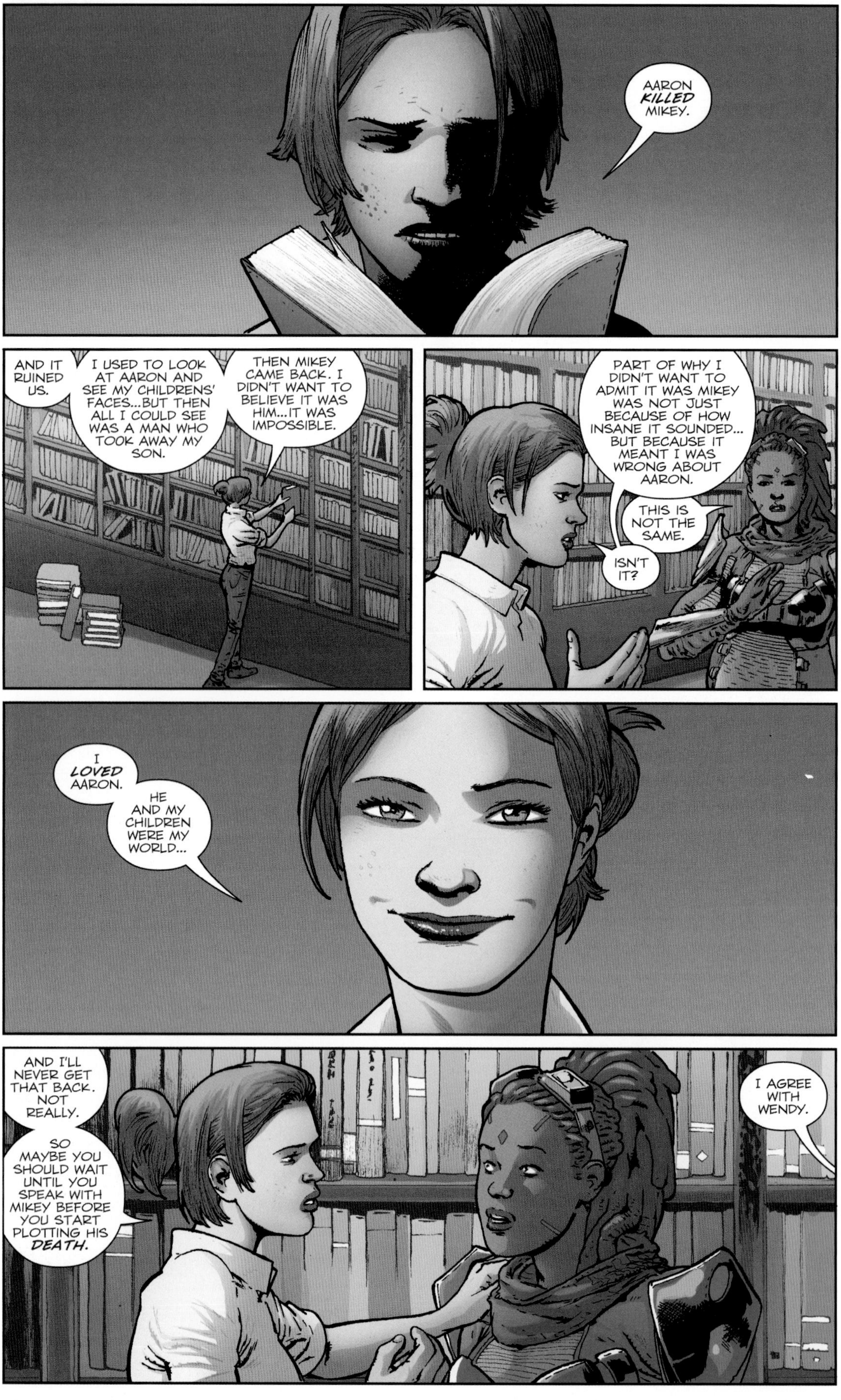
AARON *KILLED* MIKEY.
AND IT RUINED US.
I USED TO LOOK AT AARON AND SEE MY CHILDRENS' FACES...BUT THEN ALL I COULD SEE WAS A MAN WHO TOOK AWAY MY SON.
THEN MIKEY CAME BACK. I DIDN'T WANT TO BELIEVE IT WAS HIM...IT WAS IMPOSSIBLE.
PART OF WHY I DIDN'T WANT TO ADMIT IT WAS MIKEY WAS NOT JUST BECAUSE OF HOW INSANE IT SOUNDED... BUT BECAUSE IT MEANT I WAS WRONG ABOUT AARON.
THIS IS NOT THE SAME.
ISN'T IT?
I *LOVED* AARON.
HE AND MY CHILDREN WERE MY WORLD...
AND I'LL NEVER GET THAT BACK. NOT REALLY.
SO MAYBE YOU SHOULD WAIT UNTIL YOU SPEAK WITH MIKEY BEFORE YOU START PLOTTING HIS *DEATH.*
I AGREE WITH WENDY.

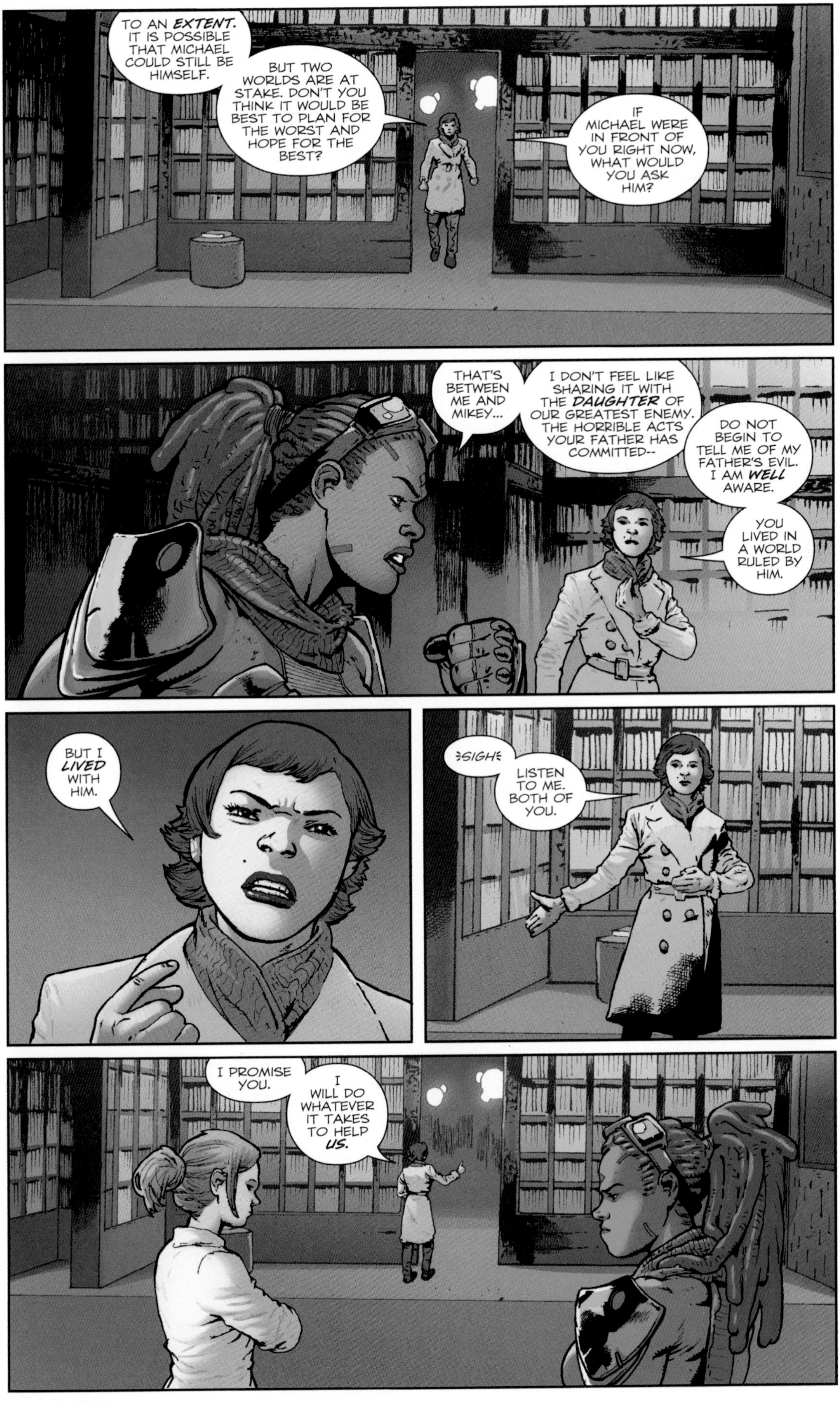
TO AN EXTENT. IT IS POSSIBLE THAT MICHAEL COULD STILL BE HIMSELF.
BUT TWO WORLDS ARE AT STAKE. DON'T YOU THINK IT WOULD BE BEST TO PLAN FOR THE WORST AND HOPE FOR THE BEST?
IF MICHAEL WERE IN FRONT OF YOU RIGHT NOW, WHAT WOULD YOU ASK HIM?
THAT'S BETWEEN ME AND MIKEY...
I DON'T FEEL LIKE SHARING IT WITH THE DAUGHTER OF OUR GREATEST ENEMY. THE HORRIBLE ACTS YOUR FATHER HAS COMMITTED--
DO NOT BEGIN TO TELL ME OF MY FATHER'S EVIL. I AM WELL AWARE.
YOU LIVED IN A WORLD RULED BY HIM.
BUT I LIVED WITH HIM.
SIGH
LISTEN TO ME. BOTH OF YOU.
I PROMISE YOU.
I WILL DO WHATEVER IT TAKES TO HELP US.

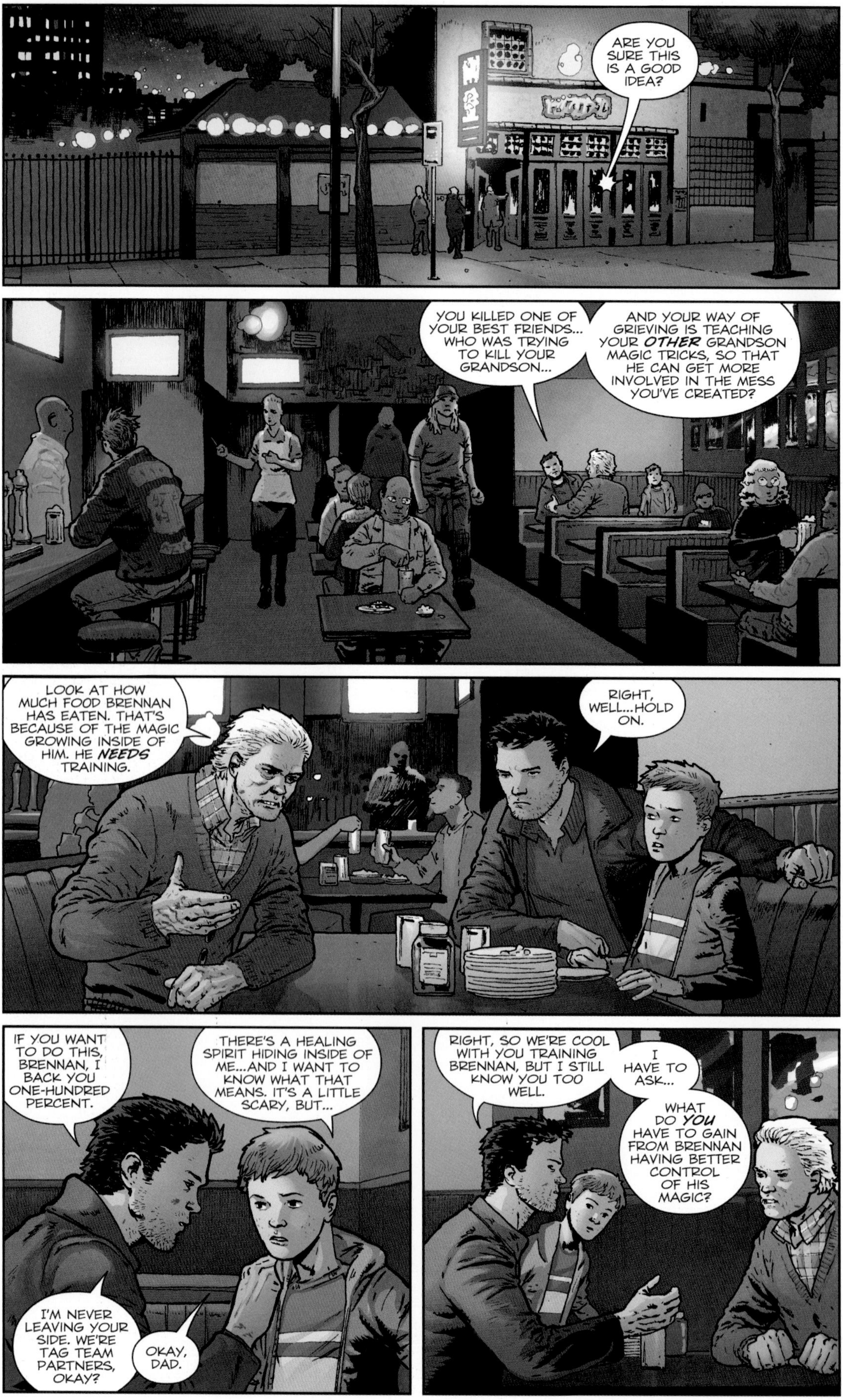
ARE YOU SURE THIS IS A GOOD IDEA?
YOU KILLED ONE OF YOUR BEST FRIENDS... WHO WAS TRYING TO KILL YOUR GRANDSON...
AND YOUR WAY OF GRIEVING IS TEACHING YOUR OTHER GRANDSON MAGIC TRICKS, SO THAT HE CAN GET MORE INVOLVED IN THE MESS YOU'VE CREATED?
LOOK AT HOW MUCH FOOD BRENNAN HAS EATEN. THAT'S BECAUSE OF THE MAGIC GROWING INSIDE OF HIM. HE NEEDS TRAINING.
RIGHT, WELL...HOLD ON.
IF YOU WANT TO DO THIS, BRENNAN, I BACK YOU ONE-HUNDRED PERCENT.
THERE'S A HEALING SPIRIT HIDING INSIDE OF ME...AND I WANT TO KNOW WHAT THAT MEANS. IT'S A LITTLE SCARY, BUT...
I'M NEVER LEAVING YOUR SIDE. WE'RE TAG TEAM PARTNERS, OKAY?
OKAY, DAD.
RIGHT, SO WE'RE COOL WITH YOU TRAINING BRENNAN, BUT I STILL KNOW YOU TOO WELL.
I HAVE TO ASK...
WHAT DO YOU HAVE TO GAIN FROM BRENNAN HAVING BETTER CONTROL OF HIS MAGIC?

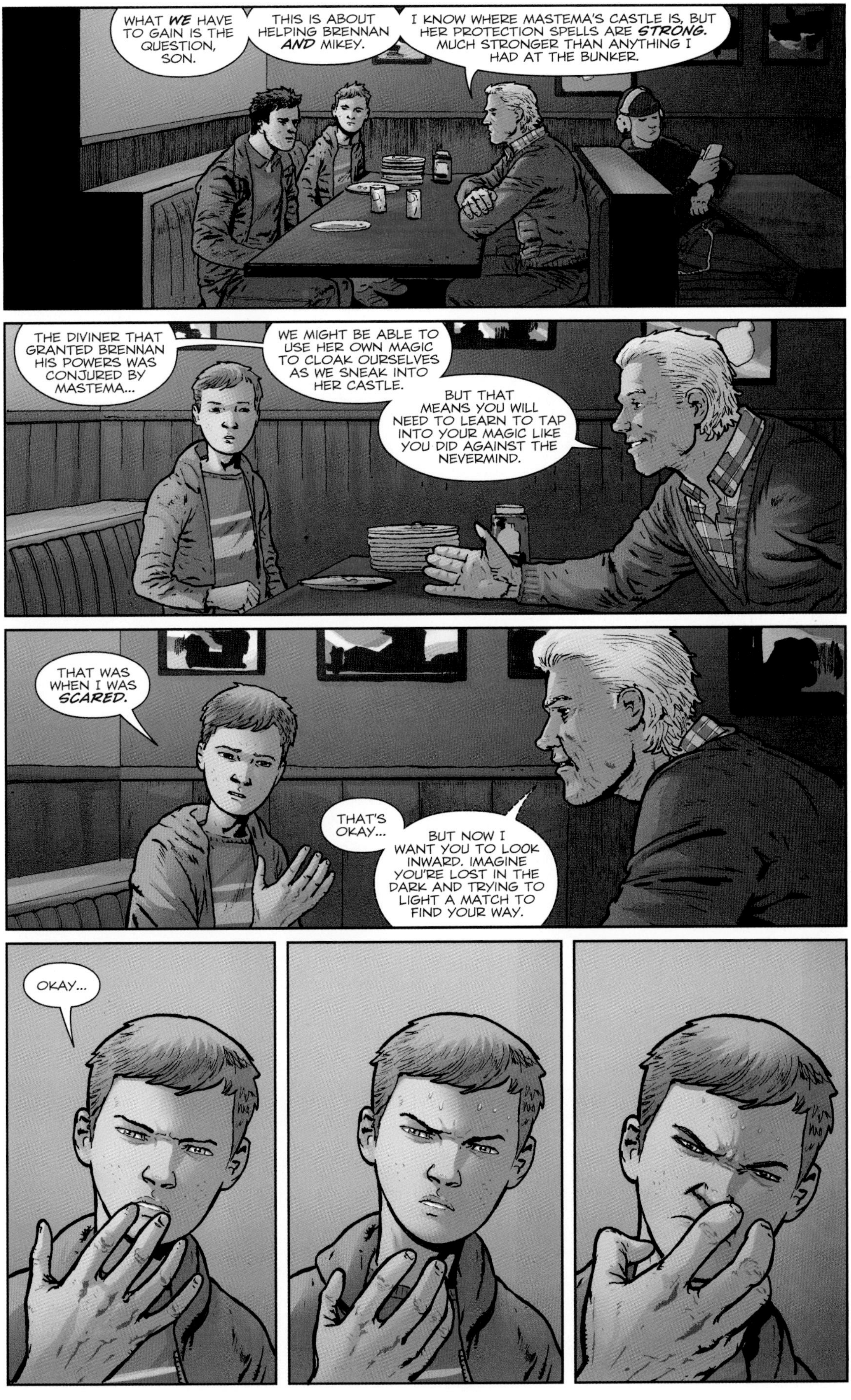
WHAT WE HAVE TO GAIN IS THE QUESTION, SON.
THIS IS ABOUT HELPING BRENNAN AND MIKEY.
I KNOW WHERE MASTEMA'S CASTLE IS, BUT HER PROTECTION SPELLS ARE STRONG. MUCH STRONGER THAN ANYTHING I HAD AT THE BUNKER.
THE DIVINER THAT GRANTED BRENNAN HIS POWERS WAS CONJURED BY MASTEMA...
WE MIGHT BE ABLE TO USE HER OWN MAGIC TO CLOAK OURSELVES AS WE SNEAK INTO HER CASTLE.
BUT THAT MEANS YOU WILL NEED TO LEARN TO TAP INTO YOUR MAGIC LIKE YOU DID AGAINST THE NEVERMIND.
THAT WAS WHEN I WAS SCARED.
THAT'S OKAY...
BUT NOW I WANT YOU TO LOOK INWARD. IMAGINE YOU'RE LOST IN THE DARK AND TRYING TO LIGHT A MATCH TO FIND YOUR WAY.
OKAY...

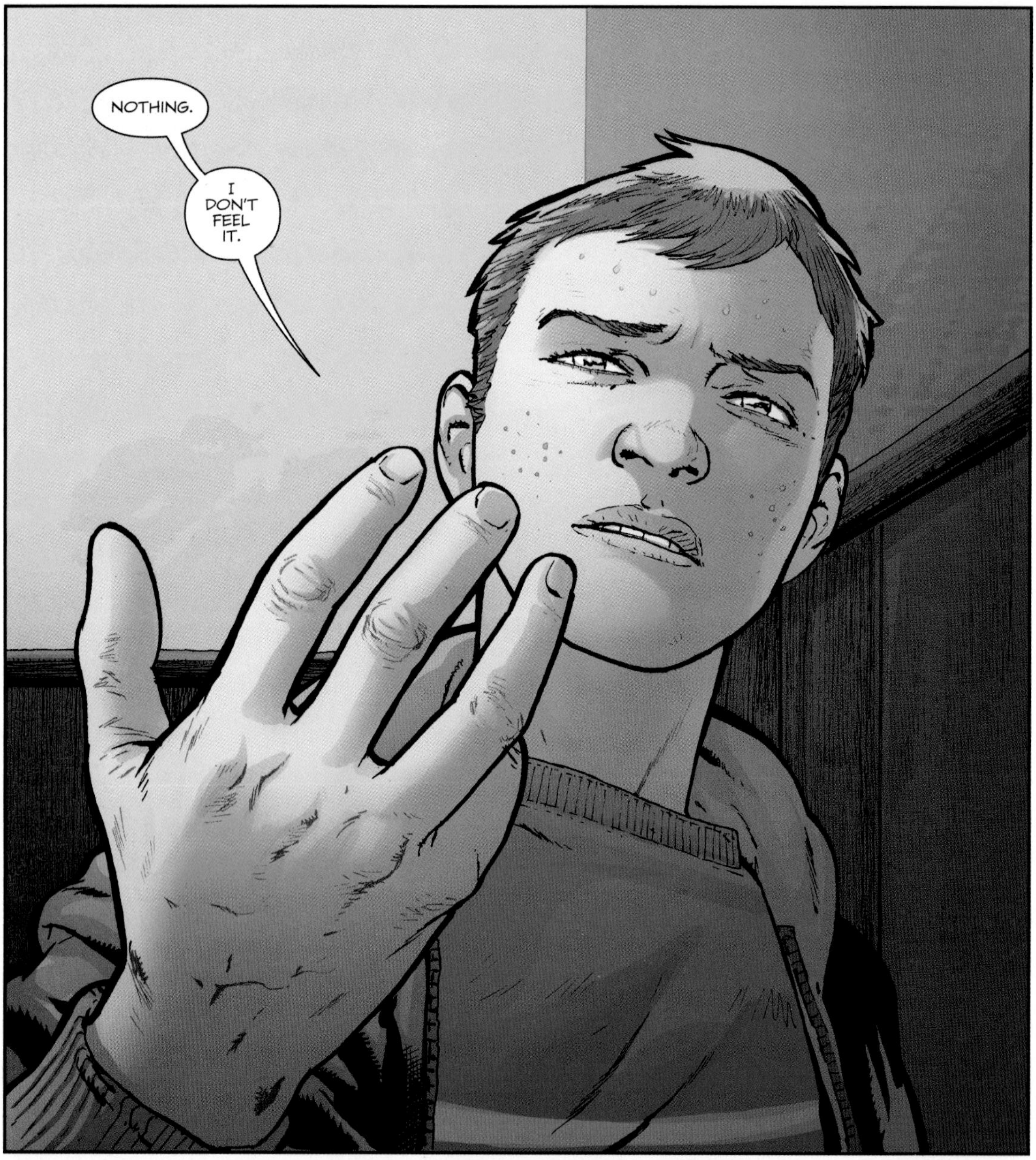
NOTHING.
I DON'T FEEL IT.

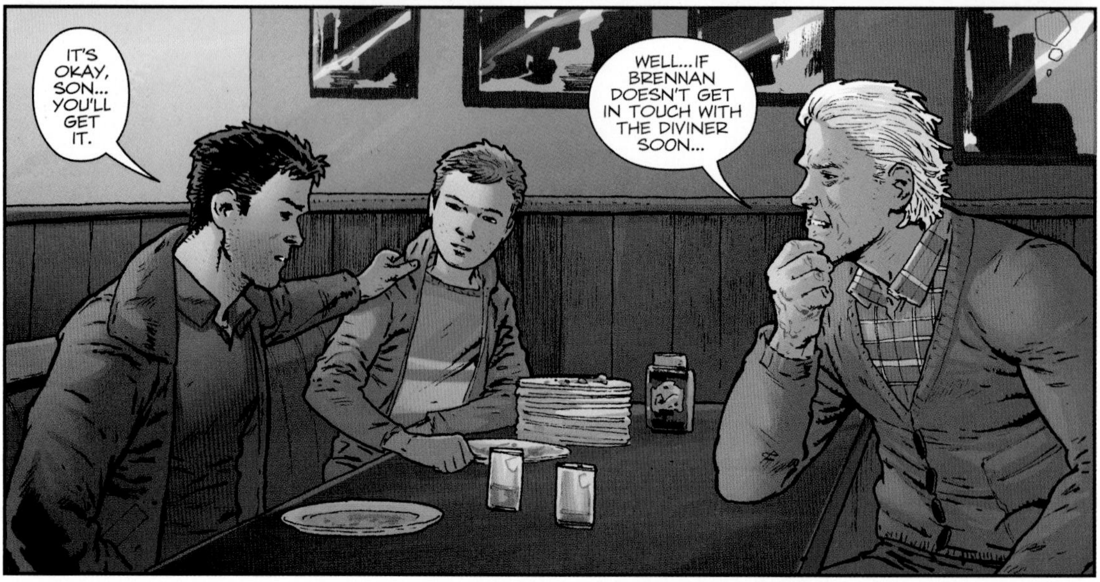
IT'S OKAY, SON... YOU'LL GET IT.
WELL...IF BRENNAN DOESN'T GET IN TOUCH WITH THE DIVINER SOON...

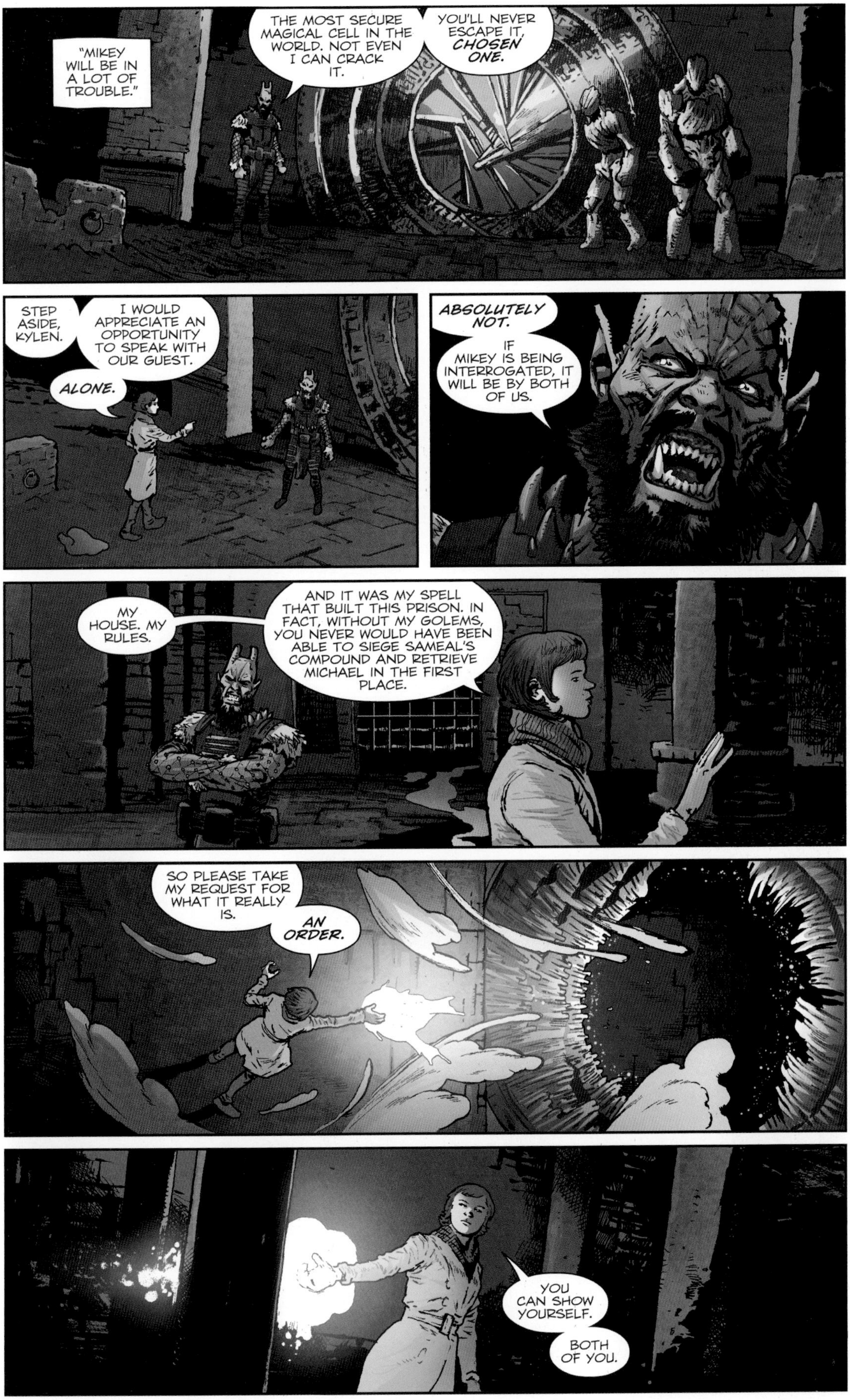
"MIKEY WILL BE IN A LOT OF TROUBLE."
THE MOST SECURE MAGICAL CELL IN THE WORLD. NOT EVEN I CAN CRACK IT.
YOU'LL NEVER ESCAPE IT, *CHOSEN ONE.*
STEP ASIDE, KYLEN.
I WOULD APPRECIATE AN OPPORTUNITY TO SPEAK WITH OUR GUEST.
ALONE.
ABSOLUTELY NOT.
IF MIKEY IS BEING INTERROGATED, IT WILL BE BY BOTH OF US.
MY HOUSE. MY RULES.
AND IT WAS MY SPELL THAT BUILT THIS PRISON. IN FACT, WITHOUT MY GOLEMS, YOU NEVER WOULD HAVE BEEN ABLE TO SIEGE SAMEAL'S COMPOUND AND RETRIEVE MICHAEL IN THE FIRST PLACE.
SO PLEASE TAKE MY REQUEST FOR WHAT IT REALLY IS.
AN ORDER.
YOU CAN SHOW YOURSELF.
BOTH OF YOU.

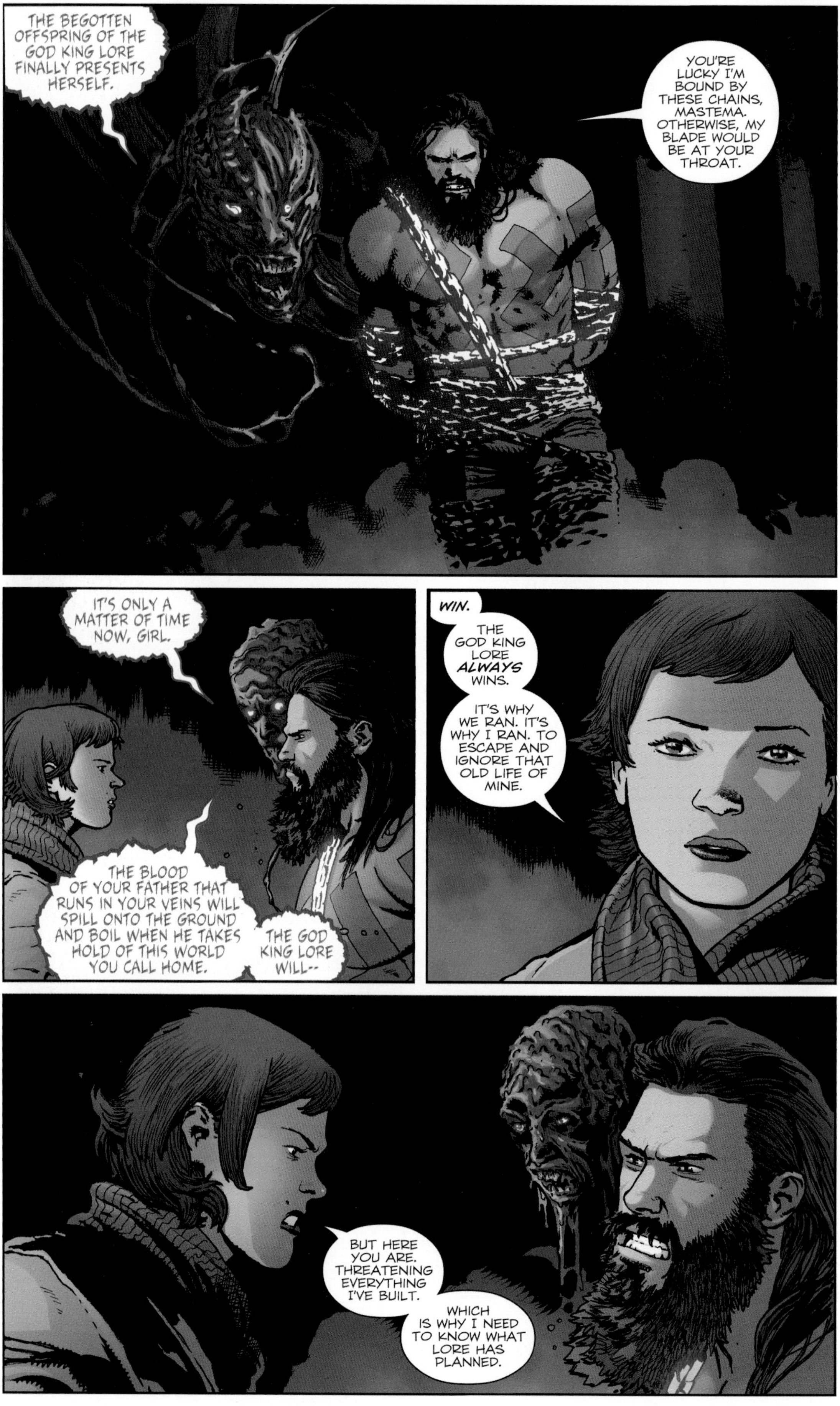
THE BEGOTTEN OFFSPRING OF THE GOD KING LORE FINALLY PRESENTS HERSELF.
YOU'RE LUCKY I'M BOUND BY THESE CHAINS, MASTEMA. OTHERWISE, MY BLADE WOULD BE AT YOUR THROAT.
IT'S ONLY A MATTER OF TIME NOW, GIRL.
THE BLOOD OF YOUR FATHER THAT RUNS IN YOUR VEINS WILL SPILL ONTO THE GROUND AND BOIL WHEN HE TAKES HOLD OF THIS WORLD YOU CALL HOME.
THE GOD KING LORE WILL--
WIN.
THE GOD KING LORE ALWAYS WINS.
IT'S WHY WE RAN. IT'S WHY I RAN. TO ESCAPE AND IGNORE THAT OLD LIFE OF MINE.
BUT HERE YOU ARE. THREATENING EVERYTHING I'VE BUILT.
WHICH IS WHY I NEED TO KNOW WHAT LORE HAS PLANNED.

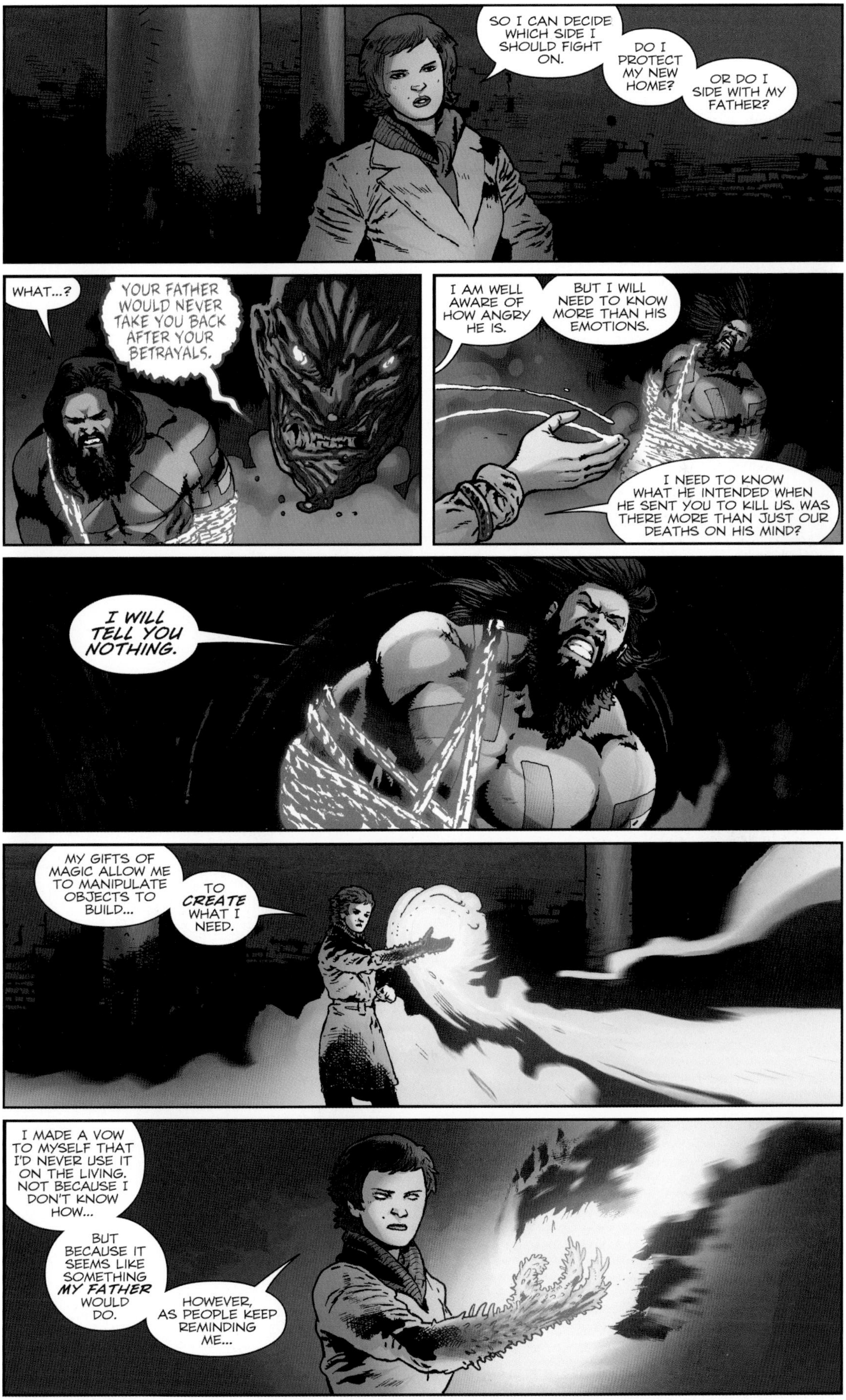
SO I CAN DECIDE WHICH SIDE I SHOULD FIGHT ON.
DO I PROTECT MY NEW HOME?
OR DO I SIDE WITH MY FATHER?
WHAT...?
YOUR FATHER WOULD NEVER TAKE YOU BACK AFTER YOUR BETRAYALS.
I AM WELL AWARE OF HOW ANGRY HE IS.
BUT I WILL NEED TO KNOW MORE THAN HIS EMOTIONS.
I NEED TO KNOW WHAT HE INTENDED WHEN HE SENT YOU TO KILL US. WAS THERE MORE THAN JUST OUR DEATHS ON HIS MIND?
I WILL TELL YOU NOTHING.
MY GIFTS OF MAGIC ALLOW ME TO MANIPULATE OBJECTS TO BUILD...
TO CREATE WHAT I NEED.
I MADE A VOW TO MYSELF THAT I'D NEVER USE IT ON THE LIVING. NOT BECAUSE I DON'T KNOW HOW...
BUT BECAUSE IT SEEMS LIKE SOMETHING MY FATHER WOULD DO.
HOWEVER, AS PEOPLE KEEP REMINDING ME...

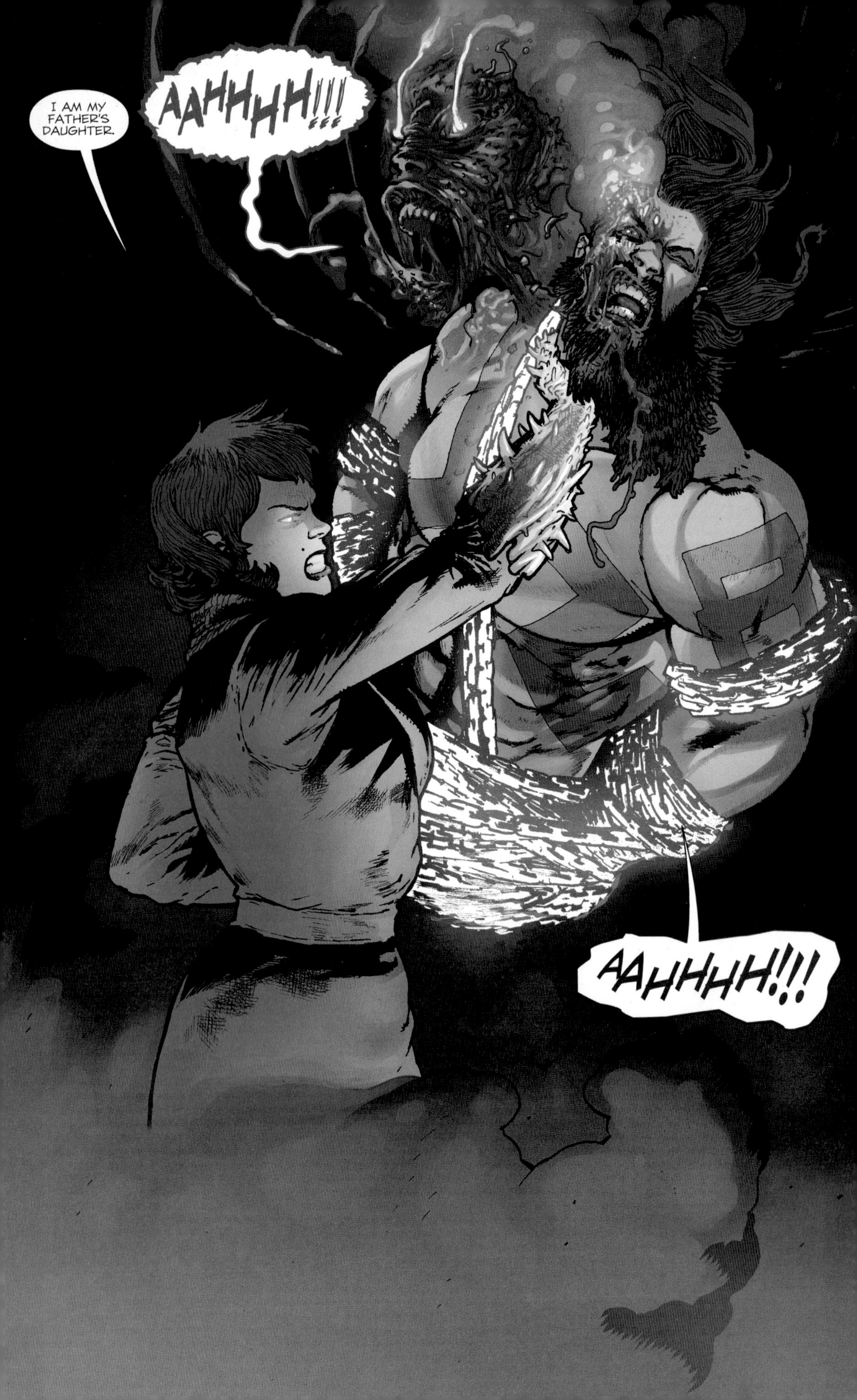
I AM MY FATHER'S DAUGHTER.
AAHHHH!!!
AAHHHH!!!

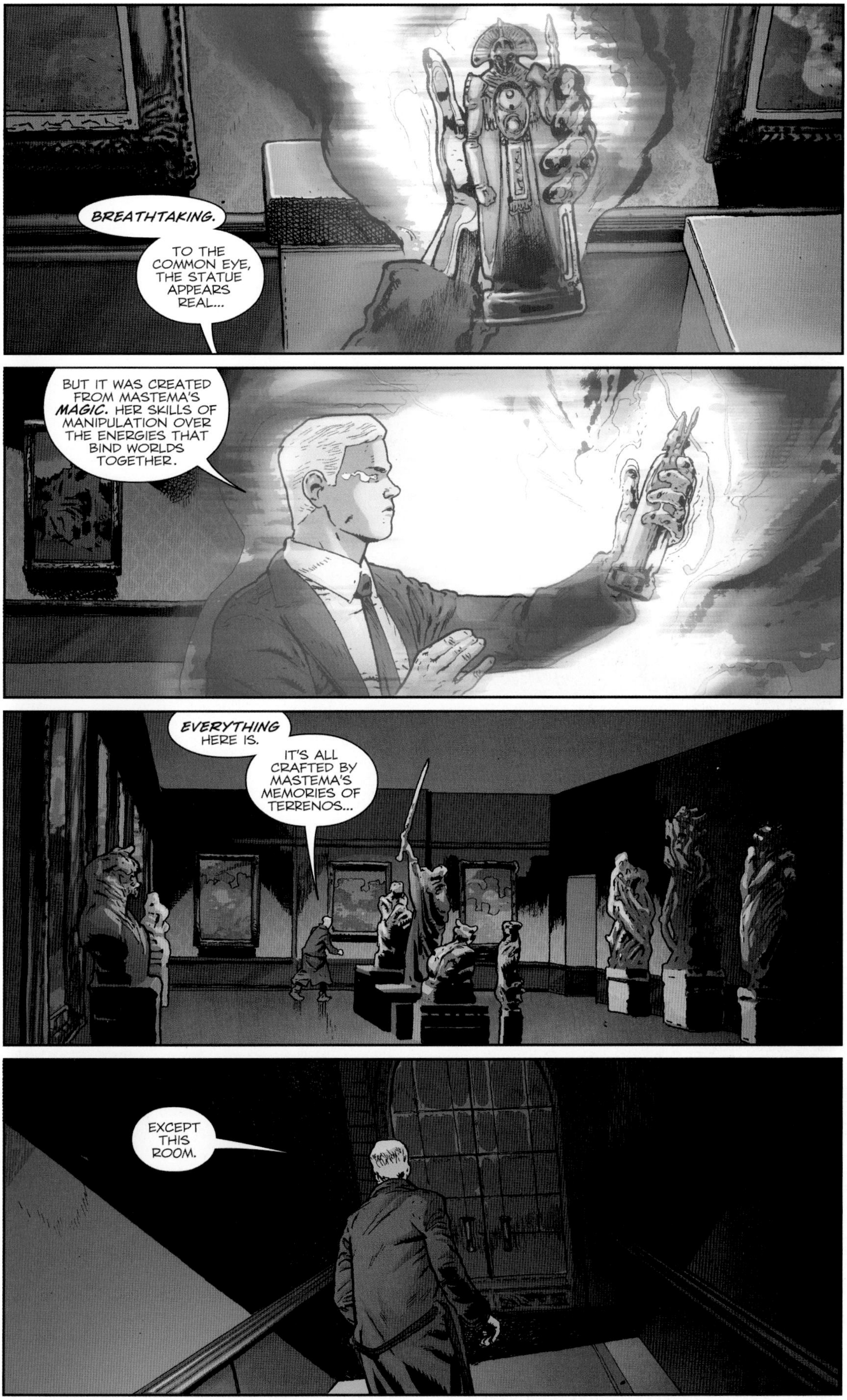
BREATHTAKING.
TO THE COMMON EYE, THE STATUE APPEARS REAL...
BUT IT WAS CREATED FROM MASTEMA'S MAGIC. HER SKILLS OF MANIPULATION OVER THE ENERGIES THAT BIND WORLDS TOGETHER.
EVERYTHING HERE IS.
IT'S ALL CRAFTED BY MASTEMA'S MEMORIES OF TERRENOS...
EXCEPT THIS ROOM.

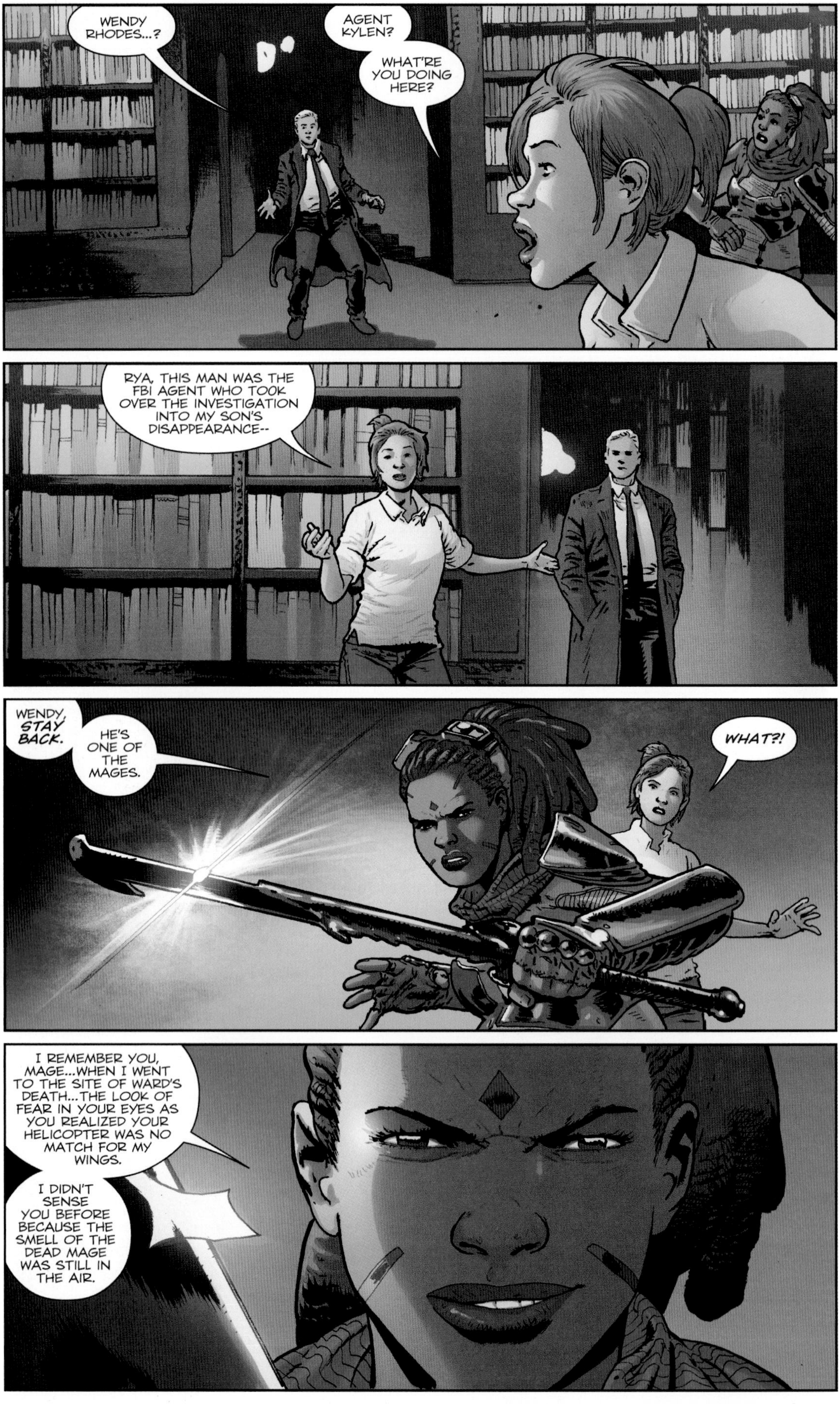

WENDY RHODES...?
AGENT KYLEN?
WHAT'RE YOU DOING HERE?
RYA, THIS MAN WAS THE FBI AGENT WHO TOOK OVER THE INVESTIGATION INTO MY SON'S DISAPPEARANCE--
WENDY, STAY BACK.
HE'S ONE OF THE MAGES.
WHAT?!
I REMEMBER YOU, MAGE...WHEN I WENT TO THE SITE OF WARD'S DEATH...THE LOOK OF FEAR IN YOUR EYES AS YOU REALIZED YOUR HELICOPTER WAS NO MATCH FOR MY WINGS.
I DIDN'T SENSE YOU BEFORE BECAUSE THE SMELL OF THE DEAD MAGE WAS STILL IN THE AIR.

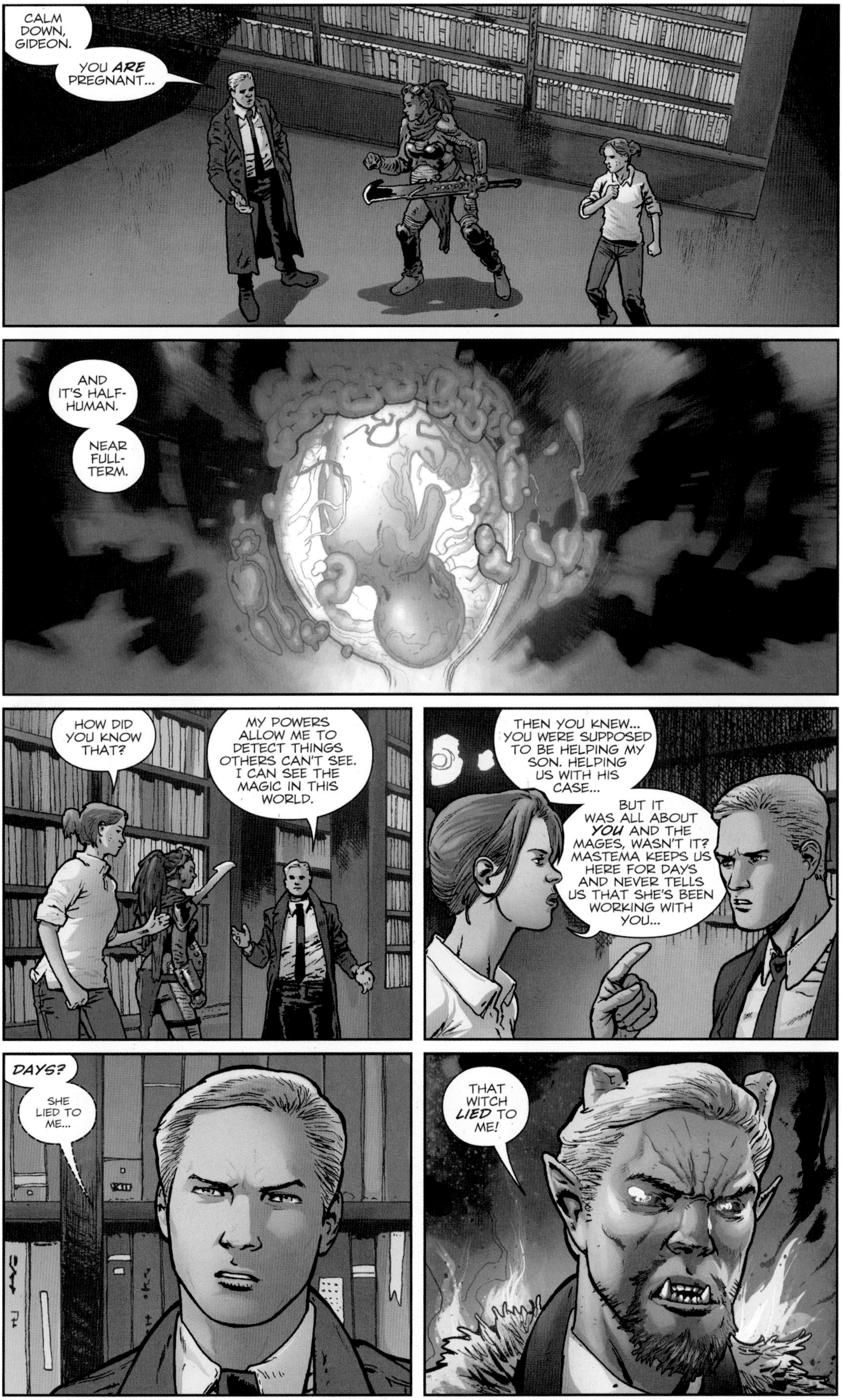
CALM DOWN, GIDEON.
YOU ARE PREGNANT...
AND IT'S HALF-HUMAN.
NEAR FULL-TERM.
HOW DID YOU KNOW THAT?
MY POWERS ALLOW ME TO DETECT THINGS OTHERS CAN'T SEE. I CAN SEE THE MAGIC IN THIS WORLD.
THEN YOU KNEW... YOU WERE SUPPOSED TO BE HELPING MY SON. HELPING US WITH HIS CASE...
BUT IT WAS ALL ABOUT YOU AND THE MAGES, WASN'T IT? MASTEMA KEEPS US HERE FOR DAYS AND NEVER TELLS US THAT SHE'S BEEN WORKING WITH YOU...
DAYS?
SHE LIED TO ME...
THAT WITCH LIED TO ME!

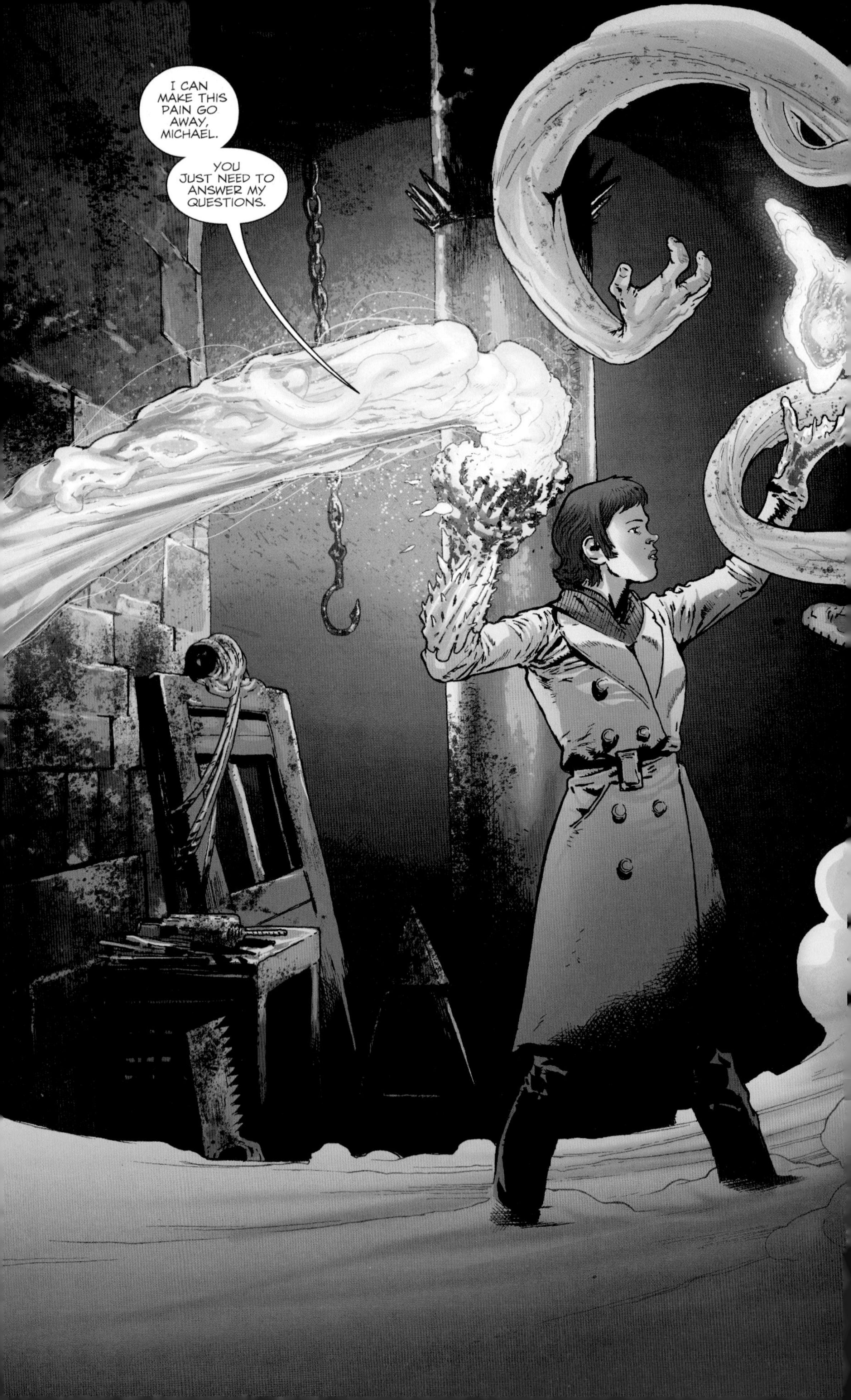
I CAN MAKE THIS PAIN GO AWAY, MICHAEL.
YOU JUST NEED TO ANSWER MY QUESTIONS.

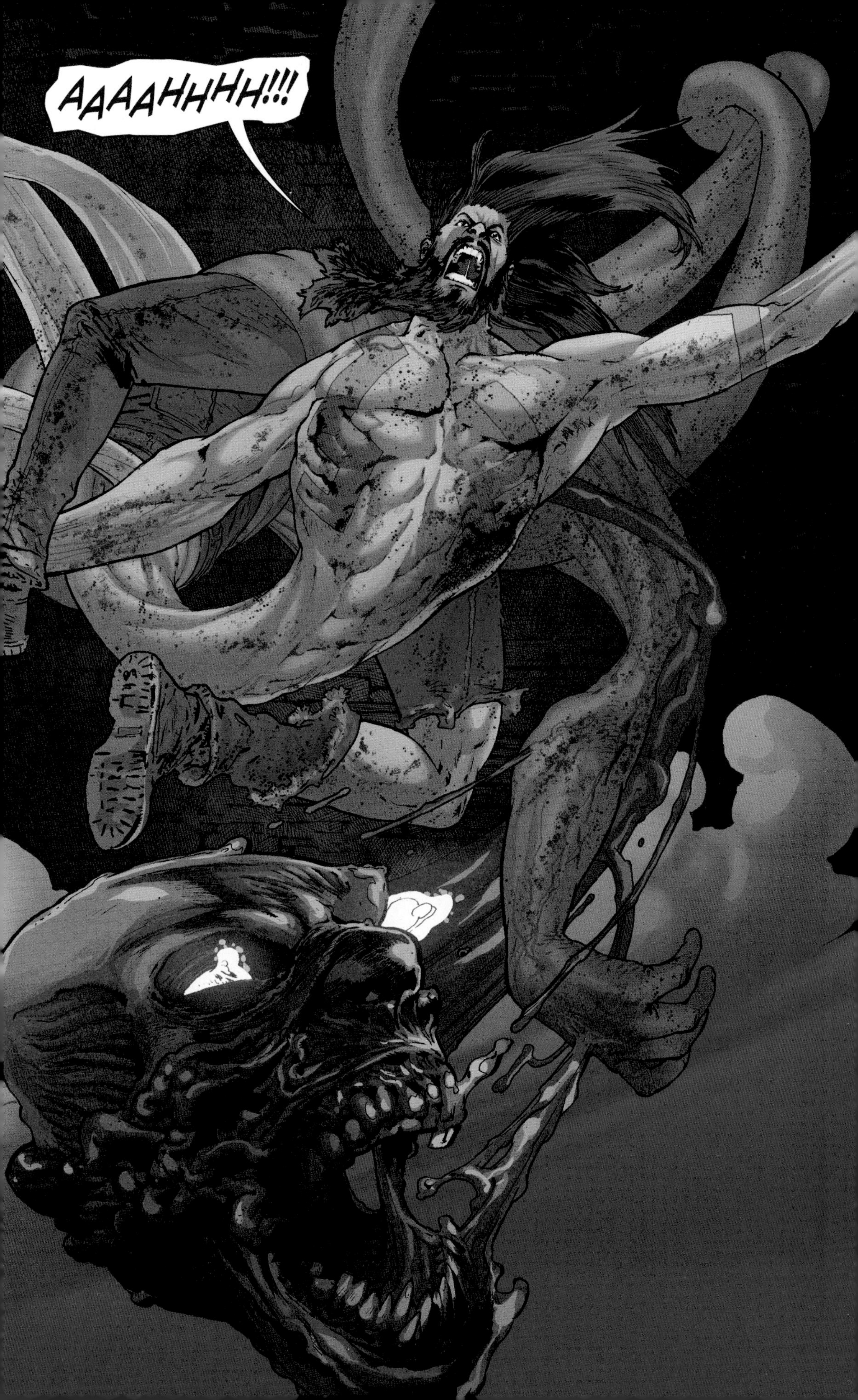
AAAAHHHH!!!

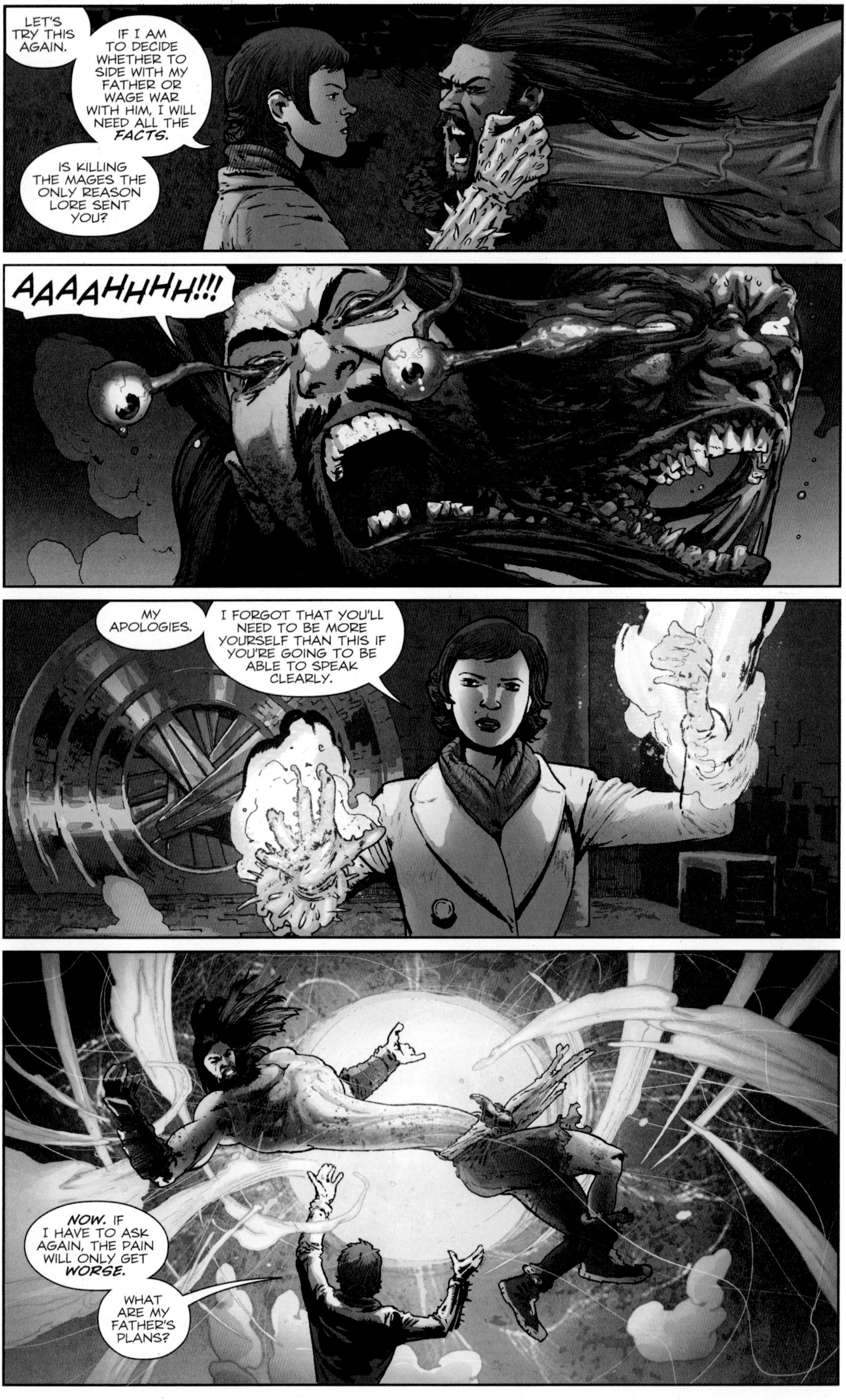
LET'S TRY THIS AGAIN.
IF I AM TO DECIDE WHETHER TO SIDE WITH MY FATHER OR WAGE WAR WITH HIM, I WILL NEED ALL THE *FACTS*.
IS KILLING THE MAGES THE ONLY REASON LORE SENT YOU?
AAAAHHHH!!!
MY APOLOGIES.
I FORGOT THAT YOU'LL NEED TO BE MORE YOURSELF THAN THIS IF YOU'RE GOING TO BE ABLE TO SPEAK CLEARLY.
NOW. IF I HAVE TO ASK AGAIN, THE PAIN WILL ONLY GET ***WORSE.***
WHAT ARE MY FATHER'S PLANS?

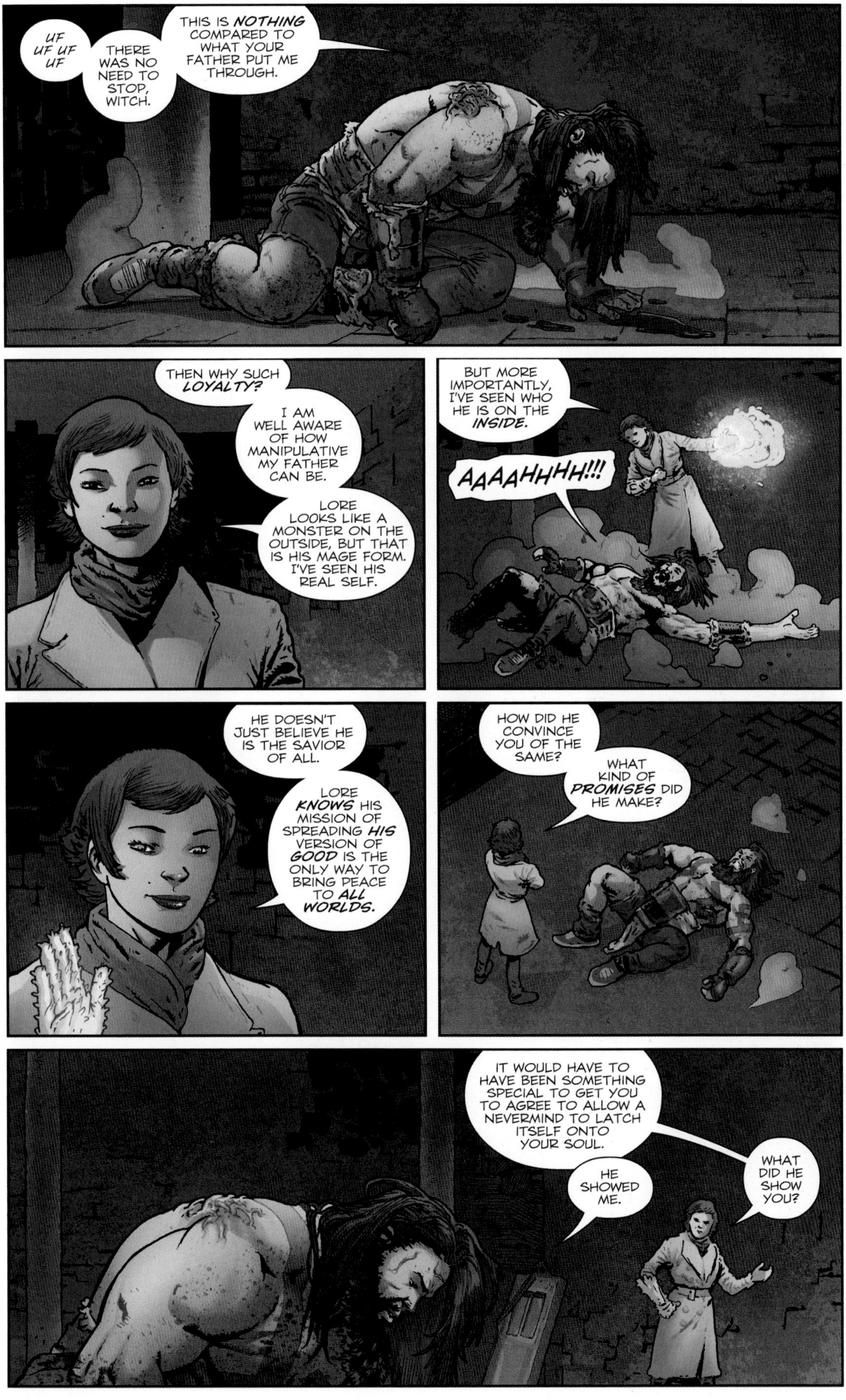
UF UF UF UF
THERE WAS NO NEED TO STOP, WITCH.
THIS IS NOTHING COMPARED TO WHAT YOUR FATHER PUT ME THROUGH.
THEN WHY SUCH LOYALTY?
I AM WELL AWARE OF HOW MANIPULATIVE MY FATHER CAN BE.
LORE LOOKS LIKE A MONSTER ON THE OUTSIDE, BUT THAT IS HIS MAGE FORM. I'VE SEEN HIS REAL SELF.
BUT MORE IMPORTANTLY, I'VE SEEN WHO HE IS ON THE INSIDE.
AAAAHHHH!!!
HE DOESN'T JUST BELIEVE HE IS THE SAVIOR OF ALL.
LORE KNOWS HIS MISSION OF SPREADING HIS VERSION OF GOOD IS THE ONLY WAY TO BRING PEACE TO ALL WORLDS.
HOW DID HE CONVINCE YOU OF THE SAME?
WHAT KIND OF PROMISES DID HE MAKE?
IT WOULD HAVE TO HAVE BEEN SOMETHING SPECIAL TO GET YOU TO AGREE TO ALLOW A NEVERMIND TO LATCH ITSELF ONTO YOUR SOUL.
HE SHOWED ME.
WHAT DID HE SHOW YOU?

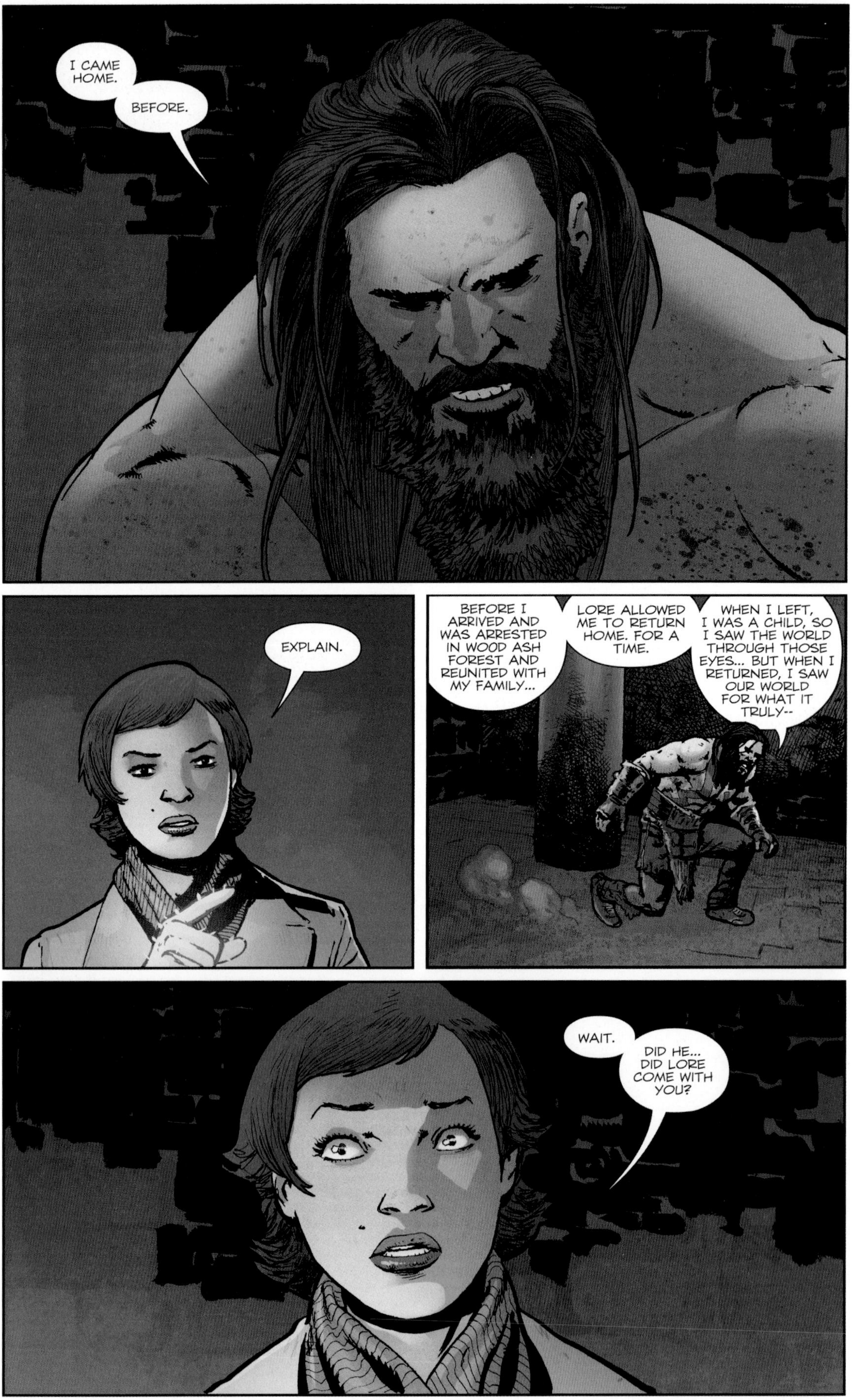
I CAME HOME.
BEFORE.
EXPLAIN.
BEFORE I ARRIVED AND WAS ARRESTED IN WOOD ASH FOREST AND REUNITED WITH MY FAMILY...
LORE ALLOWED ME TO RETURN HOME. FOR A TIME.
WHEN I LEFT, I WAS A CHILD, SO I SAW THE WORLD THROUGH THOSE EYES... BUT WHEN I RETURNED, I SAW OUR WORLD FOR WHAT IT TRULY--
WAIT.
DID HE... DID LORE COME WITH YOU?

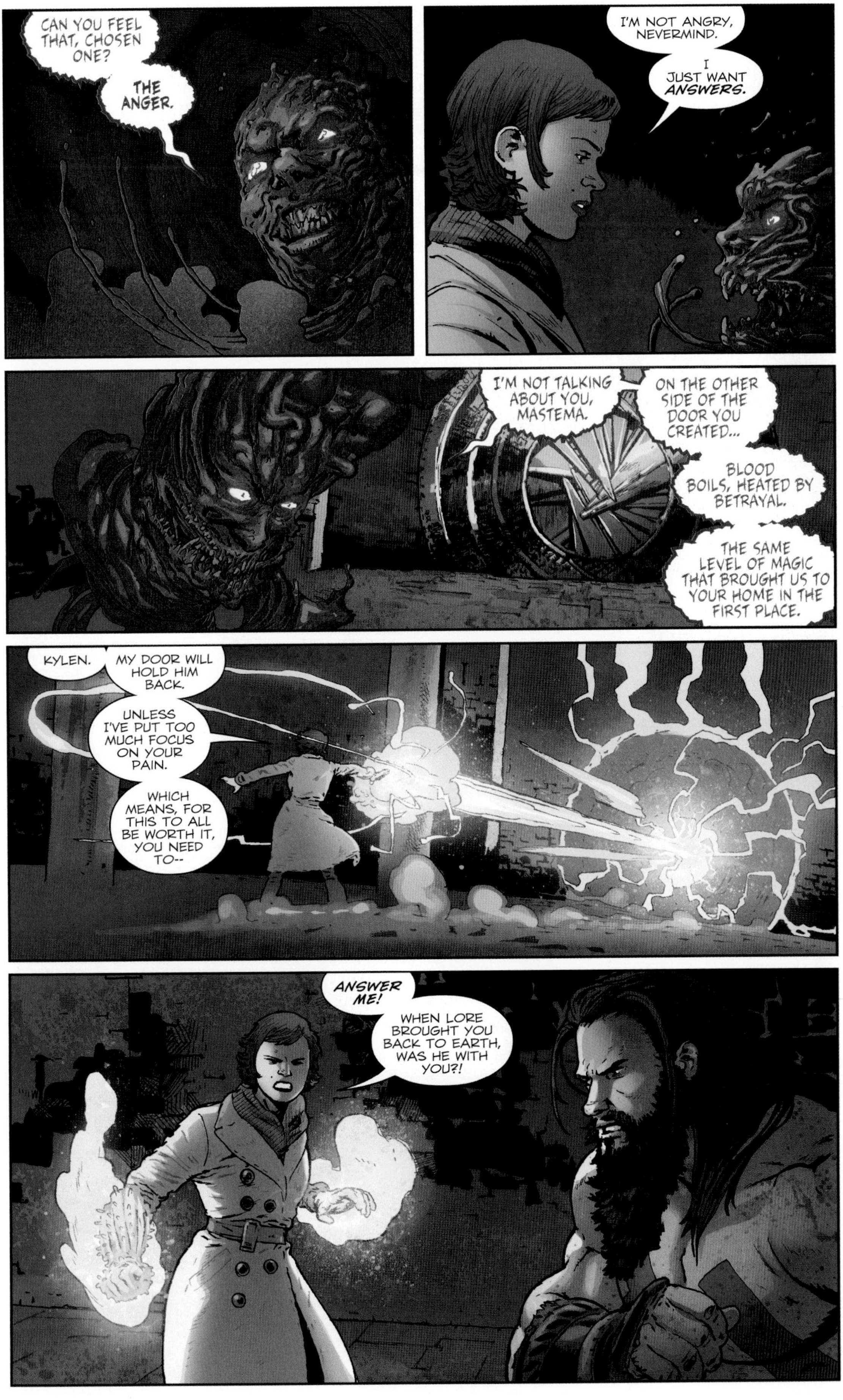
CAN YOU FEEL THAT, CHOSEN ONE?
THE ANGER.
I'M NOT ANGRY, NEVERMIND.
I JUST WANT ANSWERS.
I'M NOT TALKING ABOUT YOU, MASTEMA.
ON THE OTHER SIDE OF THE DOOR YOU CREATED...
BLOOD BOILS, HEATED BY BETRAYAL.
THE SAME LEVEL OF MAGIC THAT BROUGHT US TO YOUR HOME IN THE FIRST PLACE.
KYLEN.
MY DOOR WILL HOLD HIM BACK.
UNLESS I'VE PUT TOO MUCH FOCUS ON YOUR PAIN.
WHICH MEANS, FOR THIS TO ALL BE WORTH IT, YOU NEED TO--
ANSWER ME!
WHEN LORE BROUGHT YOU BACK TO EARTH, WAS HE WITH YOU?!

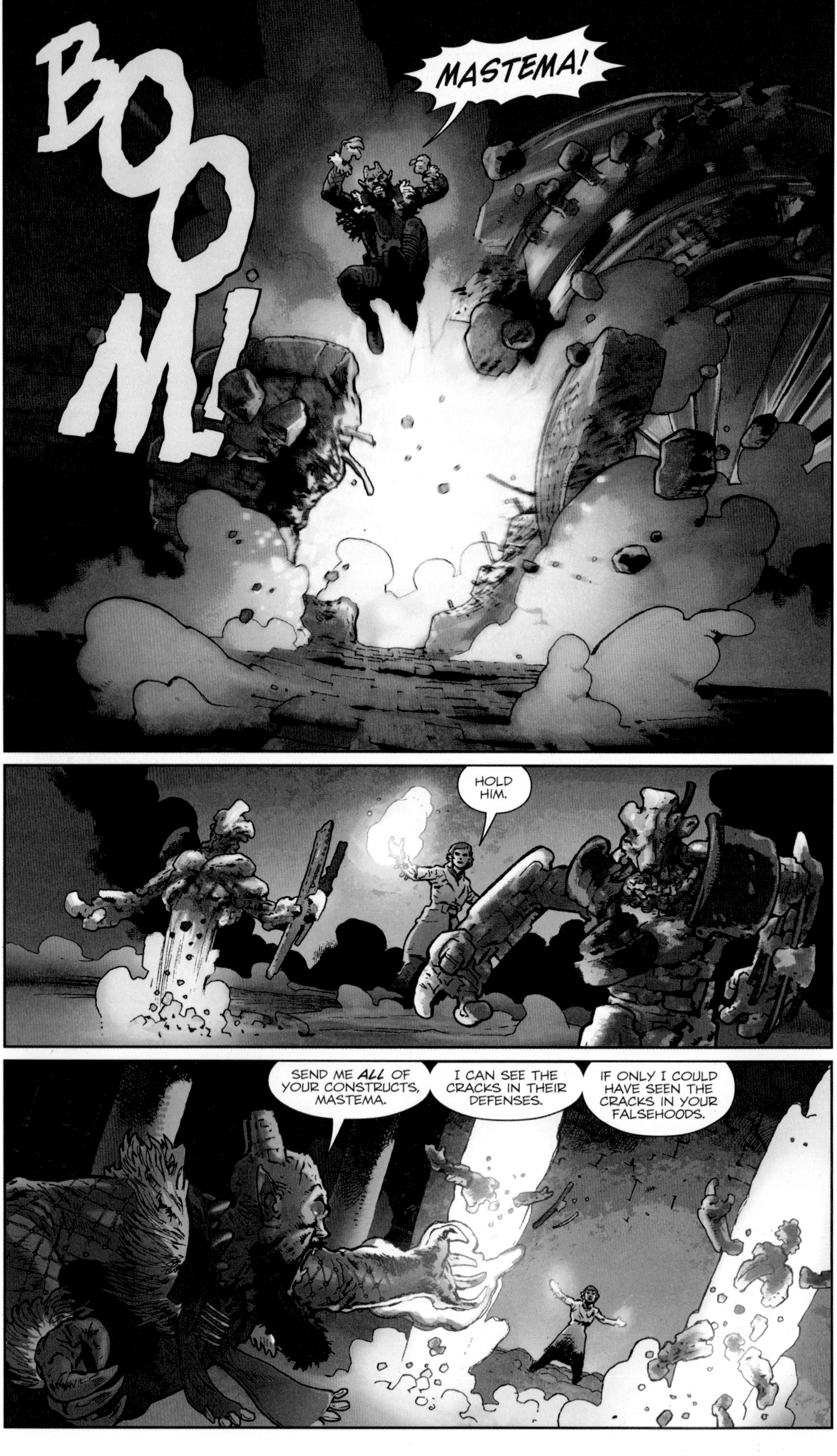
BOOOM!
MASTEMA!
HOLD HIM.
SEND ME ALL OF YOUR CONSTRUCTS, MASTEMA.
I CAN SEE THE CRACKS IN THEIR DEFENSES.
IF ONLY I COULD HAVE SEEN THE CRACKS IN YOUR FALSEHOODS.

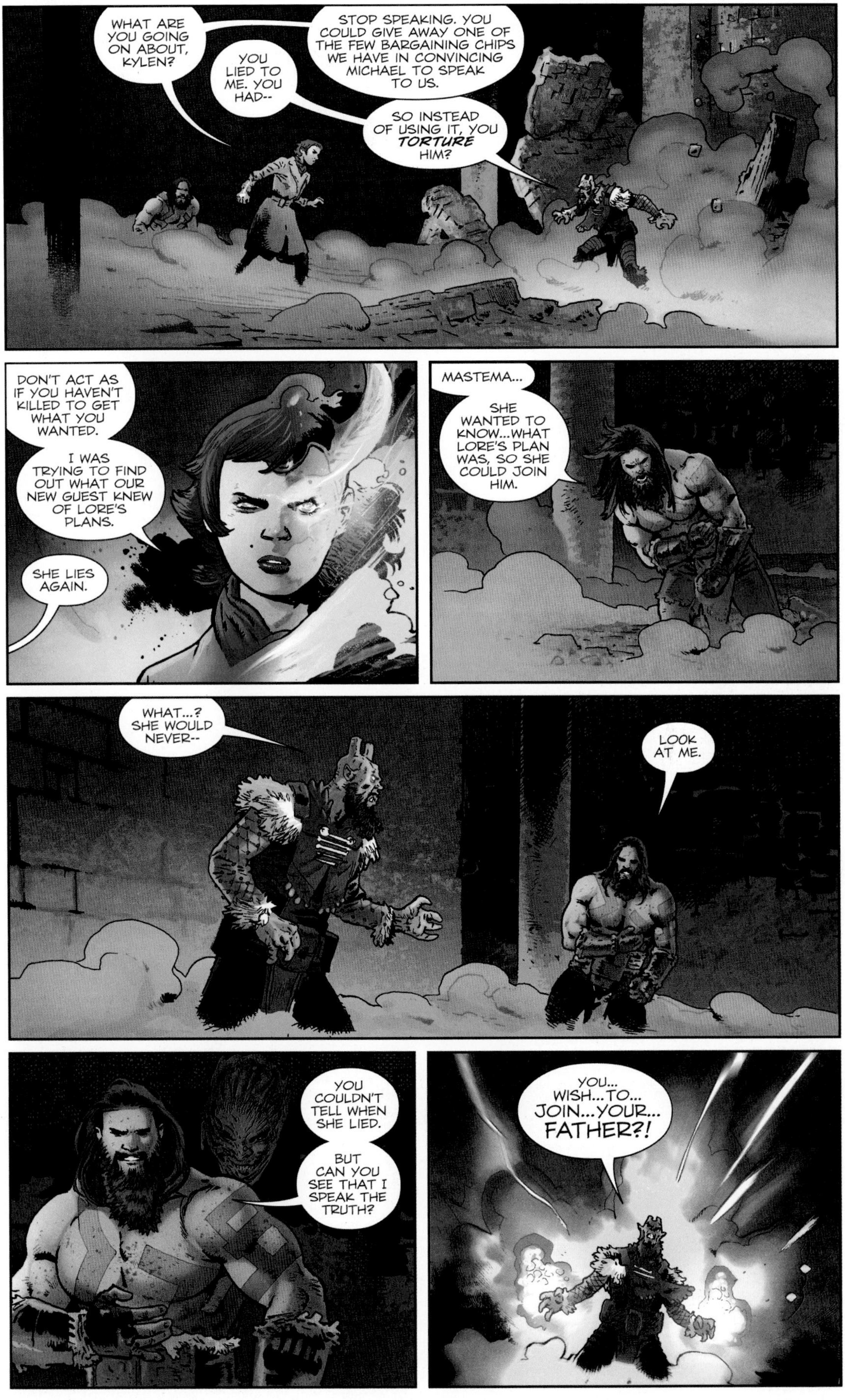
WHAT ARE YOU GOING ON ABOUT, KYLEN?
YOU LIED TO ME. YOU HAD--
STOP SPEAKING. YOU COULD GIVE AWAY ONE OF THE FEW BARGAINING CHIPS WE HAVE IN CONVINCING MICHAEL TO SPEAK TO US.
SO INSTEAD OF USING IT, YOU *TORTURE* HIM?
DON'T ACT AS IF YOU HAVEN'T KILLED TO GET WHAT YOU WANTED.
I WAS TRYING TO FIND OUT WHAT OUR NEW GUEST KNEW OF LORE'S PLANS.
SHE LIES AGAIN.
MASTEMA...
SHE WANTED TO KNOW...WHAT LORE'S PLAN WAS, SO SHE COULD JOIN HIM.
WHAT...? SHE WOULD NEVER--
LOOK AT ME.
YOU COULDN'T TELL WHEN SHE LIED.
BUT CAN YOU SEE THAT I SPEAK THE TRUTH?
YOU... WISH...TO... JOIN...YOUR... FATHER?!

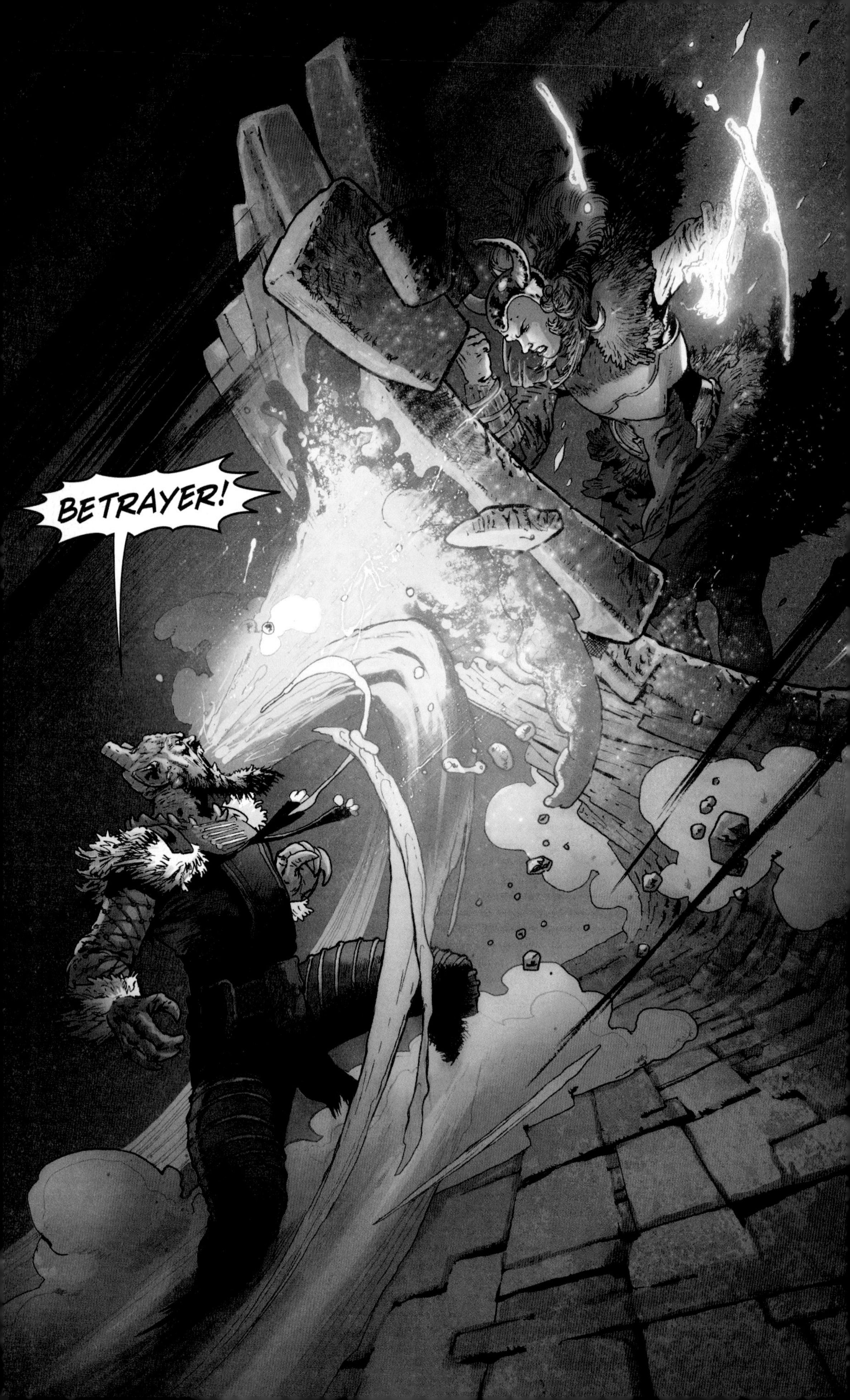
BETRAYER!

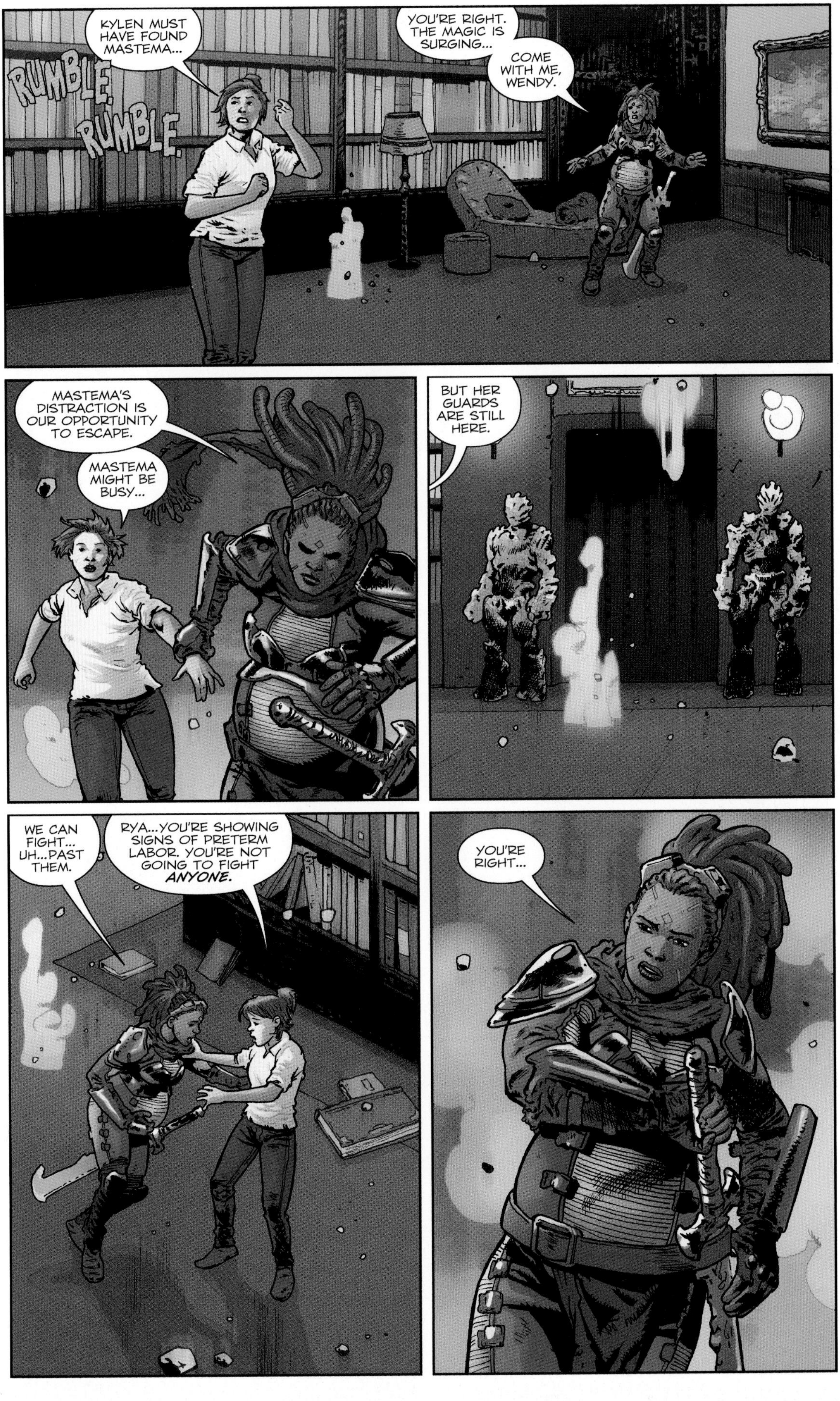
KYLEN MUST HAVE FOUND MASTEMA...
RUMBLE, RUMBLE.
YOU'RE RIGHT. THE MAGIC IS SURGING...
COME WITH ME, WENDY.
MASTEMA'S DISTRACTION IS OUR OPPORTUNITY TO ESCAPE.
MASTEMA MIGHT BE BUSY...
BUT HER GUARDS ARE STILL HERE.
WE CAN FIGHT... UH...PAST THEM.
RYA...YOU'RE SHOWING SIGNS OF PRETERM LABOR. YOU'RE NOT GOING TO FIGHT ANYONE.
YOU'RE RIGHT...

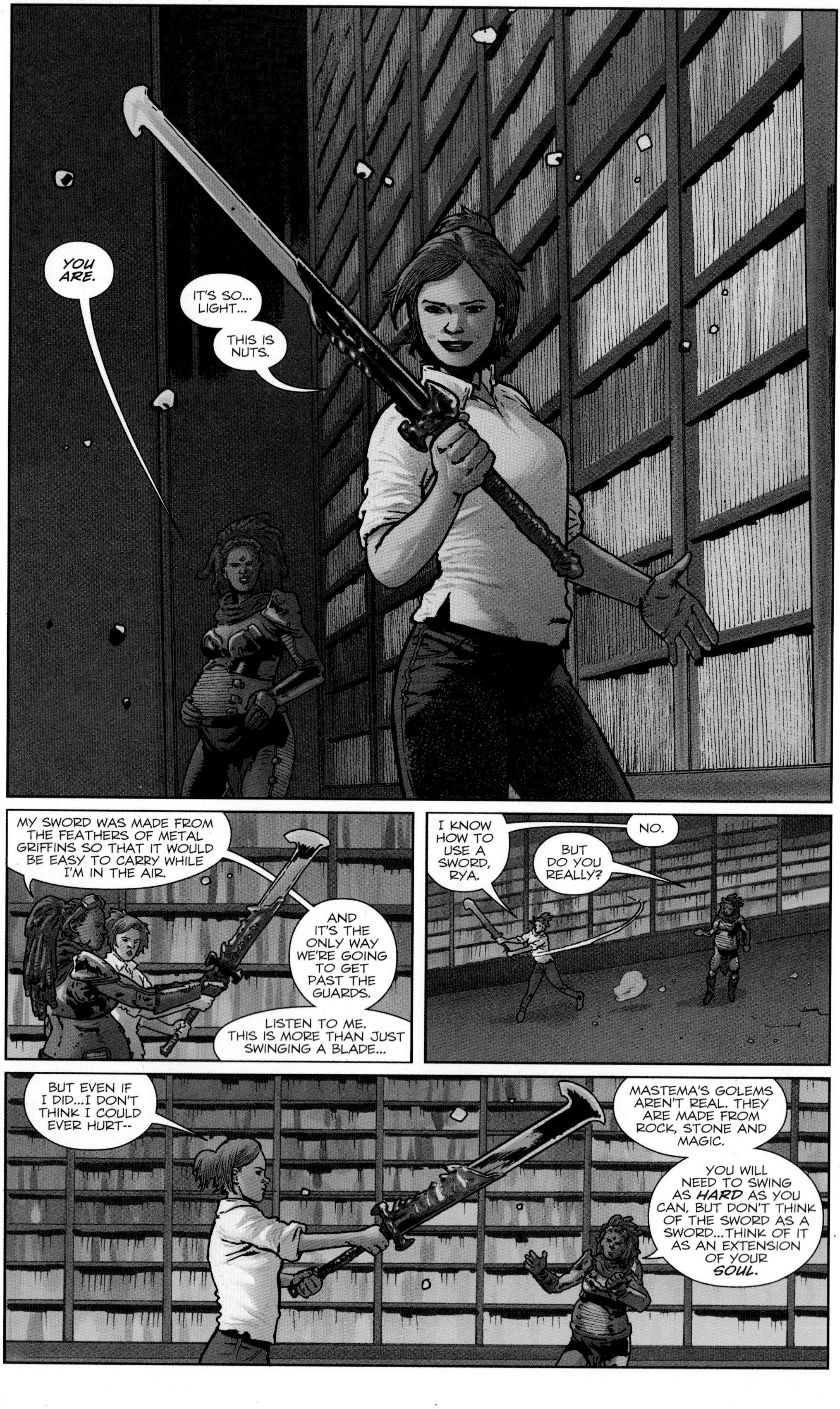
YOU ARE.
IT'S SO... LIGHT...
THIS IS NUTS.
MY SWORD WAS MADE FROM THE FEATHERS OF METAL GRIFFINS SO THAT IT WOULD BE EASY TO CARRY WHILE I'M IN THE AIR.
AND IT'S THE ONLY WAY WE'RE GOING TO GET PAST THE GUARDS.
LISTEN TO ME. THIS IS MORE THAN JUST SWINGING A BLADE...
I KNOW HOW TO USE A SWORD, RYA.
NO.
BUT DO YOU REALLY?
BUT EVEN IF I DID...I DON'T THINK I COULD EVER HURT--
MASTEMA'S GOLEMS AREN'T REAL. THEY ARE MADE FROM ROCK, STONE AND MAGIC.
YOU WILL NEED TO SWING AS HARD AS YOU CAN, BUT DON'T THINK OF THE SWORD AS A SWORD...THINK OF IT AS AN EXTENSION OF YOUR SOUL.

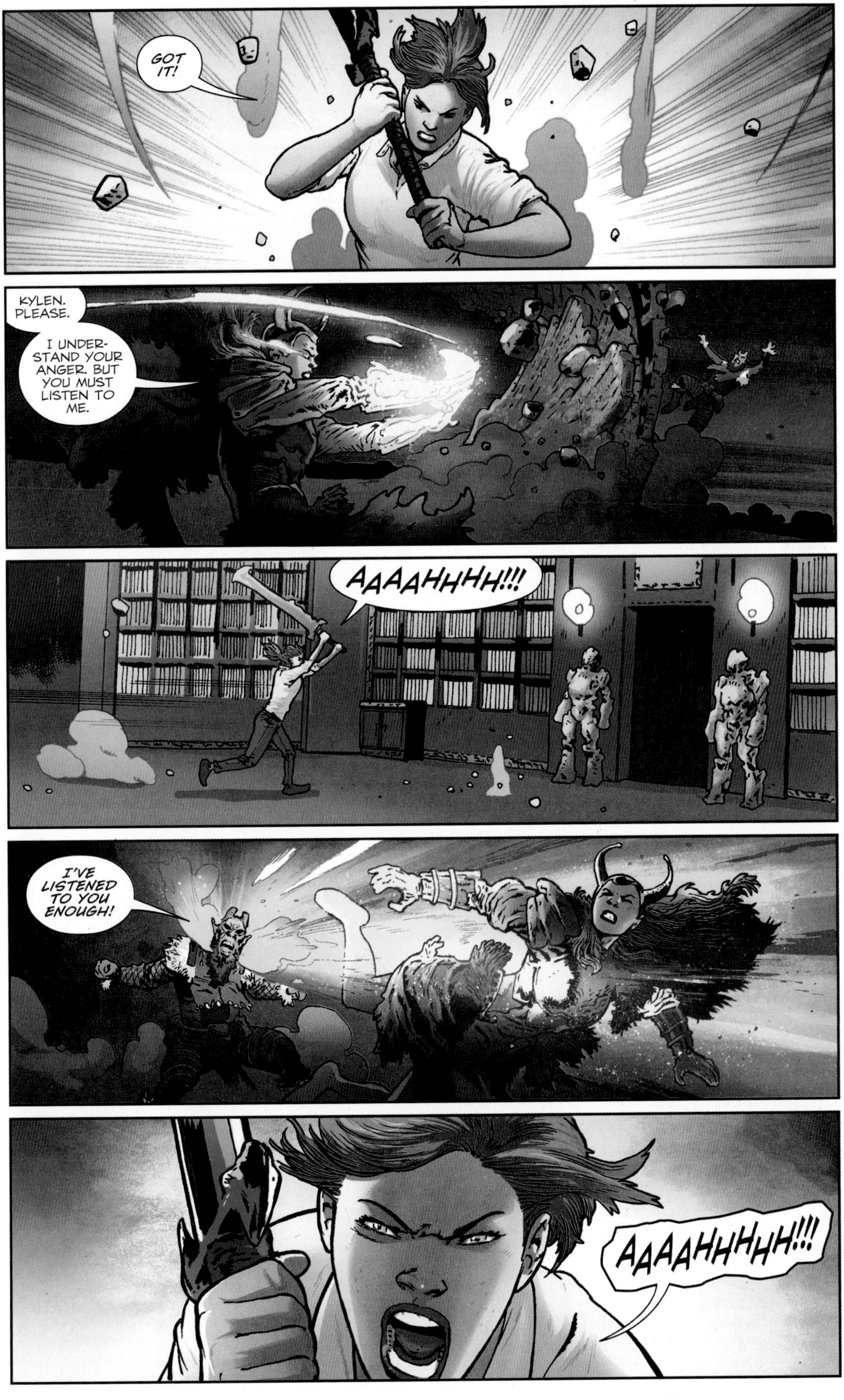
GOT IT!
KYLEN. PLEASE.
I UNDERSTAND YOUR ANGER. BUT YOU MUST LISTEN TO ME.
AAAAHHHH!!!
I'VE LISTENED TO YOU ENOUGH!
AAAAHHHHH!!!

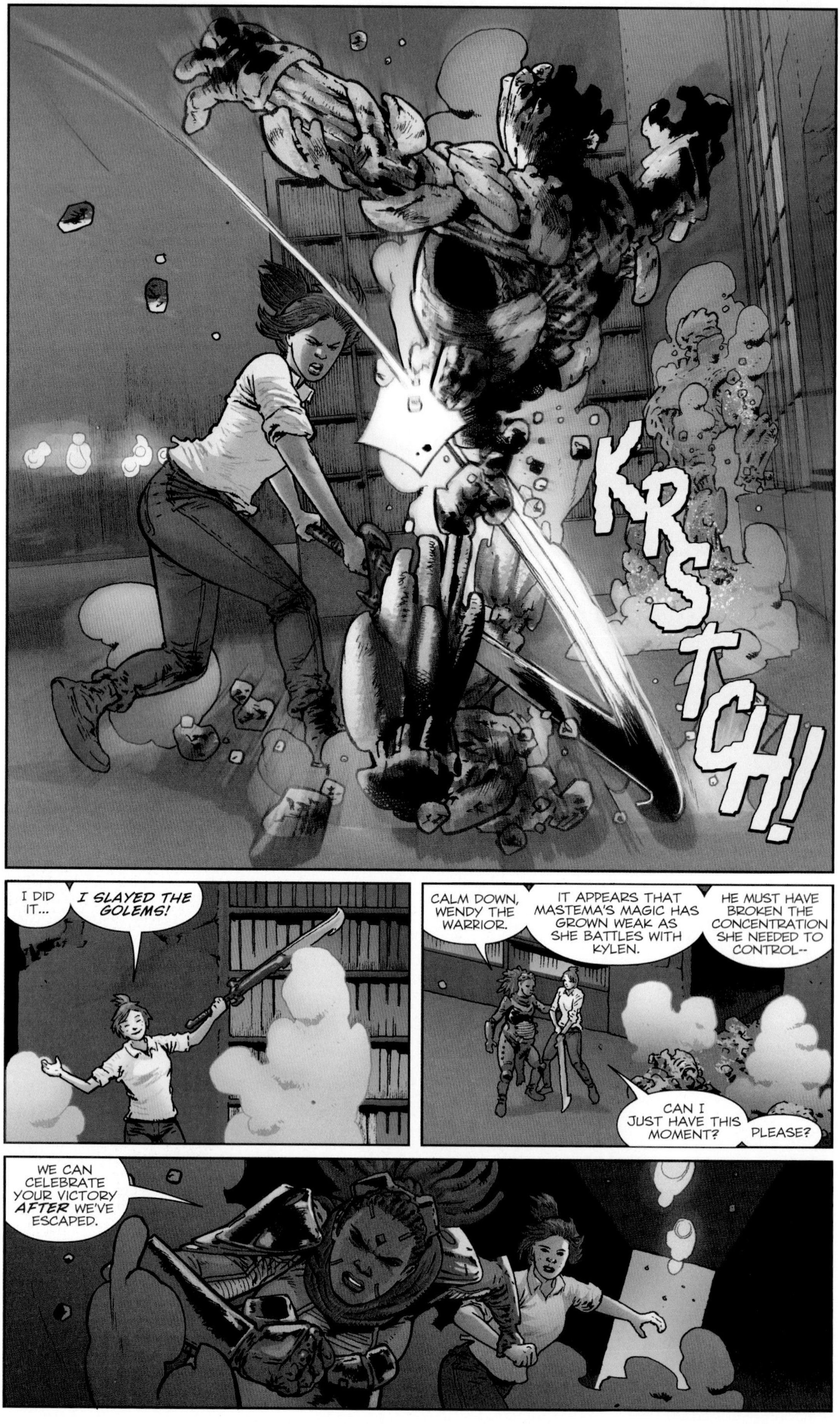
KRSTCH!
I DID IT...
I SLAYED THE GOLEMS!
CALM DOWN, WENDY THE WARRIOR.
IT APPEARS THAT MASTEMA'S MAGIC HAS GROWN WEAK AS SHE BATTLES WITH KYLEN.
HE MUST HAVE BROKEN THE CONCENTRATION SHE NEEDED TO CONTROL--
CAN I JUST HAVE THIS MOMENT?
PLEASE?
WE CAN CELEBRATE YOUR VICTORY AFTER WE'VE ESCAPED.

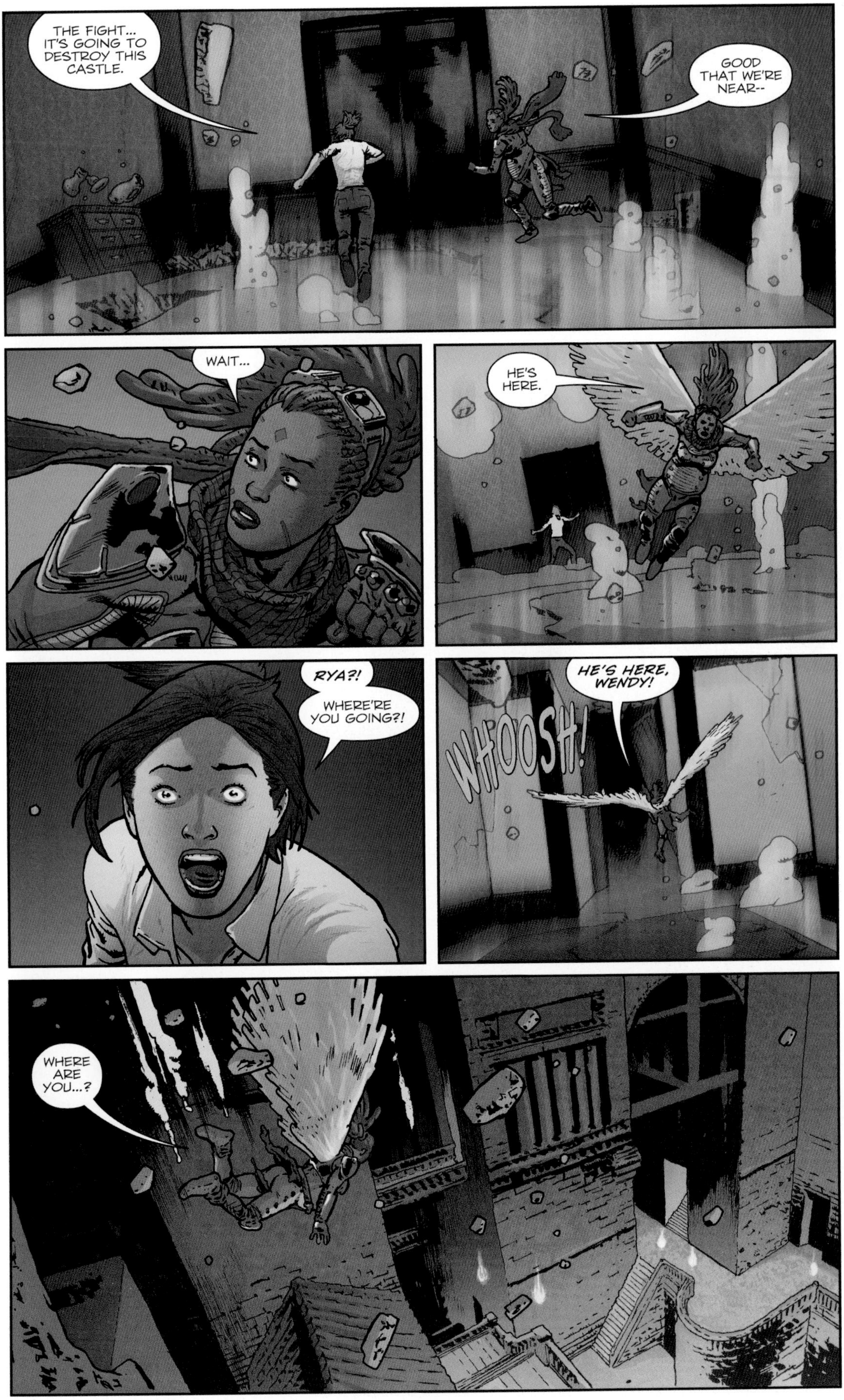
THE FIGHT... IT'S GOING TO DESTROY THIS CASTLE.
GOOD THAT WE'RE NEAR--
WAIT...
HE'S HERE.
RYA?!
WHERE'RE YOU GOING?!
WHOOSH!
HE'S HERE, WENDY!
WHERE ARE YOU...?

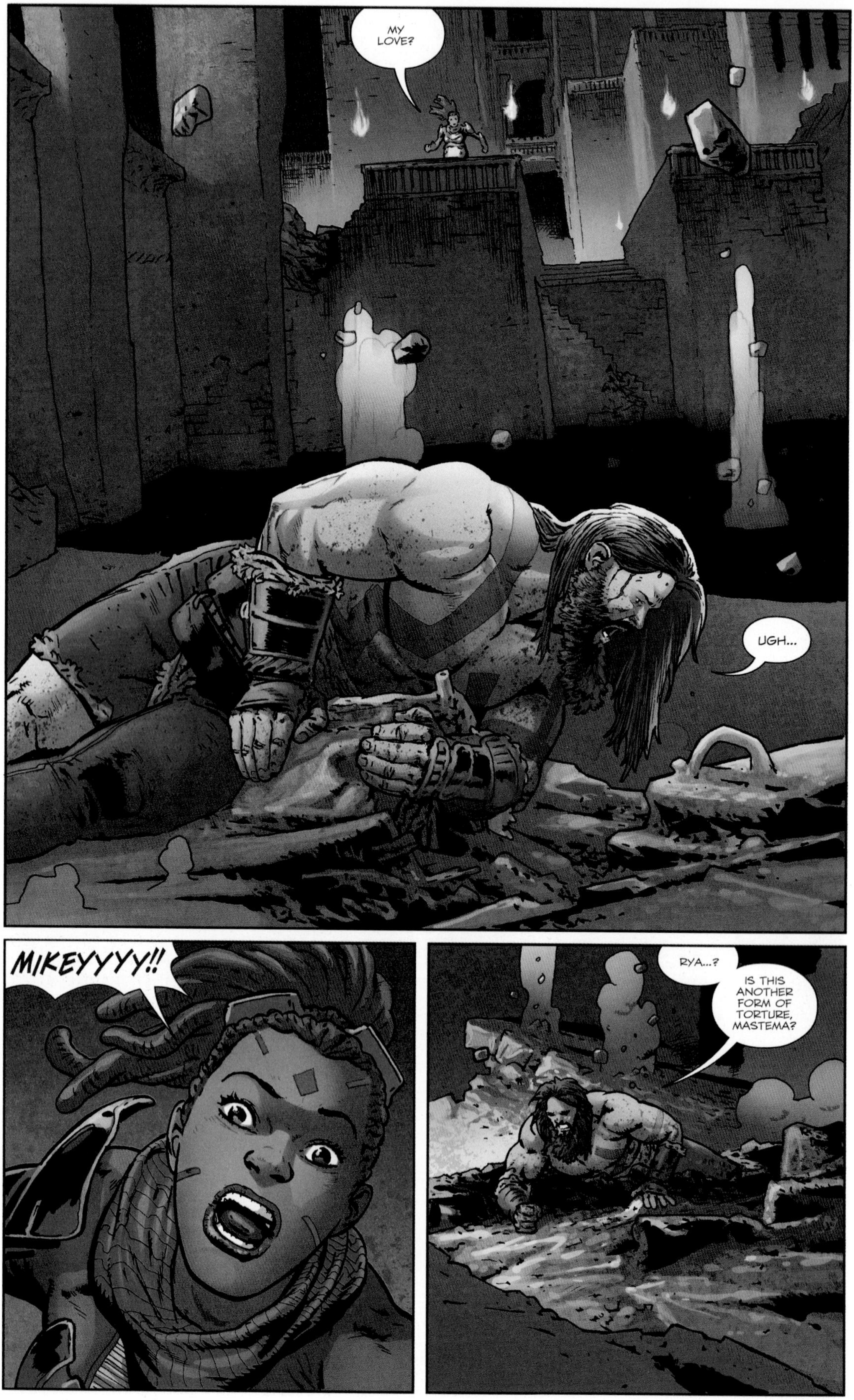

MY LOVE?
UGH...
MIKEYYYY!!
RYA...?
IS THIS ANOTHER FORM OF TORTURE, MASTEMA?

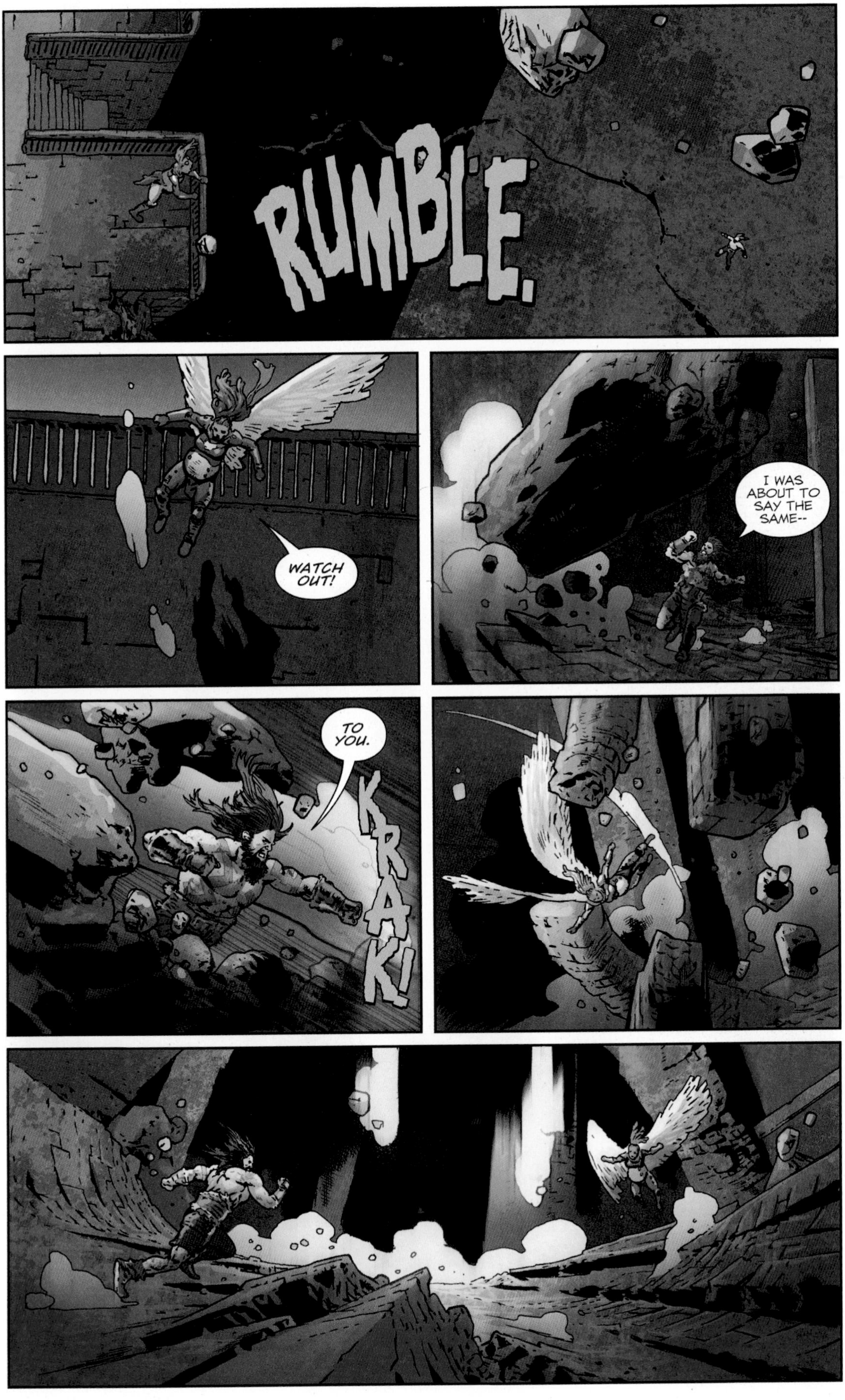
RUMBLE.
WATCH OUT!
I WAS ABOUT TO SAY THE SAME--
TO YOU.
KRAK!

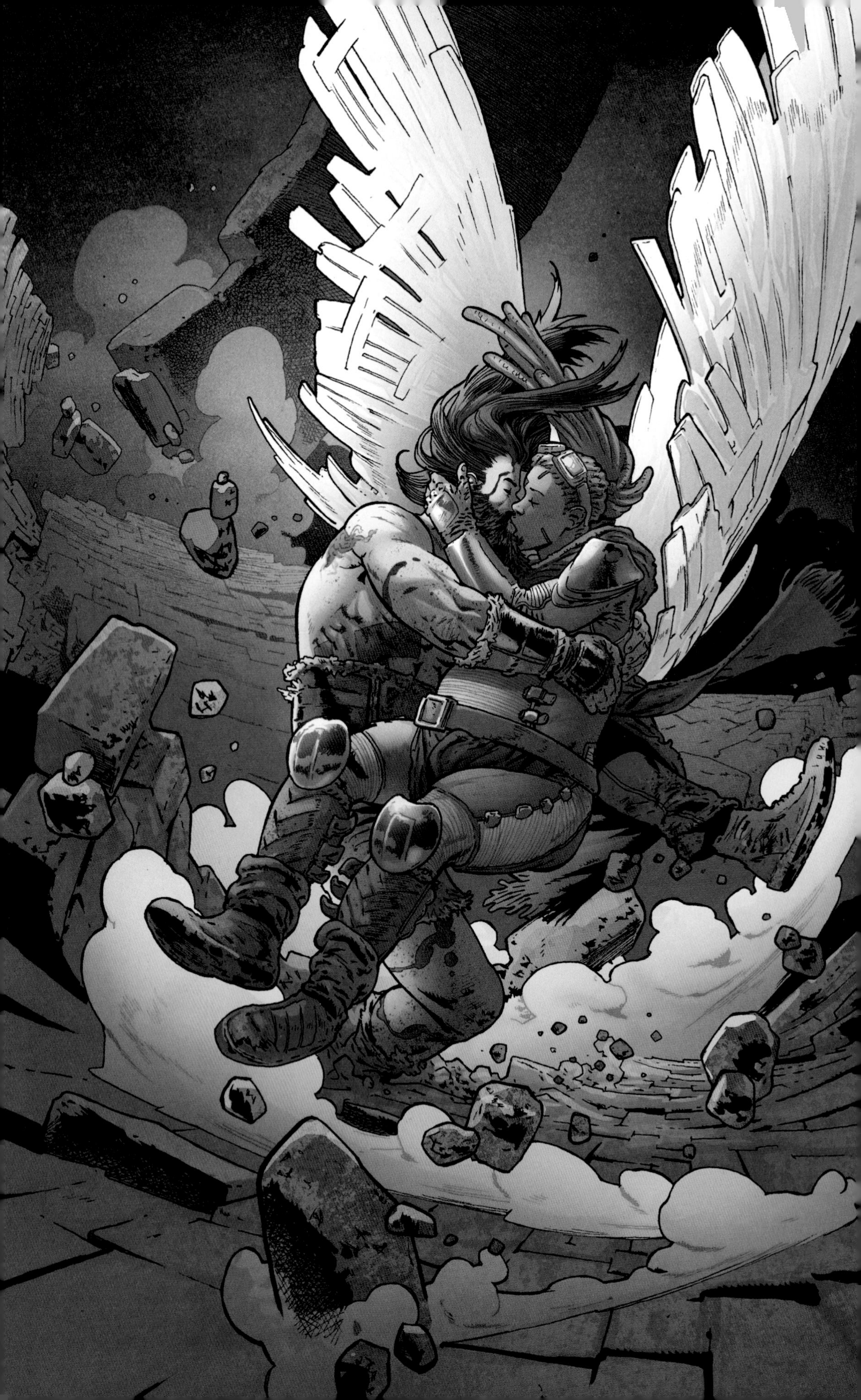

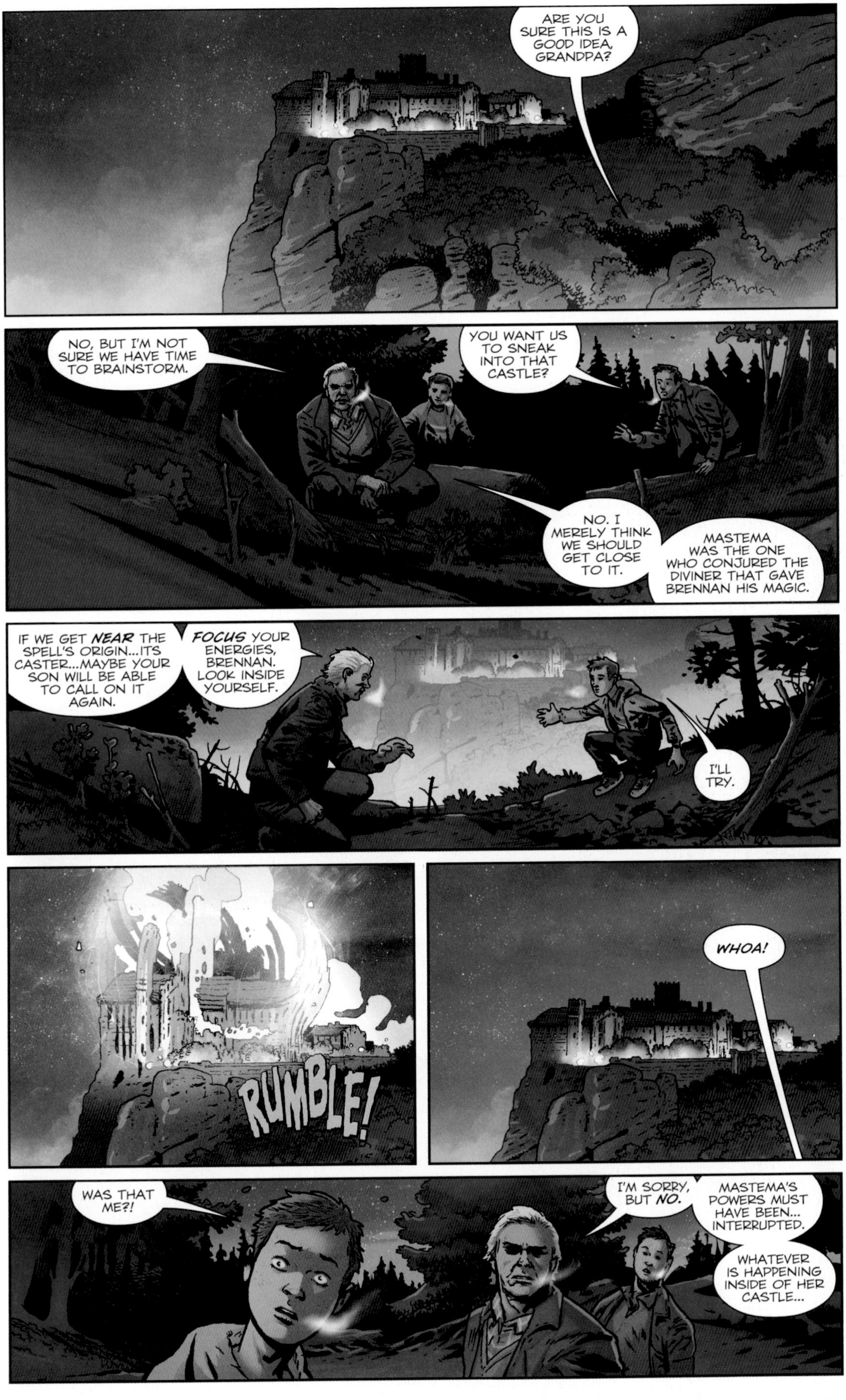
ARE YOU SURE THIS IS A GOOD IDEA, GRANDPA?
NO, BUT I'M NOT SURE WE HAVE TIME TO BRAINSTORM.
YOU WANT US TO SNEAK INTO THAT CASTLE?
NO. I MERELY THINK WE SHOULD GET CLOSE TO IT.
MASTEMA WAS THE ONE WHO CONJURED THE DIVINER THAT GAVE BRENNAN HIS MAGIC.
IF WE GET NEAR THE SPELL'S ORIGIN...ITS CASTER...MAYBE YOUR SON WILL BE ABLE TO CALL ON IT AGAIN.
FOCUS YOUR ENERGIES, BRENNAN. LOOK INSIDE YOURSELF.
I'LL TRY.
RUMBLE!
WHOA!
WAS THAT ME?!
I'M SORRY, BUT NO.
MASTEMA'S POWERS MUST HAVE BEEN... INTERRUPTED.
WHATEVER IS HAPPENING INSIDE OF HER CASTLE...

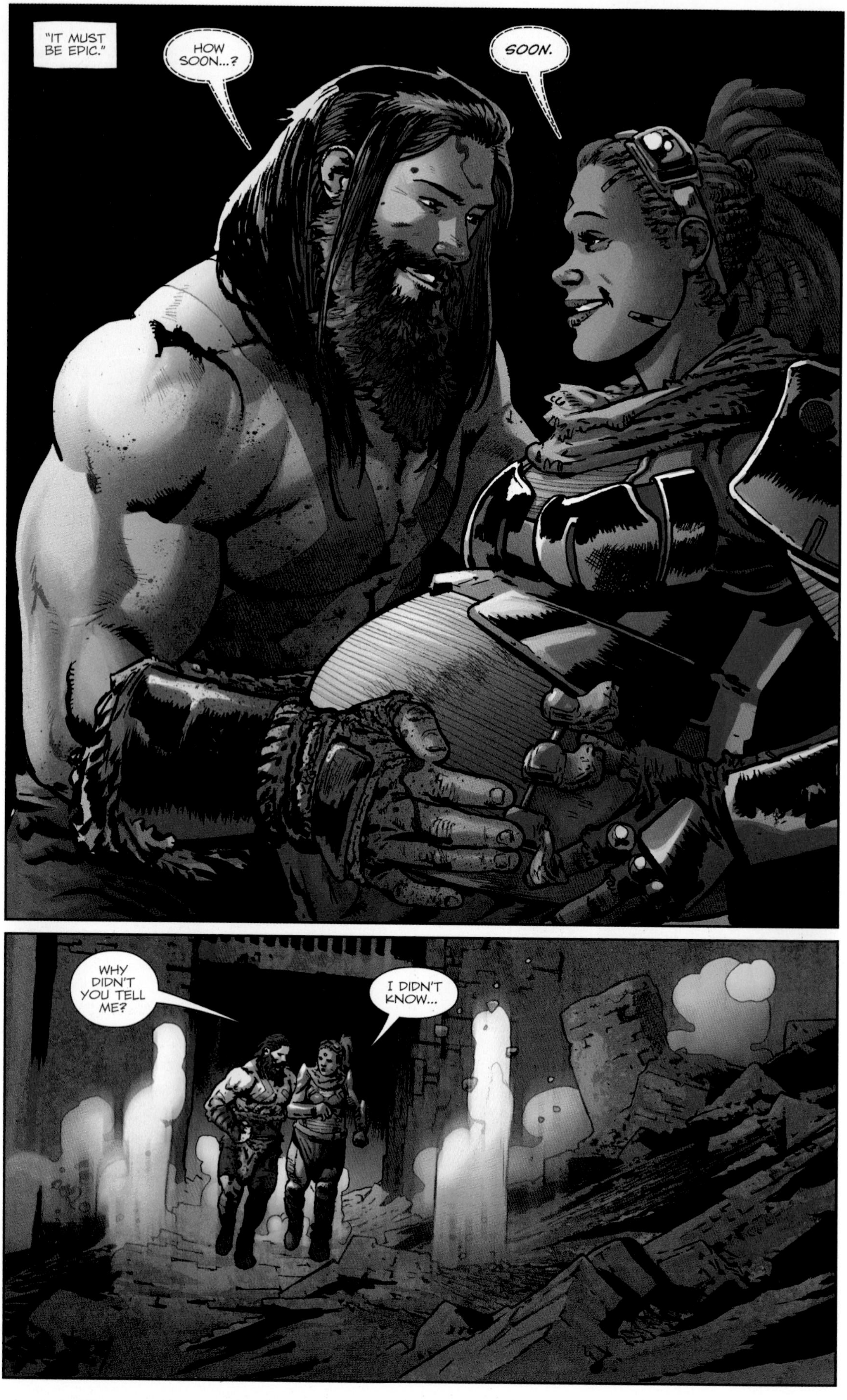
"IT MUST BE EPIC."
HOW SOON...?
SOON.
WHY DIDN'T YOU TELL ME?
I DIDN'T KNOW...

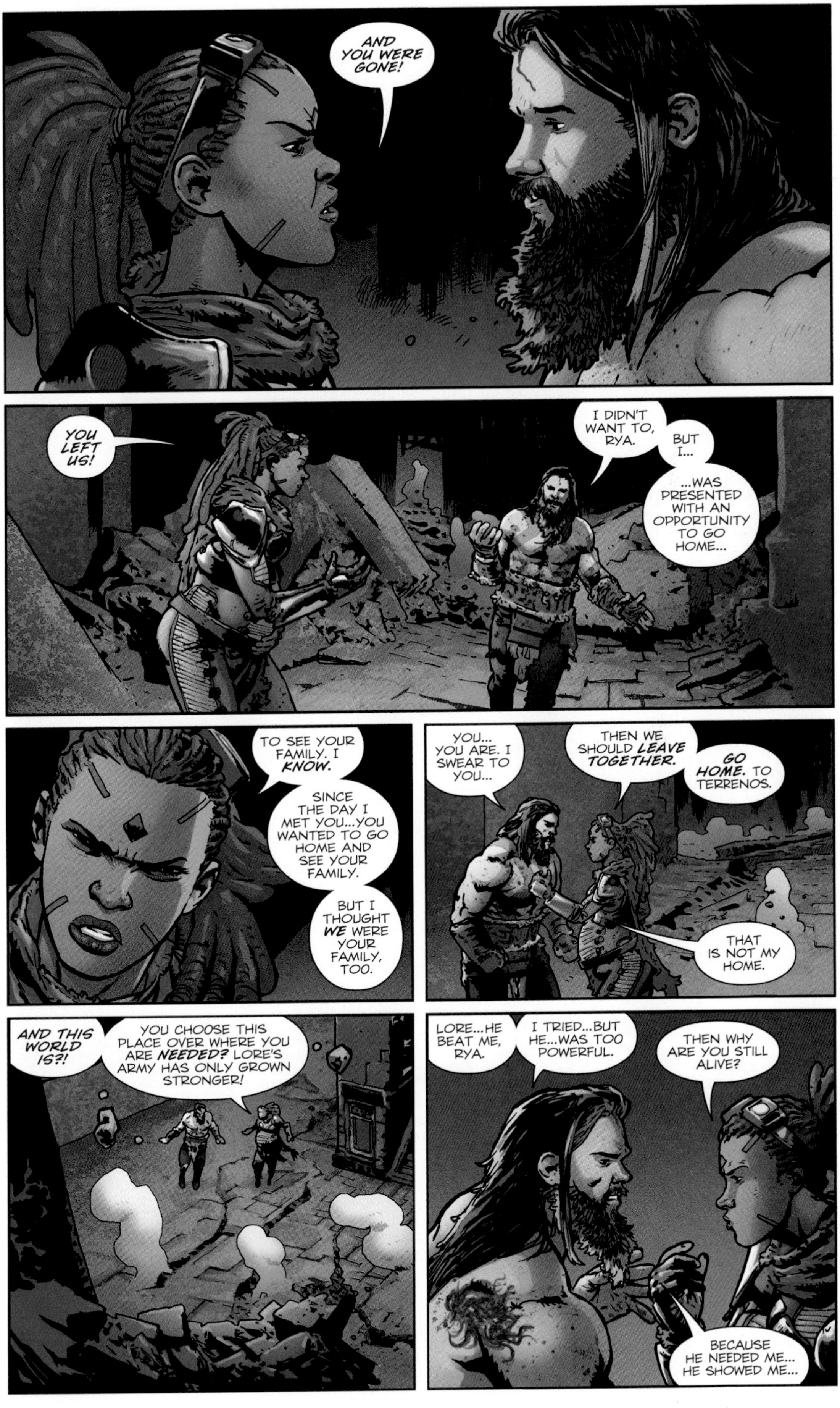
AND YOU WERE GONE!
YOU LEFT US!
I DIDN'T WANT TO, RYA.
BUT I...
...WAS PRESENTED WITH AN OPPORTUNITY TO GO HOME...
TO SEE YOUR FAMILY. I KNOW.
SINCE THE DAY I MET YOU...YOU WANTED TO GO HOME AND SEE YOUR FAMILY.
BUT I THOUGHT WE WERE YOUR FAMILY, TOO.
YOU... YOU ARE. I SWEAR TO YOU...
THEN WE SHOULD LEAVE TOGETHER.
GO HOME. TO TERRENOS.
THAT IS NOT MY HOME.
AND THIS WORLD IS?!
YOU CHOOSE THIS PLACE OVER WHERE YOU ARE NEEDED? LORE'S ARMY HAS ONLY GROWN STRONGER!
LORE...HE BEAT ME, RYA.
I TRIED...BUT HE...WAS TOO POWERFUL.
THEN WHY ARE YOU STILL ALIVE?
BECAUSE HE NEEDED ME... HE SHOWED ME...

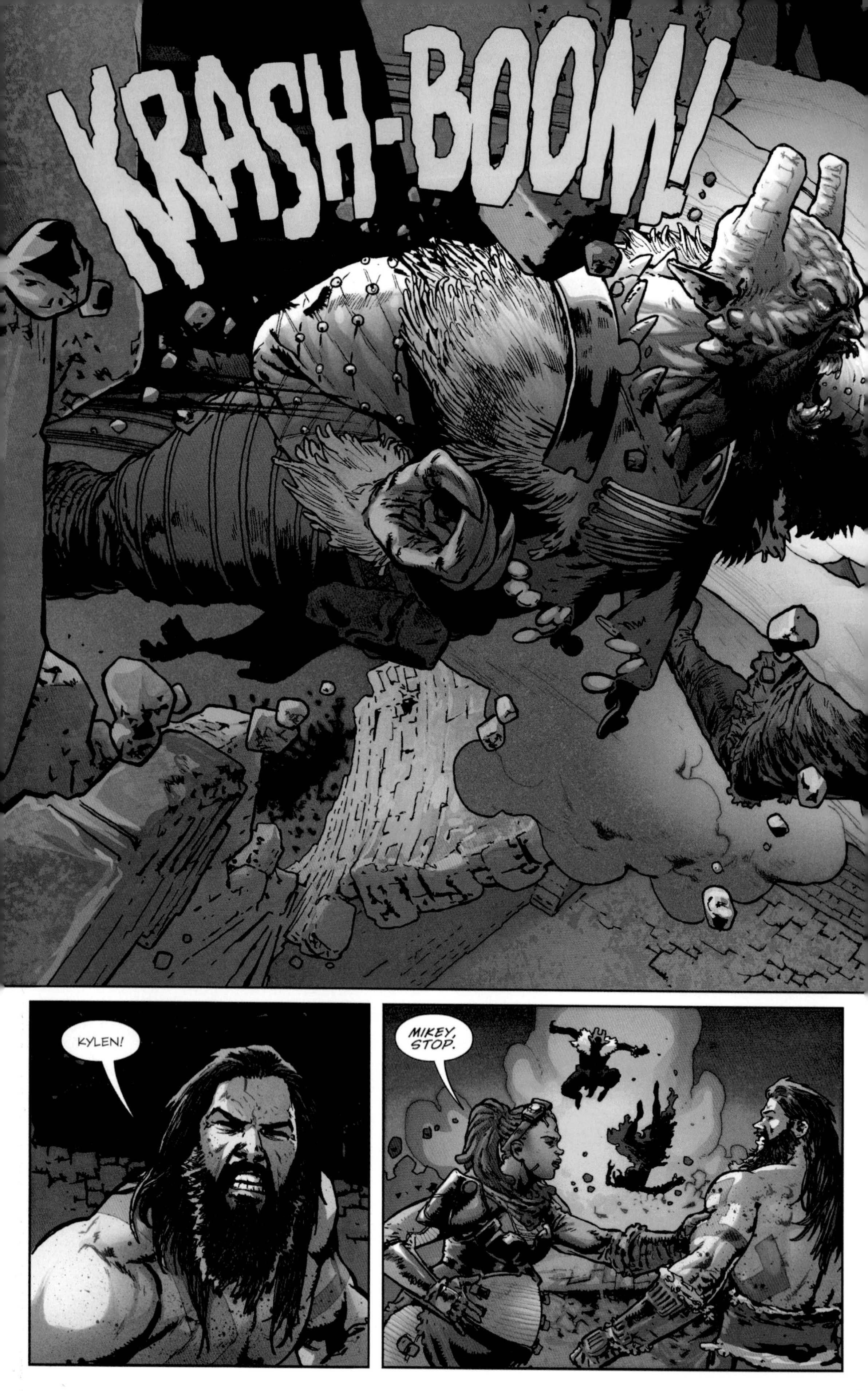
KRASH-BOOM!
KYLEN!
MIKEY, STOP.

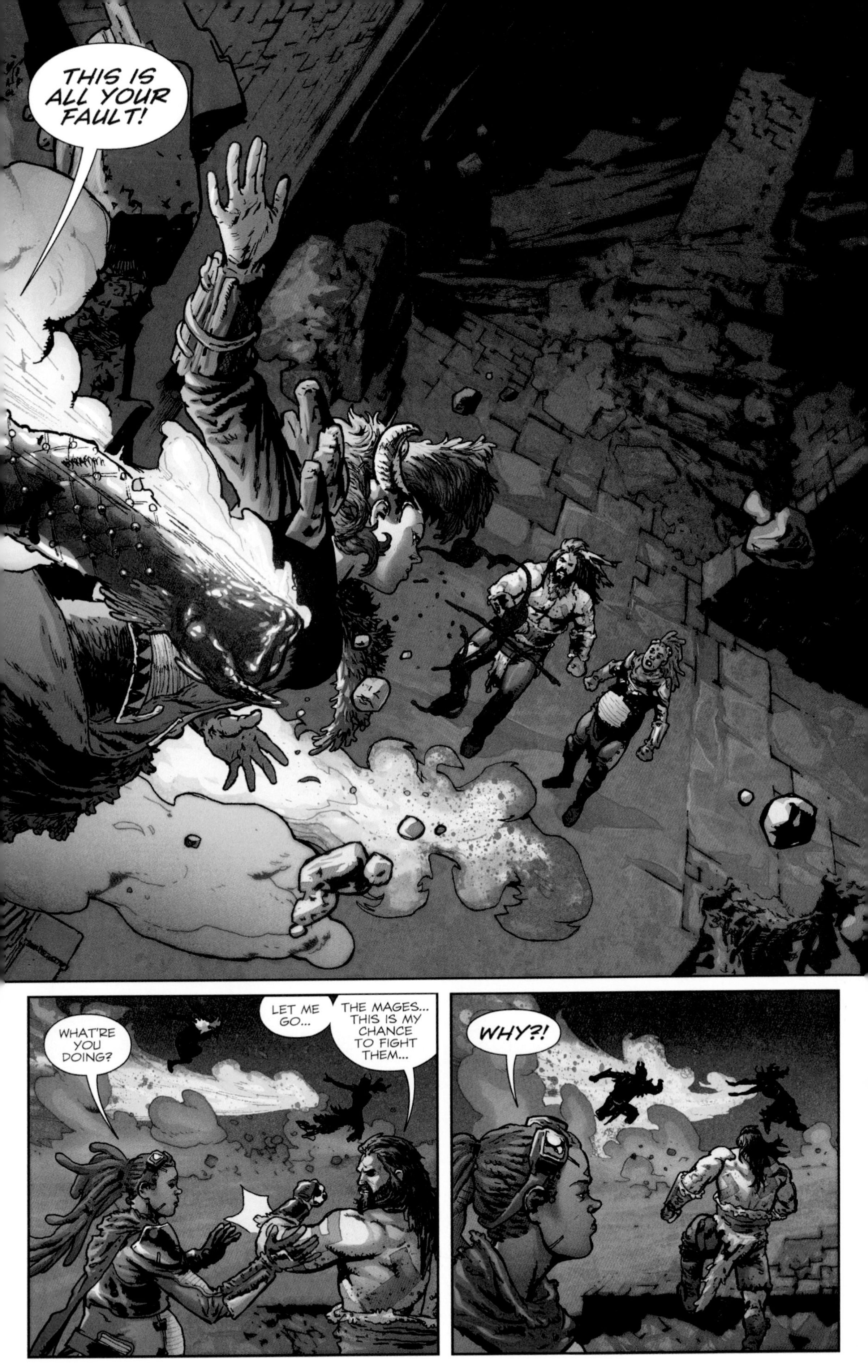
THIS IS ALL YOUR FAULT!
WHAT'RE YOU DOING?
LET ME GO...
THE MAGES... THIS IS MY CHANCE TO FIGHT THEM...
WHY?!

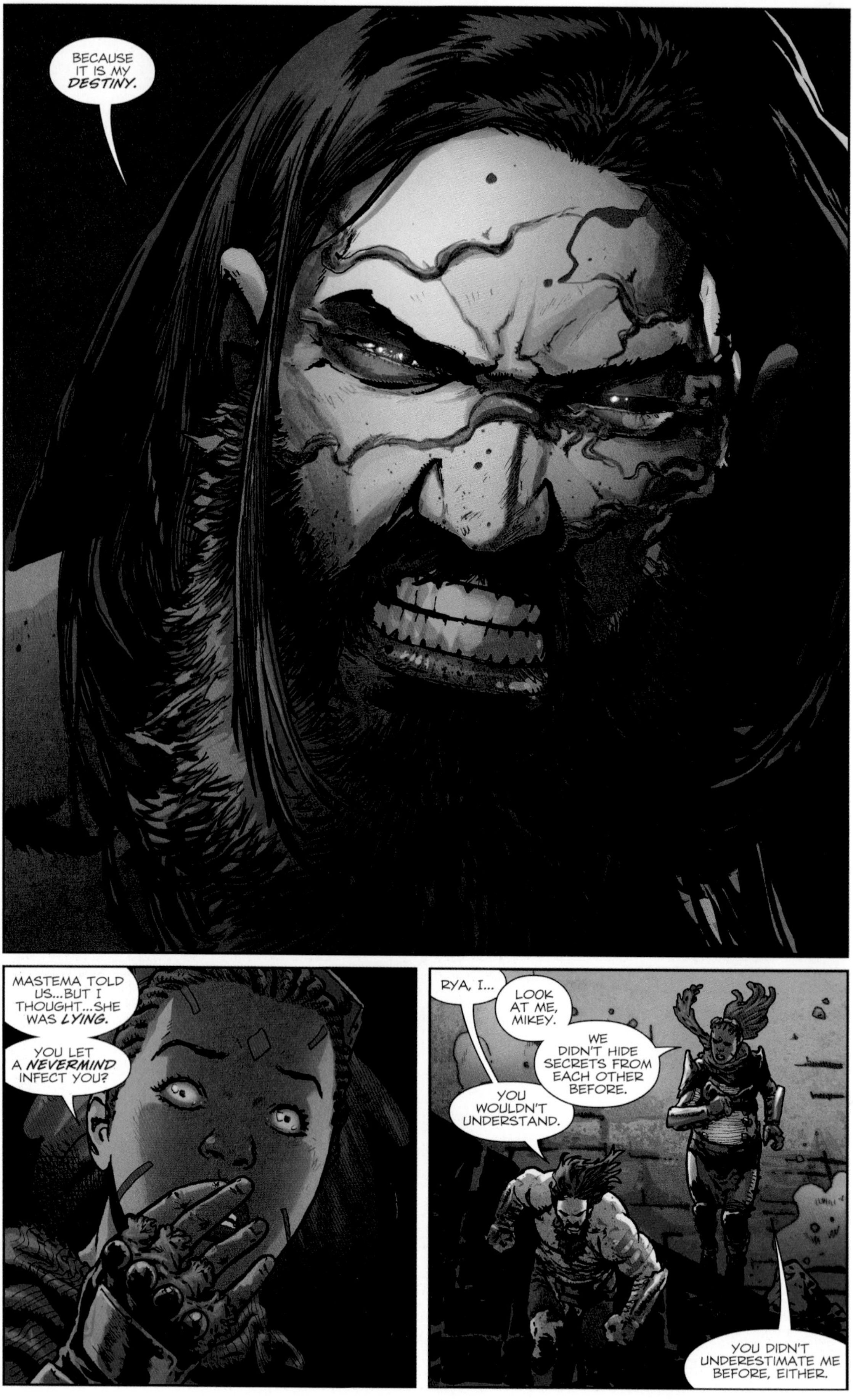
BECAUSE IT IS MY *DESTINY*.
MASTEMA TOLD US...BUT I THOUGHT...SHE WAS *LYING*.
YOU LET A *NEVERMIND* INFECT YOU?
RYA, I...
LOOK AT ME, MIKEY.
WE DIDN'T HIDE SECRETS FROM EACH OTHER BEFORE.
YOU WOULDN'T UNDERSTAND.
YOU DIDN'T UNDERESTIMATE ME BEFORE, EITHER.

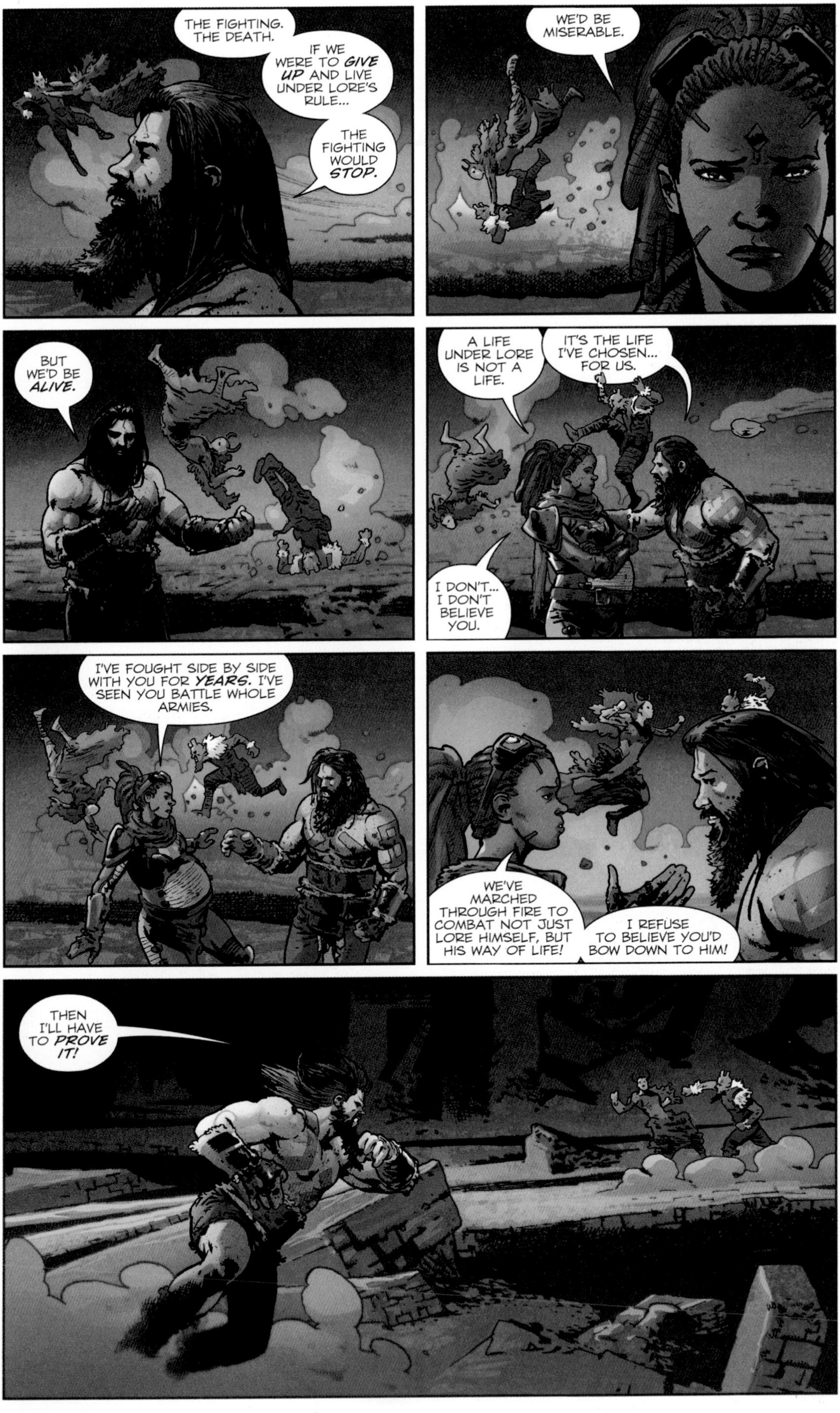
THE FIGHTING. THE DEATH.
IF WE WERE TO *GIVE UP* AND LIVE UNDER LORE'S RULE...
THE FIGHTING WOULD *STOP.*
WE'D BE MISERABLE.
BUT WE'D BE *ALIVE.*
A LIFE UNDER LORE IS NOT A LIFE.
IT'S THE LIFE I'VE CHOSEN... FOR US.
I DON'T... I DON'T BELIEVE YOU.
I'VE FOUGHT SIDE BY SIDE WITH YOU FOR *YEARS.* I'VE SEEN YOU BATTLE WHOLE ARMIES.
WE'VE MARCHED THROUGH FIRE TO COMBAT NOT JUST LORE HIMSELF, BUT HIS WAY OF LIFE!
I REFUSE TO BELIEVE YOU'D BOW DOWN TO HIM!
THEN I'LL HAVE TO *PROVE IT!*

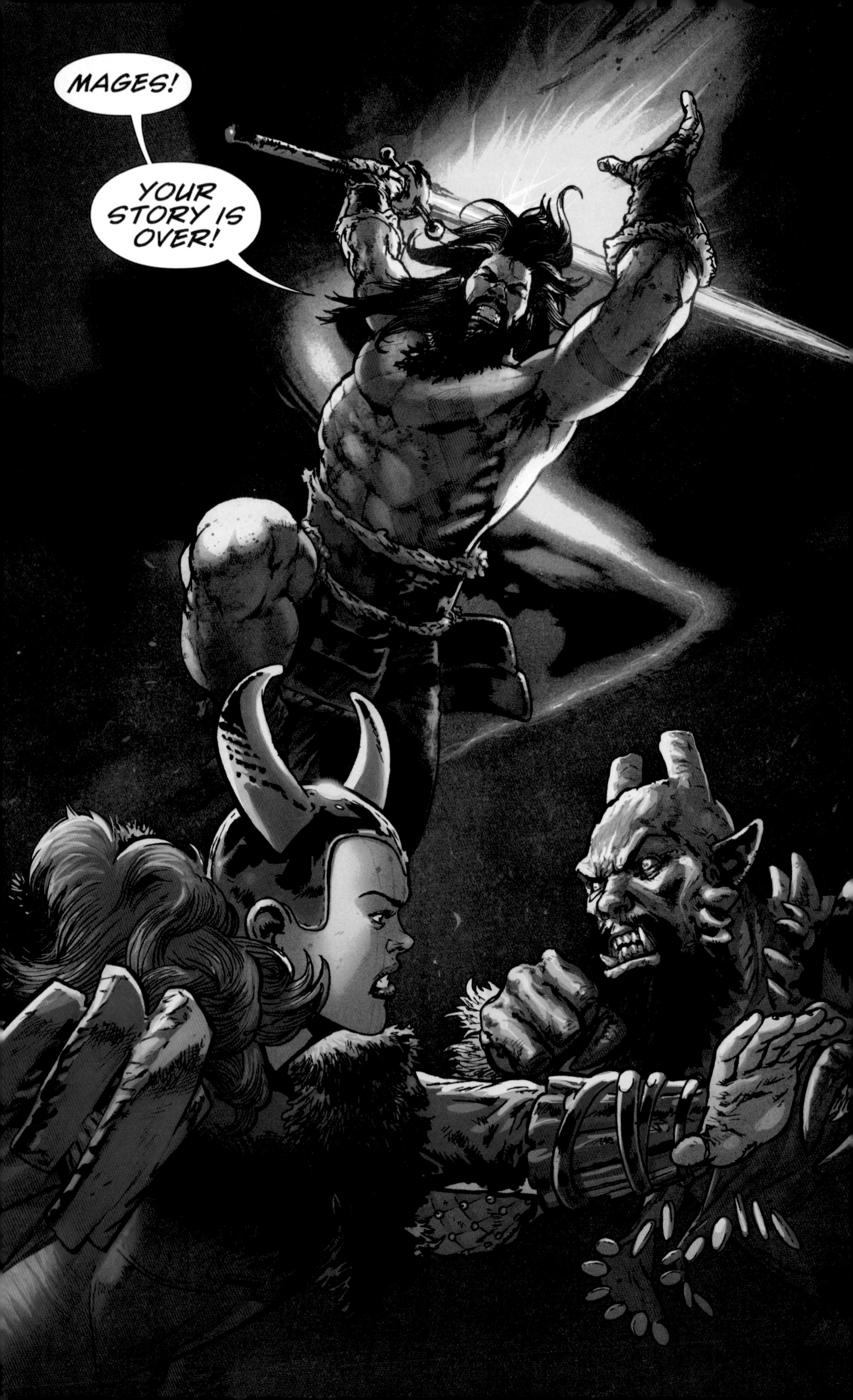
MAGES!
YOUR STORY IS OVER!

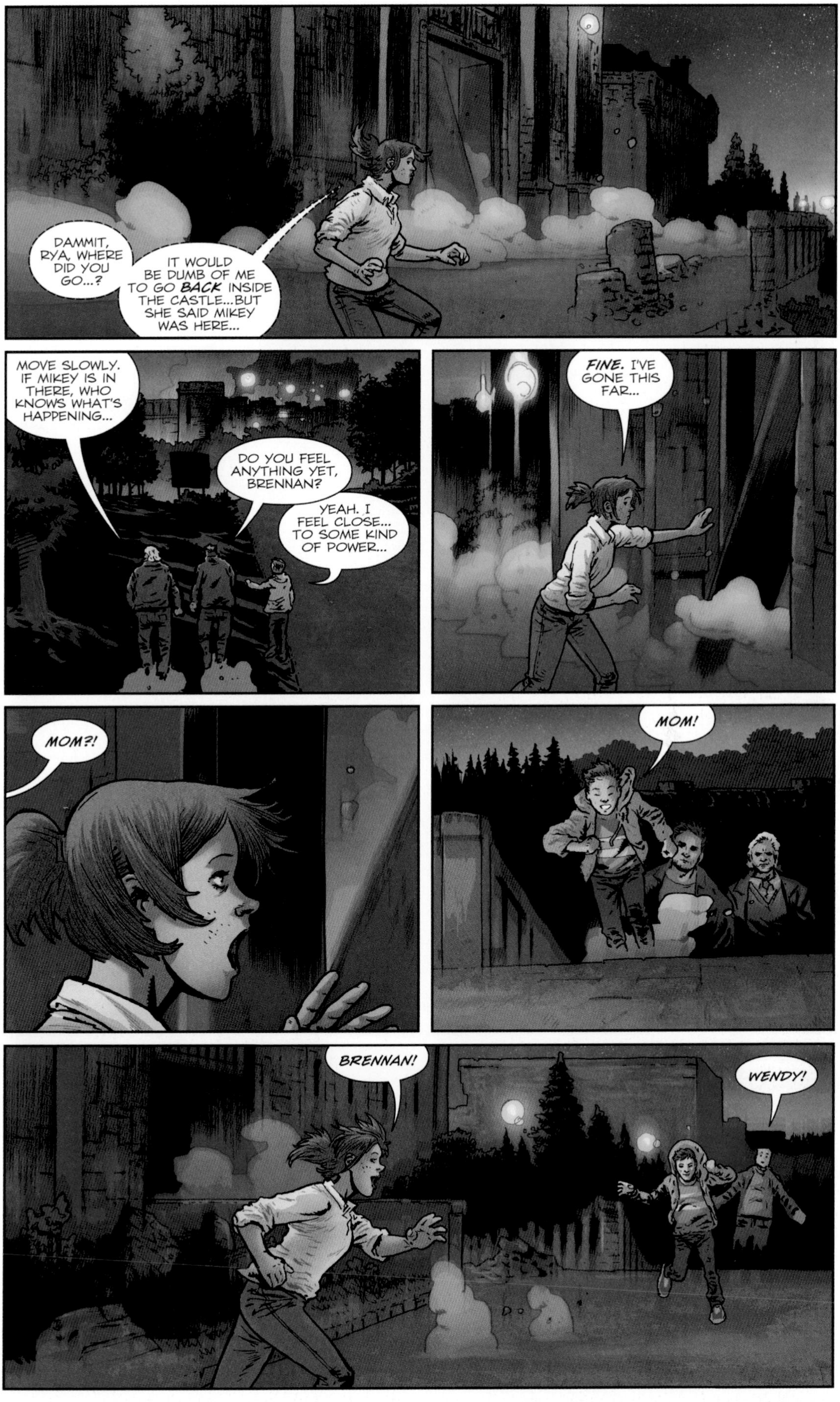

DAMMIT, RYA, WHERE DID YOU GO...?
IT WOULD BE DUMB OF ME TO GO BACK INSIDE THE CASTLE...BUT SHE SAID MIKEY WAS HERE...
MOVE SLOWLY. IF MIKEY IS IN THERE, WHO KNOWS WHAT'S HAPPENING...
DO YOU FEEL ANYTHING YET, BRENNAN?
YEAH. I FEEL CLOSE... TO SOME KIND OF POWER...
FINE. I'VE GONE THIS FAR...
MOM?!
MOM!
BRENNAN!
WENDY!

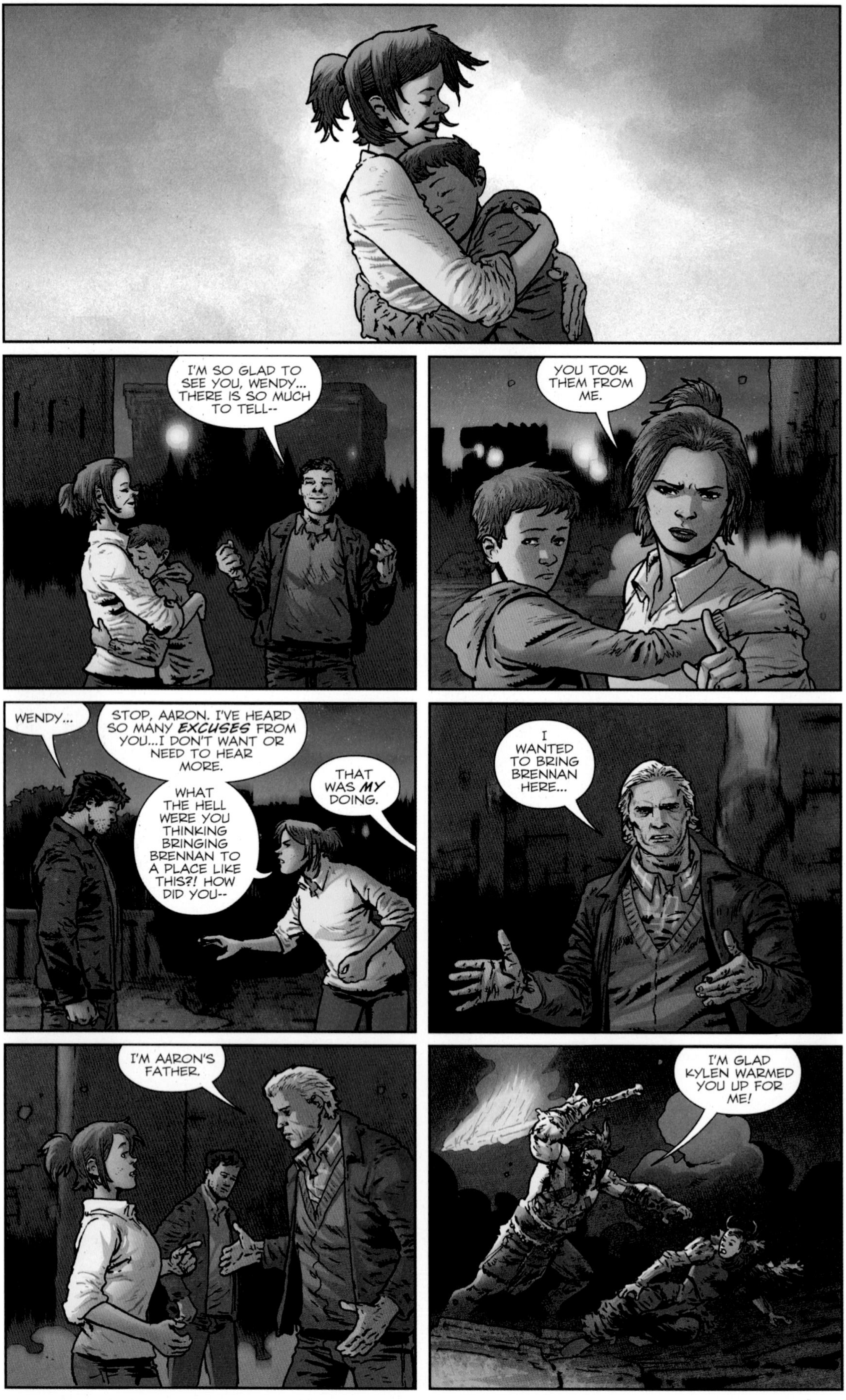
I'M SO GLAD TO SEE YOU, WENDY... THERE IS SO MUCH TO TELL--
YOU TOOK THEM FROM ME.
WENDY...
STOP, AARON. I'VE HEARD SO MANY *EXCUSES* FROM YOU...I DON'T WANT OR NEED TO HEAR MORE.
WHAT THE HELL WERE YOU THINKING BRINGING BRENNAN TO A PLACE LIKE THIS?! HOW DID YOU--
THAT WAS *MY* DOING.
I WANTED TO BRING BRENNAN HERE...
I'M AARON'S FATHER.
I'M GLAD KYLEN WARMED YOU UP FOR ME!

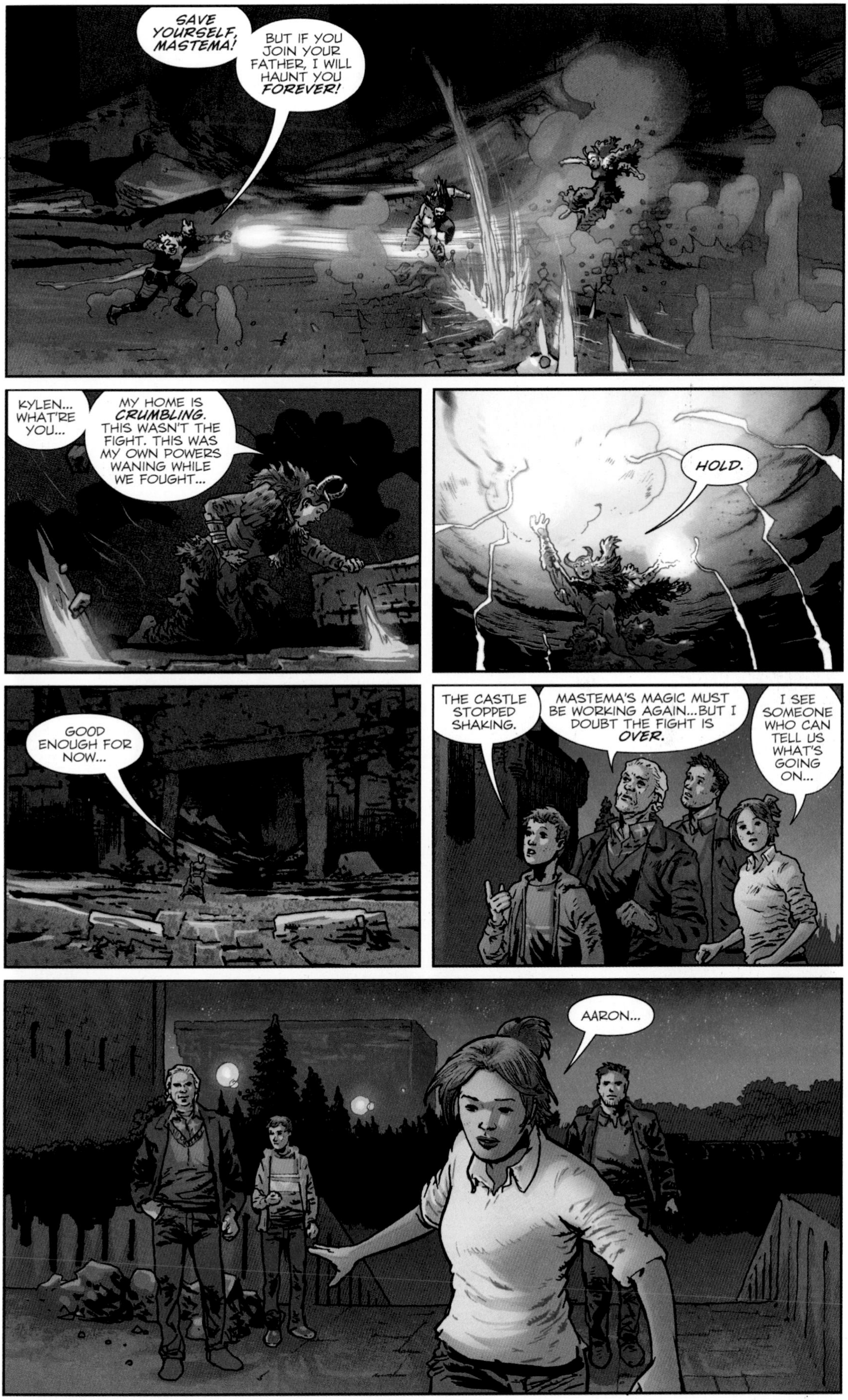
SAVE YOURSELF, MASTEMA!
BUT IF YOU JOIN YOUR FATHER, I WILL HAUNT YOU FOREVER!
KYLEN... WHAT'RE YOU...
MY HOME IS CRUMBLING. THIS WASN'T THE FIGHT. THIS WAS MY OWN POWERS WANING WHILE WE FOUGHT...
HOLD.
GOOD ENOUGH FOR NOW...
THE CASTLE STOPPED SHAKING.
MASTEMA'S MAGIC MUST BE WORKING AGAIN...BUT I DOUBT THE FIGHT IS OVER.
I SEE SOMEONE WHO CAN TELL US WHAT'S GOING ON...
AARON...

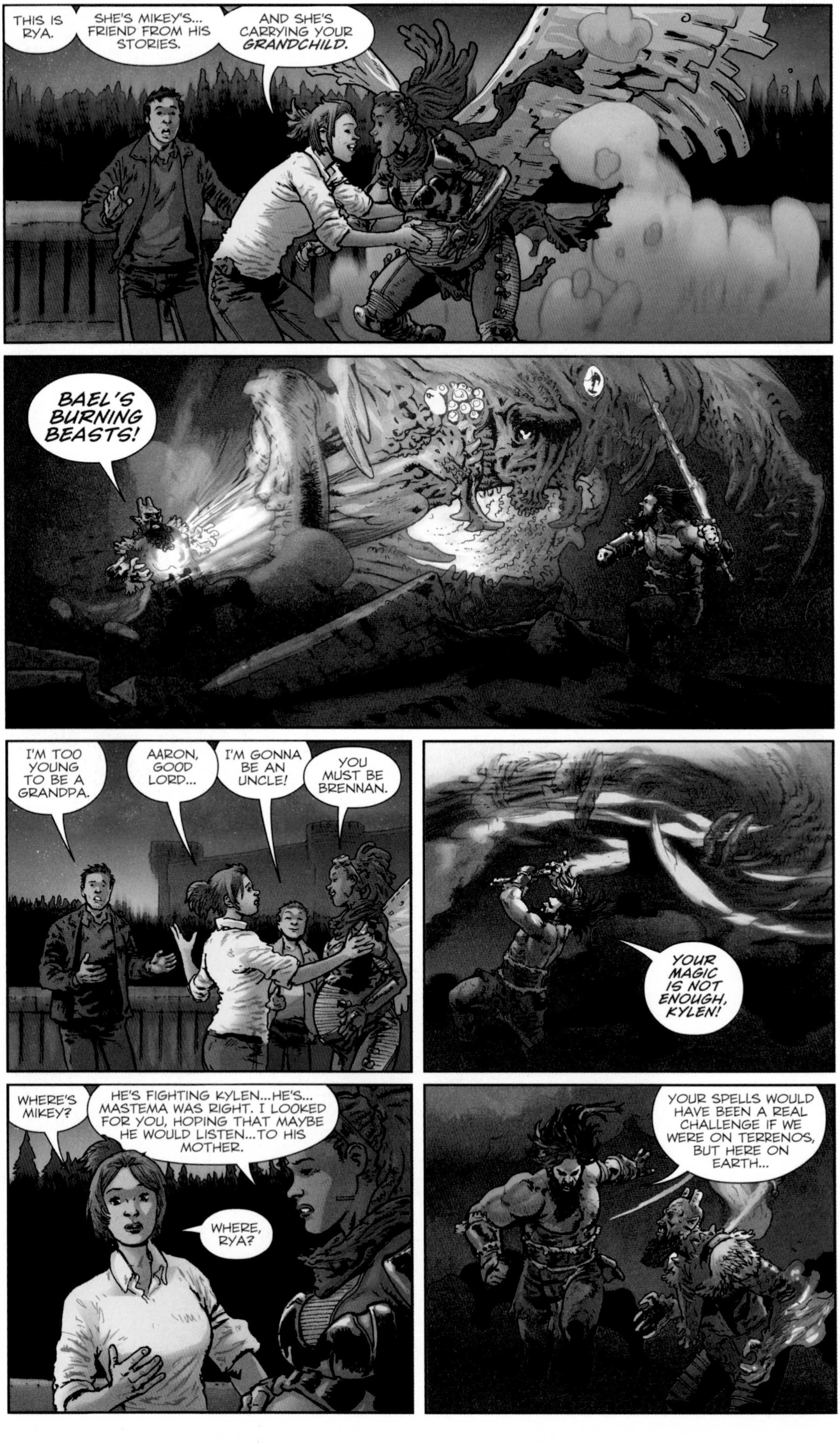
THIS IS RYA.
SHE'S MIKEY'S... FRIEND FROM HIS STORIES.
AND SHE'S CARRYING YOUR GRANDCHILD.
BAEL'S BURNING BEASTS!
I'M TOO YOUNG TO BE A GRANDPA.
AARON, GOOD LORD...
I'M GONNA BE AN UNCLE!
YOU MUST BE BRENNAN.
YOUR MAGIC IS NOT ENOUGH, KYLEN!
WHERE'S MIKEY?
HE'S FIGHTING KYLEN...HE'S... MASTEMA WAS RIGHT. I LOOKED FOR YOU, HOPING THAT MAYBE HE WOULD LISTEN...TO HIS MOTHER.
WHERE, RYA?
YOUR SPELLS WOULD HAVE BEEN A REAL CHALLENGE IF WE WERE ON TERRENOS, BUT HERE ON EARTH...

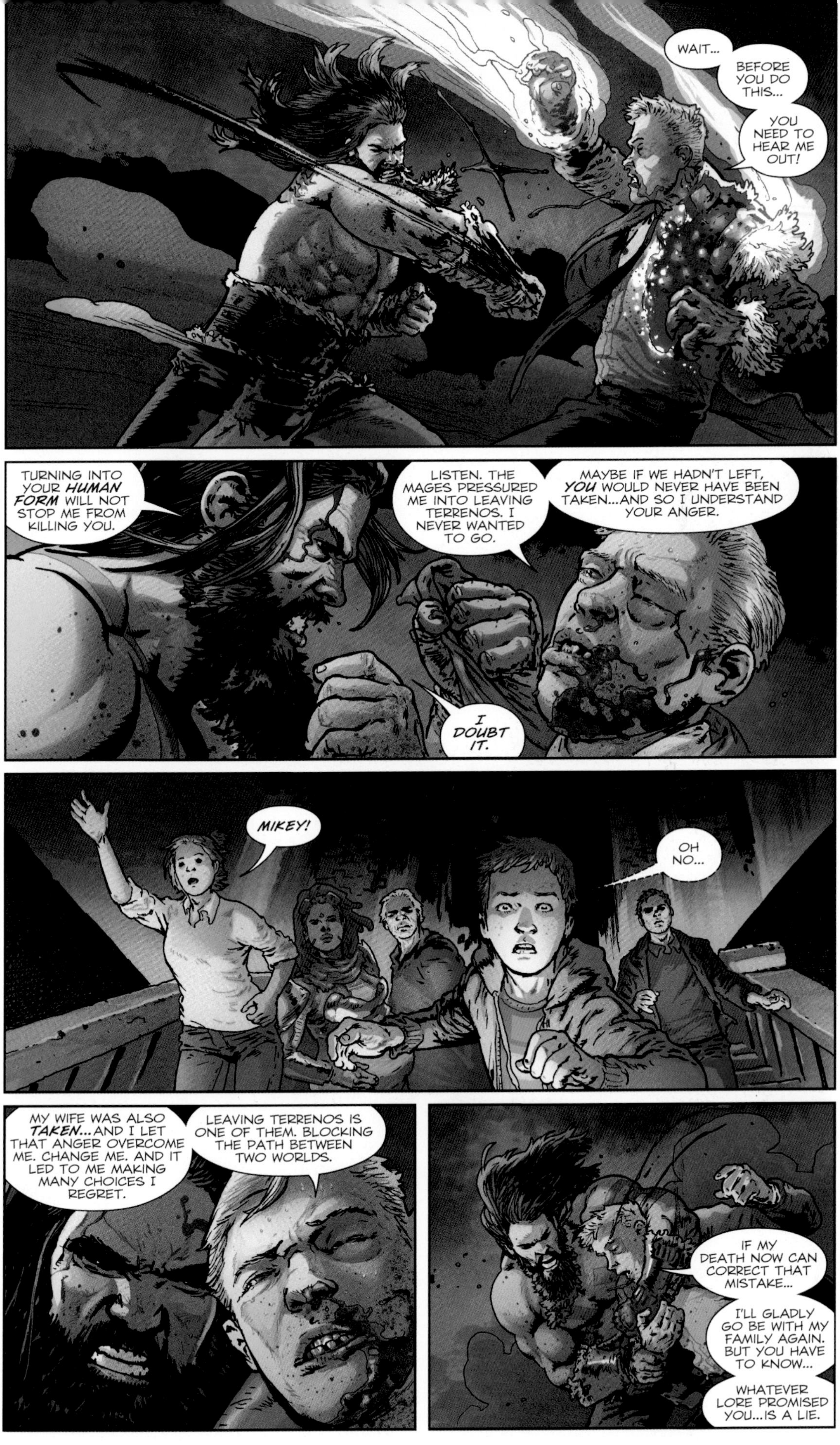
WAIT...
BEFORE YOU DO THIS...
YOU NEED TO HEAR ME OUT!
TURNING INTO YOUR HUMAN FORM WILL NOT STOP ME FROM KILLING YOU.
I DOUBT IT.
LISTEN. THE MAGES PRESSURED ME INTO LEAVING TERRENOS. I NEVER WANTED TO GO.
MAYBE IF WE HADN'T LEFT, YOU WOULD NEVER HAVE BEEN TAKEN...AND SO I UNDERSTAND YOUR ANGER.
MIKEY!
OH NO...
MY WIFE WAS ALSO TAKEN...AND I LET THAT ANGER OVERCOME ME. CHANGE ME. AND IT LED TO ME MAKING MANY CHOICES I REGRET.
LEAVING TERRENOS IS ONE OF THEM. BLOCKING THE PATH BETWEEN TWO WORLDS.
IF MY DEATH NOW CAN CORRECT THAT MISTAKE...
I'LL GLADLY GO BE WITH MY FAMILY AGAIN. BUT YOU HAVE TO KNOW...
WHATEVER LORE PROMISED YOU...IS A LIE.

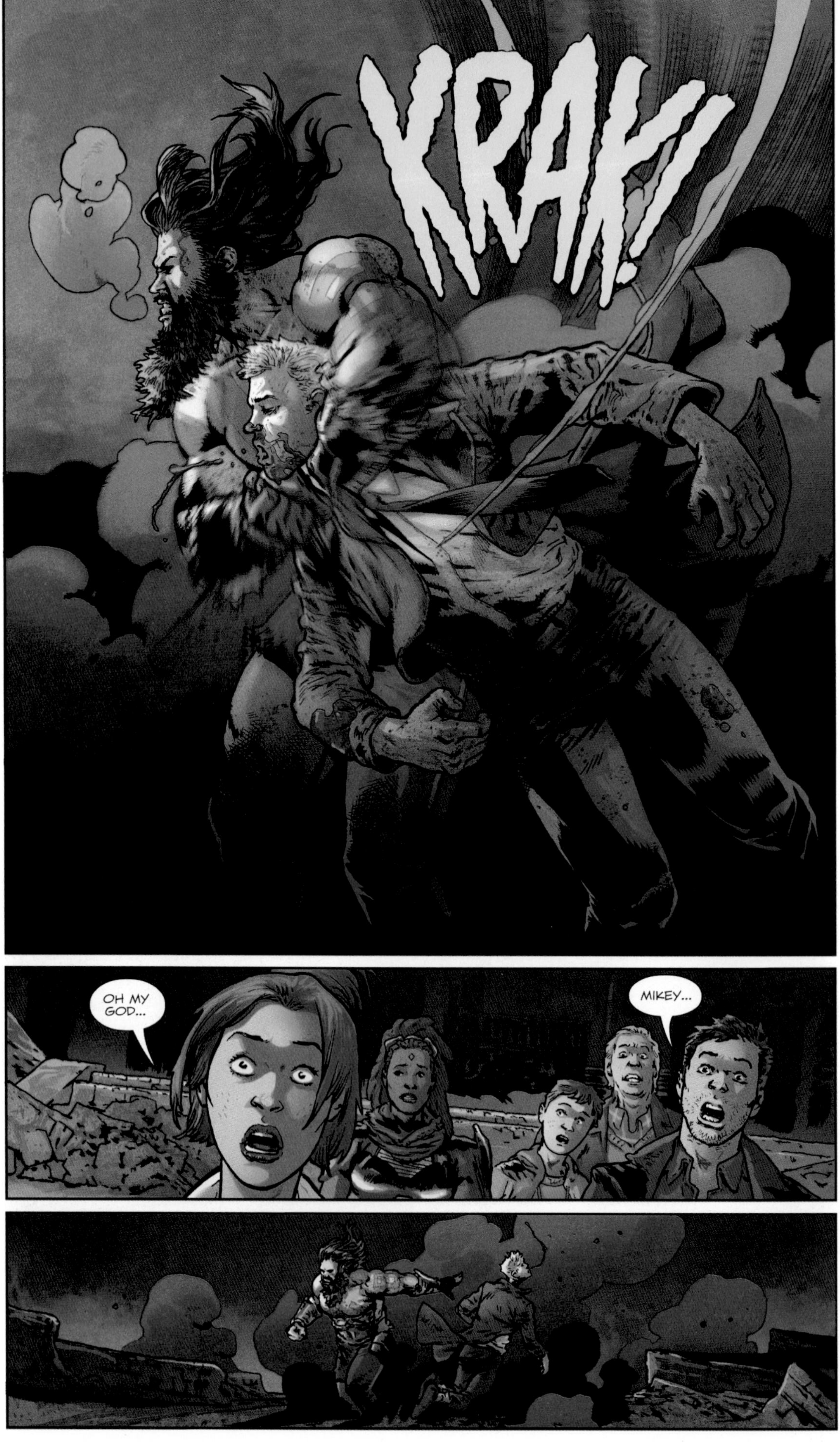
KRAK!
OH MY GOD...
MIKEY...

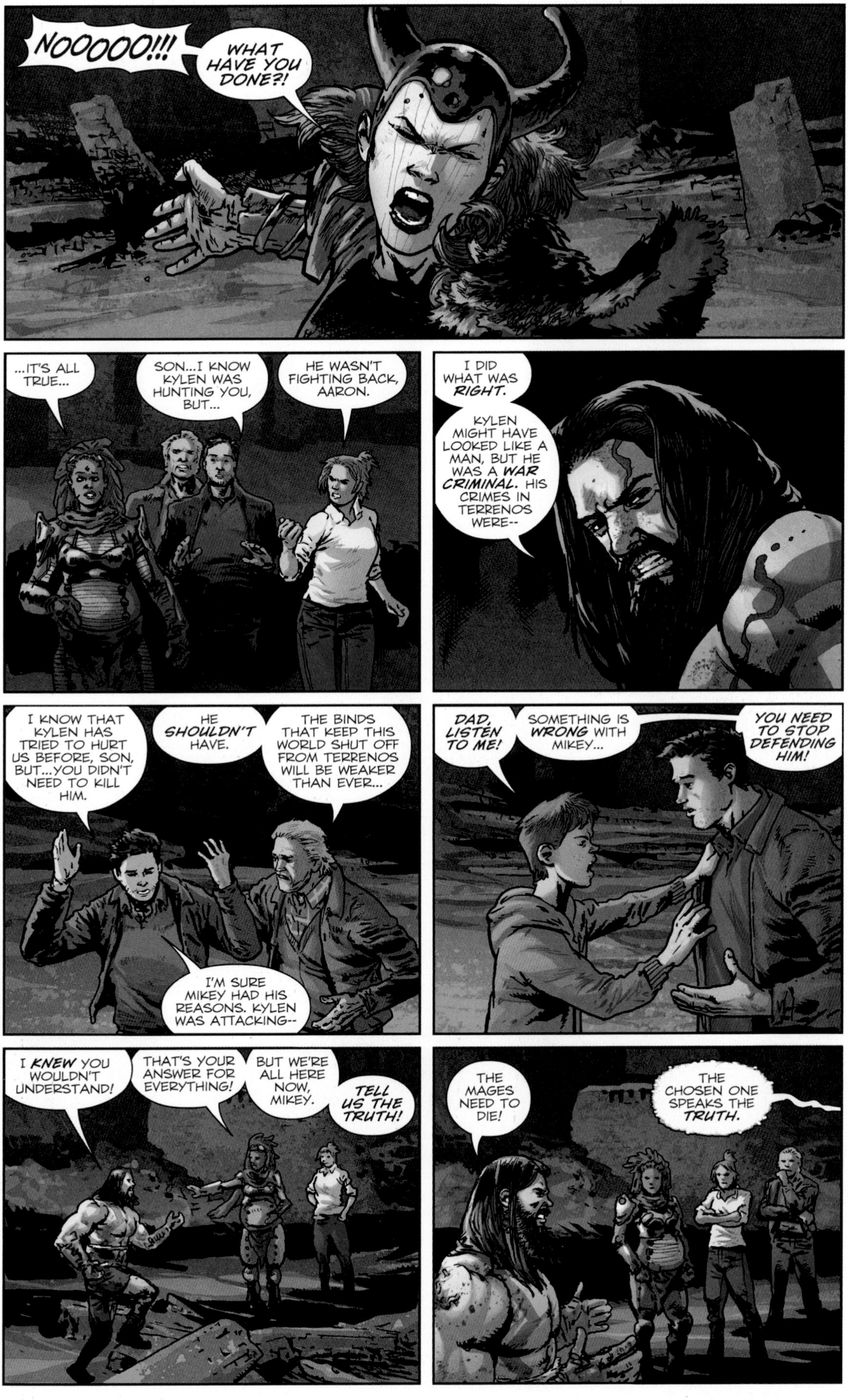
NOOOOO!!!
WHAT HAVE YOU DONE?!
...IT'S ALL TRUE...
SON...I KNOW KYLEN WAS HUNTING YOU, BUT...
HE WASN'T FIGHTING BACK, AARON.
I DID WHAT WAS RIGHT.
KYLEN MIGHT HAVE LOOKED LIKE A MAN, BUT HE WAS A WAR CRIMINAL. HIS CRIMES IN TERRENOS WERE--
I KNOW THAT KYLEN HAS TRIED TO HURT US BEFORE, SON, BUT...YOU DIDN'T NEED TO KILL HIM.
HE SHOULDN'T HAVE.
THE BINDS THAT KEEP THIS WORLD SHUT OFF FROM TERRENOS WILL BE WEAKER THAN EVER...
I'M SURE MIKEY HAD HIS REASONS. KYLEN WAS ATTACKING--
DAD, LISTEN TO ME!
SOMETHING IS WRONG WITH MIKEY...
YOU NEED TO STOP DEFENDING HIM!
I KNEW YOU WOULDN'T UNDERSTAND!
THAT'S YOUR ANSWER FOR EVERYTHING!
BUT WE'RE ALL HERE NOW, MIKEY.
TELL US THE TRUTH!
THE MAGES NEED TO DIE!
THE CHOSEN ONE SPEAKS THE TRUTH.

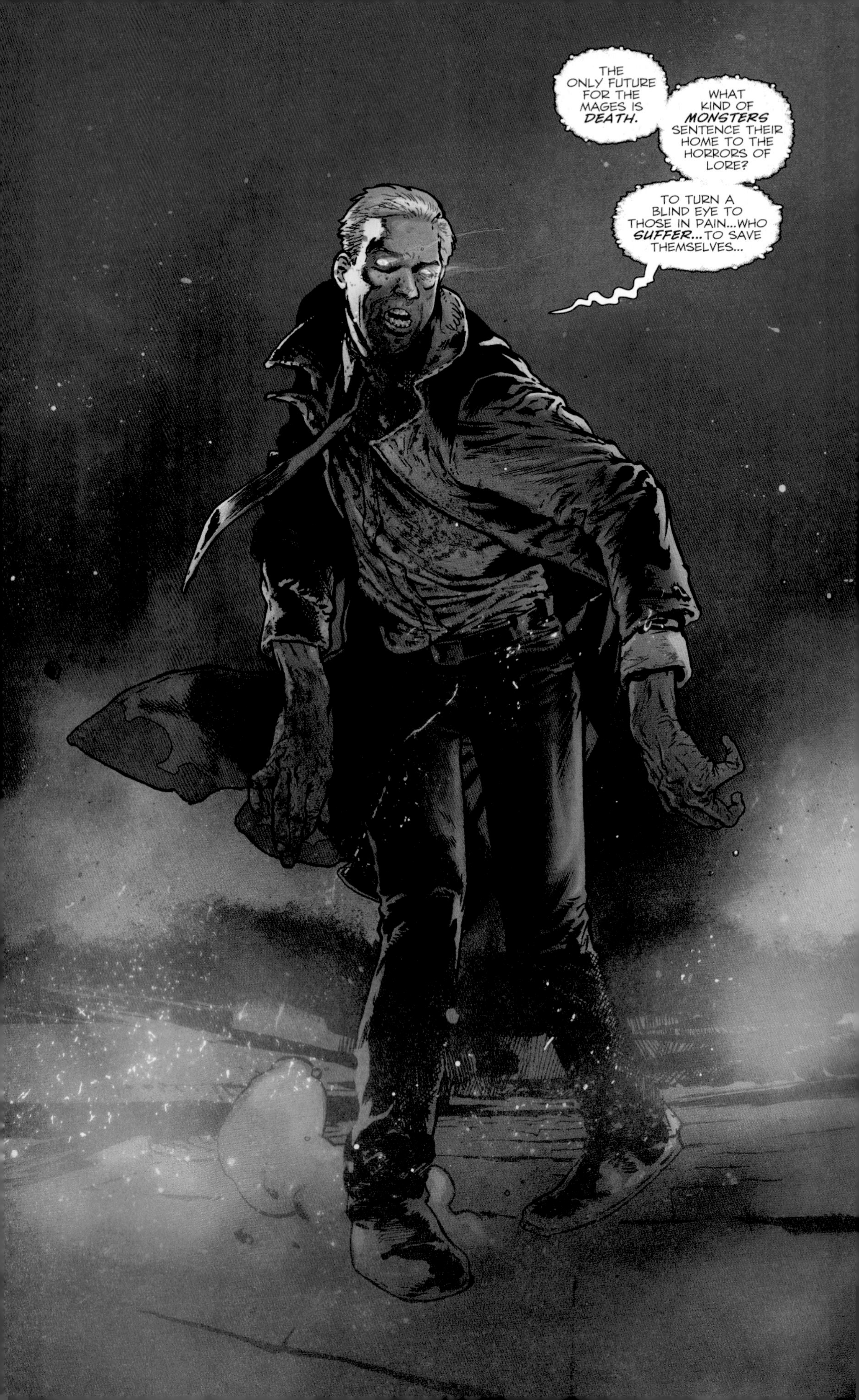
THE ONLY FUTURE FOR THE MAGES IS *DEATH.*
WHAT KIND OF ***MONSTERS*** SENTENCE THEIR HOME TO THE HORRORS OF LORE?
TO TURN A BLIND EYE TO THOSE IN PAIN...WHO ***SUFFER...*** TO SAVE THEMSELVES...

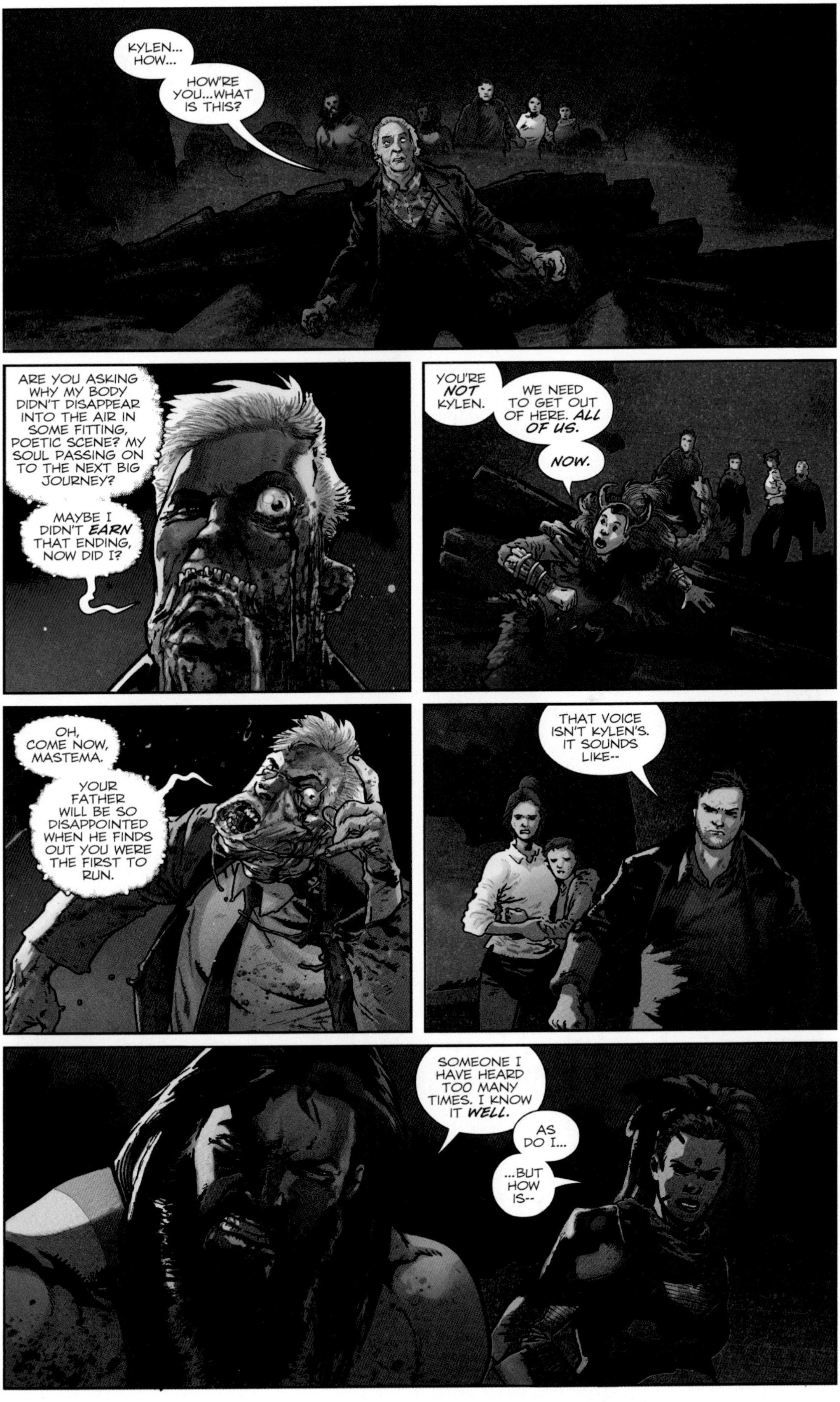
KYLEN... HOW...
HOW'RE YOU...WHAT IS THIS?
ARE YOU ASKING WHY MY BODY DIDN'T DISAPPEAR INTO THE AIR IN SOME FITTING, POETIC SCENE? MY SOUL PASSING ON TO THE NEXT BIG JOURNEY?
MAYBE I DIDN'T *EARN* THAT ENDING, NOW DID I?
YOU'RE *NOT* KYLEN.
WE NEED TO GET OUT OF HERE. *ALL OF US.*
NOW.
OH, COME NOW, MASTEMA.
YOUR FATHER WILL BE SO DISAPPOINTED WHEN HE FINDS OUT YOU WERE THE FIRST TO RUN.
THAT VOICE ISN'T KYLEN'S. IT SOUNDS LIKE--
SOMEONE I HAVE HEARD TOO MANY TIMES. I KNOW IT *WELL.*
AS DO I...
...BUT HOW IS--

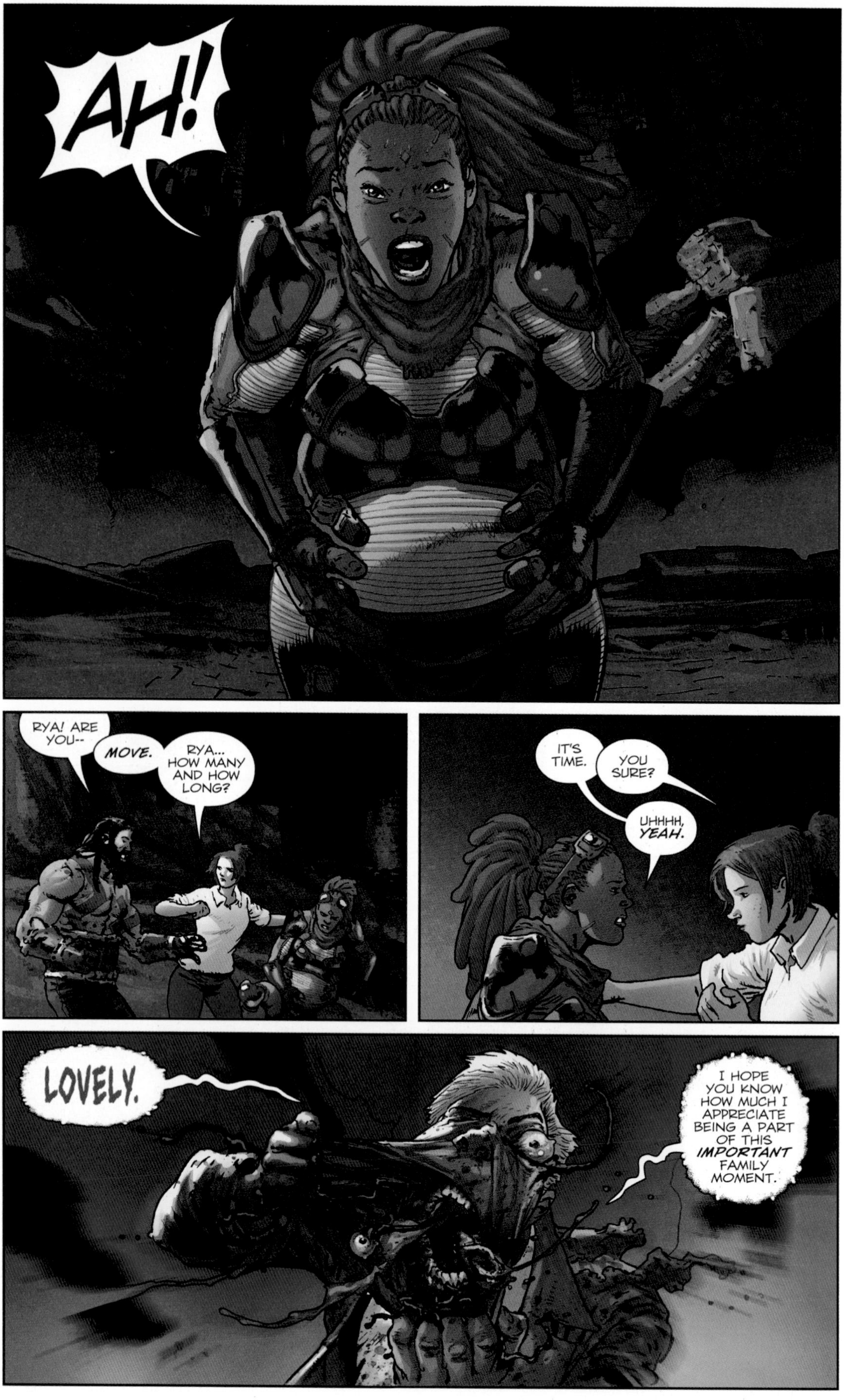
AH!
RYA! ARE YOU--
MOVE.
RYA... HOW MANY AND HOW LONG?
IT'S TIME.
YOU SURE?
UHHHH, YEAH.
LOVELY.
I HOPE YOU KNOW HOW MUCH I APPRECIATE BEING A PART OF THIS IMPORTANT FAMILY MOMENT.

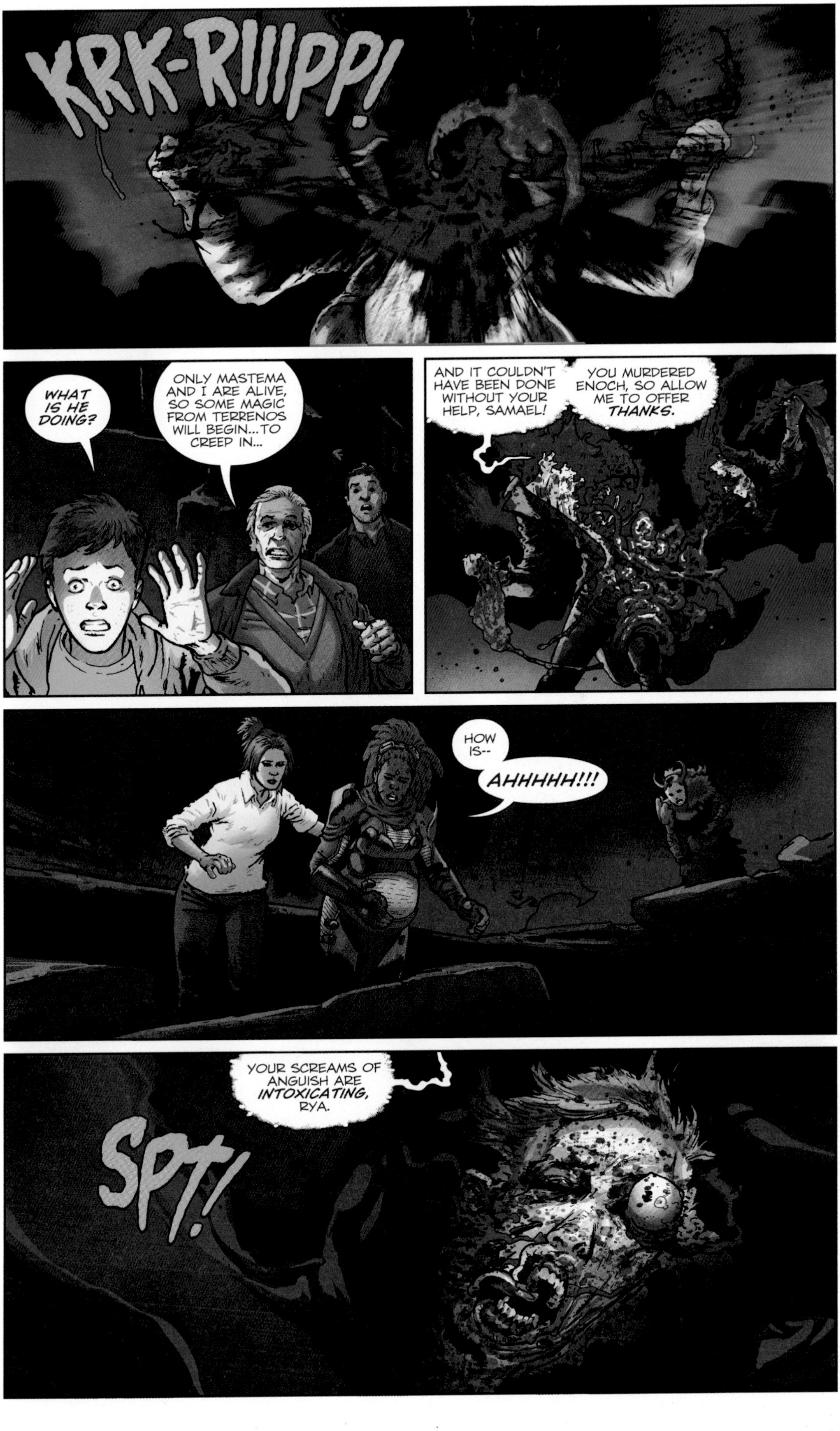
KRK-RIIIPP!
WHAT IS HE DOING?
ONLY MASTEMA AND I ARE ALIVE, SO SOME MAGIC FROM TERRENOS WILL BEGIN...TO CREEP IN...
AND IT COULDN'T HAVE BEEN DONE WITHOUT YOUR HELP, SAMAEL!
YOU MURDERED ENOCH, SO ALLOW ME TO OFFER THANKS.
HOW IS--
AHHHHH!!!
YOUR SCREAMS OF ANGUISH ARE INTOXICATING, RYA.
SPT!

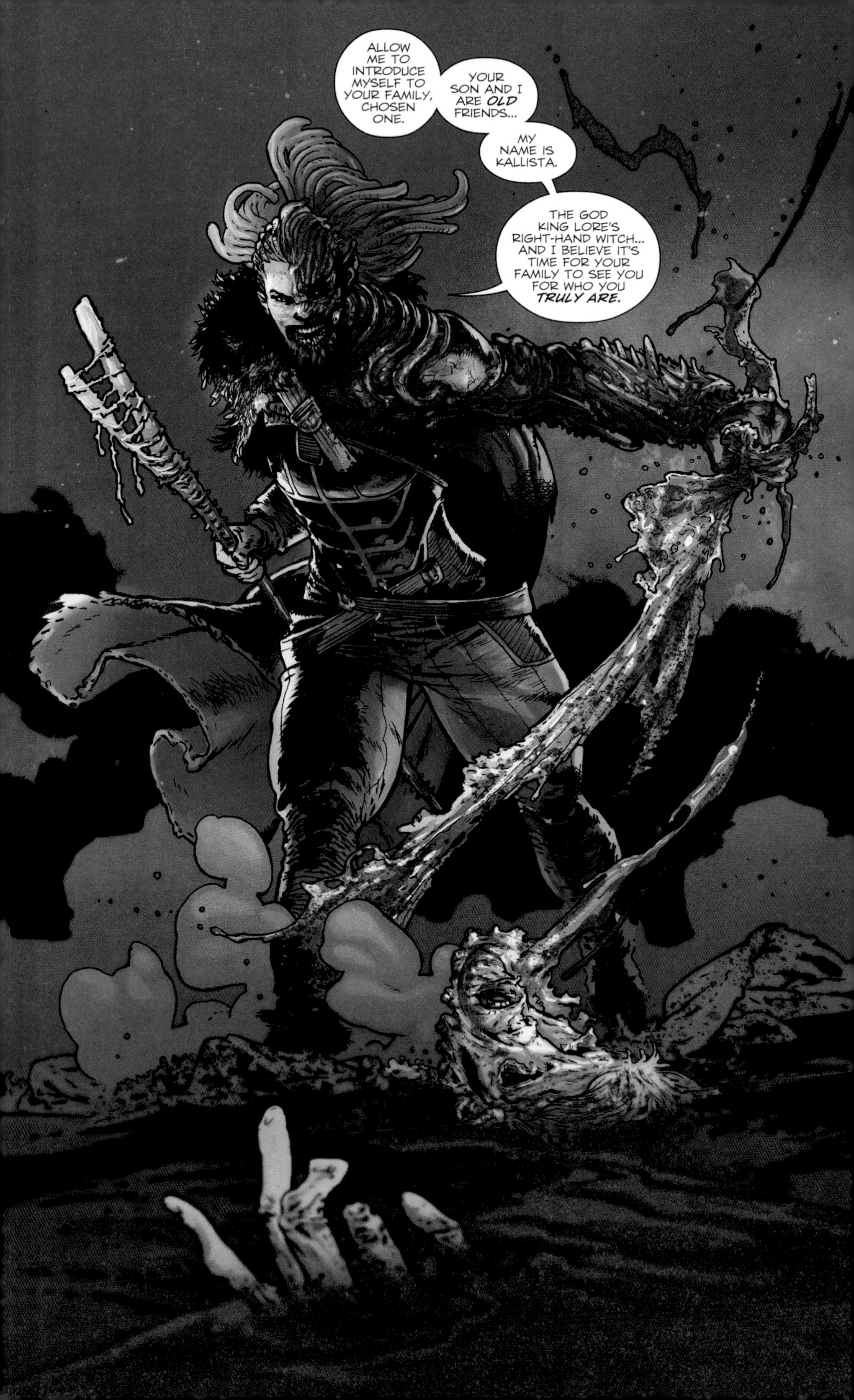
ALLOW ME TO INTRODUCE MYSELF TO YOUR FAMILY, CHOSEN ONE.
YOUR SON AND I ARE *OLD* FRIENDS...
MY NAME IS KALLISTA.
THE GOD KING LORE'S RIGHT-HAND WITCH... AND I BELIEVE IT'S TIME FOR YOUR FAMILY TO SEE YOU FOR WHO YOU *TRULY ARE.*

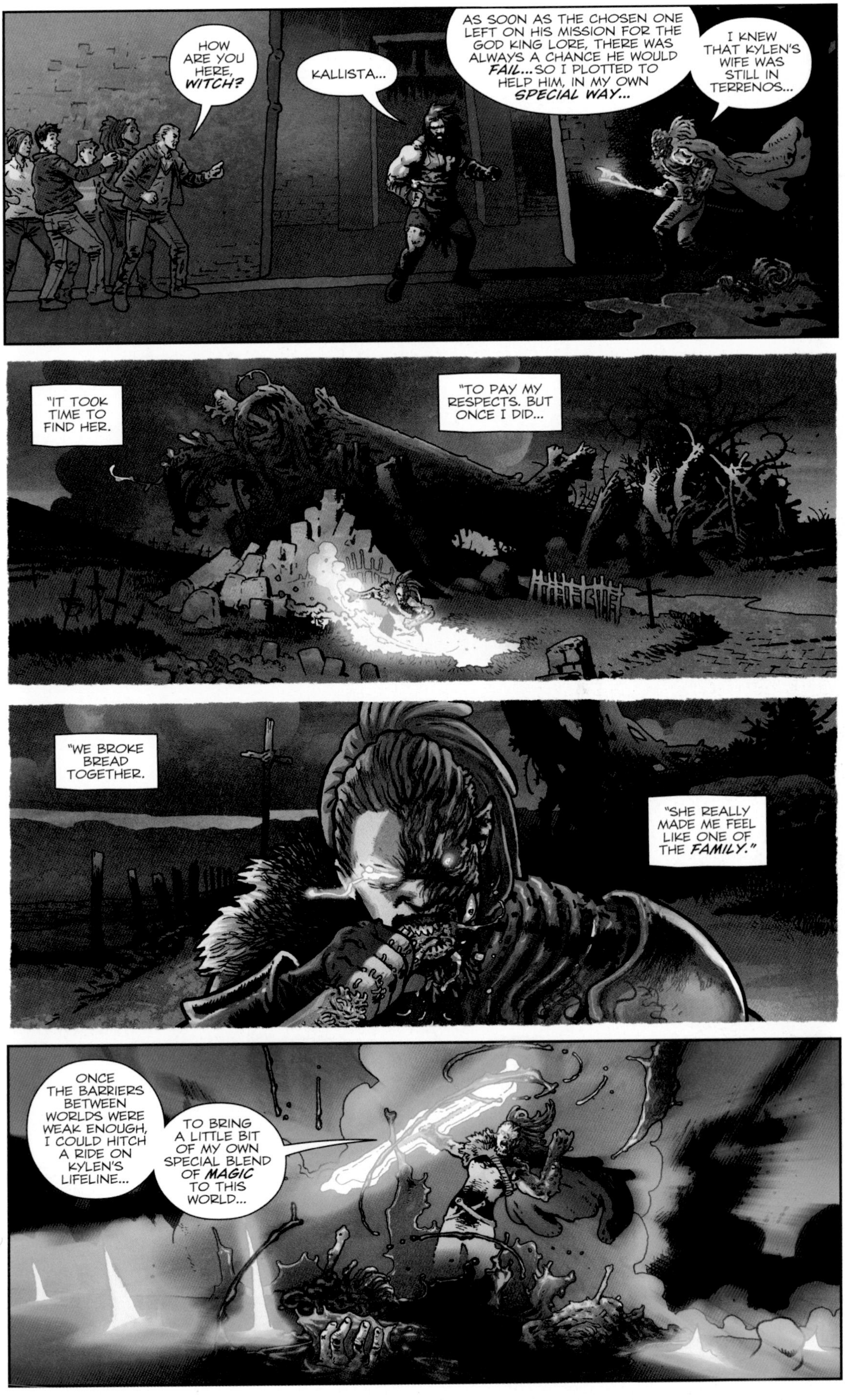

HOW ARE YOU HERE, WITCH?
KALLISTA...
AS SOON AS THE CHOSEN ONE LEFT ON HIS MISSION FOR THE GOD KING LORE, THERE WAS ALWAYS A CHANCE HE WOULD FAIL... SO I PLOTTED TO HELP HIM, IN MY OWN SPECIAL WAY...
I KNEW THAT KYLEN'S WIFE WAS STILL IN TERRENOS...
"IT TOOK TIME TO FIND HER.
"TO PAY MY RESPECTS. BUT ONCE I DID...
"WE BROKE BREAD TOGETHER.
"SHE REALLY MADE ME FEEL LIKE ONE OF THE FAMILY."
ONCE THE BARRIERS BETWEEN WORLDS WERE WEAK ENOUGH, I COULD HITCH A RIDE ON KYLEN'S LIFELINE...
TO BRING A LITTLE BIT OF MY OWN SPECIAL BLEND OF MAGIC TO THIS WORLD...

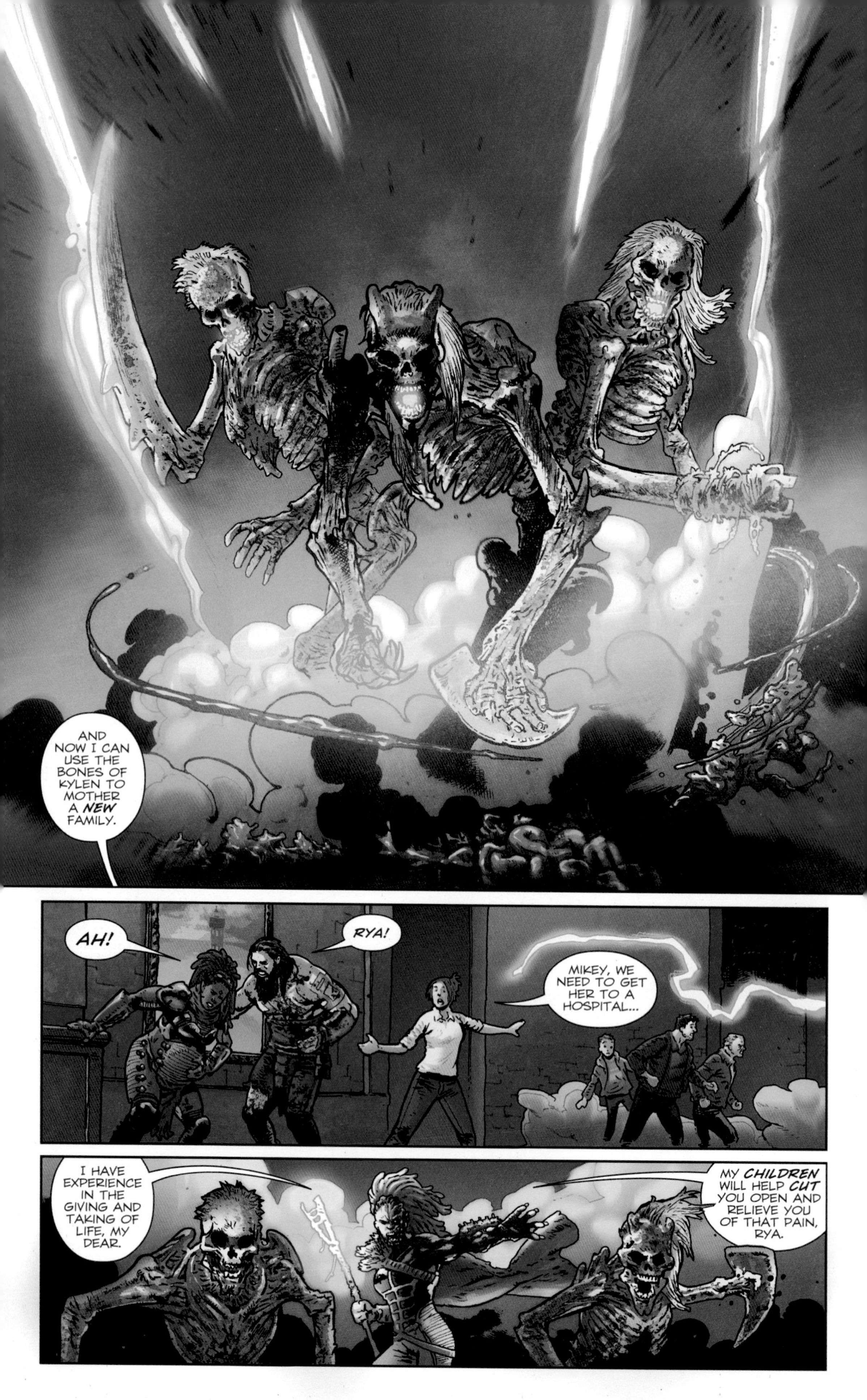
AND NOW I CAN USE THE BONES OF KYLEN TO MOTHER A *NEW* FAMILY.
AH!
RYA!
MIKEY, WE NEED TO GET HER TO A HOSPITAL...
I HAVE EXPERIENCE IN THE GIVING AND TAKING OF LIFE, MY DEAR.
MY ***CHILDREN*** WILL HELP ***CUT*** YOU OPEN AND RELIEVE YOU OF THAT PAIN, RYA.

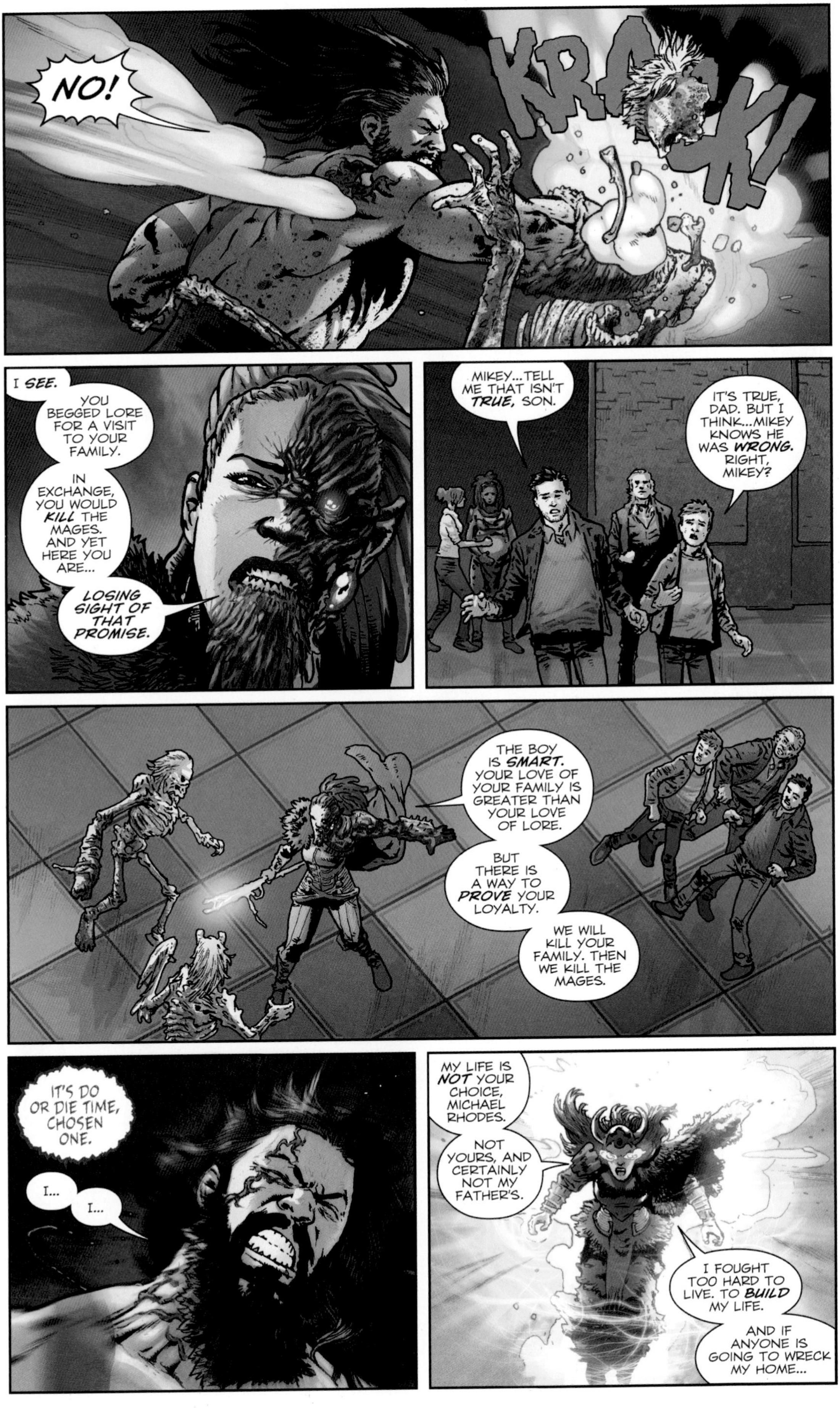
NO!
KRAACK!
I SEE.
YOU BEGGED LORE FOR A VISIT TO YOUR FAMILY.
IN EXCHANGE, YOU WOULD KILL THE MAGES. AND YET HERE YOU ARE...
LOSING SIGHT OF THAT PROMISE.
MIKEY...TELL ME THAT ISN'T TRUE, SON.
IT'S TRUE, DAD. BUT I THINK...MIKEY KNOWS HE WAS WRONG. RIGHT, MIKEY?
THE BOY IS SMART. YOUR LOVE OF YOUR FAMILY IS GREATER THAN YOUR LOVE OF LORE.
BUT THERE IS A WAY TO PROVE YOUR LOYALTY.
WE WILL KILL YOUR FAMILY. THEN WE KILL THE MAGES.
IT'S DO OR DIE TIME, CHOSEN ONE.
I...
I...
MY LIFE IS NOT YOUR CHOICE, MICHAEL RHODES.
NOT YOURS, AND CERTAINLY NOT MY FATHER'S.
I FOUGHT TOO HARD TO LIVE. TO BUILD MY LIFE.
AND IF ANYONE IS GOING TO WRECK MY HOME...

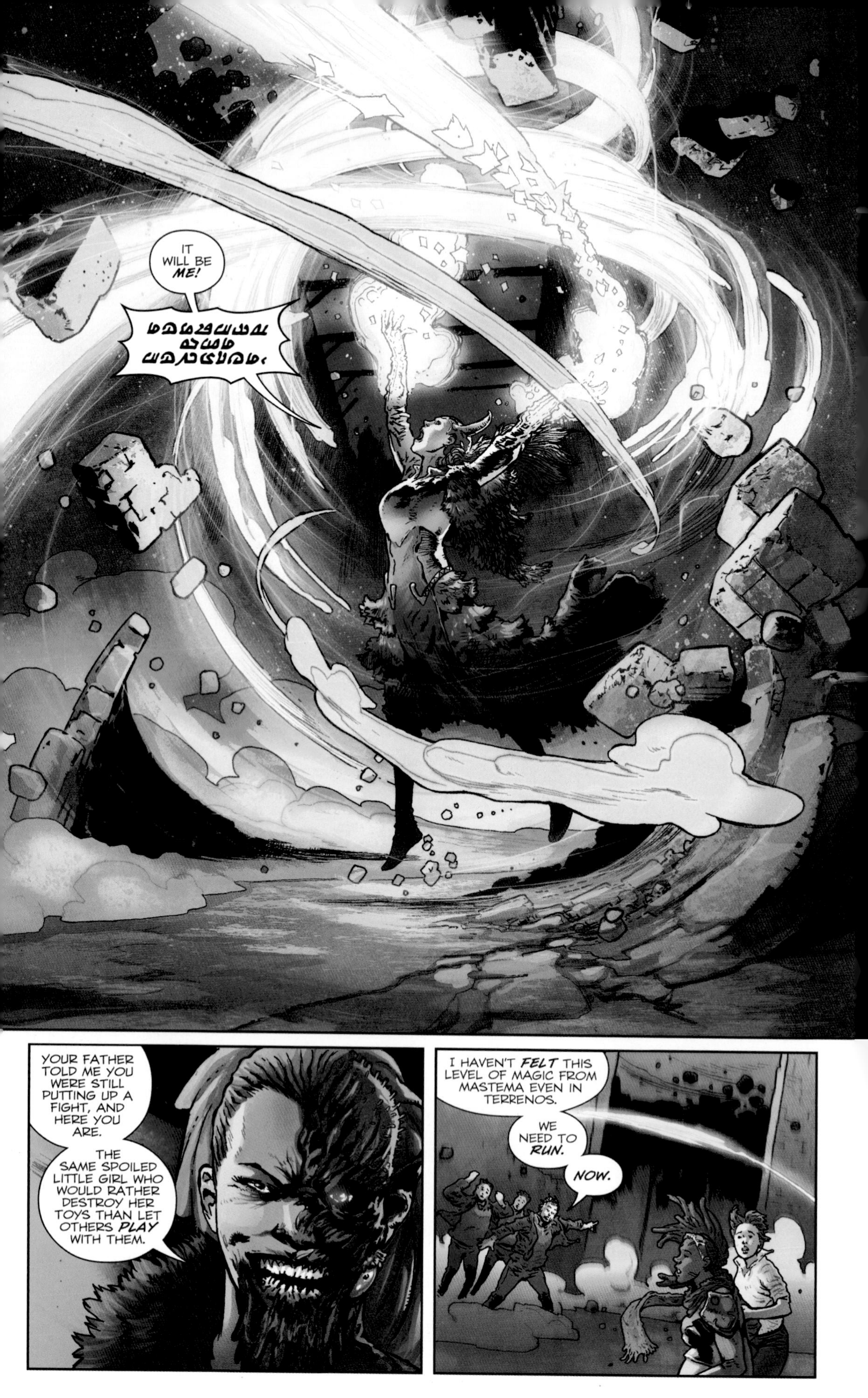
IT WILL BE ME!
YOUR FATHER TOLD ME YOU WERE STILL PUTTING UP A FIGHT, AND HERE YOU ARE.
THE SAME SPOILED LITTLE GIRL WHO WOULD RATHER DESTROY HER TOYS THAN LET OTHERS PLAY WITH THEM.
I HAVEN'T FELT THIS LEVEL OF MAGIC FROM MASTEMA EVEN IN TERRENOS.
WE NEED TO RUN.
NOW.

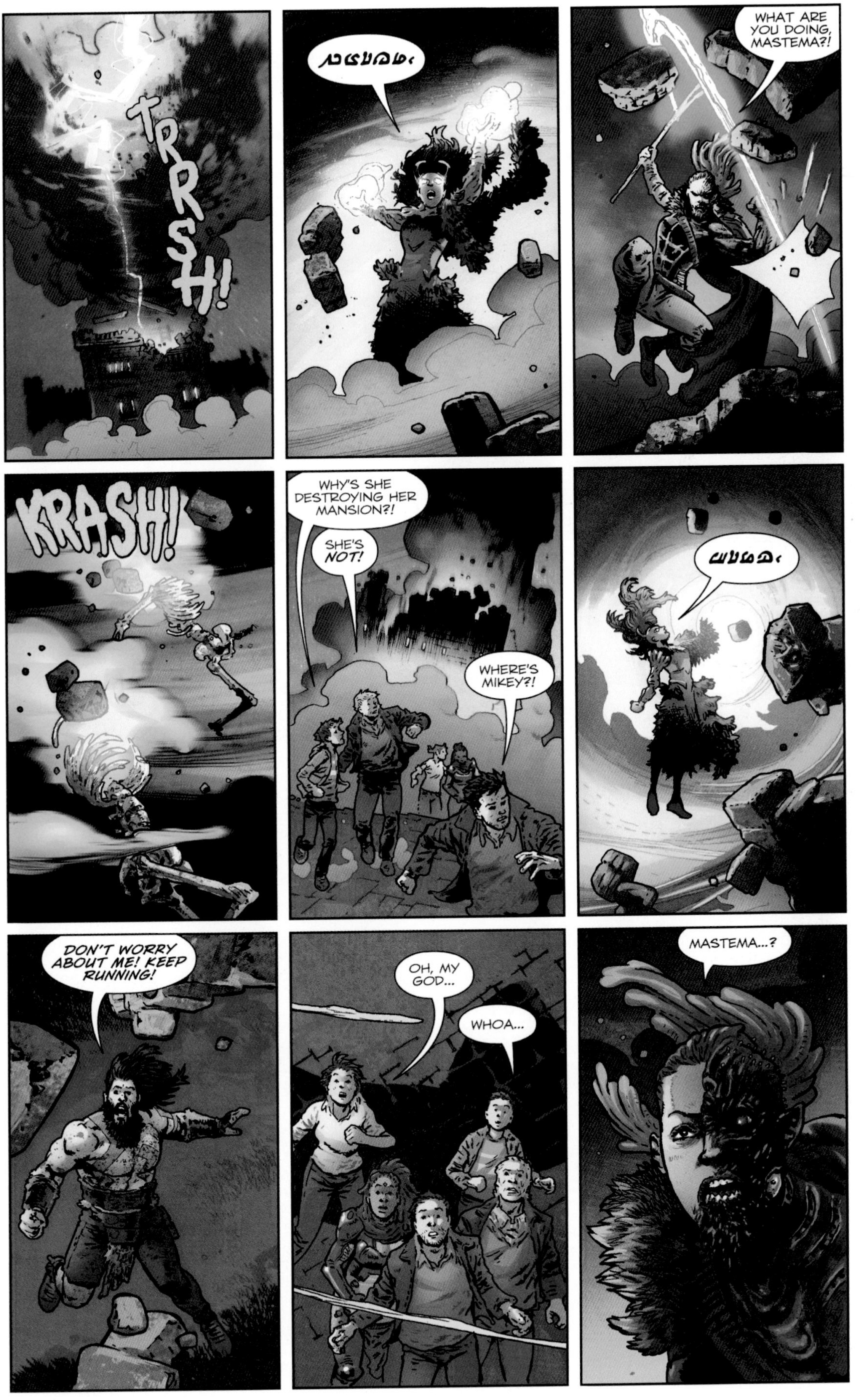
TRRSH!
WHAT ARE YOU DOING, MASTEMA?!
KRASH!
WHY'S SHE DESTROYING HER MANSION?!
SHE'S *NOT*!
WHERE'S MIKEY?!
DON'T WORRY ABOUT ME! KEEP RUNNING!
OH, MY GOD...
WHOA...
MASTEMA...?

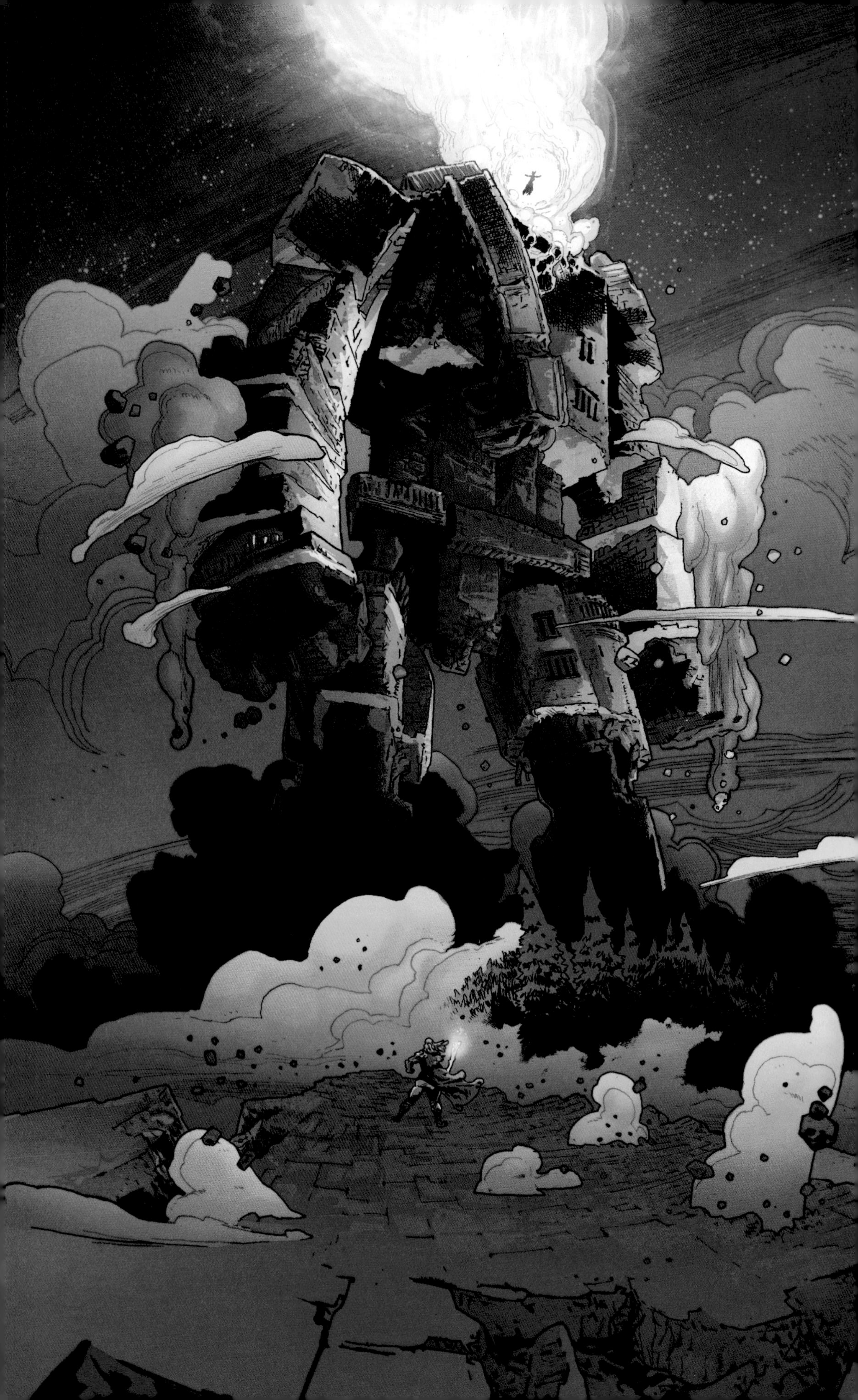

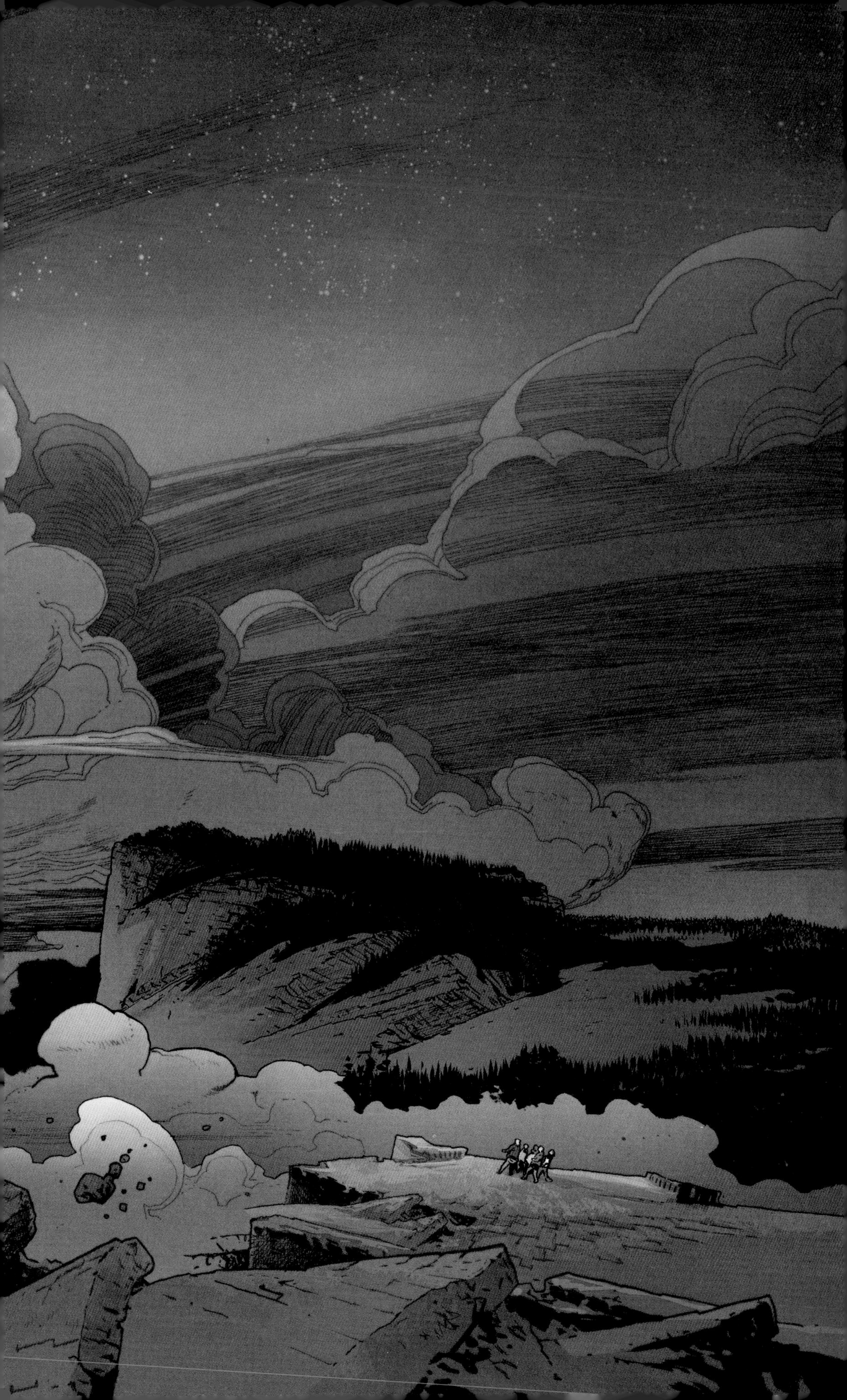

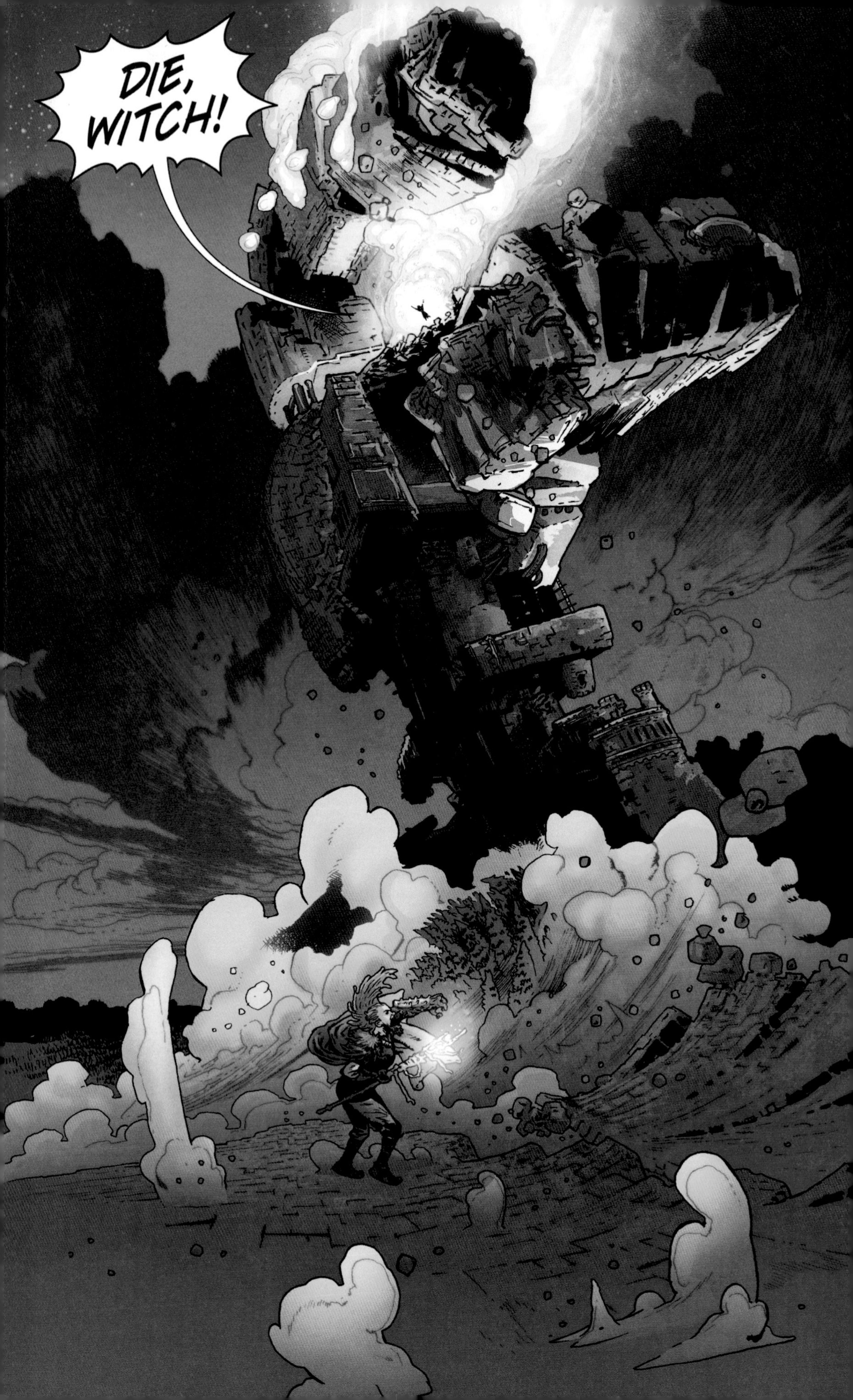
DIE, WITCH!

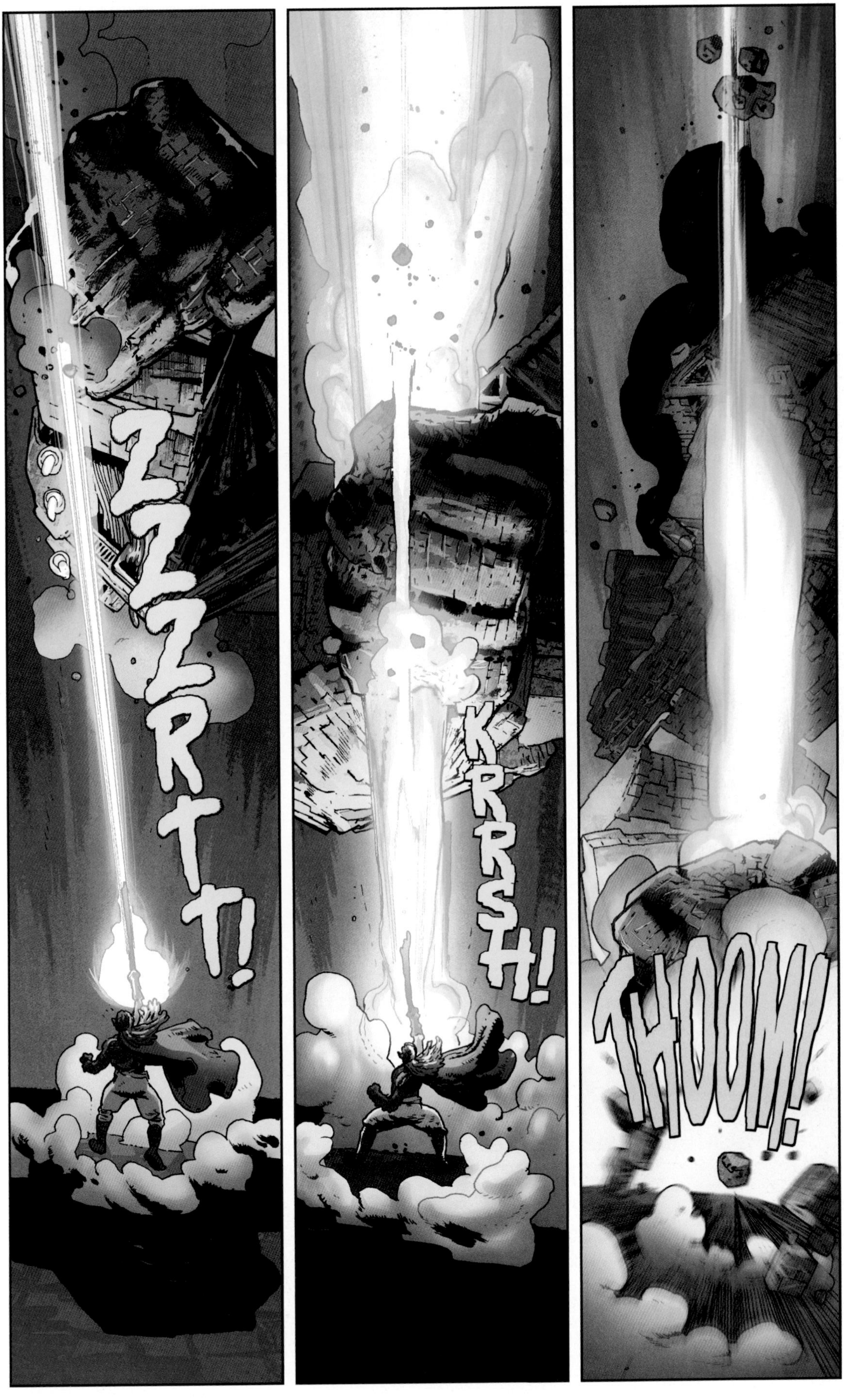
ZZZRTT!
KRRSH!
THOOM!!

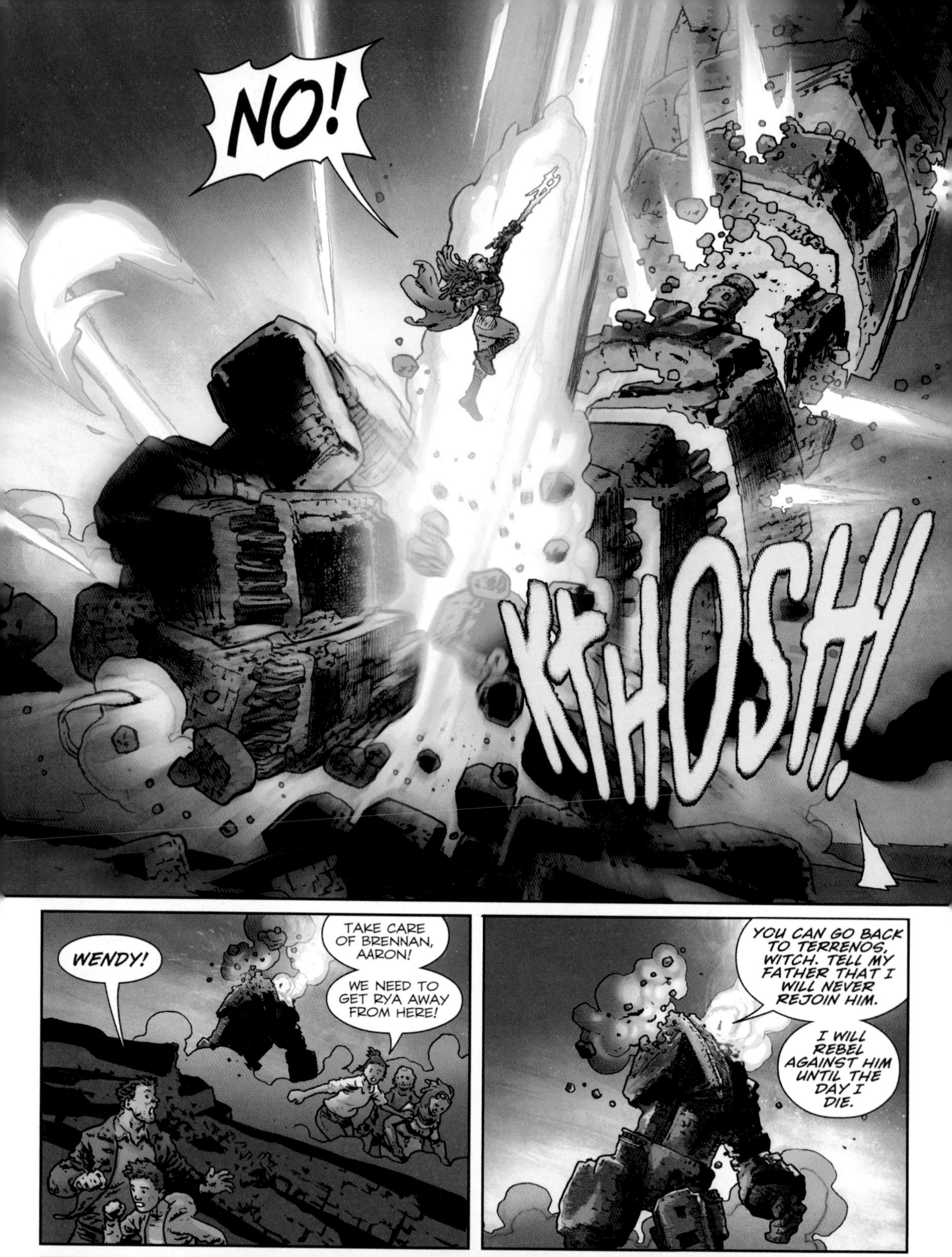
NO!
KTHOSH!
WENDY!
TAKE CARE OF BRENNAN, AARON!
WE NEED TO GET RYA AWAY FROM HERE!
YOU CAN GO BACK TO TERRENOS, WITCH. TELL MY FATHER THAT I WILL NEVER REJOIN HIM.
I WILL REBEL AGAINST HIM UNTIL THE DAY I DIE.
NOW IS YOUR CHANCE, MIKEY. MASTEMA'S DESPERATE SHOW OF POWER HAS CREATED THE CHAOS THAT YOU NEED.
KILL EVERYONE HERE, EVEN KALLISTA, AND TAKE YOUR RIGHTFUL PLACE AT LORE'S SIDE.
WHEN I KILLED KYLEN, I COULD SEE IN THEIR EYES THAT MY FAMILY...

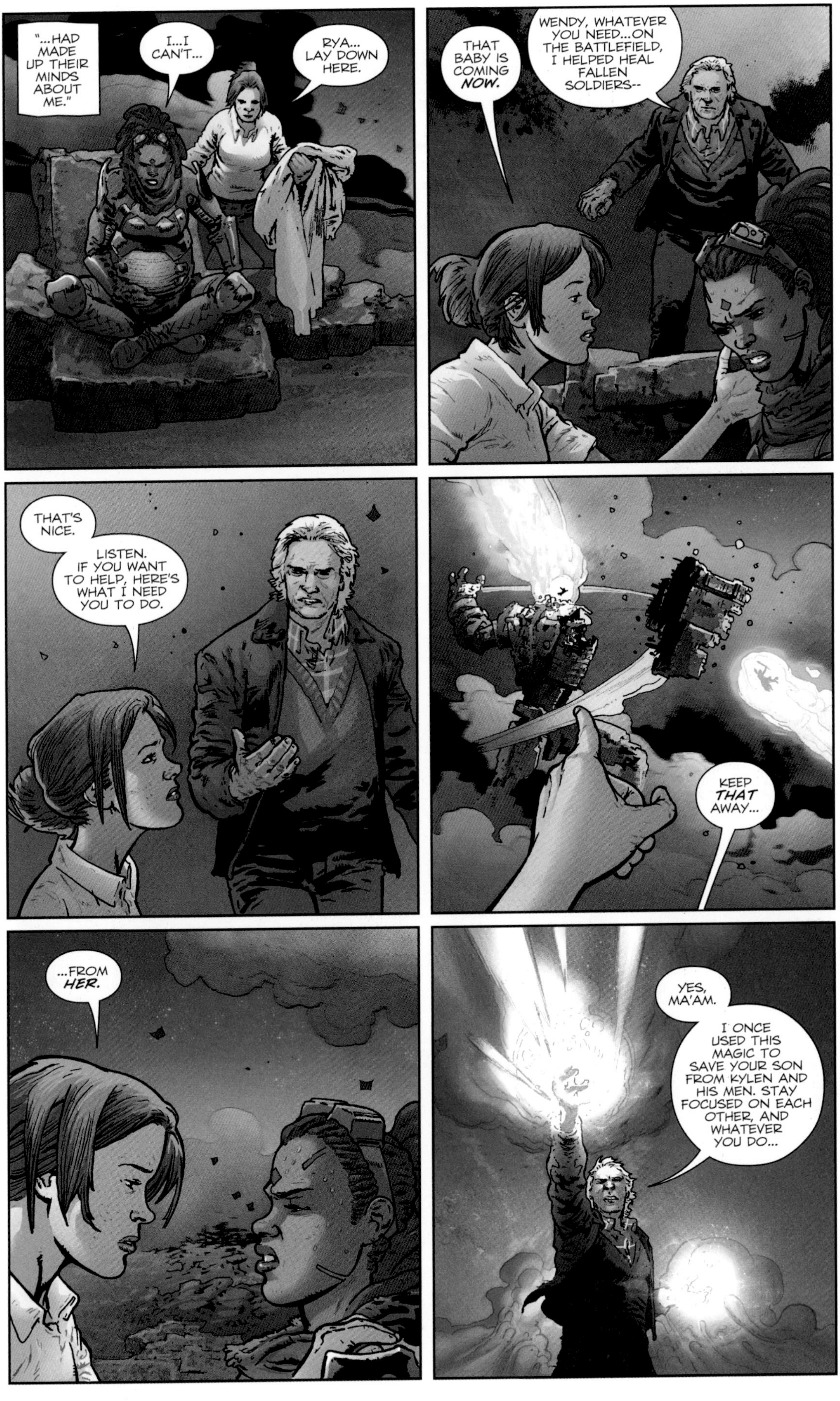
"...HAD MADE UP THEIR MINDS ABOUT ME."
I...I CAN'T...
RYA... LAY DOWN HERE.
WENDY, WHATEVER YOU NEED...ON THE BATTLEFIELD, I HELPED HEAL FALLEN SOLDIERS--
THAT BABY IS COMING NOW.
THAT'S NICE.
LISTEN. IF YOU WANT TO HELP, HERE'S WHAT I NEED YOU TO DO.
KEEP THAT AWAY...
...FROM HER.
YES, MA'AM.
I ONCE USED THIS MAGIC TO SAVE YOUR SON FROM KYLEN AND HIS MEN. STAY FOCUSED ON EACH OTHER, AND WHATEVER YOU DO...

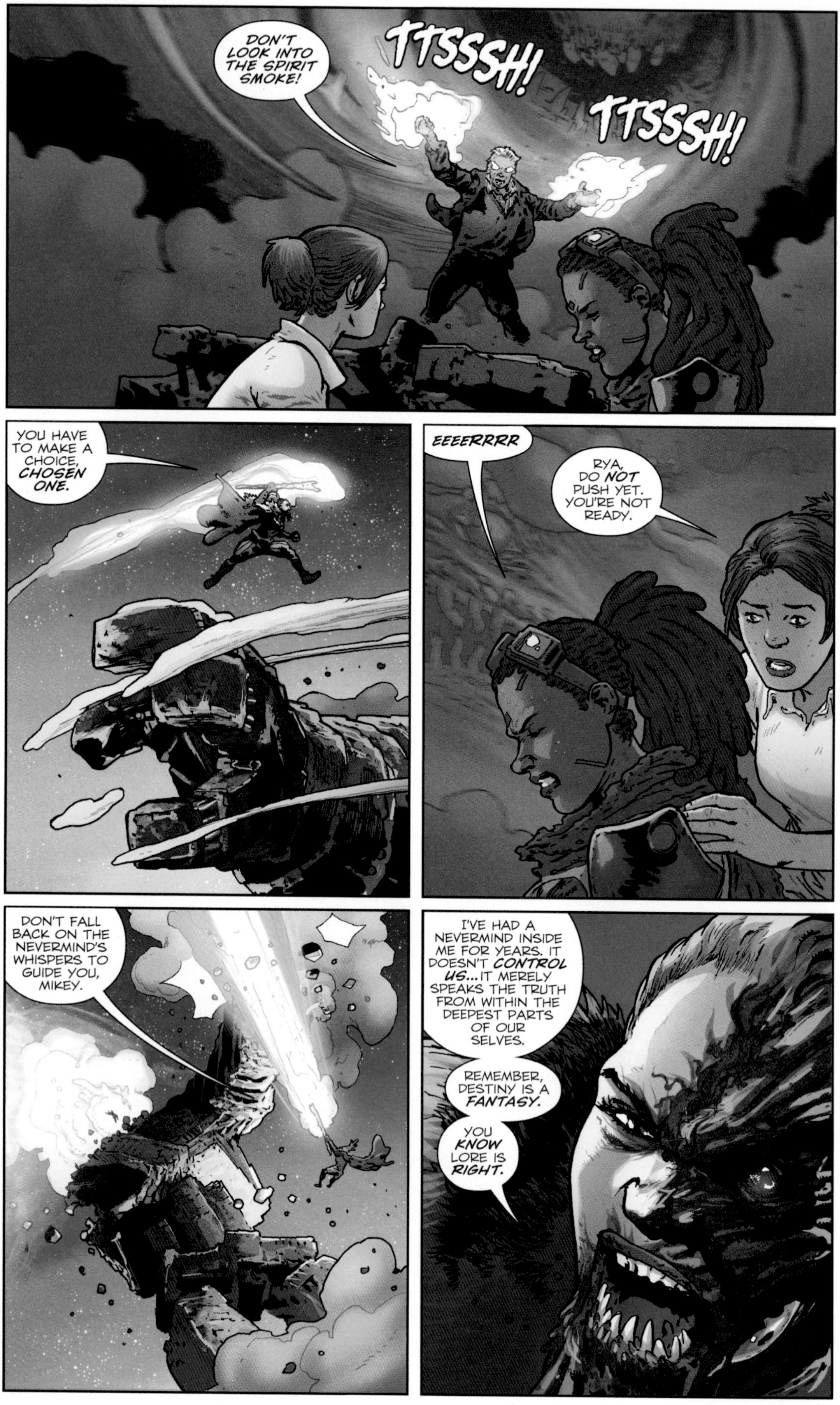
DON'T LOOK INTO THE SPIRIT SMOKE!
TTSSSH!
TTSSSH!
YOU HAVE TO MAKE A CHOICE, CHOSEN ONE.
EEEERRRR
RYA, DO NOT PUSH YET. YOU'RE NOT READY.
DON'T FALL BACK ON THE NEVERMIND'S WHISPERS TO GUIDE YOU, MIKEY.
I'VE HAD A NEVERMIND INSIDE ME FOR YEARS. IT DOESN'T CONTROL US... IT MERELY SPEAKS THE TRUTH FROM WITHIN THE DEEPEST PARTS OF OUR SELVES.
REMEMBER, DESTINY IS A FANTASY.
YOU KNOW LORE IS RIGHT.

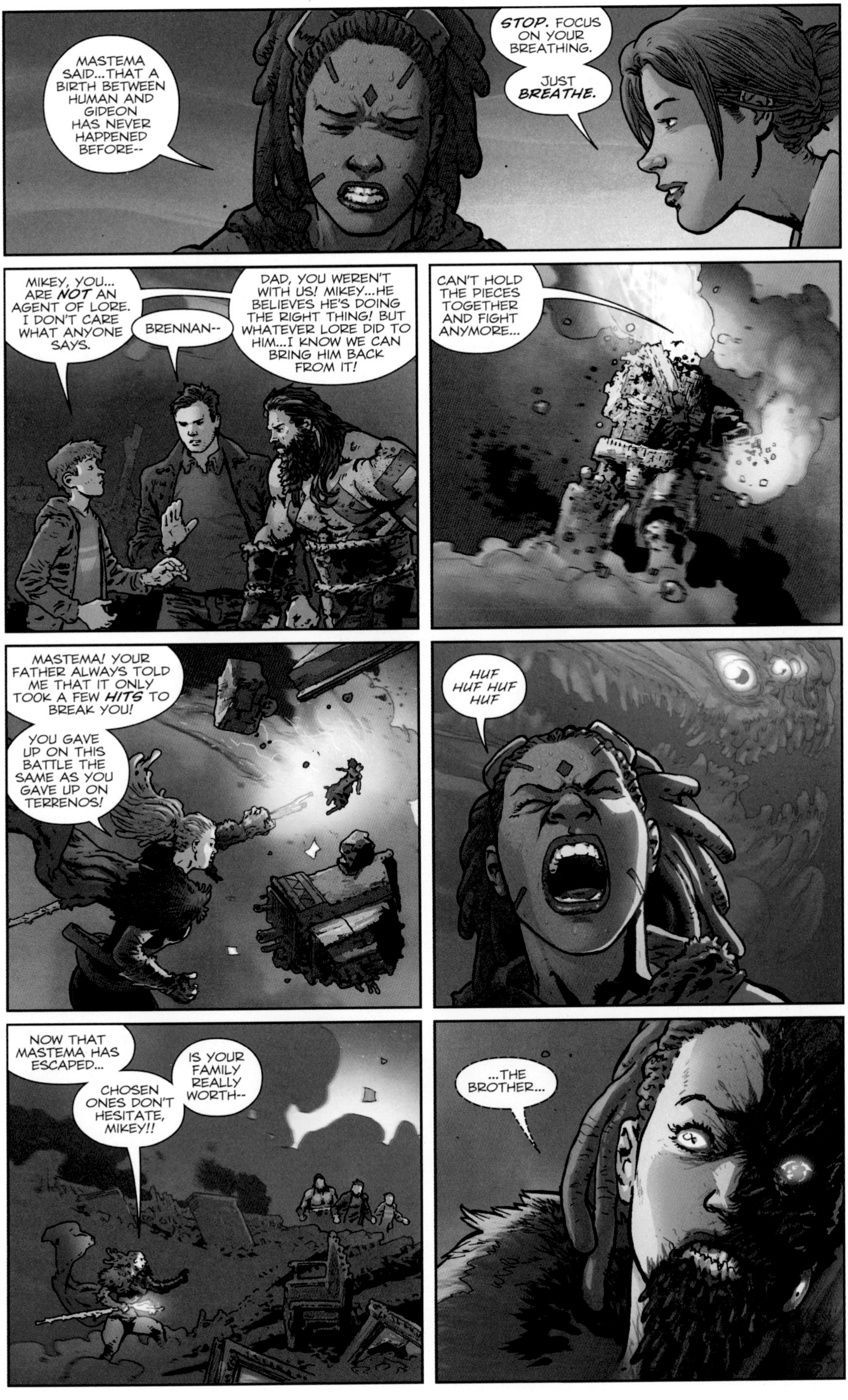
MASTEMA SAID...THAT A BIRTH BETWEEN HUMAN AND GIDEON HAS NEVER HAPPENED BEFORE--
STOP. FOCUS ON YOUR BREATHING.
JUST BREATHE.
MIKEY, YOU... ARE NOT AN AGENT OF LORE. I DON'T CARE WHAT ANYONE SAYS.
BRENNAN--
DAD, YOU WEREN'T WITH US! MIKEY...HE BELIEVES HE'S DOING THE RIGHT THING! BUT WHATEVER LORE DID TO HIM...I KNOW WE CAN BRING HIM BACK FROM IT!
CAN'T HOLD THE PIECES TOGETHER AND FIGHT ANYMORE...
MASTEMA! YOUR FATHER ALWAYS TOLD ME THAT IT ONLY TOOK A FEW HITS TO BREAK YOU!
YOU GAVE UP ON THIS BATTLE THE SAME AS YOU GAVE UP ON TERRENOS!
HUF HUF HUF HUF
NOW THAT MASTEMA HAS ESCAPED...
IS YOUR FAMILY REALLY WORTH--
CHOSEN ONES DON'T HESITATE, MIKEY!!
...THE BROTHER...

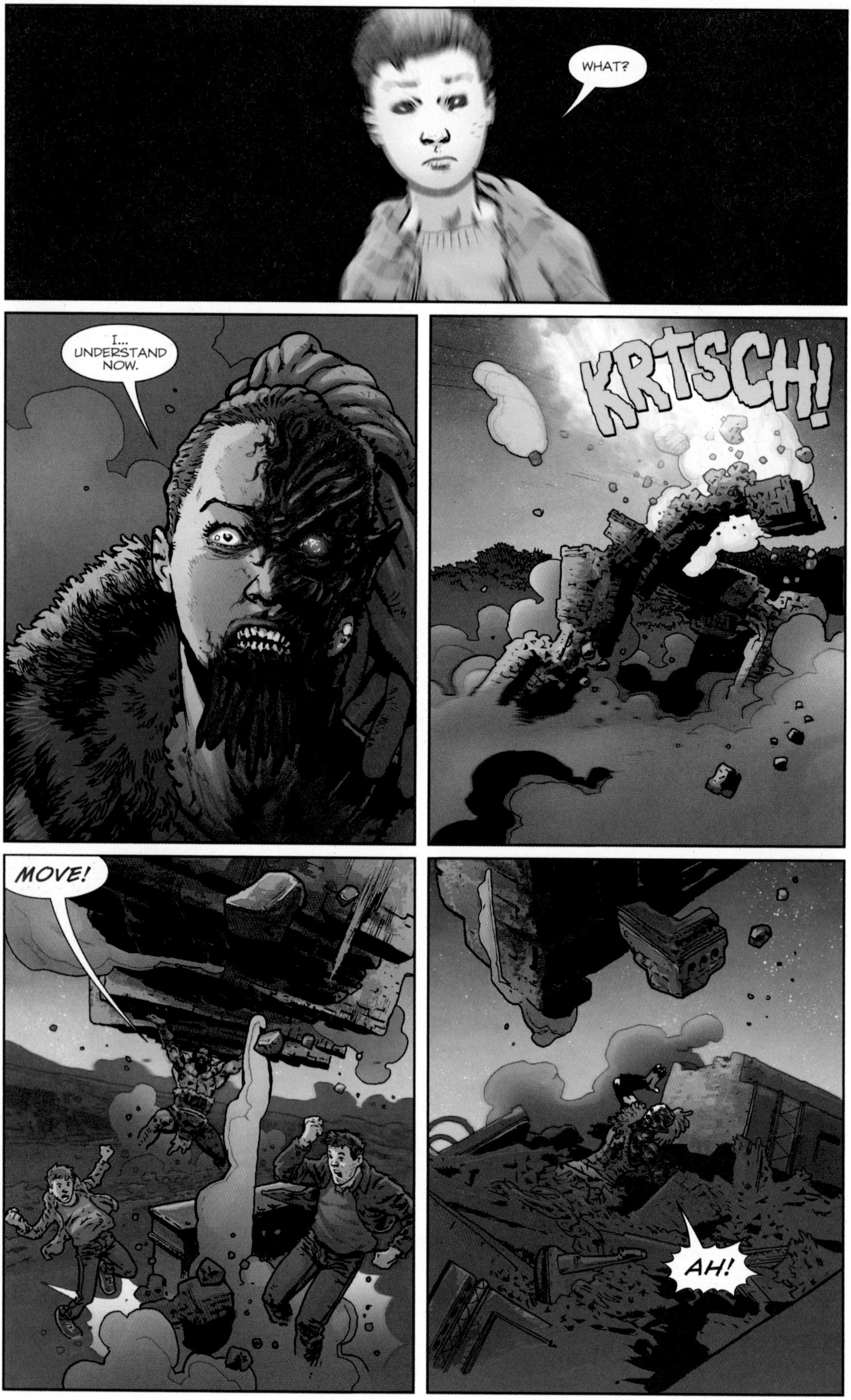
WHAT?
I... UNDERSTAND NOW.
KRTSCH!
MOVE!
AH!

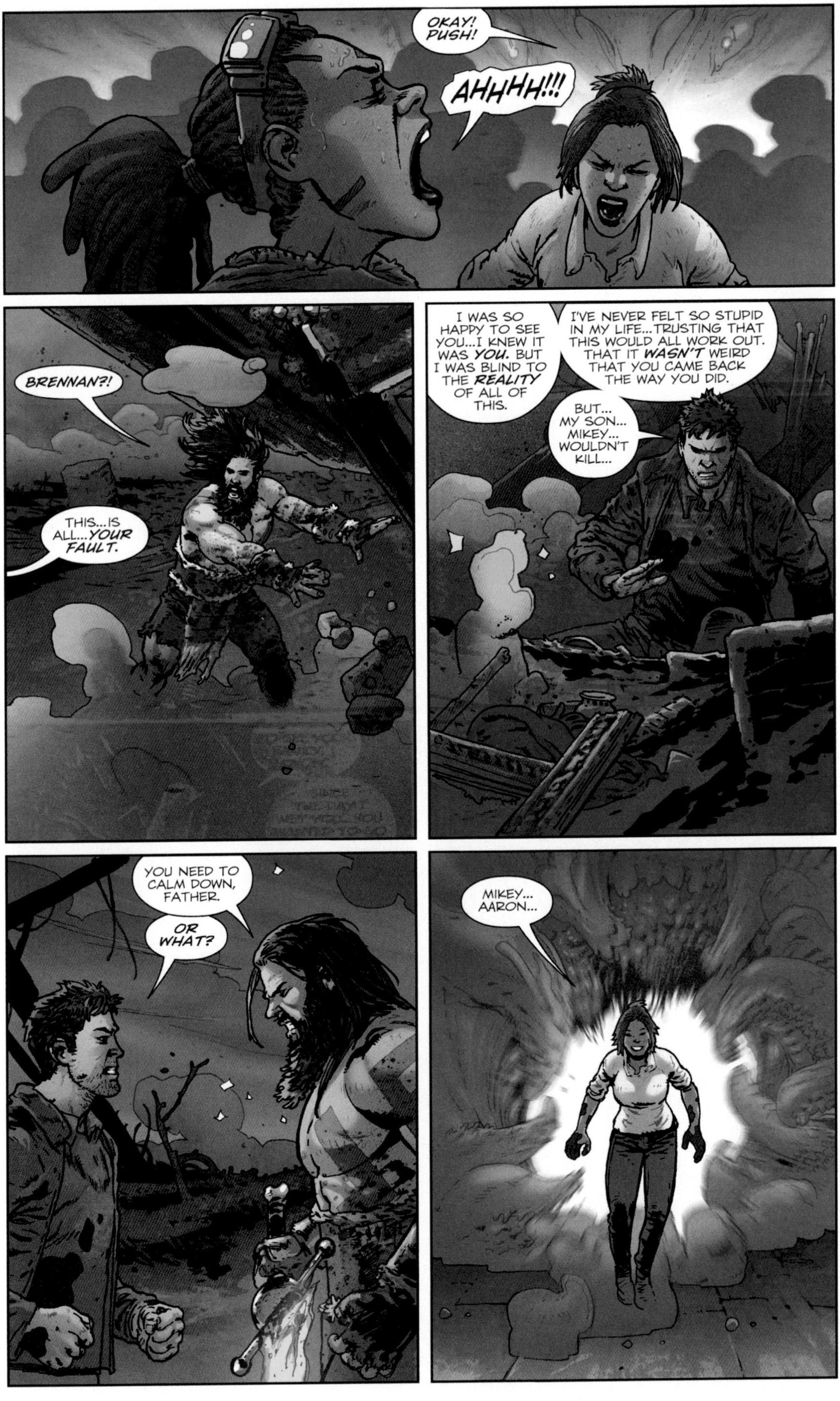
OKAY! PUSH!
AHHHH!!!
BRENNAN?!
THIS...IS ALL...YOUR FAULT.
I WAS SO HAPPY TO SEE YOU...I KNEW IT WAS YOU. BUT I WAS BLIND TO THE REALITY OF ALL OF THIS.
I'VE NEVER FELT SO STUPID IN MY LIFE...TRUSTING THAT THIS WOULD ALL WORK OUT. THAT IT WASN'T WEIRD THAT YOU CAME BACK THE WAY YOU DID.
BUT... MY SON... MIKEY... WOULDN'T KILL...
YOU NEED TO CALM DOWN, FATHER.
OR WHAT?
MIKEY... AARON...

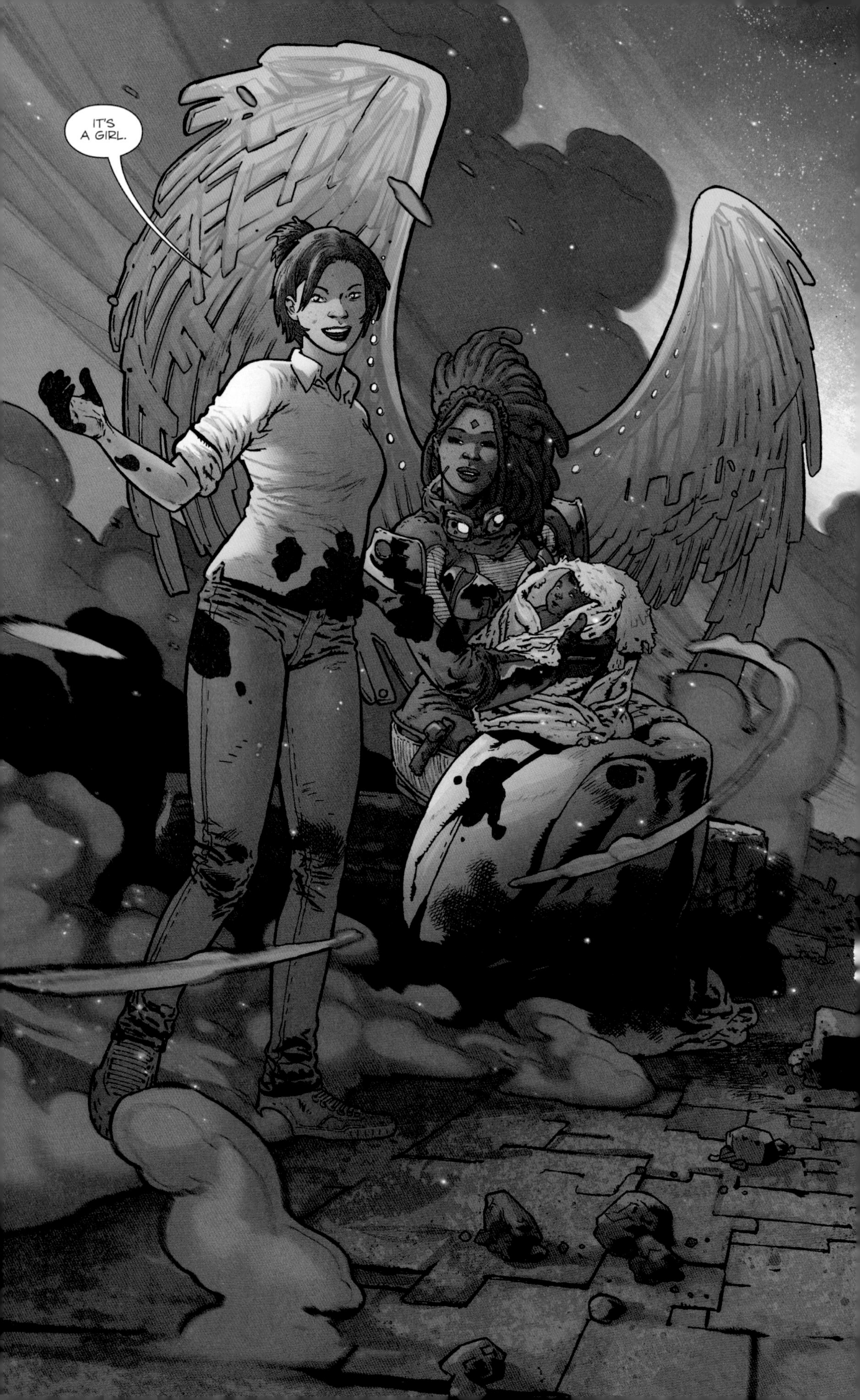
IT'S A GIRL.

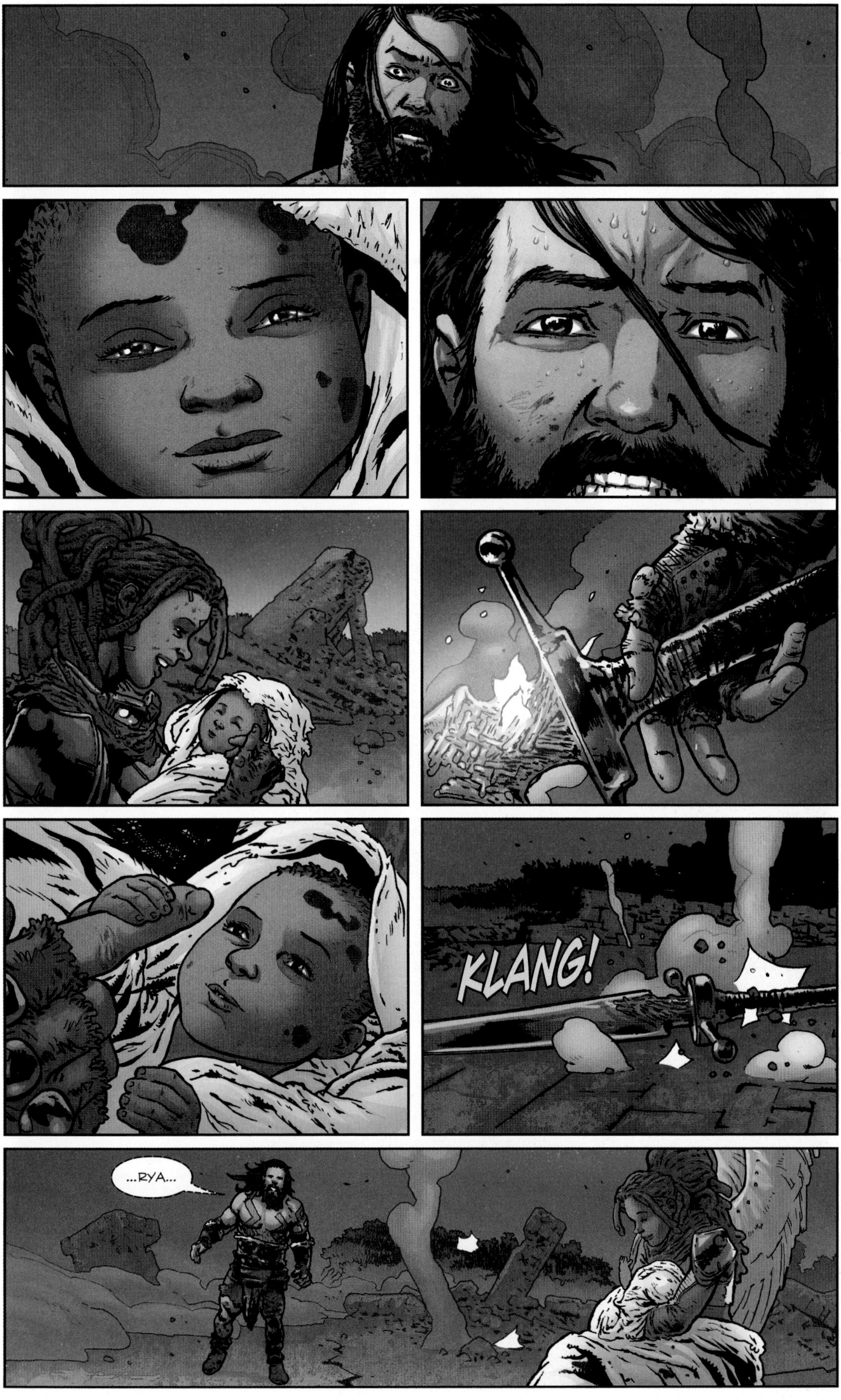
KLANG!
...RYA...

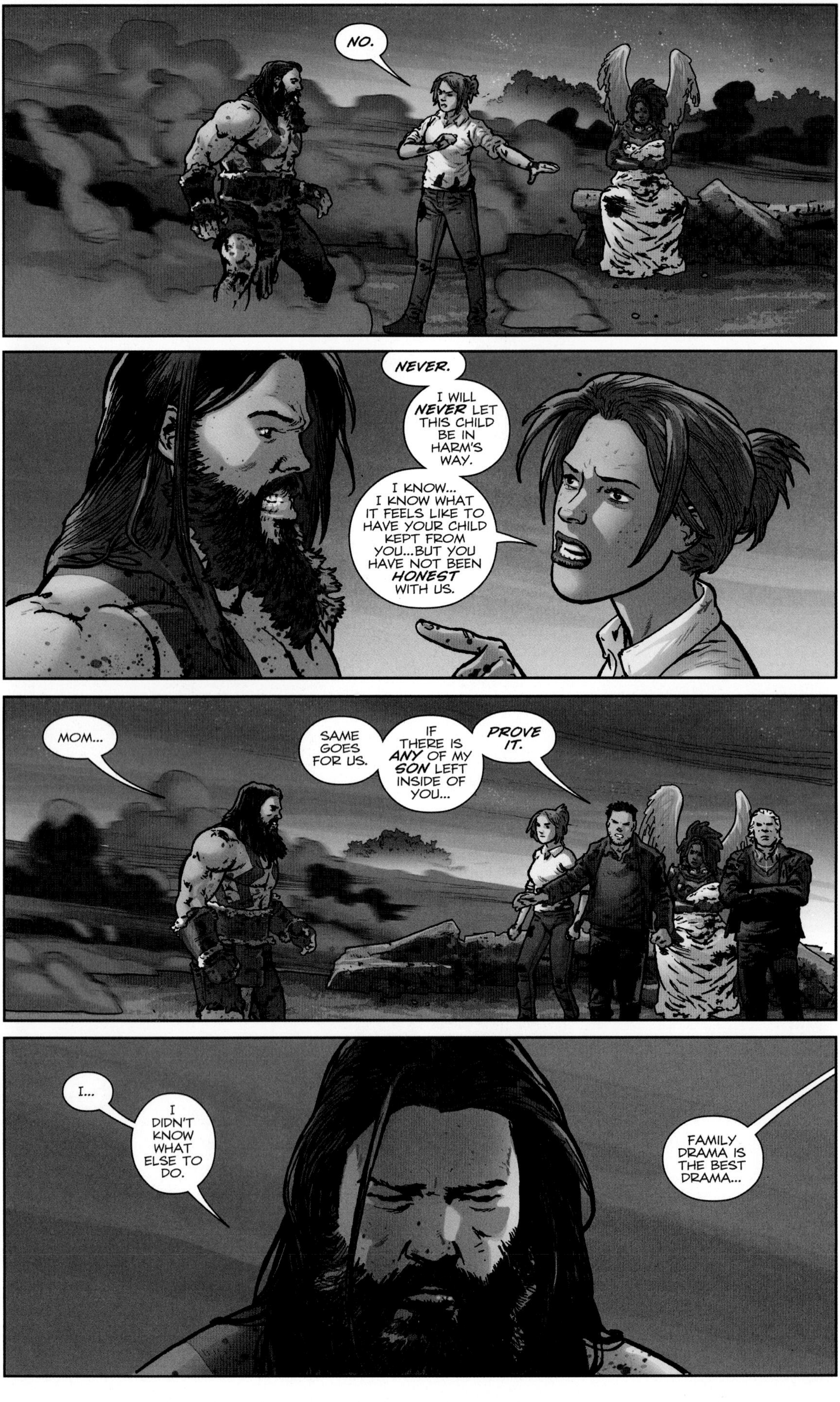
NO.
NEVER.
I WILL NEVER LET THIS CHILD BE IN HARM'S WAY.
I KNOW... I KNOW WHAT IT FEELS LIKE TO HAVE YOUR CHILD KEPT FROM YOU...BUT YOU HAVE NOT BEEN HONEST WITH US.
MOM...
SAME GOES FOR US.
IF THERE IS ANY OF MY SON LEFT INSIDE OF YOU...
PROVE IT.
I...
I DIDN'T KNOW WHAT ELSE TO DO.
FAMILY DRAMA IS THE BEST DRAMA...

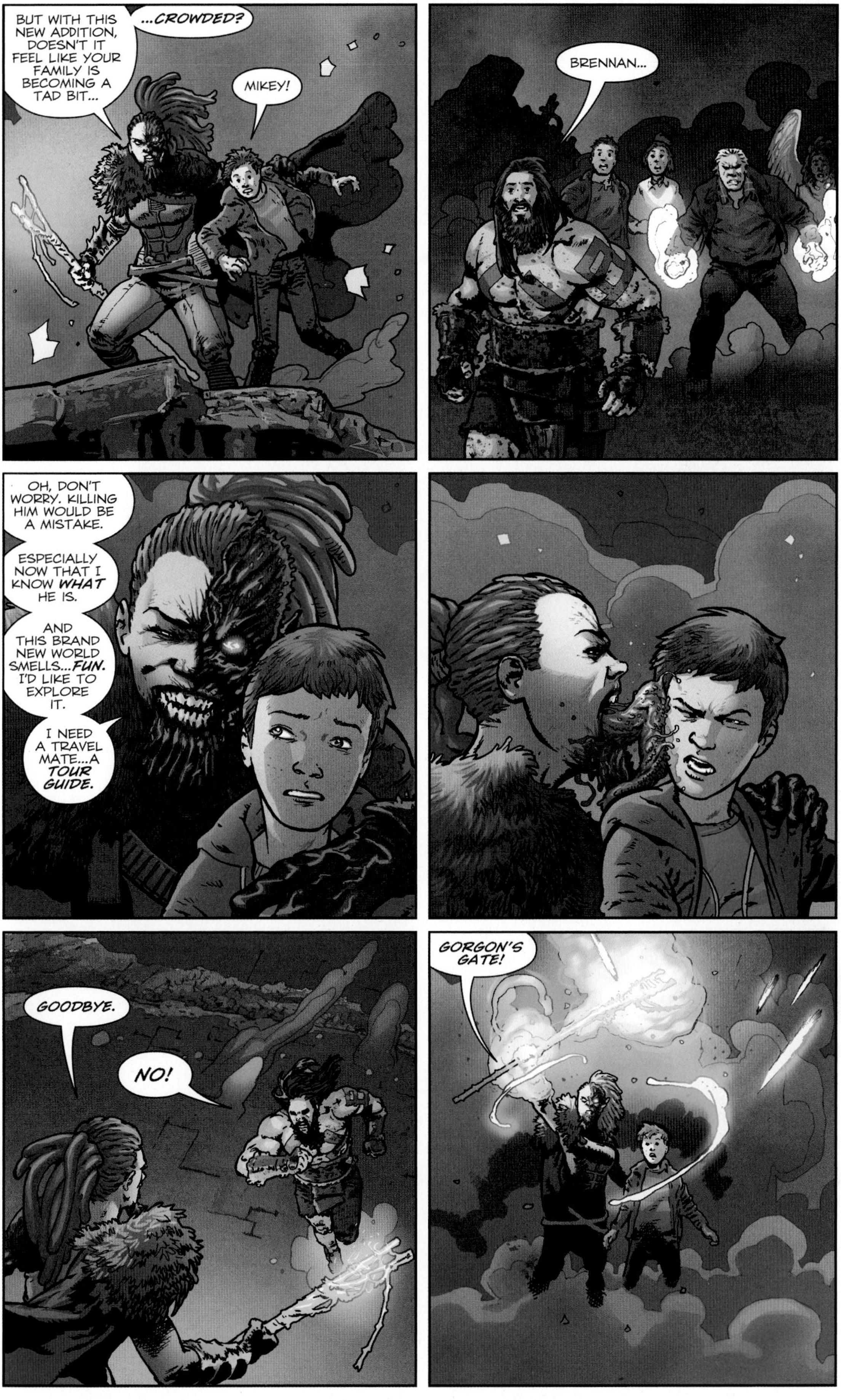
BUT WITH THIS NEW ADDITION, DOESN'T IT FEEL LIKE YOUR FAMILY IS BECOMING A TAD BIT...
...CROWDED?
MIKEY!
BRENNAN...
OH, DON'T WORRY. KILLING HIM WOULD BE A MISTAKE.
ESPECIALLY NOW THAT I KNOW WHAT HE IS.
AND THIS BRAND NEW WORLD SMELLS...FUN. I'D LIKE TO EXPLORE IT.
I NEED A TRAVEL MATE...A TOUR GUIDE.
GOODBYE.
NO!
GORGON'S GATE!

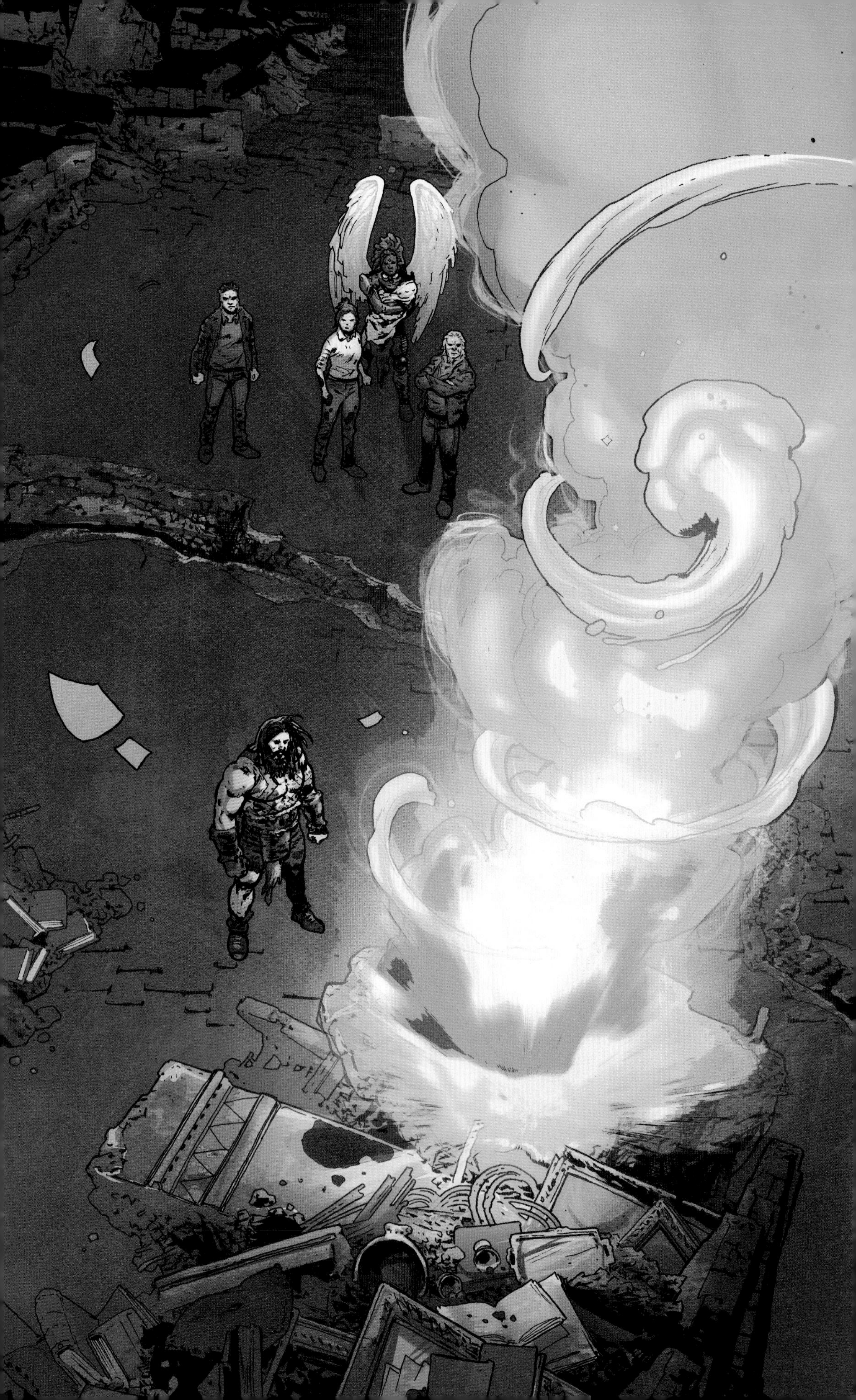

To be continued...

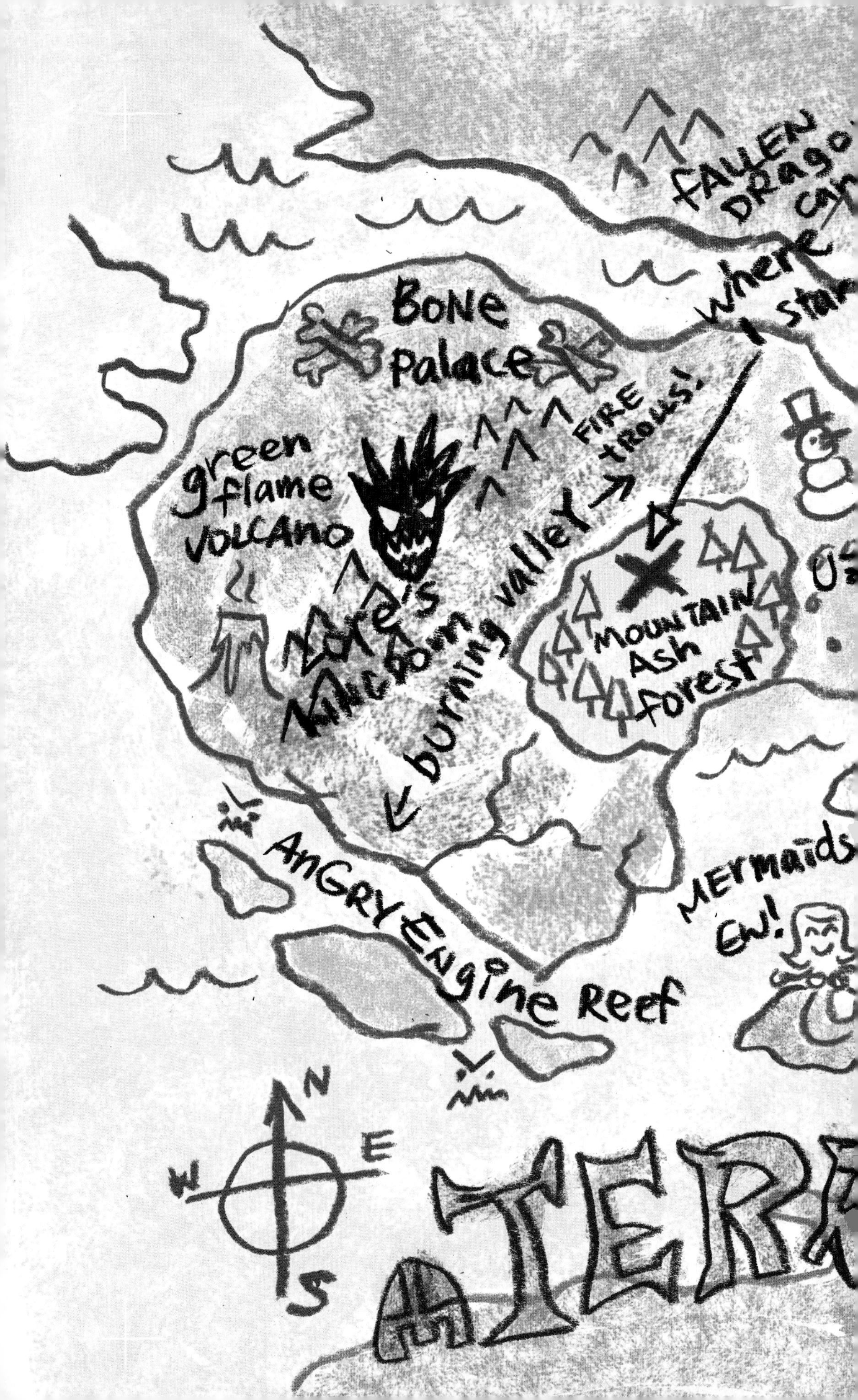

FALLEN
where
I
Bone Palace
FIRE trolls!
green flame VOLCANO
burning valley
MOUNTAIN Ash forest
AnGRY Engine Reef
MERmaids
Ew!
N
E
W
S

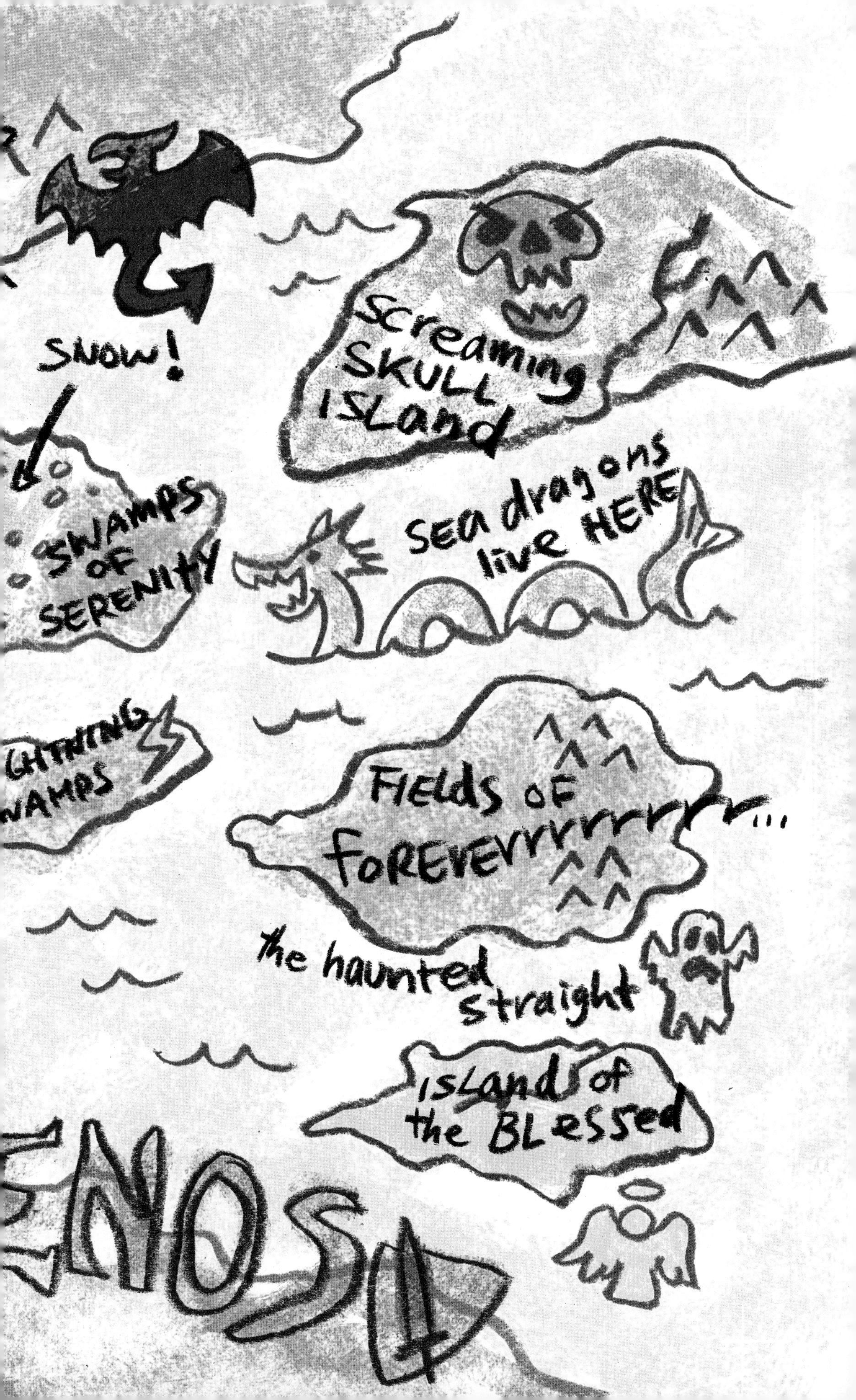

SNOW!
Screaming SKULL ISLand
SWAMPS OF SERENITY
Sea dragons live HERE
GHTNING WAMPS
FIELDS OF fOREverrrrrrrr...
the haunted straight
ISLand of the BLessed

“I could feel it in my heart…

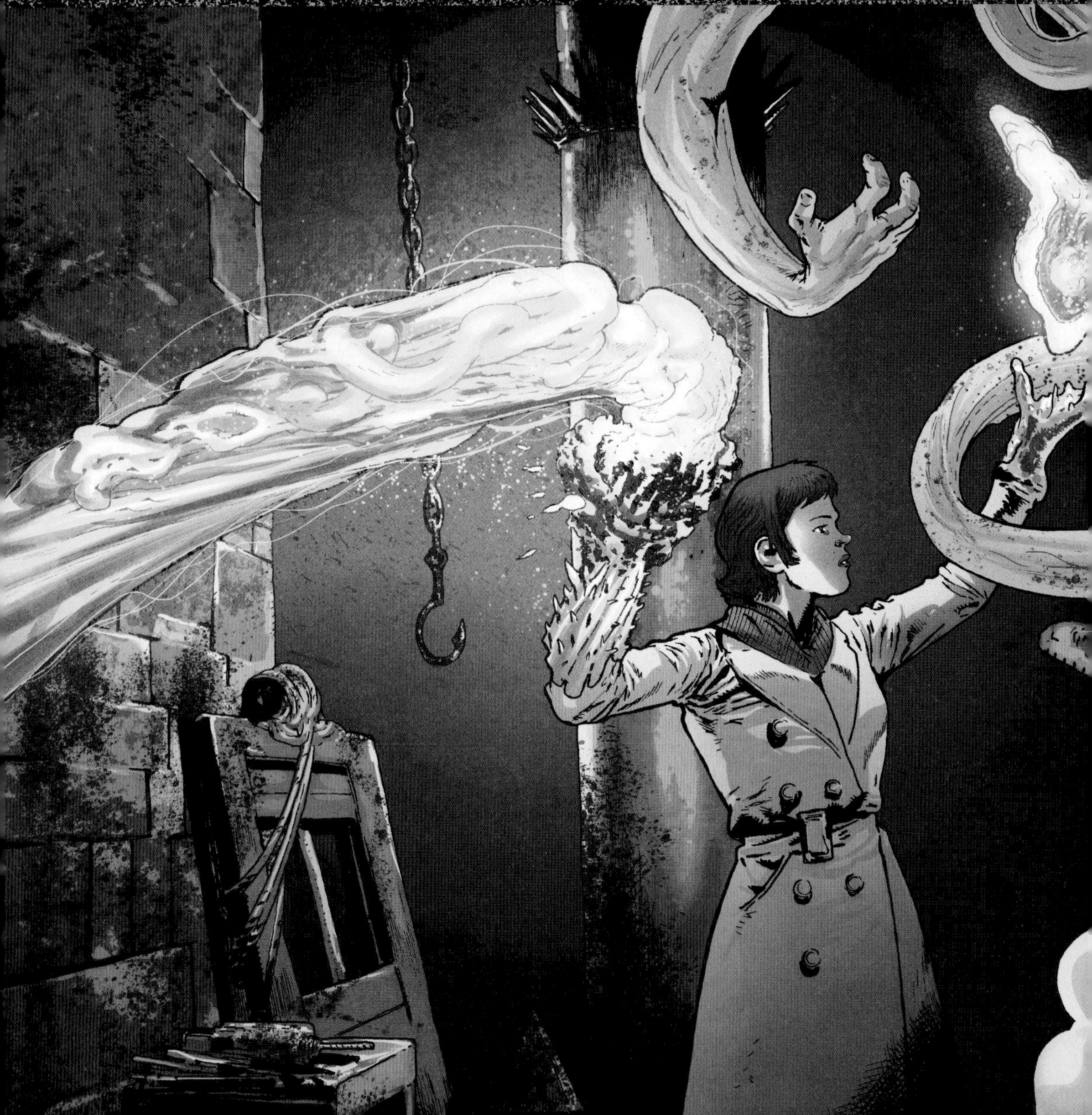

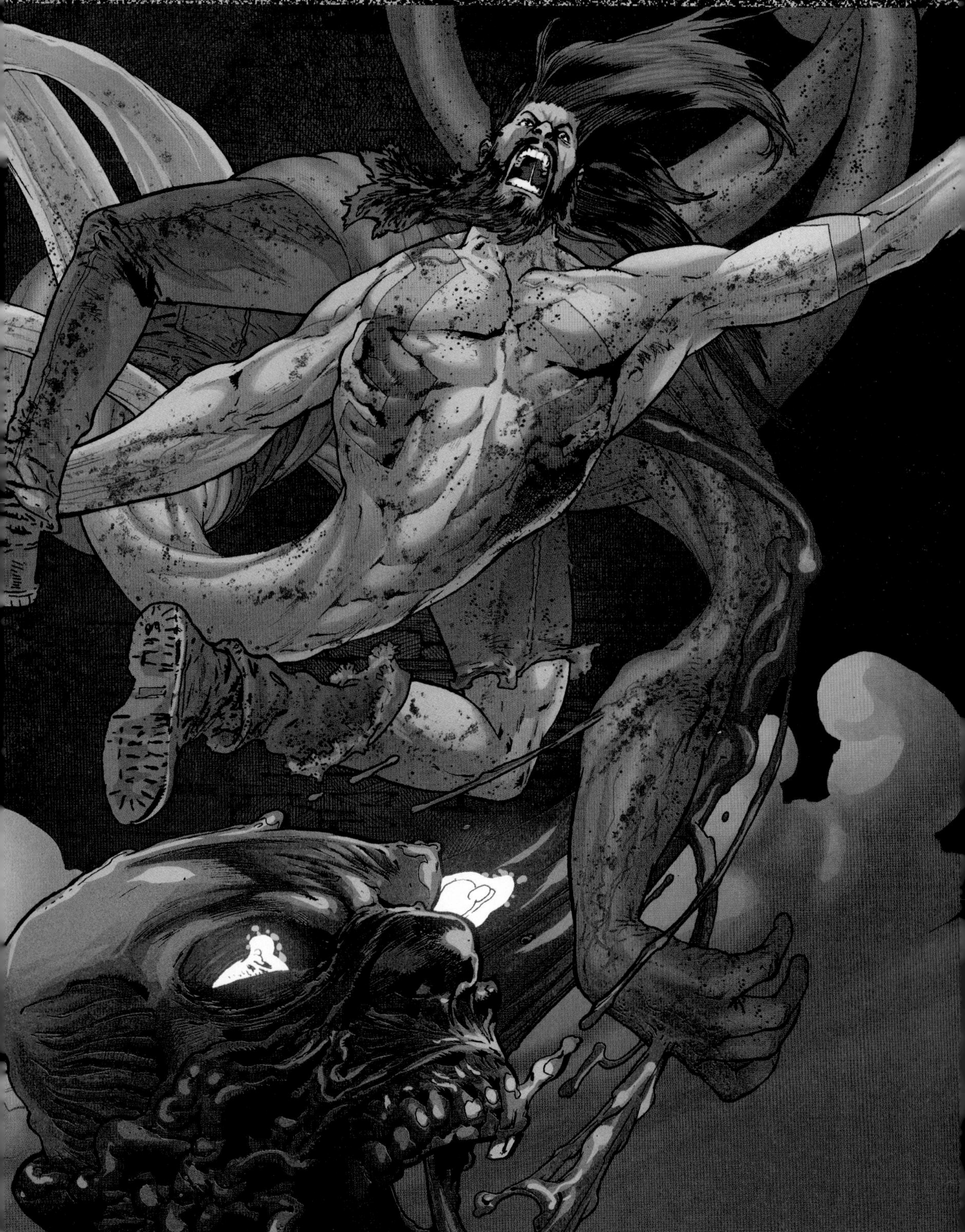

the fight was far from over.”

FOR MORE OF THE WALKING DEAD

TRADE PAPERBACKS

ROBERT KIRKMAN TONY MOORE
THE WALKING DEAD
VOLUME 1
DAYS GONE BYE

VOL. 1: DAYS GONE BYE TP
ISBN: 978-1-58240-672-5
$14.99

VOL. 2: MILES BEHIND US TP
ISBN: 978-1-58240-775-3
$14.99

VOL. 3: SAFETY BEHIND BARS TP
ISBN: 978-1-58240-805-7
$14.99

VOL. 4: THE HEART'S DESIRE TP
ISBN: 978-1-58240-530-8
$14.99

VOL. 5: THE BEST DEFENSE TP
ISBN: 978-1-58240-612-1
$14.99

VOL. 6: THIS SORROWFUL LIFE TP
ISBN: 978-1-58240-684-8
$14.99

VOL. 7: THE CALM BEFORE TP
ISBN: 978-1-58240-828-6
$14.99

VOL. 8: MADE TO SUFFER TP
ISBN: 978-1-58240-883-5
$14.99

VOL. 9: HERE WE REMAIN TP
ISBN: 978-1-60706-022-2
$14.99

VOL. 10: WHAT WE BECOME TP
ISBN: 978-1-60706-075-8
$14.99

VOL. 11: FEAR THE HUNTERS TP
ISBN: 978-1-60706-181-6
$14.99

VOL. 12: LIFE AMONG THEM TP
ISBN: 978-1-60706-254-7
$14.99

VOL. 13: TOO FAR GONE TP
ISBN: 978-1-60706-329-2
$14.99

VOL. 14: NO WAY OUT TP
ISBN: 978-1-60706-392-6
$14.99

VOL. 15: WE FIND OURSELVES TP
ISBN: 978-1-60706-440-4
$14.99

VOL. 16: A LARGER WORLD TP
ISBN: 978-1-60706-559-3
$14.99

VOL. 17: SOMETHING TO FEAR TP
ISBN: 978-1-60706-615-6
$14.99

VOL. 18: WHAT COMES AFTER TP
ISBN: 978-1-60706-687-3
$14.99

VOL. 19: MARCH TO WAR TP
ISBN: 978-1-60706-818-1
$14.99

VOL. 20: ALL OUT WAR PART ONE TP
ISBN: 978-1-60706-882-2
$14.99

VOL. 21: ALL OUT WAR PART TWO TP
ISBN: 978-1-63215-030-1
$14.99

VOL. 22: A NEW BEGINNING TP
ISBN: 978-1-63215-041-7
$14.99

VOL. 23: WHISPERS INTO SCREAMS TP
ISBN: 978-1-63215-258-9
$14.99

VOL. 24: LIFE AND DEATH TP
ISBN: 978-1-63215-402-6
$14.99

VOL. 25: NO TURNING BACK TP
ISBN: 978-1-63215-612-9
$14.99

VOL. 26: CALL TO ARMS TP
ISBN: 978-1-63215-917-5
$14.99

VOL. 27: THE WHISPERER WAR TP
ISBN: 978-1-5343-0052-1
$14.99

VOL. 1: SPANISH EDITION TP
ISBN: 978-1-60706-797-9
$14.99

VOL. 2: SPANISH EDITION TP
ISBN: 978-1-60706-845-7
$14.99

VOL. 3: SPANISH EDITION TP
ISBN: 978-1-60706-883-9
$14.99

VOL. 4: SPANISH EDITION TP
ISBN: 978-1-63215-035-6
$14.99

HARDCOVERS

THE WALKING DEAD
BOOK ONE
a continuing story of survival horror.

BOOK ONE HC
ISBN: 978-1-58240-619-0
$34.99

BOOK TWO HC
ISBN: 978-1-58240-698-5
$34.99

BOOK THREE HC
ISBN: 978-1-58240-825-5
$34.99

BOOK FOUR HC
ISBN: 978-1-60706-000-0
$34.99

BOOK FIVE HC
ISBN: 978-1-60706-171-7
$34.99

BOOK SIX HC
ISBN: 978-1-60706-327-8
$34.99

BOOK SEVEN HC
ISBN: 978-1-60706-439-8
$34.99

BOOK EIGHT HC
ISBN: 978-1-60706-593-7
$34.99

BOOK NINE HC
ISBN: 978-1-60706-798-6
$34.99

BOOK TEN HC
ISBN: 978-1-63215-034-9
$34.99

BOOK ELEVEN HC
ISBN: 978-1-63215-271-8
$34.99

BOOK TWELVE HC
ISBN: 978-1-63215-451-4
$34.99

BOOK THIRTEEN HC
ISBN: 978-1-63215-916-8
$34.99

COMPENDIUMS

The ultimate edition of The New York Times bestseller!
THE WALKING DEAD
COMPENDIUM ONE

COMPENDIUM TP, VOL. 1
ISBN: 978-1-60706-076-5
$59.99

COMPENDIUM TP, VOL. 2
ISBN: 978-1-60706-596-8
$59.99

COMPENDIUM TP, VOL. 3
ISBN: 978-1-63215-456-9
$59.99

SPECIALTY BOOKS

THE WALKING DEAD
THE COVERS

THE WALKING DEAD: THE COVERS, VOL. 1 HC
ISBN: 978-1-60706-002-4
$24.99

THE WALKING DEAD: ALL OUT WAR HC
ISBN: 978-1-63215-038-7
$34.99

THE WALKING DEAD COLORING BOOK
ISBN: 978-1-63215-774-4
$14.99

THE WALKING DEAD RICK GRIMES COLORING BOOK
ISBN: 978-1-5343-0003-3
$14.99

OMNIBUS

THE WALKING DEAD

OMNIBUS, VOL. 1
ISBN: 978-1-60706-503-6
$100.00

OMNIBUS, VOL. 2
ISBN: 978-1-60706-515-9
$100.00

OMNIBUS, VOL. 3
ISBN: 978-1-60706-330-8
$100.00

OMNIBUS, VOL. 4
ISBN: 978-1-60706-616-3
$100.00

OMNIBUS, VOL. 5
ISBN: 978-1-63215-042-4
$100.00

OMNIBUS, VOL. 6
ISBN: 978-1-63215-521-4
$100.00

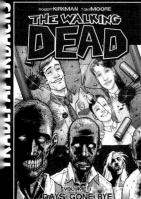

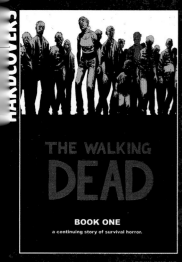

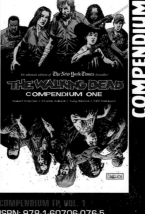

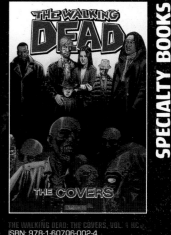

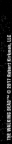

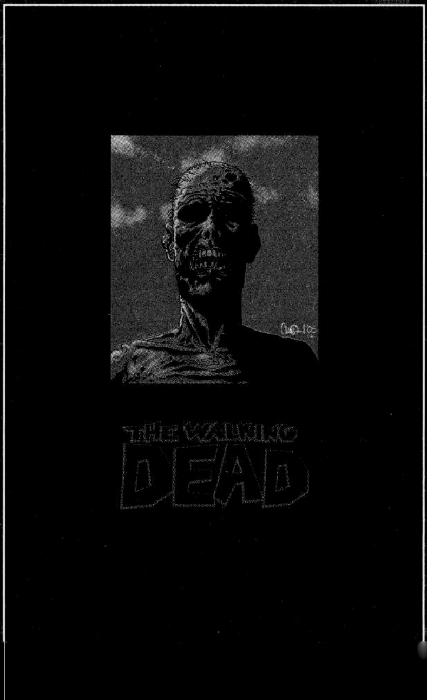

For more tales from ROBERT KIRKMAN and SKYBOUND

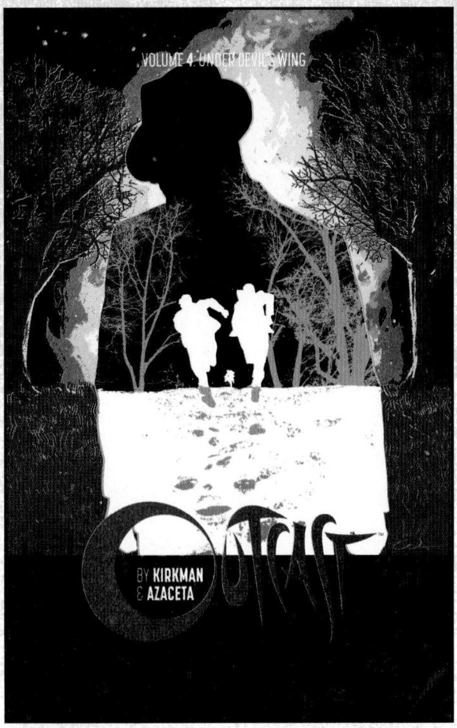
VOLUME 4 UNDER DEVIL'S WING
OUTCAST
BY KIRKMAN & AZACETA

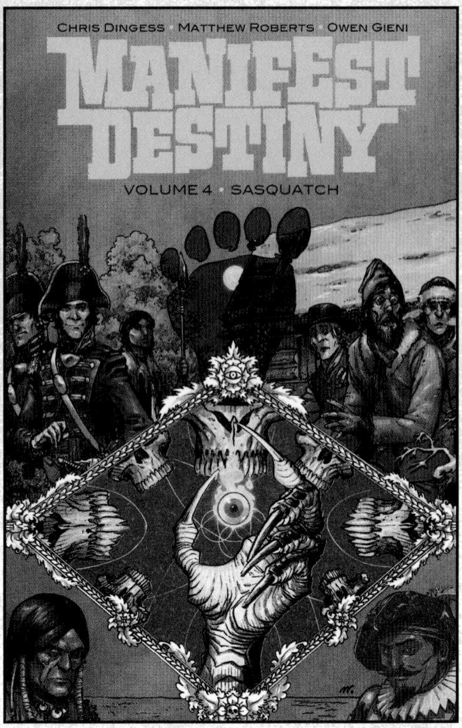
CHRIS DINGESS · MATTHEW ROBERTS · OWEN GIENI
MANIFEST DESTINY
VOLUME 4 · SASQUATCH

VOL. 1: A DARKNESS SURROUNDS HIM TP
ISBN: 978-1-63215-053-0
$9.99

VOL. 2: A VAST AND UNENDING RUIN TP
ISBN: 978-1-63215-448-4
$14.99

VOL. 3: THIS LITTLE LIGHT TP
ISBN: 978-1-63215-693-8
$14.99

VOL. 4: UNDER DEVIL'S WING TP
ISBN: 978-1-5343-0050-7
$14.99

VOL. 1: FLORA & FAUNA TP
ISBN: 978-1-60706-982-9
$9.99

VOL. 2: AMPHIBIA & INSECTA TP
ISBN: 978-1-63215-052-3
$14.99

VOL. 3: CHIROPTERA & CARNIFORMAVES TP
ISBN: 978-1-63215-397-5
$14.99

VOL. 4: SASQUATCH TP
ISBN: 978-1-63215-890-1
$14.99

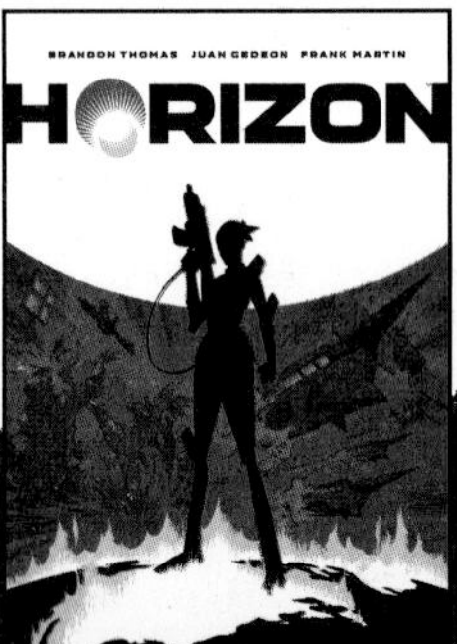
BRANDON THOMAS JUAN GEDEON FRANK MARTIN
HORIZON

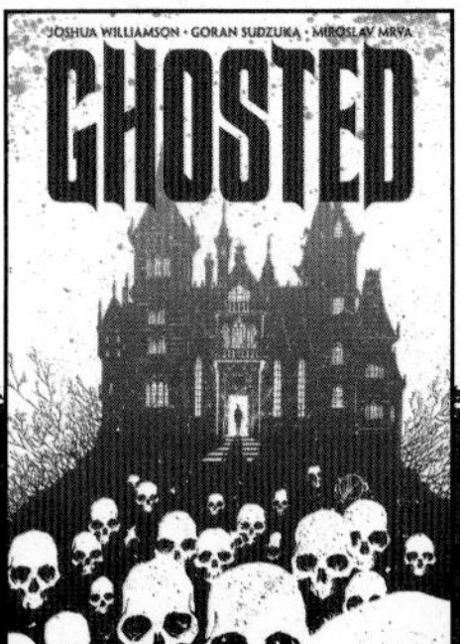
JOSHUA WILLIAMSON · GORAN SUDZUKA · MIROSLAV MRVA
GHOSTED
VOLUME ONE · HAUNTED HEIST

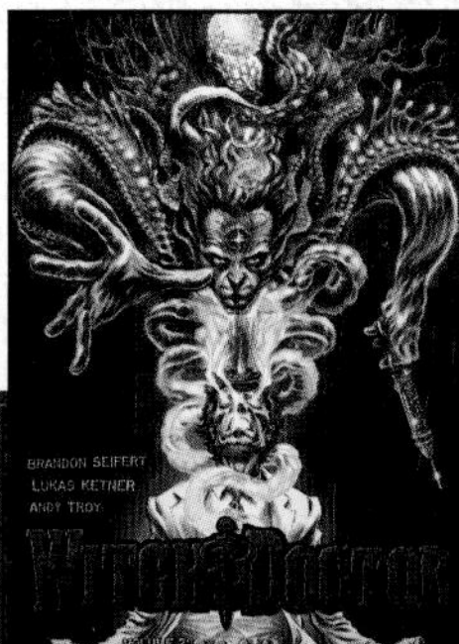
BRANDON SEIFERT
LUKAS KETNER
ANDY TROY
WITCH DOCTOR
VOLUME 2
MAL PRACTICE

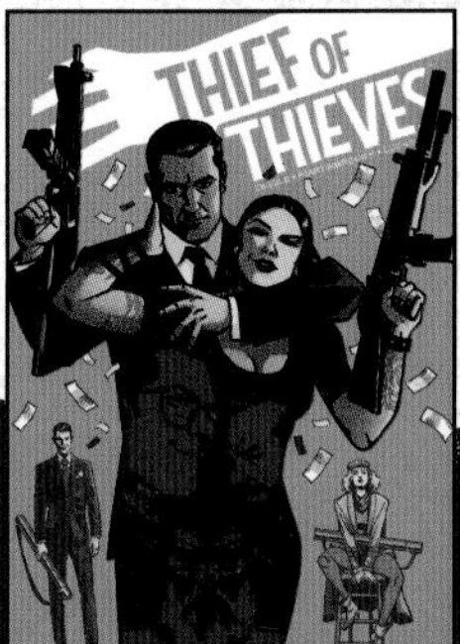
THIEF OF THIEVES
VOLUME 6
"GOLD RUSH."

VOL. 1: REPRISAL TP
ISBN: 978-1-5343-0047-7
$9.99

VOL. 1: HAUNTED HEIST TP
ISBN: 978-1-60706-836-5
$9.99

VOL. 2: BOOKS OF THE DEAD TP
ISBN: 978-1-63215-046-2
$12.99

VOL. 3: DEATH WISH TP
ISBN: 978-1-63215-051-6
$12.99

VOL. 4: GHOST TOWN TP
ISBN: 978-1-63215-317-3
$12.99

VOL. 1: UNDER THE KNIFE TP
ISBN: 978-1-60706-441-1
$12.99

VOL. 2: MAL PRACTICE TP
ISBN: 978-1-60706-693-4
$14.99

VOL. 1: "I QUIT."
ISBN: 978-1-60706-592-0
$14.99

VOL. 2: "HELP ME."
ISBN: 978-1-60706-676-7
$14.99

VOL. 3: "VENICE."
ISBN: 978-1-60706-844-0
$14.99

VOL. 4: "THE HIT LIST."
ISBN: 978-1-63215-037-0
$14.99

VOL. 5: "TAKE ME."
ISBN: 978-1-63215-401-9
$14.99

VOL. 6: "GOLD RUSH."
ISBN: 978-1-53430-037-8
$14.99